SUNBORN

SUNBORN

VOLUME FOUR OF
THE CHAOS
CHRONICLES

JEFFREY A. CARVER

TOR®

A TOM DOHERTY ASSOCIATES BOOK
NEW YORK

SUNBORN

Copyright © 2008 by Jeffrey A. Carver

Edited by James Frenkel

A Tor Book
Published by Tom Doherty Associates, LLC
175 Fifth Avenue
New York, NY 10010

www.tor-forge.com

Tor® is a registered trademark of Tom Doherty Associates, LLC.

Library of Congress Cataloging-in-Publication Data

Carver, Jeffrey A.
    Sunborn / Jeffrey A. Carver.—1st ed.
        p.   cm.—(The chaos chronicles ; v. 4)
    "A Tom Doherty Associates book."
    ISBN-13: 978-0-312-86453-8
    ISBN: 10: 0-312-86453-1
    1. Life on other planets—Fiction.   2. Cataclysmic variable stars—Fiction.
3. Cosmology—Fiction.   I. Title.

PS3553.A7892 S86 2008
813'.54—dc22

                                                                    2008034301

First Edition: November 2008

Printed in the United States of America

0 9 8 7 6 5 4 3 2 1

This one is for Chuck,
who helped make it possible.

It's also for you readers,
who have waited patiently for too many years.

I thank you all.

ACKNOWLEDGMENTS

This book has been long, long in the making, and there were times I thought I would never finish it. Without the help of the people I'm about to thank, I probably would not have. I know acknowledgment pages can start to sound like a broken record, the same people being thanked over and over, book after book. There's a good reason for that: the assistance of generous, smart, caring, loyal friends and family who help unceasingly, year after year, book after book. So it has been in my writing life.

Without my family, forget it. You wouldn't have a book to hold. My wife, Allysen, and my daughters, Julia and Alexandra, continue to be indispensable sources of love, encouragement, and critical feedback. My brother, Chuck, has encouraged in ways large and small, and my sister, Nancy, as well.

Without my writing group, several decades old now, you might have a book to hold, but you wouldn't enjoy it as much. Craig Gardner, Richard Bowker, Victoria Bolles, Mary Aldridge: four people working in the background who have helped me improve this novel in every conceivable way. You don't even want to know how many drafts they read and marked up; I lost count, myself. They even helped me confirm that the title the story has carried for the many years since its gestation was the one it should keep.

Jim Frenkel edited this book as he has so many in the past—slowly and with great care. Thanks, Jim, as always. And thanks to Tom Doherty of Tor Books for his patience and faith, and to Patrick Nielsen Hayden and all the other folk at Tor who provide such a fertile ground for books to grow in. And thanks also to my agent, Richard Curtis, who, if he had doubts, kept them to himself.

A special mention goes to the members of Park Avenue Congregational Church of Arlington, Massachusetts, who have taken a special interest in this one—especially Nick Iacuzio and the much-missed Arlene Brown, whose generosity spawned several important characters in the story.

And finally, you, the readers, who have been waiting patiently (or impatiently) for a new Chaos book for far too many years. Many of you have let me know you are waiting, and a more loyal bunch of readers no writer could ask for. This one's for you.

SUNBORN

PROLOGUE

Somewhere in the fire-scored darkness of space, a being that was neither matter nor energy slipped through spacetime like a whisper, a breath, a rustle of a curtain in the night. The being called itself by a name that, if spoken aloud, would have sounded something like *De-ee-ee-ee-ee-ee-ahh-b-b*, trailing off into extremely low-frequency reverberations. In visible light, it looked like a cloud of coal dust—except when it shrank to a single particle, or stretched to the breadth of a planet.

Deeaab moved with ease through the many dimensions of space. Time was a clay to be molded by its thoughts. It had slipped into this universe out of deep time, across a boundary few could even detect, the membrane dividing one universe from the next. It had fled the fading glow of a universe that was dying.

The crossing was perilous, with no chance of return. Deeaab had seen at least one of its fellows succeed in crossing at the same time, but others had not. Those who had failed were lost forever. The loss was never far from Deeaab's thoughts; it was like an ever-present pull of gravity.

Wandering through the star-spiral it now took for home, Deeaab listened to slow mutterings in spacetime that seemed to come from very large bodies—and also to the quick chittering of strange little creatures that flickered in and out of Deeaab's awareness like shadows. Much that Deeaab heard it did not understand, whether from the great or from the tiny. But it was astonished when it finally realized that the *stars* were the great bodies that were speaking—that they were alive with thought and awareness. Could this be? Deeaab had never heard a star speak before.

Marveling, Deeaab approached one sun, at the edge of a cloud. Understanding came with difficulty, but Deeaab could *feel* the star's thought. The star seemed glad of its presence, and Deeaab lingered, seeking deeper contact. In time it began to understand the star's feelings; and what it felt was disturbing. Deeaab felt pain, and fear, and a certainty that this sun was dying—but not of natural causes. Deeaab called the sun ✳Bravelight✳, and wished it could help. But how? There was an inimical force here, unseen, bringing death where there should only be life.

✳Bravelight✳ swelled and reddened. Deeaab drew away, but continued to keep watch . . . until the shocking moment when its friend flared with sudden, blinding intensity, exploding with a death-convulsion that sent Deeaab tumbling away.

After the death of ✳Bravelight✳, Deeaab wandered again, numb with grief and fear. It heard other murmurings, and troubling rumors of other stars dying young and in pain. What could Deeaab do? Had it fled the demise of a universe that was simply dying of old age, only to find a worse place, where death was even crueler and more capricious? Was this just the way things *were* in this universe?

In time, it came to another star-cloud, a place where suns were being born, one after another. Compelled by the memory of ✳Bravelight✳, Deeaab felt drawn to the cloud, seeking new friends. But when it felt death lurking here, too, Deeaab withdrew.

But Deeaab did not leave that region of space. Instead, it stayed nearby, waiting . . . hoping that understanding might come, and a course of action be made clear.

Deeaab pondered, and prayed.

1

WAYSTATION

 The company sped across the light-years for what felt like an eternity, enclosed only by a faintly glimmering force-field bubble. Behind them they had left an ocean world; ahead was the unknown. Inside the star-spanner transport, John Bandicut felt a distinct sense of time and space passing by as a physical stream—stretching ahead of them, flowing around and behind them. He watched as the stars outside the bubble streaked past against the backdrop of space.

Ik, the Hraachee'an, was the first to notice the gradual appearance of a ghostly, rose-colored nebula ahead. Soon after Ik pointed that out to the others, Bandicut observed the star field crinkling, as though someone were rippling the fabric of space like clear cellophane. A moment later a shock wave rocked the star-spanner bubble. "What—" *rasp rasp* "—was that?" cried Li-Jared, several of the Karellian's words dropping out in translation.

Whatever had hit them blazed golden around them, and for a moment they all seemed to turn transparent and luminous. Bandicut could scarcely breathe.

Entering new flight regime. Approaching interstellar waystationx.

Bandicut blinked at the words of the translator-stones embedded in his wrists. Interstellar waystation?

"Something's changing ahead," said Ik.

Bandicut pressed his face to the front of the bubble. "I think I see it—some kind of shadow ahead, between us and the nebula."

"Hrah. It looks like a channel of some kind."

Antares pressed close behind Bandicut, her breath warm on his cheek. "How could there be such a thing in space?"

No one had an answer, but what had looked to Bandicut like a patch of shadow grew larger quickly, then abruptly wrapped around the bubble like a tunnel. Suddenly they were flying like a high-speed train through a not-quite-solid tube, which began to glow with a pale blue light.

They felt a series of soft jolts, as though the star-spanner bubble were decelerating in discrete increments. With no further warning, it glided into a platform that reminded Bandicut of a subway station on Earth. The bubble softened and vanished with a twinkle. Bandicut and the others looked at each other. "I guess we're invited to get out," Bandicut said. His two robots went first, clambering out onto the surface and pronouncing it solid and apparently safe. Together with his companions, Bandicut followed them onto the platform. It was a strange and wonderful sensation to feel something solid beneath his feet again. /What do you think, Charlie? I mean Charlene?/ he asked silently, speaking to the quarx—presently female—in his head.

/// I think we're about to meet someone. ///

/Oh?/ He turned. A new robot was floating toward them. Or perhaps a holo-image of a robot. It was tall and vaguely humanoid. A silver band encircled its head where eyes might have been. Small clusters of sparkling jewels floated independently along the band—apparently the robot's eyes, moving to focus on all the members of the company at once. "My name is Jeaves," it said in a deep voice that sounded both human and familiar. They had heard that voice during their passage in the star-spanner. "Welcome to the Cloudminder Interstellar Waystation. I have been asked to serve as your host, though I am a visitor here myself. The station is largely uninhabited at this time."

"Hrah," said Ik. "Where are—?"

"I'll explain everything once we're inside, and do my best to make you comfortable here," Jeaves continued. "Including servicing your robots, if you like."

"Yes, we—"

"I have many questions for you, as I'm sure you do for me. But before we can enter the station proper, I must ask you all to stand by just a little longer. I believe you are familiar with the normalization procedure?"

"Of course," rumbled Ik. The others muttered agreement. On Shipworld, the vast structure outside the galaxy where the four had met, each had gone through normalization—a mysterious application of alien technology that adjusted their physiologies for local food, air, and so on. It had happened again when they'd gone to the ocean world.

/// John, I get the feeling
this isn't going to be just a pit stop ... ///

Bandicut missed the rest of the quarx's words. He suddenly felt light-headed, and was enveloped in a cottony glow. He started to call out to his companions. But the glow blurred not just his vision but his thoughts and his balance. He felt himself falling, his thoughts leaking out into the light . . .

JEAVES PROCEDURAL DIARY: 384.14.8.7

Preliminary debriefing of the newly arrived company is complete. I performed the procedure during a light trance-state induced during normalization, with the assistance of the translator-stones each member of the company carries.

Summary:

The company includes representatives of four organic species, each from a different homeworld (John Bandicut, Human of Earth; Ik, Hraachee'an; Li-Jared, Karellian; and Antares, empathic Thespi Third-female). In addition, there are two robots of Earth manufacture—Napoleon and Copernicus—enhanced to the point of sentience (but not by their original makers). They seem to share a personal bond with John Bandicut. Finally, there is one noncorporeal symbiote—Charlie (or Charlene) the quarx—resident in John Bandicut's mind.

The group came together on Shipworld, and by all accounts, distinguished themselves during the crisis brought on by the boojum incursion. (Report on boojum crisis available in Shipworld archives.) Due to urgent need, they were dispatched immediately afterward to assist with a situation on the ocean world known as Astar-Neri, in the Sagittarian arm—where they prevented a deep-sea entity known locally as the Maw of the Abyss from destroying an undersea civilization. Their discovery of the true nature of the Maw—a damaged, near-sentient stargate—is recorded separately in a detailed report.

The success of this just-completed mission owed largely to their exceptional teamwork and negotiating skills. The broad spectrum of their intelligences, empathy, courage, and problem-solving abilities make this company a formidable agent of change. Compared with other operatives who might be called into service in the Starmaker crisis, this company in my judgment offers by far the best hope for success. Plus, of course, they are here now, and available. With the instability in the Starmaker Nebula growing at an alarming rate, time appears to be critical.

All members of the group emoted a desire for extended rest and relaxation—hardly unreasonable, given their recent service. I can certainly allow them a day to rest and adjust to their new surroundings, which I have attempted to shape for their comfort. However, given the urgency of the situation, I have little choice: I must move quickly to persuade this group to join us in the Starmaker mission. The consequences of failure could redound far beyond the nebula . . .

2

MISSION UNWELCOME

 The robot's holographic image floated like a ghostly silver mannequin above the dull red cavern floor. "I trust you have enjoyed your respite, however brief," he said to the assembled company. "A day and a night isn't much. But now we must speak of a matter that cannot wait. A matter of great urgency."

Bandicut groaned. The quarx had been right. This *wasn't* just a pit stop at the waystation. Li-Jared answered first, though. "A new *job*?" he snapped, his electric-blue eyes sparking with anger. Vaguely simian in form, the Karellian paced energetically over what looked like the floor of a water-carved sandstone ravine in the middle of a desert. Somewhere beneath all that rock was the deck of the space station. "Has it occurred to you," Li-Jared drawled, "that we might not *want* a new job?"

We certainly do not, Bandicut thought. Not anytime soon,

and certainly not dropped on us the way the last one was. They had just spent a pleasant evening in idyllic surroundings, eaten good food, and even been fitted with new clothes while their old ones were cleaned and mended. They had slept in comfort, and awakened to stroll through several carefully maintained environments, each in a different section of the station. Had all of that been a softening-up for this moment? He felt an echoing feeling from Antares, who stood at his side.

"Hrah," agreed Ik. The tall, bony Hraachee'an stroked his sculpted, blue-white head with long fingers and turned both ways to note the reactions of his companions. "After what we have been through, we thought we had earned some time to relax and . . ." Ik paused, raising his hands, at a loss for words.

See to our own needs? Bandicut thought, completing Ik's sentence. Yes. They had just saved a world. And had done plenty more before that.

"I understand," said Jeaves. The holo of the robot's cylindrical body extended its arms toward them in an apparent gesture of conciliation. The sparkling eyes in the band around its head came together to become just two eyes. They softened. "But the need is urgent. You are the only ones in a position to—"

John Bandicut shook his head. "We've heard *that* bef—" he started to say. But he was interrupted by a sudden shudder that passed through the ground, shaking them all. "What the—?"

"Please wait while this passes," Jeaves said sharply as the shaking continued. "This will likely be the equivalent of a mild seismic quake on a planetary surface. It should end soon."

"Uhhll, seismic quake?" said Antares, her voice tinged with uncertainty. "I don't understand."

Bandicut gripped her arm to steady her. "It means the ground shaking—maybe pretty hard." Right now, it was starting to feel as if a freight train were passing by. "Jeaves, what's causing this?" He looked up. Overhead, an enormous clear dome protected them from the vacuum of interstellar space. It reminded him of domes on Shipworld, a pretty solid place; but they were not on Shipworld. As the ground continued to quake, he wondered about the strength of this dome.

Li-Jared swung his gaze from left to right. "What the hell is—" *bwang* "—going on, Jeaves?" he echoed, with a froglike twanging sound that seemed to emerge from deep in his throat.

Over the rumbling, Jeaves said, "It's a hypergravity shock wave. It's part of the problem I was telling you about. We've been getting them intermittently for some time, but they're growing in frequency and severity."

"When's it going to stop?" Bandicut yelled, waving a hand uselessly against the dust now rising from the ground.

"Soon, I hope," Jeaves answered, raising his own voice to a shout. "It's a disturbance in spacetime, propagating through n-dimensional space. Once it passes, I'll show you where it came from."

Li-Jared was scowling, which on a Karellian face looked something like a leer. "This doesn't have something to do with the Maw of the Abyss, does it? We thought we'd gotten away from the Maw!"

"Not that we know of—" Jeaves began. His words cut off when the station shuddered harder, and the ground heaved violently, knocking all four of the company into the dust. The ground bucked in waves. Bandicut cursed, sliding on his elbows and knees, trying to protect Antares, who had fallen half under him. Jeaves shouted something he couldn't hear. But he *did* hear the cracking of stone walls. Then he heard Jeaves's words, amplified: *". . . into the shelter! Get into the shelter!"*

Bandicut could barely lift his head. Shelter? What shelter? Then he saw a row of blazing marker lights leading down into a deep cut in the ground . . .

"Quickly!" Jeaves shouted, and Li-Jared yelled, "This way, Ik!" and hauled on the Hraachee'an. Bandicut did likewise with Antares; they couldn't stand up to run, but together they crawled toward the opening, falling through after Ik and Li-Jared, and nearly on top of them.

A light came on as a door slid shut. They untangled themselves enough to realize that they were still bouncing up and down, but less violently and on a padded surface. They were apparently in a sealed emergency shelter not much larger than the star-spanner bubble. Jeaves reappeared in their midst—a smaller projection—and asked, "Are you all right? Is anyone injured?" When no one seemed hurt, he continued, "You can ride out the shock wave here. This is the worst we have experienced—and I must tell you, it alarms me."

"My robots!" Bandicut called. "Are they all right?" The last time he had seen Napoleon and Copernicus, they'd been heading off to another sector of the station for servicing.

Jeaves flickered. "We're experiencing broken communication to that area. But the service bays are well protected."

/// They're being seen to by the shadow-people.
I'm sure they're in excellent hands, ///
the quarx murmured silently, in Bandicut's head.

/I know, I know./ The shadow-people, fractal-creatures who looked like torn shreds of darkness and appeared to have no material form, were the ones who seemed to keep things running on Shipworld—and apparently here, too. /But still . . . /

"How much longer?" Li-Jared asked in a voice quavering from the vibration, and maybe from fear.

Jeaves did not answer at once. The shaking seemed to lessen, as though it were being muffled. "We are trying to create a compensation field around the shelter, so we can talk," Jeaves said finally.

"When is it going to *end*?" Antares asked.

"I don't know. None has lasted this long before."

Bandicut squeezed Antares's hand. The Thespi female leaned against him, her long auburn hair falling against his shoulder, and together they settled back against the padding to ride it out. He felt her anxiety vibrate through him along with the continuing shudders of the quake. He slipped an arm around her shoulder to reassure her.

"You said you would tell us where this was coming from," Ik said.

"All right, then, let's start," Jeaves answered. "Please look up." As he spoke, the light in the shelter dimmed, and the ceiling and upper walls seemed to disappear, replaced by the night sky. To Bandicut, the view looked like a clear sky on a dark night on the North American plain. A great, breathtaking swath of the Milky Way arched across the field of view—except that the star patterns were all unfamiliar. "I need to tell you something about the neighborhood this waystation is located in," the robot said. "We are about twenty-four thousand light-years from the center of the galaxy."

"In the disk plane?" Li-Jared asked.

"Yes. Now notice the nebula." The view rotated about thirty degrees.

It was hard *not* to notice the wispy, ethereal cloud of glowing gas and dust floating slightly offset from the band of the galaxy. Bandicut raised his hands and held them side by side. They didn't quite cover the glowing cloud.

"We are presently a few hundred light-years from the nebula," Jeaves continued. "It is known locally as Starmaker. But you may know it by another name, John."

Everyone turned to look at Bandicut. He peered up at the cloud and the star patterns, then shook his head.

"It is well known on your homeworld," said the robot. "In fact, it is visible to the naked eye from your northern hemisphere. But we're seeing it from what you would think of as the back side. Your astronomers call it the Great Orion Nebula."

Bandicut drew a sharp breath. *"The Orion Nebula?"* he whispered, stunned. "My God." Of course he knew it; in the constellation Orion the Hunter, it was the middle "star" in the sword hanging from the Hunter's belt. A profound feeling of homesickness overtook him. Not since his exile from Earth's solar system had he seen anything that offered even this much connection with home. Now . . . he had a place again in the galaxy; he knew where he was.

Jeaves was still talking. "The Orion Nebula, besides being located some fifteen hundred light-years to this side of John's homeworld, Earth, is one of the great star-forming nebulas of the Milky Way galaxy."

Bandicut breathed out again. */Fifteen hundred light-years.* Still a long way home./

///Yes, but we're closer now than before.
Didn't we guess Shipworld was about
fifteen thousand light-years? ///

/Yah./ It had been a wild guess, though. All they really knew was that the enormous artificial habitat known as Shipworld floated somewhere outside the Milky Way, above the galactic disk. He and the others had lived there for a comparatively short time, before being hurled back into the galaxy to the Neri world.

He suddenly realized that Antares was holding a steadying hand on him.

/// You're trembling, John. ///

Was he? "I'm fine," he murmured aloud. But there was no hiding his feelings from the empathic Thespi. Antares could read his emotions perfectly.

Jeaves continued. "I'm going to magnify the image now . . ." The view of the cloud swelled until it dominated the sky. "And enhance the colors and brightness . . ." The nebula took on a deeper rose hue, streaked with blue- and green-tinged gases. Individual stars within it became visible by the score, as well as a great many blobs of condensing matter that might one day become stars. The nebula seemed to unfold like a flower. Deep within its inner clouds was a cave with wispy, mysterious walls—and within that interior sanctum blazed four intensely bright stars. Bandicut thought he recognized the cluster from photos.

Jeaves's pointer winked in the sky, breaking the moment of wonder. "Human astronomers call this bright star-group the Trapezium. And just to the left of the Trapezium, *here,* is the area where the hypergrav shock waves seem to originate—somewhere in this star-birthing area. We have sent several probes to the region to investigate. None has returned."

"Hrrm, tell us more of these probes," Ik said.

"And tell us this station is holding together out there," Li-Jared added. "I still feel a lot of shaking."

Jeaves paused, seemingly gathering his thoughts. "The station is holding together, yes. The shock wave is subsiding." Bandicut pressed his hand against the padding; he still felt vibrations, but they were fading. "And to answer Ik's question," Jeaves went on, "three robotic missions have been launched from this station that I know of."

"And you say none returned?"

"That's correct. We don't know why. The second transmitted *some* information, the others none at all."

Li-Jared jumped to his feet. "And you're about to say you ex-pect *us* to go next?"

"Our robots seem insufficient for the job," said Jeaves. "Stars may be dying there. And judging by the gravity waves, the situation is deteriorating rapidly."

"Well, *that* really makes me want to fly into it!" Li-Jared snapped. He flicked his thumbs and fingers against each other in a gesture of sarcasm.

"I do not ask for a commitment just now," Jeaves said. "I merely ask that you listen. Please."

Li-Jared growled, but sat back down.

"Whatever is happening in this star nursery," Jeaves said, "may soon have far-reaching effects, well beyond the nebula. The shock waves we have been experiencing are just the immediate symptom, and they are dangerous enough. But they likely signal far graver dangers." He paused a moment. "The quake has passed. As soon as we can run some system and structural checks, we'll get you out of this shelter. We have a visitor you need to meet."

"Visitor?" Bandicut asked.

Jeaves was silent a moment. Then: "Just a few more checks." Then: "Good." The door that had sealed them into the shelter slid open with a hiss. Jeaves's holo winked out, and his voice rolled in from outside the shelter. "You may come out now."

3

ED AND THE STARS

 Emerging from underground, they found the surround-ings as they had left them, except for a jagged crack in one of the stone walls and a slowly settling cloud of dust. "Looks like the place is still standing," Bandicut muttered.

Before anyone could answer, a clattering sound came from around the stone wall to their left. A moment later, a jointed metal robot trotted into view. It looked a little like an upright praying mantis, with a spring in its two-legged gait. "Napoleon!" Bandicut shouted in delight. "You're all right! Where's Copernicus?" Even as he spoke, Copernicus rolled up behind Napoleon. Copernicus was shaped like a short barrel on its side, propelling itself on four wheels that looked like fat, horizontal ice cream cones. The tapping sound of his greeting lifted Bandicut's heart. The two robots had traveled with him since leaving Triton, back in the solar system. They were now his oldest friends.

"H'lo, Cap'n," answered Napoleon. "We left the upgrade center to check on you. Are *you* all right?"

"We're fine."

"Guess who we saw in the maintenance section," Napoleon continued. "The shadow-people!"

"I heard," Bandicut said. "Listen, did you two get any useful readings on that quake?"

Copernicus tapped. "Cap'n, it was very severe. If we experience any more of them, I would be concerned for—"

The robot was interrupted by a sound like a soft rumble of timpani. "Is that another quake?" Li-Jared squawked, looking around worriedly.

"No," Jeaves said. "That is our visitor."

Antares pointed. "Look."

Something was creeping toward them over the desert floor. It looked like an enormous fried egg, sunny-side-up. Its motion was slow but not quite continuous. When Bandicut blinked, it seemed to surge forward with a twinkle. It was about a meter across—purple, with an orange yolk. "What the hell *is* it?" Bandicut asked. "Is *it* making that rumbling noise?"

"I believe so," said Ik, approaching it cautiously. "Do you suppose it's talking?"

There was another rumble. *"Bzzzz-rawl-l-lp . . ."*

The shape began to creep partway up the wall of a stone outcropping. *"Brrr-huup-p . . ."* A breathier sound came this time, and with it the thing's top surface vibrated.

"Jeaves?" Bandicut asked quietly. "Is this thing alive?"

"Yes," Antares said. "It is."

Bandicut gave her a startled glance. "You sense it?"

"Yes. It is aware of us."

The quarx was stirring in Bandicut's mind.

/// I think it might be aware of me, *actually. ///*

Antares had the same thought, apparently. She pointed as the being moved with a twinkling shuffle toward Bandicut. "I believe, uhhll, that it wants to make contact with you, Bandie John Bandicut."

Bandicut swallowed. "Me?" He turned. "Napoleon? Copernicus? You getting any readings from this thing?"

"Trying, Cap'n." *Tap tap.* "It is difficult to view with sensors, for some reason."

"Haa-loooo-p." That was from the fried egg.

"You think it's really trying to speak to us?" Bandicut crouched close to it. "Hello! Can you understand us?" The fried egg was near enough now that he could see faint pulsations along its "white," while the "yolk" appeared to be rotating in changing directions.

"Trryyy-ng-ng-ng . . ."

The quarx spoke softly.

/// Perhaps if you touch it with your hand,
the stones could help with the translation. ///

Bandicut shuddered.

/// I sense no danger. ///

He looked up. "You think it would be safe to touch that thing?" he asked Ik.

"Safe? Hrrm—"

"John Bandicut, please do not do anything foolish," Antares said. "You may be only a human—" and she whistled, a Thespi approximation of a chuckle "—but I would hate to lose you."

Bandicut rubbed the back of his neck. "I'd hate to lose me, too. But Charlie thinks the stones might be able to . . ." He paused and glanced at his wrists, where the two tiny, embedded translator-stones pulsed. The stones had been given to him by an alien device back on Triton. Without them, he would not be able to communicate with his companions here, and he might have died a hundred different ways by now. He looked up at his robots. "Napoleon, how's it look? Any sign of dangerous radiation or reactive chemicals?"

"Multispectrum EM radiation, Cap'n. Nothing harmful that I

can see. Spectrographic scanning shows . . . no clear chemical signatures at all."

"Huh?"

"I cannot explain. It does not seem to occupy physical space. But neither does it look like a hologram or other image. I must await further information."

Bandicut blinked. "Yah. Let's see if we can get some." The thing had stopped moving. Still crouching, he edged close enough to touch it. He felt Antares's hand on his shoulder, reassuring him. Or perhaps using him as an empathic conduit.

The egg-surface quivered as his hand approached. Its purple skin looked slick, with oily, iridescent ripples spreading outward from the point directly beneath his hand. Would it dissolve his skin?

/// You've seen too many movies . . . ///

"Maybe." His hand touched the surface. It felt cool and slippery . . .

A muffled gasp from Antares startled him. "Are you—?" he began, and then a wave of voices hit the inside of his skull, layer after layer. Or maybe . . . a *single* voice, full of harmonics and dissonance.

His translator-stones spoke softly. ✷*Attempting to filter and translate.*✷

He felt a shuddering sensation—not *his* shudder, but the sounds being squeezed through translation routines, like fruit through a juicer. Suddenly he was surrounded by fractured images of light and dark, as though he had been dropped into a space full of broken mirrors. Mountains: there were jagged mountains of ochre and maroon. The image shattered and came together again, changed. Canyons now, shifting and re-forming. Images of this creature's world, deciphered by the translator-stones? The images continued breaking and reassembling, tumbling over one another—dizzying cliffs, broken plains, and layers of harsh, blazing light.

The translator-stones did something else, and Bandicut's attention shifted to a new sound, welling up like a choir. He could almost make out . . . not words, exactly . . . but sounds distantly suggestive of a human voice. He strained to hear.

Best translation: the entity describes its species as 'Those whose appearance is to the real self as the tip of a cone is to the wide, round base.'

/Huh?/

The precise meaning is still emerging.

/It looks like a fried egg. What does that description have to do with a fried egg?/

Charlene explained.

/// The egg is the tip of the cone.
Its real self, its real being if you could see it,
is much fuller, more complexly dimensioned.
The base of the cone. ///

/It doesn't look even remotely like a cone./

/// Not literally, perhaps. ///

The quarx detoured into a brief discourse with the stones. Finally it spoke again.

/// The stones believe it is a hyperdimensional cone.
What we see is merely a cross-section of its body
where it intersects our spacetime continuum. ///

/You got all that out of what we just heard? This thing is a living . . . hyperdimensional? . . . cone? What does that *mean*? Does it have a name?/

/// The stones are still working on that. ///

Bandicut nodded dizzily. He wondered if his friends were seeing these tortured landscape images, too. Were his translator-stones communicating with theirs, conveying all that they were unraveling? He saw new movement in the jagged mountain landscape—twinkling movement, of indistinct shapes. Other hypercones? He heard something like . . . a buzz of conversation? There was a rhythm to the sound, and to the movements. The pulse of life on this being's world?

The hypercone spoke again, and now he managed to make out some of the sounds. Its voice was like sand flowing down a series of resonating steps, changing pitch with each step: *"Ehh-h-hed . . . g-gonn-nn-t-to-g-get-t-t hhh-helll-ellp-p-p-p."*

Bandicut blinked. /Did you catch that? It sounded like—/

/// Ed-gone-to-get-help? ///

/Yes. Is that its mission?/

Attempting clarification, whispered the stones.

Bandicut closed his eyes, trying to focus. Then:

We have refined the translation. That is its name. You may try to speak.

Bandicut blinked his eyes open. The hypercone's outer rim was now blue. What do you say to a fried egg? "Hello . . . Ed-gone-to-get-help. Would it . . . be okay if I called you 'Ed'?"

The cone shivered faintly. *"Eh-hd. Yeh-hss. Long-ng naaame difffff-icult-t."*

Bandicut drew a slow breath. "Yes. *My* name is . . . *John.*"

"Johhhnnn." The cone sounded like a French horn, full of harmonics, as it repeated Bandicut's name. Its outer portion shimmered.

"That's right." Bandicut paused. So much to ask. What first? "Where . . . do you come from, Ed? And what is it you came to speak about? To ask help for?"

The cone started to quiver. *"S-sshowww . . ."*

The visual images became steadier, but at the same time began to glow more brightly. The dull orange and maroons of the mountains turned luminous, becoming intense with heat, difficult to look at. Fire licked at the sky overhead. The beings twinkling along the rock faces, beings whose shapes he could not comprehend, were moving more quickly now. There was a dissonant buzzing in the air.

/// I sense distress. ///

/Definitely. But why? /

/// Uncertain . . . ///

Bandicut became aware of Antares whispering, "There is great fear. I don't know of what. But those . . . whatever they're called . . ."

"Cones. Hypercones."

Antares's eyes suddenly filled with concern; her hazy gold irises dilated into a thin gold ring surrounding large, jet-black pupils. "They fear for their lives."

Ed began changing color again. The quivering beneath Bandicut's hand intensified. The deep blue of the outer ring was developing a magenta swirl. Ed spoke again, breathily, with a sound like a large pot of thick liquid boiling. *"Day-hay-hayn-jerr. Dayn-jerr."*

"Danger?" Bandicut asked. "What kind of danger?"

"Dan-gerr ffrom the s-skyyy."

Bandicut felt Antares's hand tighten on his arm, as the sky be-hind the mountains flickered and danced. He glimpsed what looked like a sun, roiling and fuming. *That doesn't look too stable,* he thought.

"Ed? Is that sun a danger to your homeworld?"

The cone trembled. *"Alll . . . alll in dangerr. S-s-sun sh-shaking-ng. Many-y-y suns-s-s."*

"Why? Why is your sun shaking?"

The creature made a rumbling sound. *"Intrrrud-errrs!"*

"And you came—?"

"Seek-k help-p."

Bandicut shook his head. "I don't understand. What can *we* do to help? We don't even know where your world is."

Ed rumbled again, but the sound was softer, and Ed was be-coming thinner under Bandicut's hand. *"Neeed-d help-p."* And then he twinkled and vanished.

Bandicut straightened up, blinking. He rubbed his tingling hand. "Did you all see—?"

"Ed is gone," Antares said quietly. "I no longer feel his pres-ence."

"That's because it—*he*—whatever—was making a stretch to become visible here, and he couldn't do it for long," Li-Jared said, blinking like an owl.

A pale column of light appeared, and turned into Jeaves. "Your suppositions are correct. Now that you've met Ed-gone-to-get-help, you probably have even more questions. May I try to explain?"

Bandicut drew a deep breath. "All right. Let's have it."

The robot's gaze took in each of the company. "Please sit." Jeaves gestured, and behind them, a glint of blue light expanded horizontally, then vanished. In its place was a flat bench. "Let's start with the long view . . ."

✳

Jeaves displayed Starmaker, the Orion Nebula, overhead. "Under any circumstances, a stellar nursery is a dangerous place. The birth of a star releases enough energy and radiation to destroy just about any inhabited world in the vicinity. Of course, there usually aren't civilizations *in* stellar nurseries—not by your standards, where biolife such as you would have evolved. Ed's world may be exceptional; we think it *is* located in the Starmaker Nebula. But it is apparently in grave danger."

"Is that why you got involved with the nebula?" Bandicut asked.

"Not initially. Long before we encountered Ed, or started experiencing hypergrav disturbances here, we knew that something out there was killing stars. It was happening deeper in the galaxy, and has been marching steadily outward."

"Killing stars?" Antares echoed. "How can you kill a star? And what's killing them?"

"We don't know. But when you kill a star in a nursery like this—well, let me show you." The image changed slightly. "This is a recording made about three hundred years ago." Jeaves's pointer moved to the edge of the nebula, where a star suddenly flared to a brilliance that turned the sky to daytime.

"Hrahh, supernova," murmured Ik.

"Exactly. A young star named Blue Hope died, hundreds of millions of years before its time. And then—" Jeaves pointed out smaller, cascading explosions "—it took several other stars with it. And who knows how many planets with fledgling life, in outlying areas."

Antares squinted in puzzlement. "You speak of the stars as if they were . . . uhll . . . what exactly *do* you mean by . . . star *life*?"

"What do I—?" Jeaves's gaze flickered for a moment. "Oh, dear. You know, don't you—that stars, most of them, are living beings?"

Antares shook her head.

Jeaves's gaze swept the company. "Living—sentient—?"

"Okay, hold on," Bandicut said. "Just wait a minute, okay?" He looked around at the others, then back at Jeaves. "Are you saying, sentient, like *thinking*? Like we could *communicate* with a star?"

Jeaves seemed to consider his words carefully. "In principle, yes. Communication would be very difficult. However, I myself did once, under most extreme circumstances, brush the living thought of a star. It was an astonishing experience."

Air hissed from Antares's lips, as Bandicut whispered to the quarx, /I feel you twitching, Charlie. Do you know something about this?/ Was he about to tap into the crazy-quilt of the quarxian memory? Charlie/Charlene existed in a series of brief, closely connected lives, and his/her memory was at times a patchwork of ancient quarx-memory and recent history.

/// I may have . . . once.

This is bringing back echoes. ///

Bandicut felt the universe shifting beneath him again. Echoes of stars as living, thinking beings?

"This—" said Li-Jared with a bonging sound "—is not so surprising." He gazed at the others, his eyes vertical gold slivers, with bright bands of electric-blue across the middle. He appeared energized by the subject.

"It is, hrrm, to *me,*" said Ik.

"Why is it not surprising to you?" Antares asked Li-Jared.

"Because—" *bong* "—stars are such layered and energetic creations," the Karellian said. "They are defined by exceedingly complex and turbulent electromagnetic fields, and contain long-lived internal structure. It would almost be surprising if intelligence did *not* evolve there. Plus—" he waggled his hands in traceries through the air "—the highly energetic sky of my own world has shown possible signs of awareness, and it is less complex than a star."

Good Lord, Bandicut thought. He turned back to Jeaves. "So you're saying the star we just watched going supernova was a *sentient star?*"

"Indeed," said Jeaves. "And there could be more coming. My friends, the severity of that last quake has me worried. We may have less time than I'd thought. Would you mind if I brought in some friends to augment the learning process? It could make all of this go much faster." ·

Bandicut closed his eyes and thought wistfully of the respite he had been hoping for.

"I am willing," he heard Antares say. He sighed, opened his eyes, and along with Ik and Li-Jared said, "Okay."

The desert surroundings faded into the background, and two intersecting arcs of smooth stone wall became highlighted by hidden light sources, creating a focused space around them. "Prepare yourselves for contact," Jeaves said. "This will require the help of your translator-stones."

Antares's hand went to her throat, Ik's to his temples, Li-Jared's to his chest.

Whoop! Whoop! Whoop!

The alarm sound came from overhead. Three rings of golden light soared into view, skating across the sky. They grew to meter-wide haloes, then descended, orbiting one another, making a sound like wind chimes. One halo turned ruby, one pale emerald, and the third shimmering aquamarine. After a few moments, the blue one glided to the center and floated directly over their heads, making a sound like a steel hoop whirling around a pole.

/Charlie? Char?/

/// I'm not sure . . .
they're alive, I know that. ///

✳Establishing contact. Translating now,✳ muttered the stones in his wrists.

The hoop sound dropped away, and Bandicut felt himself blinking as he slipped helplessly into a dream-state. He seemed to fall through emptiness as the voices of the haloes, like soft-spoken angels, told him about the life and death of stars in a nebula called Starmaker . . .

✳

The story was almost incomprehensibly old, in human terms. Yet in other ways it was familiar: birth and life, life and death. But in this story, the players were different; the story spoke of the birth of stars, the life and death of stars. Some were wise, some foolish, some noble, some dull, some none of those things.

In the beginning, in the deepness of time, there were no players; only cold gas and dust, and coiling magnetic fields, and clenching gravity wells. No one spoke; none were alive. For a long time, there was only endless rotation of gases in the cold, and slow contraction. But as the matter condensed, compressed, and heated, there came a dull reddish glow. It was not yet life, but it was the crucible from which life would emerge.

Even so, true life might never have appeared in most of the clumps of gas, were it not for a few particularly massive balls that crushed inward and burst into fusion-fire. These first stars burned bright, burned fast, died violently as supernovas—and in death sent cataclysmic shock waves crashing through the gathering medium. From those compression waves new fusion-fires ignited, new stars kindling in the darkness.

These stars lived and died; and in their convulsions of birth and death, yet more shock waves cascaded through the nebula, creating still newer life from death.

And eventually, there were some stars who awoke. Not just to heat and light, but to more.

Some who thought.

Who felt.

Who knew.

According to the stories passed down through the ages, the first to achieve consciousness were named *Dazzle* and *Glare*—not by themselves, but by others who followed. They lived brightly and died brightly, in new supernovas that salted the clouds with heavy elements to enrich the worlds to come. None lived now who remembered *Dazzle* and *Glare* firsthand, but the story of their lives had not been forgotten. Thought by some to be more myth than reality, they nevertheless remained—whether actually or symbolically—the progenitors of their race.

Generations followed, one upon another.

In time, knowledge turned into wisdom, and the community of stars prospered through the long, slow turns of the galaxies.

Until much later, when the change came, with the arrival of the intruders . . .

*

Antares found it all rather hard to follow, but she understood clearly that there were not just living, sentient stars in this story. There were *families—histories—* of sentient stars. It reminded her of her own people, except on a vastly greater scale. These histories wound their threads through billions of years, with creatures she could barely comprehend—living stars! And there were so many of them, with such rich lives.

But something had gone terribly wrong. And that something had come from the outside.

At first it seemed only a strain in the sea of dust and energy in which they lived. But existence in the nebula was practically *defined* by strains, by shock waves, by enormous turbulences that gave life and took life away. Many eons passed before the changes were noticed. But there was a presence here that no sun had ever felt before. Changes were occurring in newborns—some emerging as lifeless balls of fusion-fire, others aware but dangerously unstable. Some of the older stars were growing confused, possibly psychotic.

That was how it started. Then came premature supernovas—which, as often as not, took not just one life, but many. And not just the lives of stars, but of worlds hundreds of light-years away, scoured sterile by the radiation—inhabited worlds, worlds filled with people. Not Thespi, maybe—but people.

Antares found the stories strange, yet also moving. But what, she wondered, could it have to do with the four of them here? It was one thing to hear about sentient stars, but quite another to think they could actually interact with them.

And as for *helping* them . . .

She empathized; given her nature, she could not help doing so. But what could they possibly *do*?

4

FOOD FOR THOUGHT

 By the time Jeaves called a halt, the haloes had filled Bandicut's head with enough background information to leave him reeling. He was feeling numb when Jeaves suggested they return to the lodge where they had spent the previous night. "You could all use a good night's rest."

"You think?" Bandicut muttered.

"You need time to absorb the information. A ship is being prepared. But it isn't ready for departure yet, in any case."

"Ship?" Ik boomed as they trooped together up the desert trail. "What ship? Who's preparing it?"

"Exploratory vessel. The shadow-people are modifying it. They provide maintenance for the entire station."

"The shadow-people I trust. I'd like to know more about this ship, though. Do we have time to think about your, hrrm . . . request?" Ik asked.

"We'll talk in the morning," said Jeaves.

They approached what looked like a hanging bead curtain, with waves of heat shimmer rippling up its strands. Was this the same transport device they had come through during their walk-around tour of the station this morning? Bandicut hesitated, but when Jeaves ushered them through, he let the curtain part around him. He felt a slight warming and stepped, followed by the others, into a now-familiar forest clearing. In the center of the clearing stood the lodge. The building, with gray stone walls, wooden beams, and a shingle roof, reminded Bandicut of Earth. Wood smoke issued from a wide, brick chimney. Last night, bringing them here, Jeaves had explained that he'd designed the look of the lodge himself, trying his best to make it comfortable. But, he'd admitted, he had more knowledge of human architecture than of Thespi, Karellian, or Hraachee'an. He'd gotten the exterior right, anyway, Bandicut thought.

Antares, Li-Jared, and Ik entered through a heavy wooden door. Bandicut paused for a last word with Napoleon and Copernicus, who would spend the night reconnoitering the area. "See what you can find out, all right?"

"Wilco," said Napoleon.

"And be careful." Finally, Bandicut followed the others inside. The interior seemed to owe more to human medieval fantasy than to anything Bandicut had ever encountered on Earth itself. The main common room was a broad, dimly lit, low-ceilinged area, with flames cracking from a log in a huge fireplace set in the far wall. Wisps of smoke hung in the air above a cluster of benches, sofas, and low tables near the fire. This was where they'd dined last night and this morning. It already felt a little like home.

Ik and Li-Jared had made their way to the fireside sofas, with

Antares right behind them. Soon they were all sitting before the log fire, with plates piled with food, and a variety of drinks: a mug of ale for Bandicut and another for Ik, who wanted to see what Bandicut's favorite beverage tasted like. Antares had a reddish nectar in a tall glass, and Li-Jared held a milkshake-like concoction. One or two of the living haloes floated in and out of the darkened room, not speaking to them but making a kind of music that sounded like a blend of steel drum and harp.

Bandicut took a deep draft of ale, pleased by its rich malt flavor and hoppy aftertaste. He lowered the mug with a sigh, grateful to contemplate something simple for a while. "What do you think?" he asked Ik.

"Most bracing," Ik pronounced, stroking the two thumbs of his left hand together along his hard-surfaced lips. "If this is a sample of your Earth drinks, I believe I approve." With that, he turned his attention to the dinner on his plate.

The food was a respectable reproduction of Hraachee'an food bars, whole-grain bread rolls, cheese, and apples; and various fruits and other samplings of Hraachee'an, Karellian, and Thespi foods. They ate quietly for a time, before Antares broke the silence, wondering aloud what the others had thought of the haloes' presentation. Li-Jared sputtered for a moment, but Ik answered first. "Truthfully," he said, "I find it hard to fathom this business of living stars."

Li-Jared blinked, the bright blue and gold of his eyes going dark, then blazing again. "Well, remember, Ik, your people had only just ventured into space when your sun exploded—"

"I hadn't forgotten," Ik said, his deep-set eyes narrowing, giving him an even more skeletal appearance than usual.

Li-Jared drummed his fingers in exasperation. "I just meant that you had not had time to become intimately acquainted with your own star, or others. Would you have *known* it if your sun were sentient?"

"Rrrm, what I was going to say was, I am willing to *entertain* the notion of sentient suns."

"Well, I hope you aren't entertaining the notion that we might *go* there!"

"I do not know. But, Li-Jared—" Ik turned his left hand

palm-up, his long, bony fingers extended "—if there are whole worlds in danger, and there is something we can do to help—"

Waving his arms, Li-Jared jumped up and stalked around in a fury. "Moon and stars—why must it be us, *always us*? We saved Shipworld! We saved the Neri! Are we the only ones in the galaxy who can do these things? Do we just keep doing it until one day we die?" He wheeled around and glared into the fire, his back to Ik.

As Ik stirred, Bandicut tried to say something. But his voice caught; it jarred him to see the two argue—and the truth was, he agreed with both of them.

"Friends, please—" Antares began, and then she too seemed at a loss for words.

Finally Ik stretched out his long limbs. "I can only guess, hrrm, there are some things only we are in a position to do."

Li-Jared's eyes narrowed visibly. "Yah, maybe we're just handy and maybe we're just—" *rasp* "—suckers."

"Hrah, maybe so. But maybe the need is still there." Ik turned to Bandicut. "Hrrrm, Bandie, would you join me in having another one of these ales?"

*

Antares was beginning to wish she'd never started the conversation. It all felt like too much to think about right now: whether to go, or not go, on a dangerous mission to do something about *sentient stars.* Or worse, some mysterious agent attacking sentient stars. And wondering whether they were going to have a choice in the matter, any more than they had chosen to plunge into the ocean of the Neri world. Antares was very fond of Li-Jared and Ik; but she suddenly realized that right now, she needed *not* to be listening to this. The arguments were clamoring in her mind like a thousand voices . . .

She rested her head against the sofa back and shifted her gaze to the fire. As she watched its dancing flames, she thought, *How strange this little company is. I have known these people such a short time, and they are such a part of me now. To think how much I trust them! And John Bandicut—we've had so little time to really get to know each other. I wish we could put everything else aside for a while.*

Though her gaze was turned away from the others, she was aware of John Bandicut's physical presence beside her. She was almost close enough to detect his feelings, but they were more like an aura, a shadow she couldn't quite grasp. *Time . . . I just need some time . . .*

★

Li-Jared had sat back down, but still looked disgruntled, as Ik returned from the food table with two full mugs of ale. Bandicut accepted one and took a swallow. *Ahh.* Sighing, he glanced at Antares. She was turned toward the fire, but her eyelids were half shut. "You okay?"

"I wish to sleep soon." She shifted her eyes toward him. "John Bandicut, will you join me?"

"Of course." He took another swallow, then paused to eye his nearly full mug. "Do you mean now?"

She whispered a chuckle. "I can wait."

Bandicut took another gulp, then caught her eye again. *She means now.* He raised his mug ruefully toward Ik. "Would you mind if we continued this later?"

Antares leaned toward Ik and Li-Jared. "My friends, would you forgive us?"

Ik sipped his ale and clacked his mouth shut. "Indeed. Rest well—both of you."

Li-Jared tapped his chest with his fingers and snapped, "What is to forgive? Ik and I will continue the—" *brr-dang* "—learned discussion. Good night."

As Antares rose, Bandicut took a last, long swallow of ale. He joined her in threading past the tables to the back of the room, where Jeaves was waiting. He floated ahead of them down a short hallway. "I wanted to make sure you were not in need of anything . . ."

"Nothing, no," Antares answered.

"Then I will take my leave. We will discuss these matters further in the morning. Good night." Jeaves left them at the door to their quarters.

They entered a modest-sized room that contained a resilient, matlike floor and a single sleeping pad large enough for two people to stretch out on comfortably. The door materialized closed behind them. Bandicut sat on the sleeping pad and looked up at Antares. "You okay? Just tired?"

"And overwhelmed." She came and sat beside him, smoothing out the red, satiny fabric of her pantsuit. He squeezed her hand. "So much to think about," she said, her breath hissing out. "Can we talk about something other than thinking stars, and missions to places we might rather not go to?"

"Sure." He was certain she did not have physical intimacy on her mind, but he felt her empathic touch at the edge of his thoughts. "Anything in particular?"

"I don't know. Bandie John Bandicut, so much has happened to us, so quickly. How long have we actually known each other?"

Not that long. Only a short time on Shipworld, in the midst of chaotic and near-catastrophic events, before they were hurled to the Neri world—and similarly perilous events—until the Maw of the Abyss hurled them away again.

Antares made a soft murmuring, almost purring sound. "And here we are, being asked to intervene in cosmic events. Stars with lifetimes of millions of years! What could we have to do with them? What could they have to do with us, even if they are awake and intelligent?"

"I don't know," he murmured. *I thought we weren't going to talk about this.*

Antares leaned her head on his shoulder; her thick mane of auburn hair tumbled over him. "It's just so hard even to know how to think about these things. I could grasp it when the Neri were in danger. And I could grasp it, on Shipworld, when the ice-line was in peril from the boojum—and you and your friends, too. But stars and worlds?" She raised her hands in a gesture of helplessness.

"Is it too hard to imagine their pain?"

"To *imagine* their pain? No. But to feel their *actual* pain—that would be very different. I do not know how I can become a part of that." She raised her chin, and her golden-irised eyes caught his. And he suddenly realized, this wasn't just about making a rational decision: smart mission, dumb mission. This was about *being part of something*.

"Then—"

"I feel as if I need to grasp this before I can even consider what we should do."

"I understand," he said, and it was almost true.

"And Ik and Li-Jared's pain and anger and frustration were so strong . . . that is why I needed to get away." She closed her eyes and breathed slowly and deeply. "I could not get it clear in my own mind."

"Does their presence bother you?"

"What? *No,* my dear Bandie John Bandicut. They are my companions—" *rasp* "—friends. I would do anything for them." Her hand turned and grasped his tightly, and he felt a wave of her feelings for Ik and Li-Jared. He also felt her feelings for *him,* which were . . . *different.*

"As I would for you," she added.

He nodded, swallowing.

"And you, John—what do you feel about this?"

"You mean, what Jeaves—?"

"Yes—*no.* About that, but not only that." She shifted position to sit cross-legged, facing him directly. "Where do *you* belong?"

"Well, I don't know exactly what you—"

She stopped him. "John." Her golden-eyed gaze was intent. "Tell me . . ." She pressed her lips together. "Tell me, who did you love? Who did you leave behind? Who do you *miss*?"

He felt a sudden upwelling of buried feelings, and a sharp lump in his throat, rendering him mute. His love for Antares, for this alien woman, this Thespi Third-female, auburn-maned and empathic, abruptly felt like a betrayal of the love he'd left behind, when a slingshot maneuver around the sun and a collision with a comet changed his life forever. He didn't know what to say, or how to explain it. Antares seemed very human at times; would she feel human jealousy? But she was *not* human. She was Thespi.

*/// I think she's asking
because she really wants to know. ///*
/But where do I start?/

"John," Antares said softly. "Why don't you tell me how you came to leave your home star. Can you do that?"

He nodded. He'd told her much already in bits and pieces,

but now he put it all together for her—how he had been working on Triton, moon of Neptune, as a mining surveyor. How he had found an alien artifact, the translator—and Charlie, the quarx now in his head. How Charlie had warned him of the comet that was going to slam into Earth, and how he was the only one who could save it—by stealing a spaceship and, with the help of the translator-stones, crossing the solar system to destroy it. By slamming into it and turning it, and himself, into a cloud of dust. But a funny thing happened on the way to the funeral, because he not only didn't die, he wound up being slung halfway across the galaxy to the strange place called Shipworld—where he was almost immediately pressed into service to defeat an enemy called the boojum.

Antares made a low humming sound. "Tell me, then, who did you leave? Who do you miss?"

Bandicut suppressed a twinge. *Julie Stone—are you waiting for me, thousands of light-years from here? Or are you long dead and gone?* He forced himself to breathe. "I miss my friends Georgia and Krackey, on Triton. And my niece, Dakota, back on Earth."

Antares leaned forward, tilting her head. "Your niece?"

"My brother's daughter. My brother and my parents . . . died, about ten years ago." He barked a sudden laugh. "Ten years ago, when I *left,* I mean. I don't know how long ago, now . . ."

Antares closed her hand over the top of his. "I understand. We are both in the same . . ."

"Boat," he said. "Circumstance."

"Not knowing how much time has passed, out there. Yes, I have often wondered the same. Tell me about . . . Dakota." Antares gazed at him with what seemed a very human expression of sympathy. He wondered if he was losing his ability to distinguish between human and Thespi. Besides the three-fingered hands, the silken body hair, and the four breasts. "Is she very . . . precious to you?"

A smile came, and went. "Dakota was—or *is*—an incredibly sweet, bright kid, who was orphaned when my brother and his wife were killed in a tunnel collapse." He hadn't thought about this in a long time. It still hurt. "That left her with just me and her

mother's parents. So Dakota's the only family *I* have. And I promised her . . . I would take her up into space someday. A promise
I'll never be able to keep now."

Antares waited a moment, then touched his cheek. "Is there
something more? About Dakota?"

"Hm? I guess not."

"Nothing? And yet it sticks in you, like a—"*rasp*"—craw?"

He chuckled. "Sticks in my craw. Okay. See, I created a trust
fund for her." *How do I explain a trust fund?* "It's a savings of
money—resources—to help her go away to a good school someday."

"This is good. Why does it stick in your craw?"

"Because I don't know if she ever got it. The government
thought I was a deranged criminal, and they might have seized it;
or her grandparents might have, I don't know. So—" his breath
caught and he had to force the words "—maybe I *did* keep my
promise to her, through that. If she took the money and used it
to pay for a good education, that could get her into space." He
drew a deep breath. "That's what I *want* to think."

Antares parted her lips with a sigh. "Then perhaps that is
what you *should* think." He nodded and sighed. She gave him a
moment, then continued. "There is someone else, though, isn't
there? You've told me . . . what is her name? Julie? Why don't you
want to talk about her?"

"I—well—" Now he was struggling again. "I didn't know her
that long, really—just long enough. I really . . . hated to leave her.
Especially the way I did—not even getting to tell her what I was
doing. I can't imagine what she thought." He felt a pressure between his temples, and wondered if it was coming from Antares.

/// Don't you know? ///

/Know what? It's a hard memory to focus on./

/// I'm not even human, and I can see it,
plain as day. ///

/See what?/ Bandicut felt a scowl surface on his face. He
tried to wipe it away with his thumb and forefinger.

/// You don't want to deal with the pain. ///

Bandicut muttered a growl at Charlie. Antares squinted. "Are
you talking to me, or to Charlie?"

"Um, sorry. It's just that—"

"It hurts?"

"Well, *yeah*—"

"It's important," she said softly. "That's why I want to know about it." She clasped his hand between hers. "John Bandicut, your thoughts and feelings about *her* will have an effect on *us,* will they not?"

He nodded. "Yes, I suppose so . . ." His face grew warm again as he drew forth the memories. "She became the person I trusted the most, the one I wanted to be with all the time. I was falling in love with her just when I had to leave forever."

"And you are wondering, will you ever see her again?"

"I don't see how I ever can. Even if she's still alive, what are the chances I'll ever return to Earth?"

Antares's breath whistled out. "I do not know. And yet, in a way, does it even matter? You still feel what you feel, yes?"

He nodded, shutting his eyes. "Yah . . ."

*

For some time after Bandicut and Antares left, Ik gazed into the fire—pondering sentient stars, and unseen masters who catapulted them off on hazardous missions. Despite his misgivings, he was intrigued by the possibility of sentient stars. Intrigued and frightened. A flaring sun had destroyed his homeworld— and along with it, his lifebonder Onaka and everyone else he had cared for. Had his own sun been a sentient being? Had it known what was happening? Ik drew a long swallow of the Earthman's ale and held the half-full mug up to regard it against the dancing flames of the fire.

"Ik?"

He turned his head, looking at Li-Jared through a slight mental haze. The ale seemed to be doing more than just giving him a warm glow. /Please reassure me that my normalization is handling this ale,/ he said silently to his voice-stones. He remembered a very bad time on the Neri world, when the normalization had *not* protected him adequately from the local food. Without Bandicut and Charlie's intervention, he might have died then and there.

"Ik, are you here with me?" Li-Jared demanded. The electric-blue slits across his gold eyes reflected the flickering firelight, giving him a look of great urgency.

"I am," said Ik, still waiting for a response from his stones.

All appears within limits, reported the stones.

"Are you with me in opposing this insanity?" Li-Jared was nervously fingering the tall glass holding his cream-elixir. He raised it as though to drink a sip, then lowered it again. "Yes?" he asked.

Ik tensed. "I, like you, have serious reservations."

Li-Jared's fingers began twitching. "*Serious reservations?* Ik, this is a mad thing they want us to do! This robot, Jeaves—these Shipworld masters—they want us to take off on a suicide mission."

Ik sighed through his ears. "Possibly so."

"Don't you remember what they've put us through? How they threw us into an ocean—not once, but twice? Are we going to let them keep doing this?" Li-Jared started to rise again, looking agitated.

Ik gazed at him silently. In fact, he did remember, all too clearly. There had been another time—before the Neri, before meeting John Bandicut—when a star-spanner bubble plunged Ik and Li-Jared into the ocean of an alien world. That time, they hadn't sunk into the depths, but bobbed on the surface, where a fishing-float rescued them. The nearby coast was populated by a strange fisher folk. Intelligent but not spacefaring or highly industrial, they were in grave danger from their planet's fluctuating magnetic field and radiation from their sun. Ik and Li-Jared had the impossible task of persuading them that they *had* to shield themselves or move underground, or risk terrible losses. By the time they'd convinced the leaders of the impending catastrophe, Ik and Li-Jared were nearly executed as mutant spies.

Li-Jared was still talking. "Is there any reason why they couldn't just pull us back to Shipworld with the star-spanner, the way they did from the Matuni world? Don't we deserve a—" *rasp* "—break?"

"I don't know," said Ik.

"But we intend to find out, yes? *Truth,* Ik! Truth is what I want to hear!" Li-Jared's bright eyes glared out of his brown-haired face. When Li-Jared was angry, it made even his friend Ik want to step back.

Ik sighed again. The ale seemed to make his thoughts foggy. "Truth, yes," he said at last. "But first perhaps we should do what Bandie and Antares have done. Get some rest."

Li-Jared growled under his breath, but did not say no.

5

UNSCHEDULED DEPARTURE

 "Morning" was marked by light streaming in through translucent squares high in the bedroom walls. Bandicut blinked his eyes open, wondering for a moment where he was—until it all rushed back with a jarring urgency. He pushed himself upright, washed and dressed, and walked with Antares through the empty common room. On his way, he picked up a mug of coffee and something that looked like a scone. Antares took a dark roll and a mug of sweet tea. They ate their breakfast standing up, before pushing open the front door.

Jeaves was waiting outside. "Good morning," he said. "Did you sleep well? Would you like to stretch your legs?"

"Fair, and I suppose so. Are Ik and Li-Jared up?"

"They went to take a look at the ship. If you hurry, you can catch them. Walk that direction." Jeaves pointed to their left. "You'll find the path. It's a short walk to the docks."

Bandicut glanced at Antares. She hooked an arm through his, and they followed a narrow path winding through the woods. There was a certain surrealistic feeling in walking among trees dressed in russet and yellow—many of them reminiscent of Earth, others with strangely curved branches that ended in spherical clusters of leaves. Bandicut was about to ask Antares if there were trees on the Thespi world, when he spotted the glint of a different environment ahead through the woods. Space docks?

They quickened their steps, before they heard Li-Jared's twang: "There they are!" The path broke out of the trees into a large, high-ceilinged area with a floor of a hard, pebbly gray material. Directly ahead loomed a huge spacecraft hangar.

Most of the floor space was taken up by empty docking cradles. Li-Jared waved them toward the nearest, the only one holding a vessel. Napoleon and Copernicus circled around it, taking readings from the strange-looking craft. The size of a small yacht, it was shaped like a melted, slightly deformed lozenge. Its surface was translucent and milky orange. It was enveloped in a nearly transparent haze, which on closer inspection was filled with almost invisible, silver glitter. Nano-assemblers? Bandicut wondered, remembering a seafloor factory that had manufactured submarines.

/// Nano-shit for starships? ///
Charlene mused.

/Maybe./

Whreeeek-whreeek! The sudden sound was like a shriek of badly tuned violins. A flurry of angular black shapes, part bat and part tattered black rags, fluttered around the spacecraft—and disappeared into the hull. "Hrah! Shadow-people!" Ik cried. Fractal beings, the shadow-people only partially inhabited the familiar dimensions of spacetime; but they were a welcome sight. It appeared they were hard at work on the ship.

Antares had turned to watch the shadow-people, but now she swung back to Ik and Li-Jared. "So, is this *the* spaceship? The one Jeaves wants us to take into that nebula?"

Jeaves's holo-image appeared beside Ik. "It is."

Li-Jared strode alongside the haze-enshrouded ship, gesturing in agitation. "And we're supposed to believe that this *thing*—" he waved his hands "—can not only get us to that nebula alive, but help us do something once we're there?"

"Well, rrrm, the star-spanner bubble didn't look like much, either," Ik pointed out. "Perhaps Jeaves will enlighten us."

"I will try," said the robot.

"Starting with the empty cradles," Ik continued. "Is this the only ship on the station?"

"Yes. All of the other vessels were sent out as probes."

"The ones that didn't return?" Li-Jared asked. "Why do you think this one will do any better? What's so different about it?"

The robot seemed to pause in thought. "Well, the basic hull design is the same—but the probes were all robotic and smaller, whereas this one is being fitted to accommodate you."

"That's it? That's the difference? Has anyone considered that maybe there's a design deficiency—and *that's* why the others didn't return?" Li-Jared waved at the ship. "Look at it! That doesn't look solid enough to *stand* in, much less fly into whatever the—" *rasp* "—we'd be flying into!"

"Hrrm, I am forced to agree," Ik said. "If the other missions failed, why should we think we can do better, with the same kind of ship?"

"The other missions didn't have you," said Jeaves.

Bandicut blinked. "Huh?"

"The seven of you. The other missions had excellent robotic equipment and programming. But they didn't have you four, or the quarx, or *your* robots."

"And *that's* the difference?" Bandicut asked.

Jeaves's sparkle-eyes looked at each of them in turn. "That is the difference."

Li-Jared made a bonging sound. "Well, that's just—"

"Oh, and the others didn't have *me*," Jeaves added. "For whatever that may be worth. I have some knowledge and experience, which may prove useful."

Li-Jared lowered his head, muttering darkly.

Antares blew a strand of hair away from her face. "What is it about *us* that you find so compelling?"

The robot stretched its gleaming arms wide. "You have a proven record, working together; you have succeeded in ways no one else has. Ik—you have a remarkable ability to bring cohesion to a group. You brought this company together."

"Hrmm, yes, but surely they would have—"

"They trust you, Ik. You're careful, you're reliable, and you take the long view of things. Yes? And you, Li-Jared."

Bong. "What about me?"

"You have knowledge, wit, and common sense. You don't hide your feelings. You speak if you think someone's not being straight with you. It can be annoying to your friends, I suspect, but it's a great asset."

Li-Jared stood uncharacteristically mute.

"Antares," Jeaves continued, "the value of your empathic abilities should be obvious. But so is your combination of hardheadedness and compassion, and your loyalty to your friends. And John—or should I say, John and Charlie?—the two of you together have the ability to do things none of the others can."

"Come on."

/// It's true, you know. ///

"You healed Neri who were dying from radiation sickness—remember? Plus, you're an excellent leader, and you have the benefit of all of Charlie's knowledge and insights." Jeaves turned around, looking at each in turn. "Should I continue? You all have translator-stones, which even by the standards of Shipworld are remarkable. And then we have Napoleon and Copernicus, who have grown so much they'd be unrecognizable to the people who built them."

"Okay, we get it," Bandicut said.

"Do you? *All* of you?"

"That means me, right?" Li-Jared said. "Well, I'm flattered, but not so much that I'm ready to sign on to your mission." He made that deep-in-the-throat sound again. *Bwang.* "I think we've done enough already. I think we should take this ship and fly it home. Or just stay here and hold out for a return to Shipworld."

"But could you fly this ship yourselves?" Jeaves asked. "It is not ready for flight yet, and its AI is being prepared for a particular mission. As for transportation back to Shipworld, I have no way to offer that."

"Could you not, if we decline the mission," Ik asked, "send us away in a star-spanner bubble?"

"The star-spanner generator on Shipworld has to be able to reach out and latch on to you," Jeaves answered. "Even if I had a hotline to Shipworld to arrange that—which I don't—the distance and the interference from the hypergrav waves effectively rule it out." The robot shook his head. "No, you would need a fully independent star vessel."

Ik opened his mouth to reply, but was interrupted when a

low rumble began to throb through the ground. "Rrrm! Not another—?" The rumble grew louder and harder. A series of jolts made them all stagger.

The Jeaves holo flickered, went out, then returned. "Stand by. We're picking up warnings from the sensing satellites."

Whreeeek-whreeek-whreeeeeeek! A group of shadow-people swarmed out of the ship and divided; half flurried around the craft and the rest flew up and vanished near the ceiling. Bandicut watched them until his gaze focused on the clear dome overhead. The ceiling vibrated visibly as another shock wave rippled through the station. "Jeaves—is that ceiling going to come down on us? Should we be getting to a shelter?"

"Too far—!" Jeaves began, then blinked out.

As the shaking became more intense, Napoleon and Copernicus raced up, alarm lights blinking. Napoleon staggered, and Copernicus skidded as his wheels slipped on the vibrating deck. "This is not a safe place to be!" Napoleon twanged. There was a loud crash, somewhere on the far side of the hangar.

Jeaves blinked back on. "We have lost contact with several of our sensing units between here and the nebula. This is all—" Whatever Jeaves said next was drowned out by another crash, this time from the direction of the forest. Trees falling?

"Jeaves? Should we get back to the lodge?"

Jeaves flickered out. When he did not reappear, Ik tipped his head back and said, "I am worried about those dome sections. If they crack—"

"This will be the first place to lose pressure," Bandicut said.

"The lodge may be reinforced," said Antares.

With the ground shivering under their feet, they ran—bouncing and skittering as if on an enormous griddle—toward the woods and the lodge. They were just approaching the tree line when a thunderous series of cracking sounds in the woods ahead made them stop.

Whreeeek-whreeek-whreeek! A cluster of shadow-people flew over their heads and circled back toward the ship, crying out.

They want you to return to the ship. It's the safest place.

All four looked at each other, as though their stones had spoken to them in unison. A halo appeared, wheeling over their heads, seemingly intending to lead them.

As the ground shook again, Bandicut waved toward the ship with his arms. "Let's go!" They ran together, following the halo.

Jeaves reappeared as a ghostly image near the ship, where Napoleon and Copernicus had just careened to a stop. The appearance of the vessel had changed in the minutes since they had left. The surrounding haze was gone, and the hull had taken on a more metallic and silvery sheen. It also had sprouted slender attachments, and bristled like a sea urchin. Antennas? Bandicut wondered. Force-field generators? Spines to discourage predators?

"Please get aboard," Jeaves urged. "You'll be better protected on the ship, especially if we lose atmosphere in the hangar."

"How likely is that?" Li-Jared demanded, his voice vibrating.

"I don't know. The station is coming under significant stress. Until now, these waves have been a nuisance and a warning. But the station AI has just declared an emergency," Jeaves said, leading them toward the stern of the ship.

Bandicut felt Antares's hand on his arm. "John, what is that?" She pointed past the stern to the end of the hangar. "Is that a star-spanner bubble?"

He squinted. A pale gold sphere was gliding toward them along a silver thread that stretched across the open hangar floor. "Looks like. Is that *our* bubble?"

"It is," Jeaves confirmed.

The bubble moved quickly. As it approached the spacecraft, it began to shrink. With a sound like a sizzling frying pan, it drew up to the stern of the ship—growing smaller but brighter, until it was a blazing ball the size of a grapefruit.

Bandicut's stones suddenly spoke. *Recharge is complete.* The star-spanner bubble flared with a diamond light, then vanished with a hiss into the end of the spacecraft. There was a reverberation like a plucked harp string. *Joining phase is complete. Boarding phase has begun.*

A dark opening appeared in the side of the spaceship. "Please board here," Jeaves said. He sparkled and disappeared, and Copernicus answered his plea by rolling forward into the opening. The hangar floor shook again.

The company exchanged glances and strode aboard, with Napoleon bringing up the rear. The quaking immediately diminished. There was no airlock or entry chamber, just a passageway, luminous with a reddish orange glow. After several sharp turns, it opened into a large room, also suffused with a pale, but still orange, glow emanating from translucent walls. It looked like an intimate theater, with four padded bench seats and standing room for one or two dozen people. The floor sloped down to an open space, and a luminous front wall where a holo-screen might have been.

Jeaves's disembodied voice called, "Come on down front."

As they did so, Bandicut asked, "Where are we? And where are you?"

"You're in the operations and command center of the vessel. What you might call the bridge," Jeaves answered. "I'm not installed in the ship yet, so I'm still speaking remotely from the station."

Bridge? The space did not look even remotely like a command center. "How do we—?"

"Hrrrm, the controls," Ik asked. "The instruments. How can one fly the ship from here?"

A shimmer of light appeared in the middle of the floor. It darkened to reveal a pedestal holding a small console; lighted geometric shapes covered its top. "We can bring up controls as needed, in a variety of configurations," Jeaves said. "But the shipboard AI will be doing the flying, with help from one of the haloes. We'll keep these out of the way until we need them." The pedestal vanished. A moment later, a halo dropped out of the ceiling, circling overhead. It made the familiar ringing sound like a hoop around a pole, and seemed to echo with a sound like *"Dee-lee-lee-lie-lie-lie-lie-lie . . ."*

Jeaves said, "You have met De-li-li-li before. She is speaking her name to you."

Bandicut watched the halo circling, and was suddenly reminded of a dog he had once known, a dog named Delilah that was always running in circles, barking. "Delilah? May we call you that? I knew a Delilah once."

(Delilah,) came a soft, chiming voice. (Delilah, yes.)

"This is all very nice, I'm sure," Li-Jared said curtly. "But since you got us aboard the ship, would you mind telling us what's happening with the quake that drove us in here?"

Jeaves answered, "It is diminishing, but our remote sensors indicate that more violent shock waves will arrive shortly. The hypergrav disturbances seem to have entered a new phase; they are coming in waves of increasing severity. This is not entirely unexpected."

"Meaning what?" Bandicut asked.

"Meaning it appears to confirm a theoretical model."

"A model?"

"Yes, it predicts that the hypergrav disturbances may grow past a critical threshold, then abruptly become much more powerful, and more destructive."

Bandicut tried to absorb that. "Your model predicts this?"

"Yes," said the bodiless voice.

"That implies you know what's causing the waves."

"Negative. That's what we need to find out. We know it's coming from stars in the nebula, but little beyond that."

"Then how—?"

"It was a chaotic pattern analysis. The strength of this current set of waves is very close to one set of predictions for a multiplier effect. It is likely to get worse. *Much* worse."

"That seems like a good reason for us to leave," said Li-Jared.

"It does indeed," Jeaves said. "And the shadow-people are speeding preparations for launch. They can work very fast when they need to. They're giving it top priority, even over protection of the station."

Bandicut opened his mouth and closed it.

"When you say *launch,*" Antares asked, "you mean toward the Starmaker Nebula, don't you?"

"That is my hope."

"But if we prefer to go in another direction?"

There was a pause, and finally a grainy holo of Jeaves's body appeared where the pedestal had been. The image seemed to be shifting its gaze from one person to another, attempting in vain to make eye contact. "This ship has been outfitted for the purpose of flying to Starmaker, to discover the source of the trouble. Any other destination would negate our chances of accomplishing that mission."

"Then we're prisoners?" Antares asked. "Will you take us against our will?"

The grainy holo turned, and turned. "Not against your will, no. But truthfully—without your help, the mission has little chance of success. If it fails, then Ed's world will fall, and likely others. Perhaps *many*—"

"But if we ask you to take us to Shipworld, can you do it?" Li-Jared asked, interrupting.

"I wouldn't know how—not directly. There *are* other waystations. Possibly the trip could be made in stages, if you chose that path. I am uncertain."

"Sounds like we'd be better off staying here and trying to call for a pickup, if we made that decision," Ik said.

Jeaves's head jerked slightly. "I fear . . . your chances of survival here would not be great."

"*How* not great?" Antares asked.

"*Very* not great. The truth is . . . the shadow-people have just advised me to launch. They are finishing the essential parts of the job as we speak. The station is under increasing strain— more than predicted, actually—and with heavier shock waves forecast, the risk of structural failure is rising rapidly."

"So we don't *have* to go—" Antares began.

"But if we stay here," Bandicut said, "we get pulverized with the station?"

"More or less," Jeaves concluded.

They stood silently, looking at each other. Bandicut was aware of the two robots ticking and whirring around the room, investigating. Suddenly the floor started to vibrate more noticeably. "We can continue this discussion later! I must check on the progress of the preflight!" Jeaves said sharply. "And I must get myself loaded onto the ship. Delilah will assist you for now." The holo winked out.

Bandicut half closed his eyes, feeling the deck tremble. "This place is shaking itself to pieces."

"Hrah."

✳

The next few minutes felt intensely chaotic. Shadow-people flitted in and out of the walls like hyperactive ghosts, fluttering overhead and then gone before the eye could focus on them. The vibrations grew worse, even from within the protection of the ship. Bandicut wondered what they were like outside. He spoke aloud, to the wall: "Is there some way for us to see what's happening?"

Jeaves or Delilah or *someone* did something, because the front wall of the room dissolved, revealing the spacecraft docking bay, and the empty cradles on the far side of the ship. Shadow-people were whirling about the ship like leaves in a storm. A hoist on the far side of the hangar was sliding jerkily across the floor. Bandicut could *see* the floor and the cradles vibrating violently.

Delilah dropped out of the ceiling and spoke in a chiming voice: (The shadow-people are completing the final spaceworthiness checks. Nonessential modifications must wait.)

"Are the shadow-people coming, then?" Bandicut asked.

(No. Their place is not on a moving ship.)

Antares's gaze darkened. "Won't they die if the station is destroyed?"

(They will make their own way from here. The preflight is now nearly complete.)

Another shudder passed through the floor. A shadow-person flitted across the ceiling on the inside, emitting a *whreek!* of . . . alarm? Or was it calling out a checklist?

Abruptly *all* the walls went transparent, revealing the entire docking bay. It was as if they were suddenly standing on an open platform, with only a ghostly form of the ship surrounding them. Bandicut drew a sharp, dizzy breath—while beside him, Antares grabbed the back of a seat to steady herself. As the shaking intensified, she lowered herself into the seat, then pointed across the cavern. "Look!" The far wall of the docking bay had turned as clear as the ship—or perhaps the entire side of the bay had simply opened to space, revealing darkness and the glimmering mist of the distant nebula.

(Hangar integrity is failing,) chimed Delilah. (We will be departing in a few moments. Does anyone wish to leave the ship?) Overhead in the docking bay, structural members of the dome were starting to come apart and fall. A supporting beam fell, twisting and turning, and glanced off the top of the ship.

All four of them involuntarily ducked; but no one spoke except Li-Jared, who bonged in consternation. Delilah chimed once more, as the sharpest quake yet shook the bridge. (If you are staying, please prepare for departure . . .)

Bandicut blinked, grabbing a seat for support—and realized with a start that they were already moving.

*

There was no physical sensation of movement, but the edge of the docking bay streaked past in a blur, and suddenly they were in space. Bandicut turned to look back, and thought he glimpsed several flecks of animated blackness darting away from the ship, back toward the station. The last of the shadow-people? The waystation was shrinking behind them. Bandicut drew a sharp breath. The station wasn't just receding; it was disintegrating. "My God!" he said hoarsely, causing the others to turn as well. The station was flattening and contorting like a globule of oil in water. Large pieces of it were separating from the whole. They stood, silent, watching.

After a few moments, the ruins flared into a starburst of light. When the light faded, only a cloud of debris remained.

Bandicut swallowed hard. Before he could think of anything to say, Ik turned forward again, shouted, and pointed to glowing lines of text floating in midair beneath Delilah. They read:

Sorry for the scare. That happened much faster than expected. I regret losing the waystation—but we nearly lost you and the ship, and that would have been worse. I am now aboard, but not yet fully integrated with the shipboard AI.

Estimated time to Starmaker Nebula, if you agree to the trip, is nine days via n-space.

Estimated time to Shipworld is unknown.

Estimated time to nearest waystation, if you decide not to accept the mission, is twenty-one days.

Please think carefully about what I've said. Godspeed to us all.
—Jeaves

"Can you all read that?" Antares asked, an instant before the text vanished.

"Hrah, yes. It was in my language."

Bwang. "Mine also."

Bandicut just nodded.

Antares looked thoughtful. "So Jeaves is onboard. And it sounds as if he's giving us a choice, rather than planning to—" *rasp* "—shanghai us." Antares glanced around at the clear bubble that surrounded them and shivered. "This feels worse to me than being in the star-spanner bubble. I know it's practically the same. But I feel naked here."

They were surrounded by the stars, with almost nothing visible enclosing them except a ghostly deck of the bridge, and a tracery of surrounding hull. Bandicut had to fight back a feeling of vertigo. "Yah," he whispered. "Me, too." He called out, "Delilah— can we have some walls back, please?"

With a chime, the walls reappeared around them, leaving just the front of the bridge open to the view of space ahead. "Thank you," Bandicut sighed. He drew a long breath, then turned to the question that he assumed was on everyone's minds. "Jeaves, can you hear us? Where are we headed right now? Remember you said, *if we agree to go.*"

Jeaves's voice returned, but immediately started breaking up. "Yes, I . . . not forgotten . . . trouble with . . . voice capabil . . ."

"Jeaves? Are you all right?" Ik asked.

"Not entirely . . . software integrat . . ."

Jeaves's voice fell silent, and Delilah chimed, (Jeaves is unavailable at this time. Do you need further assistance?)

Bandicut shook his head.

Ik turned to him. "Should we be worried?"

"Damned if I know," Bandicut said. "Goddamn computers . . .

probably a different operating system on the ship. How many thousands of years have these people been making computers?"

No one answered. Bandicut looked back up at the ceiling. "Delilah, what direction are we heading right now?"

(Away from the disintegrating station. No destination set yet.)

Bandicut sighed. It really was up to them, apparently. "So how about it? Do we go along with Jeaves on this mission?" He turned his hands up and looked from one to another.

Bong. "If we go, we'll probably die."

"Hrah. If we don't go, we'll probably die."

Antares looked impatient. "Uhhl, can we forget all that for a moment, please? John Bandicut, did he not say that if we don't go, Ed's homeworld will be destroyed? And others, as well?"

"Yah. *Many* other worlds, I think, is what he said."

"And did he not also say that if we do not go—if this *thing* is not stopped—" Antares paused "—a great many *stars*—thinking, intelligent stars—may suffer?"

"Yeah, he did."

Antares nodded and pressed her lips together. "So-o-o . . ."

Li-Jared muttered and hissed, and stalked around. "Hrrm," Ik said, following Li-Jared with his gaze, "it would not be right to turn our backs on such need." Ik raised his chin slightly, and his deep-set eyes caught the orange glow of the walls. Li-Jared stopped his pacing for a moment and turned to stare at Ik.

"Much as I want to go home," Bandicut said, forcing the words out with some difficulty, partly because he had not until this moment made up his own mind, "it looks to me as if we . . . should go by way of the Orion Nebula." /I can't believe I just said that./

/// I knew you would. ///

/Why didn't you tell me, then?/

/// You needed to decide for yourself. ///

/Mmph./

Li-Jared had wheeled, scowling at Bandicut. His electric-blue eyes dimmed, as though his displeasure were sucking the life out of them. "You mean by way of the Starmaker Nebula?" he grumbled.

Bandicut nodded.

Ik's expression was firm. "I believe we must. It is the right thing to do." He clacked his mouth shut. "I am sorry, Li-Jared."

"Right for *whom?*" Li-Jared muttered, in a tone that sounded like gravel shifting.

"Do you deny the need?" Ik said. "If the four of us can help entire worlds—?"

"I don't deny the need!" Li-Jared snapped. "I do deny that it should always be up to *us* to do these things."

Ik gave a slow shrug. "I do not, rrm, disagree. But if the need exists, and we alone have the ability to help . . ." He raised his long-fingered hands.

"You and your damned *long view,*" Li-Jared muttered, pacing away from them. He paused at the far end of the room, then paced back, scowling down at the floor. When he drew close, he looked up, his eyes bright with electric-blue fire. "I suppose you are right, as you so wretchedly often are. I suppose we are only four lives, compared to worlds—and thus, as you say, it is the right thing to do." He spread his arms wide. "Must I be happy about it?"

"None of us is happy about it, Li-Jared," Ik said. "But we will do what we must. Yes?"

Li-Jared drew a weary breath and said, "Yes."

A text message appeared in the air:

Thank you. One more thing: the nebula is host to more life than you might think. We should not be afraid to ask for help, if the opportunity arises.

A moment later, Delilah reappeared, floating through a wall and ringing again like a hoop. (Would you like to look around the ship now?)

"Please," murmured Antares. "It is time we saw where we're going to be living—"

"Or dying," Li-Jared grumbled, turning with a flick of his hands to follow the halo.

6

Julie Stone sat in her room in the Triton mining station, staring at a holo of Lake Tahoe, on Earth. She had never been to Lake Tahoe, but the image of the cool still waters, the snow-capped mountains, and the blue sky soothed her mind like a balm. She had been staring at it so much she was starting to feel that this was her way of drinking alone.

But she wasn't really alone, of course, because the translator-stones were always present, rummaging silently through her mind. And their words—or the translator's words: *Something still out there trying to destroy your world . . . more data needed . . . must decide for yourself whether to trust us . . .* kept running through her mind, like a song she couldn't get out of her head. It had been weeks now since she had first felt the stones, and they continued to make her life a waking dream.

/Who are you, really?/ she asked them for the hundredth time. /How am I supposed to know whether to trust you? Wasn't it others just like you who killed John?/ She couldn't hold back the thought, and she couldn't hold back the shame that followed. She didn't want to demean John's death. He died, after all, saving Earth.

As usual, from the stones there was no answer, just a vague, humming reminder to be patient.

It had started with the translator, deep in the ice cavern beneath the surface of Triton, when it chose to speak to her and her alone. Sometimes it was hard to tell if it was the translator itself speaking in her mind or its daughter-stones, embedded in her wrists. Whichever it was, they had chosen her, just as once before the translator had chosen John. Why, she didn't know. But it was putting her in an impossible position, as the liaison to the first and only alien artifact ever found by humanity.

There is much we have to learn together . . .

Was she sane? Was she crazy? Alien voices in her head, from these pulsing jewels in her wrists? She'd tried to explain it to her best friend, Georgia, but somehow she never could. Same with her boss in exoarchaeology, Kim. Was it something the wrist-stones were doing to keep her from talking about their mission? Tomorrow she had a meeting with the top brass, and she needed some answers.

You will know us through our actions, whispered a voice, as though to reassure her.

How very biblical of you, she thought. But when do I see your actions?

Was this how John had felt, isolated and caught up in incomprehensible forces? Had he wondered, as she desperately did now, *Why is this happening to me?*

*

The meeting with the brass was not going well.

They wanted answers, and she had few to give.

Arrayed around the table were several of the station administrators—Cole Jackson, Lonnie Stelnik, and a couple of others; she was used to dealing with them. But added to the mix were visiting VIPs from various oversight bodies. A man named Mackler represented a UN agency; Dr. Takashi of MINEXFO, the Mining Expeditionary Force, was here; he was joined by his boss, Special Envoy Dr. Keith Lamarr.

And Julie, in the hot seat.

"Miss Stone," said Dr. Takashi, "in the past two months, we've tried various methods of studying the translator, none of which have produced usable data. We have tried, twice, to move it into our labs here, with spectacularly expensive results in ruined equipment. You're the only one it will talk to, and we need you to talk to us."

Julie opened her mouth to reply, but nothing came out. She wanted to say, *You don't understand, there's a danger to Earth!* But as soon as the thought crossed her mind, she felt the familiar pressure in her head—not painful or threatening, but inhibiting. The stones did not want her to talk about that yet. She drew a slow, steady breath, and said the only thing she could think of: "I don't know what you want from me." She felt like an idiot saying it. /Why won't you let me talk?/

You will be able to soon.

"Really, Miss Stone, I think we've been pretty clear about

what we expect," Dr. Lamarr said. He was a salt-and-pepper-haired man of fifty-something, and he conveyed a distinct aura of quiet power. "We expect you to initiate communication with the extraterrestrial device—"

"I *have* opened communication."

"We mean communication that is *not exclusive to you.*"

"It's not as if I haven't tried," Julie said. "I've *asked* it to speak to other people besides me. I don't know why it won't. But I can't force it." To the wrist-stones, she muttered, /Can't you give me *something* to say to them?/

The stones said nothing, but seemed to be thinking.

Cole Jackson, Director of Survey Operations, spoke up in a gravelly voice. "Doesn't seem like the thing wants to talk to much of anyone."

"It's talked to at least two people," Lamarr said with careful patience. "And I want to know—what's so special about John Bandicut and Julie Stone? Is that so unreasonable to ask?" His gaze never left Julie.

She felt her face redden. "No, it's not," she whispered. Then she felt the stones stirring, and she pressed her fingertips to her brow, half closing her eyes.

∗*Tell them this: the translator is gathering important data. When it is finished, it will have a message. And it will be requesting transport to Earth.*∗

She opened her mouth, closed it, opened it again.

"Yes, Miss Stone? Was there something you wanted to say?"

Clearing her throat, she repeated what the stones had told her. /Is that all? Nothing more?/

∗*Not at this time.*∗

Lamarr echoed her own question: "Nothing more?" She shook her head. Lamarr's exasperation was evident. "Miss Stone, if this object—"

"The translator."

"Forgive me. If the *translator* intends peaceful interaction with humanity, isn't it just logical that it would explore communication with a variety of people, not just one, or two? That it should have picked *only* you, out of all the people on Triton—it just seems odd, doesn't it?"

"It does," she acknowledged.

"Isn't it possible that—how shall I put this—?"

Julie flared. "What—that I'm lying to you?"

"I didn't say that."

"But it's what you meant, isn't it?"

Lamarr pressed his lips together, revealing no emotions.

She knew she should shut up; she'd already said too much. But . . . "It's just like the way you thought John was lying, even though the evidence was right there in front of your faces that he stopped a comet from hitting Earth."

"Evidence," Lamarr said softly. "The evidence *I* know of says that Mr. Bandicut stole and destroyed a very expensive spacecraft."

"Telescope cameras recorded the collision with the comet!"

"Cameras recorded a collision. But whether it was a comet, or our spacecraft, is another question altogether, isn't it?"

Julie raised her hands and dropped them, giving up.

"All right," Lamarr said. "I think—unless someone else has a question for Miss Stone?—we're through with this part of the meeting. Miss Stone, you may return to your duties, but we'd like to talk to you again tomorrow . . ."

✳

Julie made her way back to her office in exoarch, but didn't stay long. There was no way she could do any useful work in this state. She headed to the gym and the centrifuge room. As she jogged around the revolving track at the half-gee level, she tried to clear her mind of it all. It didn't really work. When she finished, she still had a head full of chaotic thoughts as she trooped back to her quarters for a shower. But at least she was physically tired, which made her feel that she was doing more than simply joust with the air.

As she struggled into clean clothes, there was a buzz on the comm. "What is it?" she called, pulling a sweatshirt over her head.

The system answered in the contralto voice she thought of as Hazel: "Julie Stone, you have a holo-message waiting. Origin: Earth."

"Who from?" *Please don't let it be another screed from*

Thomas. Her brother *still* couldn't understand why she'd gone to Triton in the first place, and regarded her statements about John Bandicut as pathetic fantasy. Maybe it was from her parents. She was due to hear from them, but they rarely used holo.

"Sender is Dakota Bandicut," said Hazel. "Would you like to view it on your screen?"

Dakota? "No, I'll take it in the VR room." If John's niece had gone to the expense of sending a holo, she wanted to view it in full virtual reality.

She brushed quickly at her hair, then hurried out. The rec center was on the far side of the main building, but it had three VR rooms, plus food and drink. She swore when she found all three VR rooms occupied. She sat in silence watching two men play a game of EineySteiney; when the door to Room Three opened and one of the miners emerged, she jumped up to take his place. "Hey, if you're in that much of a hurry for a good time—" he called, but she brushed past him and slammed the door without answering.

Taking the center seat, she said, "This is Julie Stone. Show me my mail."

The room darkened partially, and a figure appeared, standing in a pool of light. It was a half-height image of Dakota Bandicut. Julie had never met the girl, nor spoken to her in real-time, but her appearance was striking. John Bandicut's niece, now age twelve, had the same jaw line, the same eyes, the same intensity of expression as her uncle.

"Julie? Hi. I can't talk long, because Nan says it costs too much, so I'm paying for this with my own money." She gulped, and for a moment seemed paralyzed by the need to speak quickly. *"I just wondered ... how you've been, and have you heard anything more about what happened to Uncle John? I've just been—you know—I don't hear anything. There's nothing on the news anymore, and the government hasn't told us anything."* Her face darkened visibly.

It was all Julie could do to keep from crying out to the image. *I know how you feel! I feel the same way!* "Damn," she whispered finally, "I wish I could meet you and tell you in person what John did. What I *know* he did!"

But she was just talking to herself. With a round-trip signal lag of eight hours, she couldn't talk back to the holo, not in real-time. All she could do was listen, and compose a reply.

"I got your letter. You wouldn't believe how many people say Uncle John was lying—or crazy. I don't believe any of them. I believe Uncle John. I know you do, too." Dakota fidgeted, biting her lower lip. *"Did I tell you about the college fund he set up for me? He didn't even tell me about it, and no one told me about it until he was gone. I can't even thank him for it! But now they're saying, because he was—because they're saying he was crazy, maybe it wasn't legal, the way he set it up. I don't understand it. And Nan won't talk about it, she says I'm too young. Julie? You don't think he was crazy, do you? Please say no."*

Julie felt an anvil drop on her chest. It was all she could do to breathe. *What's the matter with you people? How can you do that to a twelve-year-old girl?* By the time she gasped out a pained breath, she realized that Dakota was saying good-bye.

"Back up thirty seconds," she commanded the system.

She listened again to Dakota's plea, and then a second plea—for Julie to get in touch again. *"It's not like I don't have friends. But sometimes it feels like you're the only one who understands, even though we've never met. Do you think, sometime, you . . . could come back to Earth and see me? I'll be waiting to hear. I have to go now. Bye."* Dakota's image froze as the recording ended.

Yes, Julie whispered to herself, eyes shut. *Yes, I very much want to do that.*

She opened her eyes. Dakota was still there, a statue. "Yes," she said softly to the still image. "Somehow. Someday . . ."

✶

Emerging from the VR, Julie saw Georgia Patwell waving her over to a table. The sight of her friend raised her spirits; they hadn't seen each other in days. "Am I glad to see you," she murmured, sliding into the booth opposite Georgia. She yanked the privacy-curtain closed and slumped in her seat. "You wouldn't believe this day."

"I heard they gave you quite the wringing out," Georgia said.

She extended a finger toward the ordering board and gave Julie an inquiring glance as her fingertip hovered over the draft beer button. Julie nodded emphatically, and Georgia pressed the button. She already had a glass of white wine at her elbow.

"So," Julie said, "did Lonnie Stelnik come and crow about it?" The operations supervisor, under Cole Jackson, had gotten in a few digs during the course of the meeting.

Georgia's beautiful dark eyes flashed with amusement. "Just as you'd expect. He seemed to think he'd one-upped you pretty well. Somehow I doubted it."

Julie chuckled bitterly, then scowled. "Damn it, if the translator won't tell *me* anything, what am I supposed to do?" When Georgia remained silent, she looked down at her open hands as if the answer might lie there. "The thing is, these people act as if they *own* it."

Georgia sipped from her wine. "Legally, don't they?"

"How? How can they?"

"Well, doesn't MINEXFO own the rights to anything they find on Triton?"

"Any *metals* they find on Triton."

"And any artifacts."

Julie's stomach churned. "How about an intelligent—and *sentient*—object that obviously has its own ideas about being independent?"

"Hey, I'm with you, girl," Georgia said. "But the consortium *did* invest about a gazillion dollars in this operation, so it's understandable that they want something back for it."

"Yeah, but they're going to have to be patient."

Georgia cocked her head, studying Julie. "Sure they have to be patient. But why do *you* feel bad?"

"Huh?"

"You do, don't you?"

Julie hesitated, startled by the question. She spread her hands on the table. "Well, yeah. I feel like I'm in danger of losing my job if they think I'm holding out on them."

Georgia gazed steadily back at her. "Are you? I think it's time for a reality check, kiddo. Aren't you the one holding the cards here? Without you, they've got nothing. Right? Nothing but a machine that eats their cranes and confounds everything they try to do."

"Well, yeah, but—"

"Jesus, girl, don't play into their hands!"

Julie flushed. "That's not—"

"They're making you feel insecure and guilty." Georgia leaned forward urgently. "But the truth is they need you more than you need them. Am I right?"

"Well, you can say that, but—" Julie's voice caught, as Georgia's words started to get through to her.

"But what? It's true, and if you step back for a minute, you'll realize it. You'll realize you have nothing to fear from them." Georgia's voice was soft but penetrating. "And you'll stop letting them scare you. Just do the best you can with the translator and quit worrying."

Julie stared back at her with her mouth open. Her head was buzzing. Was she crazy? Or was Georgia talking sense? She drew a slow breath. "Maybe you have a point . . ." She was beginning to realize that Georgia was *completely* right, and she felt a rush of embarrassment and shame that she had allowed herself to be railroaded like that. "No, you're absolutely right! I've been letting them walk all over me." She turned her head, her face burning now. "Jesus! That's got to stop. It's *going* to stop."

"That'a girl!" Georgia reached out and patted her hand soothingly. "Now, shouldn't you be getting a drink about now?"

Julie nodded and poked the privacy-curtain open to look for the waiter. The bartender was just walking by with a small tray, and she received her beer from him gratefully. She lifted the mug and took a long swallow of the amber brew. "All right, that's settled. What else is new?"

Georgia slowly raised one eyebrow. "Well, this isn't exactly a change of subject. I might have some news you haven't heard yet. Promise you won't hit the ceiling."

Julie implored with her open hands. "What?"

Georgia adjusted the privacy-curtain to close a small gap, and leaned close over the table. "I was taking a look at the in-system comm traffic and I read some things maybe I strictly shouldn't have."

"Shame on you."

"I read a few things addressed to Herr Envoy Lamarr."

"Maybe not so shameful. What did they say?"

Georgia gazed at her for a long moment. "Well, if you had any hopes that they might let the translator sit undisturbed . . . I'd forget them."

Julie felt a chill take over her body. "What are they planning?" she asked, her voice thick.

Georgia cleared her throat. "There's a shuttle arriving in twenty-nine days from the InterExploratory Coalition. Said shuttle has orders to pack the translator up and take it to Earth under the watchful eye of the Coalition. Now, you know how well MINEXFO and the IE Coalition get along—so you can bet that MINEXFO *really* doesn't want the Coalition meddling with the translator, much less trying to take custody of it. As you said, they consider it theirs."

Julie eyed her mug, but didn't drink. "And?"

"The MINEXFO ship that's here now has a launch departure window for Earth that opens in three days. I think they're planning to take the translator and run. Possession is nine-tenths of the law, and if they can be on their way back to Earth before the other shuttle arrives, there's no way to catch them."

Assuming the translator is willing to let them move it. "There'll be one hell of a legal battle back on Earth," Julie said, taking a gulp and coughing as the carbonation went the wrong way.

"Sure. But they'll have the whole trip back to make studies . . ."

And maybe establish a relationship with it?

"And they'll definitely need help from you, Julie." Georgia was peering over the top of her wineglass at her.

Julie didn't know how to react; it was too much to absorb all at once. She wanted to yell, argue, dig in her heels and fight—for something. But all she could do was stare across the table at her friend.

"*Breathe,* Julie."

She drew in a ragged breath.

"You were about to turn blue there," Georgia said, touching her wrist. "So what do you think? What will the translator do if they try to dig it up?"

"The last time they tried, it cost them twenty million dollars in ruined equipment." Julie felt a sudden tingle in her wrists, and closed her eyes. It wasn't often that the stones rang to let her know they had something to say. /Yes?/

The translator will accept an offer to travel to Earth.

Julie coughed again. /Now? You mean, now it'll go along? On the MINEXFO ship?/

Yes. You may inform your colleagues.

"Julie? You still with me?"

"What? Yes! Yes, I'm here." Julie tried to force a smile, but it came out crooked with puzzlement. "It's just that—" She shook her head and started laughing out loud. "The translator—the mokin' translator *wants* them to take it to Earth!"

Georgia could only gaze at her in amazement.

7

ALMOST LIKE HOME

The halo spoke sonorously as it led them through the ship. They peered into sleeping quarters and a common room for meals, then various work compartments. The vessel seemed cavernous, or at least endless, and the passageways all looked bewilderingly identical. The ship's facilities included what appeared to be laboratories full of incomprehensible gear, a docking bay carrying a small scout craft, and several compartments that on first glance appeared to be empty—then, when Bandicut glanced back, were humming with strange machinery.

Copernicus and Napoleon roved around taking readings. Upon crossing paths with the company, Copernicus noted aloud what Bandicut felt—that there was far more space inside the ship than they could account for, from the external dimensions.

Delilah confirmed that it was not their imagination. The space-craft did not just travel *through* n-space; it *was* an n-space projection. Its hull was not matter at all, but an orchestration of n-space force-fields.

"You mean," Bandicut asked, "the only thing between us and a hard vacuum is some clever manipulation of *dimensions?* Nothing solid?"

Delilah warbled softly. (N-space has many aspects. The outer hull is created from the boundary conditions between different layers of n-space: what you might call a force-field. Inside, we have expanded the compartments into hyperdimensional volumes to enlarge the usable space.)

"Enlarged by how much?" Ik asked.

(There is no defined limit. It stretches or contracts as we wish. It greatly increases the versatility of the craft.)

"I'm sure it does," Bandicut said.

Bong. "Could you maybe change the colors of some of the walls—so we can find our way around?"

The halo swayed gently in the air. (That is one of the refinements the shadow-people had planned. We will see.) The halo trilled briefly. (Jeaves wonders if you would like to try the dining quarters.)

"Indeed," Ik said.

(Then please follow me . . .) And as the halo passed back the way they had come, the walls turned a deep forest-green.

*

The dining room was a cozy place, with padded booth seats at right angles to each other. The room was just large enough for the four of them and the robots, though it felt larger after a wrap-around window appeared, providing a panoramic view of their destination. The view of the nebula had been enhanced and brightened so that it glowed prettily in the distance—prettily and dangerously. There had been no further quaking. Perhaps whatever layer of n-space they were traveling in was isolated from the gravitational disturbances.

They spent a couple of hours nibbling biscuits and fruit, and periodically trying to converse with Jeaves, who still couldn't get his voice to work properly. After a while, Delilah reappeared and asked if they'd like to be shown to their sleeping quarters. Bandicut and Antares looked at each other, and Antares caught Bandicut's hand and rose.

They followed the halo to their room, which turned out to be a spacious, dome-shaped compartment. Bandicut laughed when he saw his backpack on the floor. He had forgotten all about it. The halo floated across the room, showing them where, by touching the wall, they could open a passage to the shower and lav, and where another touch caused a part of the floor to rise, turning it into a bed. Then it left, saying they would be summoned when needed.

Bandicut sank onto the edge of the bed with a sigh. Antares leaned against him, resting her head on his shoulder. He put his arm around her, and they sat like that for a time, without speaking. After a while they stretched out on the bed, loosely in each other's arms. "John Bandicut," Antares murmured at last, pressing her forehead to his neck, "I am frightened, a little."

"Just a little?"

"More than a little."

He took a deep breath. "Me, too."

"But I am glad to be here with you, instead of alone."

He drew back so he could see her face. "Me, too."

Antares stared up into space. Her forehead, framed by thick auburn hair, was drawn in thought. Her eyes shone, thin gold irises floating over ebony pupils. Her mouth crinkled in response to his smile. Her gaze shifted to meet his, and the furrows faded from her brow. "John Bandicut—do you remember, back on the world of the Neri, when we were—" *rasp* "—intimate?"

He chuckled. "Did you think I was likely to forget?"

She hiccupped a laugh. "No, not really. But I wondered . . . how are you feeling about it now?" She tapped his chest with her forefinger. "I don't know what sticks in your human mind and what doesn't."

"Well, that does. Vividly. It's a very happy memory."

Antares made a soft humming noise, and he realized that she

was exploring his feelings empathically. There was a time when he'd found that unnerving. Now, he found it reassuring. "How do *you* feel about it?" he asked. "Are you still glad?"

"Uhll, yes," she said. "But . . . it's difficult for me, even so. Because, what I did with you—what I'm doing with you *now,* even—is forbidden for a Thespi Third. I—"

"Yes, I know—but Antares, you'll probably never be among the Thespi again!"

"Aiiee—" she raised an open hand toward the ceiling "—how can we know?"

"I don't think *any* of us is ever going home again. So what does it matter what your ruling class thinks?" She stiffened as he said that, and he wondered if he had pushed too far. She was uncomfortable with these thoughts, even if they were true.

/// *So are you, aren't you?*
You should tell her. ///

He sighed. "Antares? I'm sorry. We all miss our homes. And we can't just snap our fingers and forget about them. I'm sorry I said that."

Antares's hand tightened on his; she gazed into his eyes, then touched his left cheekbone, then his right cheekbone, with the three fingertips of her other hand. Her touch was soothing, so much so that he found himself not just relaxing, but actually growing drowsy. He tried, unsuccessfully, to force his thoughts awake.

"Perhaps," she said, "one day we will . . ."

He never heard the rest, as sleep stole over him.

✳

Bandicut was dreaming of a small boy standing in a wheat field. A rising wind rippled his hair. The sky was unsettled, a darkness in the west—a deep turbulence, and maybe trouble brewing. (Had he once stood in such a field as a boy? His grandfather had been a farmer, on the plains of the American Midwest. He wondered as he watched the dream unfold if this was a memory, as well as a dream.)

Still, if there was trouble in the distance, overhead the sun was dancing among the clouds. Out ahead somewhere, his dog was running through the field. Was that rustling of the wheat tops Blackie charging through the field?

Or was it something else, darker than a black dog?

✷

Antares sighed as John Bandicut slept. It wasn't quite the result she'd been aiming for. But John was bone-tired, and sleep was what he needed. She gazed at him, surprised by the depth of her affection. Finally she closed her eyes and went to sleep herself.

At some point she woke with a start, with images of the floor shaking under her. She felt nothing now. Groggily she raised her head and peered across the room. A distorted ring of greenish light was glimmering on the far wall. She thought she heard a whisper like a breeze: *"Com-m-inggg . . . are you com-inggg? Cannot-t-t fin-n-nd . . ."* She blinked in the semidarkness; there was nothing, no light, no whisper. She let her head fall back on the pillow. Had she seen that or dreamed it? She imagined she had felt the presence of the creature called Ed; but it had been so fleeting, she wasn't sure. Had something shaken the ship? She stretched a hand out and touched the floor. It was cold, still.

Turning, she studied the dark form of John Bandicut, asleep beside her. He was stirring, dreaming. Had he felt it, too? She touched his shoulder, and through it his feelings. He was dreaming, reliving something, she realized, and she found that unaccountably reassuring. Comforted by his presence, she thought of the intimacy they had shared once, under the Neri sea. She felt a growing urge to repeat it. She also felt a reluctance. She craved closeness to him; she was torn by shame for her forbidden actions. Those on her homeworld would never know, but that seemed irrelevant. *She* knew.

Sighing, she rolled onto her back and soon fell back asleep. As she slept, she dreamed of walking over shifting sands, the waters of the sea rising over her feet.

✷

Bandicut sat up, trying to recover a dream that was already skittering away. Something about a field. And an exhaust pipe. Was that what had woken him? Before he could follow the thought any further, he heard a ringing sound from the far side of the room. What was that?

A moment later, Jeaves's voice rasped from the same part of the wall: *"Come to . . . the bridge . . . as soon as . . . possible."* The robot's voice sounded as if it were being wrung out of an old, handheld radio.

"What is it, Jeaves?" he asked. Antares rolled over, and sat up, asking what was going on. "Don't know yet. Jeaves wants us. Is something wrong, Jeaves?"

"Contact approaching. Need you . . . on the bridge."

Bandicut threw off the thin blanket. "Let's go. I hope we can *find* the bridge again."

∗

They indeed nearly got lost in the luminous maze of n-space corridors. They were soon joined by Li-Jared, bonging in bewilderment, then Ik. "I swear this corridor has changed since last night," Bandicut said, and no one argued with him. Finally Delilah appeared and led them, changing the color of the corridor to crimson on the way.

The bridge now looked less like a theater and more like a lounge in two sections: the inner half enclosed and protected by three walls, and the outer half a kind of wide ledge or balcony that extended directly into space. The view, Delilah explained, was corrected to display what they would see if they were not enveloped by n-space fields. The result was a spectacular view of the rose and sapphire mists of the nebula, and an equally spectacular invitation to vertigo. Napoleon was pacing around the room, clicking furiously, while Copernicus sat at rest near the edge of the balcony, sensors swiveling.

"What have you found?" Bandicut asked Napoleon.

"Spacetime phenomenon coming into range, Cap'n." *Tick tick.*

"Spacetime phenomenon?" Bandicut turned, following the robot's movement. "What kind of spacetime phenomenon?"

"John, look there." Antares pointed out into space.

Bandicut squinted. "At what, the nebula?" It filled about half of the visible sky.

"In front of the nebula. Something really dark. I think it's moving this way." Antares strode out onto the outer bridge near Copernicus, to get a better look.

Bandicut followed her uneasily, still trying to see it. That faint patch of darkness? "There?" he asked, pointing.

"Uhhll. It *is* moving this way."

"It looks almost like a smaller nebula," said Ik.

B-gong. "Nebulas don't move like that. It's moving like something with purpose."

Copernicus turned in place, then rolled by, humming, to confer with Napoleon. "We are measuring alterations in the spacetime metrics, in that direction. Possibly related to the moving patch."

Bandicut glanced at the robot. "How can you even tell what's happening to spacetime out there?"

"It's not easy, but we are doing our best, Captain," Napoleon answered. "We are attempting to mathematically subtract the effects of our spatial threading."

There was a click and a garbled voice from the walls. It was Jeaves. "*. . . am trying . . . voice algorithm . . . can you hear me now?*"

"What's wrong with your voice?" Ik asked.

"*Apologies . . . incompatible . . . voice AIs . . .*"

"Give it to us in text," Bandicut said.

"*No, wait. I think I've got it. How's this? Can you hear me now?*"

"Yeah, that's good."

"Finally. The ship's AI wasn't designed with a compatible voice interface. I think we've got it solved."

Bong. "Happy for you," said Li-Jared. "Are you going to tell us what this is that's coming at us?"

"Yes. That dark patch you see is not a nebula, but an extremely complex spacetime fluctuation, as Napoleon and Copernicus noted. I wanted you to have a look at it as early as possible. I think it might be to our advantage to attempt contact, when it gets closer."

"Contact?" Bandicut glanced nervously at the others.

Ik made a sound deep in his throat. "Hrrm. A spacetime fluctuation, which we should contact? John Bandicut, this robot Jeaves has a strange sense of humor."

Bandicut frowned. "I haven't noticed that it has *any* sense of humor. Jeaves?"

Jeaves's disembodied voice answered, "I believe that what you see is a being, and not a simple astronomical object."

"Uh—okay. And how would we—?"

"I am not entirely certain. But Delilah is something of a spacetime fluctuation herself. She may be able to help, when the time comes."

"I see," said Antares. "And when will that be?"

"Possibly within the next ship-day. Maybe two. But you may experience preliminary effects."

Preliminary effects? Bandicut turned back to squint into space. "Can we get a clearer image?"

Delilah circled down from the ceiling. (What would you like?)

"Can you magnify?" asked Ik.

The halo didn't answer, but the view zoomed in abruptly. The dark object was now clearly visible against the distant nebula; in fact, it looked as if they were about to plow right through it. It was roiling, turbulent, black smoke. The view zoomed in still farther, and now it looked more like a weird curtain, curling and billowing in a breeze. Bandicut felt a sudden wave of dizziness; his stomach dropped out from under him. /What's happening?/ He felt himself falling, and grabbed for support on a railing.

/// Ohhh . . . ///

Bandicut steadied himself; his breath was coming hard and fast. /You too?/

/// Yah . . . don't . . . know what . . . ///

Bandicut turned his head—slowly—to look at his companions. "Do you guys—uh—?" All of the others were swaying or groaning. Antares held her head.

"Hrrrr-ahhhh! Can we . . . change the view back, please?" Ik rasped.

Chiming softly, the halo restored the more distant view. Bandicut let his breath out slowly as the dizziness subsided. He reached out to touch Antares. "You okay? Was there—?"

"Uuuoooll, yes," she murmured, rubbing her temples. "Did you feel it? The presence?"

"I just felt like I was going to keel over."

/// I felt its presence. ///

"It is alive, and it is sentient," Antares said. She still had both three-fingered hands pressed to her temples. "I think it was aware of us, but I cannot be certain."

Bandicut turned to the halo. "What just happened? Why did we feel faint like that?"

(That was unexpected. Possibly, you were sensing the being's influence on the surrounding continuum,) Delilah murmured.

"But I thought you were just magnifying the image."

(Not simply magnifying. Extending our own spatial-threading field to improve the resolution. Apparently we created a linkage to those distant fluctuations.)

Bandicut didn't entirely follow, but decided to let it go. "Then what can you tell us about this . . . entity?"

(Rather little. Our remote sensors have detected it—or something like it—in the past. We have no evidence of harmful intent.)

"Hrrm, your robot friend urged us to contact it," said Ik. "Was there a reason?"

Li-Jared's eyes narrowed to vertical gold slivers, with a tiny bar of gleaming blue across the middle. "It was not pleasant to experience. Will it continue to make us feel ill, as it gets closer?"

(We hope not. We will attempt to compensate. And you may find that you can adapt.)

"What do you think?" Bandicut asked Antares.

Antares's lips were pressed together, her eyes slitted like Li-Jared's, but horizontally. "I do not know what to make of it."

Ik stretched out a hand. "Could you feel if it intended to harm us?"

Antares pushed her hair back from her face, and her eyes relaxed a little. "No. I felt a strong presence—but what kind, I do not know. It was very strange."

"Strange, *friendly?* Or strange, *hostile?*" Bandicut asked.

"I do not know."

Bandicut spoke to the wall. "You haven't said anything, Jeaves. But you brought us here to see it."

"Yes," said the wall. "This spacetime being is known to the shadow-people. They advised me to try working with it."

Bandicut frowned. "That's not much to go on."

"No. It was a parting conversation. But the shadow-people are quite intuitive about others. I trust their instincts."

"Is there any way for us to ask them? I mean, there are no shadow-people aboard, right? Do you have any way to communicate with them?"

Delilah descended again, trilling. (What do you wish to know?)

"Well—I'd sure like to know if they could tell us more. Is there any way to reach them?"

(I can share certain elements of their knowledge with you.) The halo abruptly expanded, and something strange appeared in its center—a gray, twisting darkness. For an instant, a shadow-person seemed to writhe there, and a shrieking violin sound split the air. *(Whreeeek! Whreeeek!)* And then the shadow-voice began to be modulated in a way that sounded as if it were trying to form words.

"Hrrm, can anyone understand it?" Ik asked.

/Can you tell what it's saying?/ Bandicut asked Charlie.

/// The stones are trying to decipher. ///

Indeed, the stones in Bandicut's wrists were buzzing with activity. /And—?/

The haloes, you understand, are a life-cycle stage of the shadow-people, said the stones, startling him. *The halo is drawing upon a memory. It is remembering the name of the cloud. We are attempting to translate.*

There was a rumbling in the air, and then Bandicut heard, *(Dee-eeee-eeee-aaab.)* The reverberations seemed to continue, even after the voice stopped speaking.

Ik tried to echo the sound in his throat. "I'm not sure how to say it," he said.

(Dee-ee-ee-aap.)

Bandicut grunted. "It sounds sort of like *Deep,* the way a blue whale might say it."

Charlie considered for a moment.

/// I think you have the right idea.
It's a kind of groan,
as if it's straining to reach out
across time, or space.
'Dee-eee-eee-up,' maybe. ///

Bandicut tried, but it hurt his throat. Finally he said, "Deep. Can we just call it Deep?"

Ik gave a quick nod. "That, hrrm, seems close." He turned to Delilah, in whom the vision of the shadow-person still fluttered. "Is 'Deep' a satisfactory translation?"

(Reeeek! Ye-e-e-ssss.)

"And . . . what kind of thing is it?" Bandicut asked. "Can it communicate with us?"

(Reeeek!)

"Can it help us? Can we talk to it?"

(Whreeek! Un-n-ssurrre.)

"Then why—?" Bandicut gestured in frustration.

(Whreee-eee-eee . . .) Delilah contracted spasmodically as the shadow-image within emitted a series of frantic violin riffs.

"Delilah, what is it—what are we supposed to do—?"

The shrieks faded, and the halo returned to its normal appearance. (We are uncertain. But the shadow-people have sensed the presence of this thing, Deep, before. And they have heard stories . . .)

"Stories?"

(From far back in time. Stories of Deep, or beings like it, who spoke with stars, and retold their stories. We know little of its actions beyond that.)

"But we are flying to meet it."

(Where we are going, we would meet it anyway. We can only wait . . . see . . . hope . . .)

Bandicut felt his stomach tightening. Wait and see? He looked at his friends, then back at Delilah, who was floating away. "Is there anything else? Is that what you brought us here to see?"

Delilah answered, (We wanted you to know what was coming,) and then vanished through a wall.

"Hrrrm, and now that we know?"

"We can have nightmares about it," Antares said softly.

★

No one felt much like going back to sleep to have nightmares, so they gathered in the common lounge for breakfast, and to discuss what might be coming, and how they might prepare. Everyone was feeling off balance, Bandicut realized—not just him. It was not just apprehension about this Deep creature, but also the reminder that so far they had about as much say in this mission as puppets on a string. They had—in a leap of faith—agreed to come, yes. But they still had no detailed information, nor were their views being solicited. They didn't even know, exactly, who was in charge. Was it Jeaves? The shipboard AI? The halo?

Li-Jared was the most vocally annoyed, and he waved a pair of breakfast rolls around like small clubs as he voiced his dissatisfaction. But the usually unflappable Ik was not far behind. Even the two robots seemed agitated; they kept moving in and out of the lounge, checking things with their scanners, as though determined, by gathering data, to bring sense to their confused state. Antares had clearly been most affected by the contact with Deep. She sat in silence, eating cheese and fruit, drinking an emerald-green tea, and keeping her thoughts to herself.

Bandicut finally brought up something that was nagging at him. "This might seem trivial, but you know—we're doing something that a lot of people might consider bad luck."

Bwang. "What's that? Listening to a human-speaking robot?" Li-Jared asked, rubbing his black fingers energetically on his chest.

Bandicut's mouth opened. He wasn't sure whether to be amused or insulted. "Don't try to hide your feelings, Li-Jared. Do you trust robots or not?" He glanced at Napoleon and Copernicus, who were inspecting the base of the wall that curved around the dining tables.

"I trust *them*," Li-Jared said. "It's Jeaves I don't trust."

"Well—" Bandicut shrugged "—I don't blame you. But that wasn't actually what I was talking about. I was thinking how we're flying in a ship without a name."

"Hrah. My people, too, would find that odd," said Ik. "Uncomfortable."

Antares cocked her head. "I don't understand. What is the purpose of naming the ship? There is only one ship."

Bandicut shrugged. "To give it some personality, I guess. Doesn't a ship feel a little like a living thing to you?"

She cocked her head even more. "Should it?"

"Sure. Every ship has its own quirks, its own personality."

"I know a good name," Li-Jared said glumly. "How about the *One Way Trip*?"

"Hrrm, Li-Jared my friend, even for you, this is a gloomy view of things." Ik clacked his teeth together thoughtfully. "Although, on the other hand, I can't think just now of a better name."

"How about *The Long View*," Bandicut suggested. "You're always encouraging us to take that. Well—now we are."

Antares laughed huskily. "Judging from our experience back there on the bridge, it's an accurate name."

Li-Jared made a soft, sputtering noise.

There was a moment of awkward silence. Bandicut stirred his coffee and said, "I can't entirely argue with Li-Jared. When you think about it, we've been on something of a one-way trip since we all met." Since I left Triton, he added silently.

"I like *The Long View*," Antares said.

Li-Jared looked annoyed.

"But," she continued, "I also like the *One Way Trip*. So why can't the ship have two names? One for each mood."

Bandicut opened his mouth to protest—then thought, why not? So it was a little unconventional. But maybe only by human standards.

Ik clacked his mouth. "I like the idea. Maybe it will bring us double luck, yes?"

Li-Jared shrugged.

"Well, since that is settled, I think I am going to retire for a while," said Ik. "And make myself at home in *The Long View/One Way Trip*."

Might not be such a bad idea, getting a little more sleep, Bandicut thought. Get it while we can.

8

DEADLY ENCOUNTER

Bandicut slept dreamlessly this time. He awoke to find Antares studying him. She crinkled a smile, touched his cheek tenderly with her fingertips, then got to her feet. He followed her, rubbing the sleep from his eyes.

They met the others in the lounge. Over brunch, they came to a decision: while they were en route, the best thing they could do was to gather information. "We should learn what this ship has on it, and how to use it," Li-Jared declared, echoed by Ik, who said, "We should learn to fly it." To which Bandicut replied, "Fine, but who's going to teach us? Jeaves?" Jeaves did not seem to be present. They settled, for the time being, on trying to master the layout of the ship, and set out together to explore.

The vessel continued to be weirdly mutable. During the night, their sleeping quarters had been rearranged, and were now neatly arrayed like the arms of a sea star around the common lounge. It seemed an improvement. But the rest of the ship remained a cipher: a changing maze of corridors and compartments that seemed to unfold out of n-space, as needed. "Hrah!" Ik cried in frustration to Delilah, who floated by at one point, perhaps to make sure they were not lost. "Can you not pick a layout and stick to it?"

Delilah chimed in puzzlement, pointing out that future needs might be unpredictable.

"Please!" Ik said. Delilah replied with something undecipherable, and went away. Bandicut chuckled and kept walking.

Napoleon and Copernicus were off prowling elsewhere on the ship. Napoleon had mentioned something about download-ing literature from Jeaves, or maybe it was from the shipboard AI—so perhaps that was what they were doing. Bandicut won-dered, though, *What literature?*

Eventually, Antares went to the bridge, and Li-Jared wan-dered off on his own. Bandicut and Ik tried again to explore the compartments that they guessed to be science labs. Just about everything in them was incomprehensible: enigmatic machines that seemed to wink and turn themselves inside out, and floating images that seemed to flower open and rotate through multiple dimensions. Bandicut was at a loss, and the questions he asked Delilah—when she was around—just produced translation grid-lock.

By the end of an hour, they had all returned at least temporarily to the bridge, that being the one place where they could have at least the illusion of control. Everything seemed almost frighteningly quiet. They knew the quiet couldn't last—but what could they do? The hours passed, and the dark smudge that was Deep drew steadily closer.

*

As it happened, the robots had indeed seized a few minutes to download literature from a library Jeaves had made available to them. The library, Jeaves said, was incorporated into his memory systems—part of his original programming as a "server and personal assistant." After checking that all seemed calm on the bridge, Napoleon left to join Copernicus for a fresh download. They met in a small alcove off the main corridor, where Jeaves had prepared interface ports.

Napoleon signaled readiness, and they jacked in together. Napoleon experienced a momentary shiver of guilt, and hoped they weren't doing this too often, or being derelict in their duties. They had both found that they liked reading novels, and also found the reading something of an attention trap. They were hooked, as John Bandicut might have said. Napoleon found the literature remarkably stimulating. According to Jeaves, they were genuine originals from Earth. Napoleon had never been on Earth, not alive, though most of his components had been manufactured there. His own awakening had come on the remote outpost of Triton. He felt a longing for Earth, and reading the exploits of characters on Earth seemed to nourish that longing.

Copernicus, on the other hand, had little affinity for Earth, per se. But he loved adventure, or at least the imagining of adventure; he also felt that these novels gave him insight into human thought and action. Clearly it was useful to absorb these stories, even if they infringed a little on his work time, because they involved human passion and drive. It was for that very reason that they were called *romance* novels. The more he knew about these human qualities, the better he could serve Bandicut and the others.

Together the robots perused the titles in the library, looking for five apiece to choose. They were rationing themselves. Either of them could have absorbed the entire library with ease, but Jeaves had told them that these texts were best savored in moderation.

★

Li-Jared paused in a corridor intersection, noticing Bandicut's two robots plugged into the wall. What were they doing—recharging? Spying on the shipboard AI? Colluding with the shipboard AI?

Li-Jared had shared some tough times with Bandicut and these robots, and he harbored a growing fondness for the norgs, as Antares called them, especially as he had watched their personalities evolve. He didn't actually think they were up to anything bad. Still, there was no telling what influence Jeaves was having on them. It seemed they were always getting "upgrades" to their programming, from the shadow-people or others—though it was never very clear just what the upgrades entailed. While he had never observed a negative outcome from any of the changes, it was worth finding out what they were doing.

"Napoleon! Copernicus!" he said, approaching them. "What are you two up to?"

There was a certain amount of clicking and humming. Copernicus stayed plugged into the wall, but the taller, gangly Napoleon disconnected and turned to face him. "Greetings, Mr. Li-Jared. Is there an emergency on the bridge?"

"Not that I know of. What are you two doing?"

"We are reading books."

"Books?"

"From Earth."

"Ah."

"Novels," Copernicus offered.

"*Ah.*" As if that explained everything.

"We are downloading from Jeaves's library," Napoleon said, "and reading them internally, at our leisure."

"I see," Li-Jared said. Jeaves's library? This might bear keeping an eye on. "Well—you'll be there if we need you, right?"

"Of course," said Napoleon. "We are merely making use of spare processing cycles."

"That makes sense—I guess." Li-Jared rubbed his fingers together briskly. "Well, then—see you later." He turned to leave.

"They're helping us to understand human nature better," Copernicus called, just as Li-Jared was starting to turn back into the main passageway. Li-Jared paused, but could think of no response, so he just gestured with an open hand, and continued on his way.

✶

On the bridge, Antares maintained watch, with John. Ik had retired to his meditations, and Li-Jared was still wandering the ship. Antares, in a near-meditative state herself, sat cross-legged on a low, padded bench seat in the center of the bridge, facing the balcony view. She was aware of John's presence nearby, sometimes walking, sometimes sitting; but he was not in the center of her thoughts. He would be there if she needed him; she didn't have to think about it. Instead, she gazed at the wispy magenta-and-blue radiance of the approaching nebula.

She had stopped trying to understand the physical details of star-formation and star-birthing nebulas. She didn't have the science for it, and her interest lay elsewhere. She wanted only to sit in stillness and openness, trying to tease out anything she might detect with her empathic senses, whether from Starmaker or Deep, or anything else. She would have considered the notion crazy—they were *much* too far away—if it hadn't been for the earlier long-distance contact with Deep. Clearly things were possible in n-space that she would not have guessed. She did not want to repeat the earlier contact. But she did hope to find subtler threads that might help her prepare for whatever was coming.

Just now she felt a faint ringing sensation, at an extreme distance. She couldn't identify any specific emotions in that ringing, but she felt welling up within *herself* a breeze of sadness, overlaid with traces of pain and fear. She couldn't be sure whether these were echoes of something in the distance or from within her. But she thought they were not her own.

There was something closer, too. After a moment, she realized it was Deep. She thought she felt hints of curiosity and urgency. And something like anger.

And it was moving toward them.

⋆

Bandicut had decided that the most useful thing he could do was remain nearby, ready at hand if Antares needed him. The trouble was, watching someone meditate—even someone he cared for—got tedious. He paced; he sat on one of the small sofas behind her; he tried to think of ways to communicate better with Delilah; he tried to puzzle out Jeaves, who had spoken only briefly to say that, barring emergency, he would be unavailable for a time, due to system integration difficulties.

Bandicut started awake with a crick in his neck and a tickling in his mind. /What is it?/

/// Not sure. ///

"Do you feel it?" Antares asked, turning her head slightly. Her back was to him, and he couldn't quite see her eyes. "The disturbance is getting stronger."

"It is?" Bandicut leaned forward to stand up, but then closed his eyes instead, concentrating. "I feel—*something*—just a twinge. I don't know what to make of it."

"I don't know what to make of it, either, but it's more than just a twinge. I feel—" Antares swung around to face him, raising both hands to her forehead "—as if there's a second pulse pounding in my head. It's Deep. He's alive and he's definitely aware of us."

"He?"

"That's how it feels to me."

/// I feel it, too.
You're sensing it through me. ///

Bandicut joined Antares on the bench seat. Together they faced Starmaker and the dark cloud—except that he could no longer pick out the dark cloud. "I don't see it. Him."

"He's there," said Antares. "But I think there's something else, too."

"Something like—?"

"I don't know. Something else. I feel a great anger. I wasn't sure before, but now it's unmistakable."

"Anger toward . . . us?"

Antares's forehead creased. Her hair started to fall over her face, but she made no move to brush it back. All her concentration seemed to be directed outward. "I'm not sure," she said finally.

Bandicut's stomach knotted. "Should I call the others?"

"That might be a good idea."

"Jeaves?" Bandicut called. "Delilah? Can you call Ik and Li-Jared to the bridge? Something's coming!"

Jeaves's holo-image appeared—for the first time since their departure—flickered once, then steadied. "They're on their way. We're scanning, but so far you're learning more than we are. Do you want Delilah to magnify the link?"

"No!" Antares said, jumping to her feet. "Not yet. It'll overwhelm us."

Bwang. "Where is the danger?" Li-Jared cried, running onto the bridge. Ik followed a few seconds later. "Is it that Deep creature again?" Li-Jared asked, striding out onto the balcony. He looked to be poised to dive off into space. "Is *it* the danger?"

Antares sat down again, concentrating. "We don't know yet."

"Hrah, it has grown! It is much closer!"

Startled, Bandicut realized Ik was right. The dark cloud had become visible again. And indeed it was larger—alarmingly large, and directly in their path. "Jeaves? What's that thing doing? A minute ago it wasn't visible."

"It seems to be zigzagging," Jeaves said. "It was off to your left for a while, then cut back in front of us. I believe it may be pursuing another object."

"What object?"

Ik raised a long arm. "I see a tiny black speck out there." He was pointing a little to the right of the roiling cloud. "Do you see it?"

Bandicut shook his head.

Bong. "No."

Antares suddenly spoke, but distantly. "I don't *see* it, but I do feel Deep's awareness of it. I'm beginning to get a sense . . . it's almost a visual image . . . from Deep."

"Telepathic?" Ik asked.

Antares turned her head slightly. "I suppose, uhhll, but not like any I've ever—" She suddenly gasped, putting a hand to her head.

Bandicut returned to her side. "Are you—?"

"I'm fine—but it's changing." She drew a sharp breath. "It's as though I'm seeing—not with my eyes, but my mind. It's like seeing a dream you can't quite remember, and you *feel* it more than you see it. And yet it's still a vision, it's like something laid out on a huge field of light . . ." She pressed her fingers to the side of her head. "It's jagged things of light. I can feel parts of it that are *Deep,* and parts that are the . . . other. I can't tell, though, what's—" She closed her eyes, breathing rapidly. "It's getting stronger."

Bandicut blinked, feeling a momentary wave of dizziness.

/// Oh my, yes. ///

With a whirring sound behind them, Napoleon strode onto the bridge, followed by Copernicus. "Cap'n? We are sensing unusual stressors in the n-space field—"

Bandicut swung around. "N-space field? When did *you* start sensing n-space fields?"

Napoleon moved his upper body from left to right, flexing in his midsection like a long coil spring. Bandicut didn't remember his ever doing that before, either. The robot seemed to be scanning intently. Finally he answered. "It's an enhancement the shadow-people gave us."

Bandicut blinked. "What kind of readings are you picking up?"

Napoleon stepped closer to the front of the bridge. "Many n-space disturbances. With multiple sources. Wouldn't you agree, Copernicus?"

"Many," Copernicus agreed.

"What do you mean? Is it Deep?"

"Possibly," said Napoleon. "But we are also detecting hyperspatial gravity waves similar to the ones we experienced at the waystation. Their source may be a second object out there."

"Jeaves, can you tell us anything?" Bandicut called.

"No, but—hold a moment." Jeaves was interrupted by a single, jarring rumble through the floor, followed by a flickering of the starscape. The effect was dizzying—and in the midst of it, Delilah flew out of a wall with an urgent ringing sound.

(Image breakup. Necessary to strengthen the n-space channels for a clearer view. Possible risk. Two objects, purposes unknown.)

"Uhhll," Antares said, hugging herself. "If you magnify the way you did before . . ."

(May be necessary to obtain information.)

Antares ran her fingers through her hair. "All right. If it is necessary."

(Beginning now. Prepare for disturbances.)

Bandicut's stomach suddenly floated. The image zoomed inward. As the cloud grew before his eyes, so did the feeling of lightness. /Are you feeling this?/ he whispered.

/// Oh yes. ///

Now there was something strange, something alive, tickling at the edges of his mind. But was it Deep or the other thing? He felt a dark shroud of anger, coming toward them.

Antares murmured, "Not anger. *Malice.* I don't know which one—"

"Delilah! Jeaves! If these things come after us, can we defend ourselves?" Bandicut shouted.

Delilah dropped, ringing like a steel drum. (We are attempting to shield the ship against—)

The halo never completed her sentence. A tiny black spot swooped into view, flying in a sharp arc toward them. Everyone gasped in unison. It grew quickly—not to become huge like the cloud, but large enough to look like *something,* a probe or spacecraft. Bandicut felt a sudden wave of intense cold. It wasn't physical, exactly; it was a feeling that this thing, whatever it was, was sucking heat and life right out of them, and out of all of the space surrounding them. He couldn't move, but could only watch the black object zigzag violently, careening toward them. And close behind it rushed the roiling blackness of Deep.

Antares was staring fiercely, trying to parse the feelings cascading around her. "Deep," she whispered, "is trying to destroy—"

The black object shot across their bow, and Deep went after it, changing shape, his interior flickering. A tremendous shudder passed through the deck; the bridge lights wavered, and the viewspace went watery. Delilah shrieked something about hull integrity. *"Everyone stay where you are!"* Jeaves barked. The balcony and viewspace began to contract.

Gong! "What's happening to the ship?" Li-Jared cried.

"Instability in the n-space fields!" Jeaves said. "We're locking down." Then his holo blinked out as his voice trailed off into a series of staccato barks.

The cold deepened, became nearly unbearable.

Bandicut felt a sudden inner wrenching, as though something had grabbed hold of spacetime and *twisted* it. He reached out for Antares, but his hand went the wrong way and at the wrong speed, and he groped . . . *slowly* . . . in empty space. /Time . . . something . . . wrong . . . with . . . time . . . /

/// Yes-s-s-s . . . ///

He could see, out of the corner of his eye, everyone on the bridge veering and twisting in slow motion . . . and then as suddenly as it had started, it ended.

But in the much-reduced viewing window, the black object had slowed nearly to a halt. Bandicut had just a moment to feel dread—*it's going to attack!*—when the billowing curtain that was Deep folded around and enveloped the object. A flash of purplish light escaped, and then Deep roiled again and glided away from the ship. The intense cold suddenly vanished, and in its place was a powerful, nearly overwhelming feeling of *presence*. Bandicut reeled.

/// That's astounding. I feel . . . ///

Struggling to catch his breath, Bandicut managed to ask, /You feel . . . what?/

/// A clear sense of satisfaction. ///

"Hypergrav waves have stopped," Napoleon reported. "The small object is gone. N-space fields are stabilizing."

Bandicut stared in wonder as Deep appeared to turn and wheel back in their direction. Had Deep come all this way to take out that other object? And now, was it coming back to do the same to them?

Bandicut murmured to Antares, "What do you feel?"

Antares shook her head. "It's very alien. I can't tell."

Delilah fluttered across the top of the bridge-cavern, ringing. (Deep is intersecting with our n-space fields. Close encounter is imminent.)

Deep loomed . . . then *shrank,* abruptly . . . shrank in the space of a heartbeat to a small, intensely black point hovering directly in front of their view. The star field was distorted, as though spacetime were being twisted around a pole. Gusts of air swirled through the bridge. Bandicut felt dancing pinpricks in the backs of his eyes. His knees buckled, and he nearly went down.

Charlene cried out,

/// *Oh Jesus! I feel . . . really strange, John.* ///

/What is it, Charlene?/

/// *I don't know, I . . .*

I'm being pulled . . . into Deep . . . ///

Bandicut was trying to keep from falling over. "My God . . ." The bridge was ballooning out into a huge bubble, stretched into open space. The floor where he was struggling to stay on his feet seemed to reach far out into the emptiness . . . into the twisting fabric of spacetime. It wasn't just space, though—something was wrong inside his head.

/*Charlie?* Are you all right?/

The quarx's voice came from a hundred miles away.

/// *John, I can't . . . I don't know where I am . . .* ///

A sudden silence filled his head. /Charlene? *Charlie!* Are you there?/

Just a whisper of wind.

/*Charlie!*/

Light and darkness churned before him. *Deep.* "Help!" he whispered, reaching out for Charlie and finding nothing. Next to him, he felt Antares hunched over, felt her distress raking over him like stinging fabric. But he couldn't reach to her, not now.

/*Charlie!*/

This time he heard—or felt—a faint reply. It seemed to come

across a terribly great distance, and only with extraordinary help from the translator-stones. The quarx's voice echoed faintly:

/// John . . . ? ///

/Come back!/ Bandicut whispered inwardly—and then screamed aloud, *"Deep! Have you taken Charlie?"*

He felt a long, low moan that seemed to shake the entire ship. Bandicut stood tight with fear. And then he felt a sharp jolt in his chest, his heart, his mind—and the sudden stinging awareness of Charlie reappearing in his thoughts.

/// John—! ///

The voice was weak, but it was coming from his own head. Charlie was back. But she was hurt.

/Charlie—Charlene—what is it, what's happening?/ *Am I going to lose you?*

/// Don't know . . . I'm not . . .
John, I was inside Deep . . . don't know how, why . . .
all strange . . . powerful . . . incredible . . .
John, I'm losing my grip . . . ///

/Charlie, don't!/

/// I feel as if I'm not all . . . here . . . ///

/What happened are you hurt did that thing pull you out of me? *Jesus*, Charlie!/ Bandicut was gasping for breath. He felt as if his heart were about to pop. He could feel Deep still around him, with a hold on Charlie. /No!/ Losing Charlie to someone else was worse than losing her to death. Death the quarx could recover from. But if she went away . . .

/// John . . . so much to tell . . . ///

She was hanging by a thread. She was trying to summon memories, images . . . something, anything to show him.

/Steady—*just take it easy.*/ Bandicut shut his eyes, trying to keep *himself* steady. /What can I do? How can I help you?/

The quarx was struggling to answer. A shower of images burst into Bandicut's mind, images of the inside of a cloud, an intense fluctuation of spacetime, images that were like droplets of fire, each bearing a trace of memory—of universes colliding, of galaxies growing, of whispered conversations with stars. It was bewildering. Charlene was struggling to speak, but he felt her slipping away on a treacherous rope . . .

/Charlie, don't go—/
        /// I'm trying . . . I wish I could . . .
    John, catch as much as you can . . . oh, damn. ///
Bandicut felt a lurch, as though the quarx had lost her foot-
ing on a tightrope, and was dangling, twisting. There was another explosion of tiny images, expanding and bursting into
his consciousness; images of great loneliness, and of slipping
through rifts in spacetime, and of confronting dark and menacing machines . . .

And then an abrupt implosion as it all came collapsing back
to a point again, then vanished. The connection with Deep was
broken. And with it, something that Charlie needed, some part
of her she needed to stay alive. He felt her slipping away . . .

/Charliiiiie!/

The quarx's last words came as the faintest whisper:
            /// I'm sorry . . . ///
/Charlene—!/
        /// Bye, John. ///
His breath went out in a rush. He doubled over, hugging
himself against a flash of pain inside. A great emptiness welled
up inside him where the quarx had been. He shook in spasms,
weeping silently. /Don't go, Charlene. I can't do without you!
Don't go!/ But there was no reply, no echo of the quarx's thought
or feeling.

Charlene was gone.

Struggling to draw a breath, he looked up. The bridge was
slowly returning to its normal shape. The dark point had billowed back out into a cloud, and was backing away. And Charlie
was gone.

And on the floor beside him, Antares lay unconscious.

9

It was as though a larger-than-life Thespi choir were singing underwater. The voices were at once immediate and distant in Antares's mind. What were they saying? Something terrible had happened, something that had sent her with a silent scream into this place. From outside there was an eruption of light and darkness, and something great and strange and angry clashing with another, smaller, almost as powerful.

It was a dreamy awareness; all she could really tell was that the smaller of the two entities had died, crushed out of existence. Vast curtains of light swayed and shifted in her mind, like an aurora gone mad. Then everything darkened.

It didn't last, though, the darkness. Soon she felt something else: a pulling and tearing, stabbing beams of light, inner light. And *pain.*

Deep, penetrating pain. *Whose?*

Loss, and separation.

Charlie's voice echoed—from across a great gulf. Indistinct, afraid, confused. *Charlie has left John Bandicut and entered— joined somehow with—the dark and terrifying cloud. How can this be? And what about John—?*

Time passing confusingly.

Later, she was aware of another connection, Charlie returning to John. But it did not feel normal; the fit was all wrong; Charlie was too badly injured, and the rejoining could not succeed. Charlie cried out in pain; there were more stabbing beams of light; another cry of pain, this one from John Bandicut: *Charlie, what are you—no, Charlie, don't leave!* But Charlie was fading . . . too far, too fast . . . *fading out of existence . . .*

Then even Antares's unconscious awareness slipped away.

*

Everyone was talking at once, including the robots and the halo. Everyone except Bandicut, who crouched on his haunches holding his head and blinking back tears, half trying to see Antares and half trying to shut everyone and everything out. *Charlie's gone. Charlene. Gone. Why now?* /What did that goddamn thing do to you, Charlie? Tried to steal you away./ But there was no answer; Charlene was gone. She'd died.

"Hrrm, is Antares—?"

What? He looked up through blurry eyes. Ik was trying to say something. *Antares.*

He was kneeling over her, barely even seeing her. It was too late for Charlie. But Antares needed him now. "Antares—are you—?" His throat closed, choking off his words. With a trembling hand, he touched her cheek. Then he picked up her hand and squeezed it. "Antares, wake up." *Charlie, wake up! Can't you see I need help?*

"Rrrm, John Bandicut, are you hurt? You do not seem . . . well." Ik towered over him, rubbing his long throat nervously. Like a tree crouching, he squatted down on the other side of Antares.

Bandicut drew a ragged breath, and tried to force out, "Charlie—" He shook his head. His tongue felt thick; his voice didn't want to work. "She's . . . gone. Deep did something."

"Aaaiiii, I am sorry," Ik murmured with feeling. He had been through more than one quarx death with his human friend before. He gazed at Bandicut, then gestured down. "What happened to Antares?"

"I don't know," Bandicut whispered, brushing the line of her jaw with the backs of his fingertips. She was breathing, her chest undulating slowly, lower breasts then upper. He leaned closer. *"Antares?"*

This time she stirred slightly. After a moment, her lips parted and she expelled a soft breath: "Aaa—uuhhlll . . ."

Bandicut swallowed against a rock in his throat. He seized her hand and held it tightly. "Antares!" he whispered. "Can you hear me?"

An answering whisper: *"Hear you. Yesss . . ."*

"What happened? What did you see?" *What did you feel? Did you feel Charlie die? Can you feel what I'm feeling now?* He squeezed her hand.

Her eyes flicked open, and suddenly she was gazing up at him. "I saw . . . I *felt* . . . Deep. And then it—" she turned her head, as though trying to see the view out past the balcony "—it attacked the other . . ." She turned back to look up at Bandicut. "What was that thing?"

"I don't know," Bandicut whispered, shaking his head.

Antares nodded and closed her eyes. After a moment, she opened them again: wide, thin circlets of gold surrounding jet-black. "And then it—uhhl, *Charlie!* She's gone!"

Bandicut nodded, not trusting himself to speak.

With an effort, Antares lifted her hand and pressed her fingertips to Bandicut's chest. "She went to Deep?" she whispered. "Earlier? Before she died?"

Bandicut forced himself to speak. "Yes. Somehow. She came back, but she was *hurt.*" He hesitated, the final images from Charlene, from Deep, spinning in his head. "It was too wrenching, I think. Too much information, I don't know. She couldn't— she was already dying."

Antares gazed up at him. The images from Charlene were so intense, he barely felt Antares's empathic touch. Finally he raised his own eyes. Ik was motionless, watching them, concern etched in his deep-set eyes. Li-Jared, however, was pacing back and forth at the front of the bridge, glaring into space. Muttering under his breath, he looked both frightened and angry. Delilah was bobbing in the air like a life raft on a storm-tossed sea, chiming softly and incomprehensibly.

"Can Charlie return from a death such as this?" Antares whispered.

He let out his breath with measured slowness. "I don't know. She lost a part of herself before she died, I think. It's never happened like this. I just don't know."

Napoleon stepped forward, swiveling his head. "Friends, I observed a violent encounter between the one you call Deep and a smaller source of n-space distortion. Deep appeared to both destroy and absorb the smaller. The readings were extremely provocative."

"Rrrm, *how?*" Ik asked.

"It appeared there were differential time streams surrounding the object. I believe Deep may have torn it apart by subjecting it to a temporal shear zone."

That made Bandicut sit back. "Really."

Ik was more vocal. "Jeaves! Do you have something to tell us about this?"

There was a momentary squeal of feedback, before the holo of Jeaves reappeared. "Sorry. I have been working with the AI on a check of our systems. I believe Napoleon has the right of it—and yes, we are safe for the time being. I also believe we have just witnessed a new chapter in a very old story."

Ik cocked his head, and Antares pushed herself to a sitting position. "What—" *bwang* "—old story?" Li-Jared asked.

"Before I get into that," Jeaves said, "let me say that I believe Deep probably saved us from being destroyed, or at least seriously hindered in our mission."

"You mean by, hrrm, intercepting that—"

"Device. Probably an ancient tool. Or weapon. Its appearance has provided us with some useful information. Its behavior matches certain old, recorded patterns. The hypergrav waves are not mentioned in the records. But they suggest that devices of similar origin may be involved in the crisis we have come to investigate."

"Devices that do *what?*" Li-Jared asked sharply.

"We don't know yet. But as Napoleon observed, one thing they can do is create distortions of spacetime. Specifically, of n-space."

"Why is that so alarming? Don't *we* create distortions in spacetime?" Li-Jared asked, gesturing around in a wide sweep. "Isn't that how we fly?"

"Indeed. But we don't *project* our distortions destructively onto other bodies. Onto starships. Or, perhaps . . . stars."

"Are they the cause of what's happening to Ed's world?"

"That remains to be seen," answered Jeaves. "But I expect there are other such devices out there. And they may be causing greater harm than simply threatening our ship. This one may simply have been a sentinel."

Bandicut felt a chill. "So," he said, the pain of Charlie's death rising again in his chest, "Deep *was* acting to protect us when it . . . did whatever it did . . . to the thing."

"*I* believe so. But I must be clear—we have not yet established real communication with Deep." Jeaves rotated and gestured forward, toward the distant, dark wisp.

If Deep was on their side, Bandicut wondered, why did it kill Charlie? Had Deep snatched the quarx, trying to take her by force? Or was her death purely an accident? Had Charlene been caught in a link with Deep and simply been unable to pull free? He caught Antares's gaze, and saw his own pain reflected in her eyes.

"Deep is proceeding ahead of us," Jeaves said, "at what appears to be a safe distance."

"What, then?" Ik asked. "Is Deep, hrrrm, acting as a—" *rasp* "—*escort* to us?"

"Possibly," Jeaves said. "But that is a question that must await communication."

"And if we can't communicate with it?" Li-Jared asked.

"Well, that is one reason you were asked to come along."

All four stared at Jeaves.

"We knew Deep, or something like him, might be in the area. And we hoped *you* might be able to establish communication."

"Uhhl, why us?"

"Because you have been successful in the past. And you have translator-stones—which I, for example, do not. And you—" Jeaves spoke directly to Bandicut now "—had the quarx."

"Right," Bandicut said, fighting back the stab in his heart. "Right."

The robot image dipped its head in acknowledgment. "But before we pursue that question, there is some background that I now perceive is relevant to our situation. I believe I understand connections that I did not before. This may take some time, so why don't we move to where you can be more comfortable. May I suggest the lounge?"

∗

Whatever else, they were all hungry, and unanimous in their desire to get away from the bridge for a while. Napoleon and Copernicus remained on watch.

Once they were gathered in a semicircle with a table full of food, Jeaves floated to where they could all see him. "It's time for some historical context."

"Whose history?" Antares asked, picking apart a pastry roll.

"Really, the galaxy's history," Jeaves answered. "Because, if the device that Deep eliminated is evidence, then what's going on in Starmaker may be related to events that occurred hundreds of millions of years ago, near the galactic center."

Ik broke off a food stick in his hard mouth and munched silently, waiting for Jeaves to continue.

Bandicut found his thoughts turning to Charlie, who was the only one he knew who could even conceive of millions of years of real history. *You should be here now to hear this, Charlie.*

"There was a war," Jeaves said. "A terrible war that lasted for many thousands of years. Our knowledge of that time is sketchy, and sources of information are scattered and difficult to evaluate. But we know that a sprawling complex of civilizations once lived in a large region of space, much closer to the galactic center. We know some of their names: Alenora, Coreselia, Lo-ko-hin, K'nent."

"Once lived?" Antares asked.

"May still live. We don't know for certain. Attempts to send star-spanner probes from Shipworld into the region have largely ended in failure. But we do know that some of their artifacts still live. And I might add that these civilizations not only took part in the most terrible war in the history of the galaxy, they also created some of the most beautiful works of art. John, you are familiar with the Horsehead Nebula?"

Startled, Bandicut said, "Of course." To the others, he explained, "It's a nebula famous on my world. It has a distinctive shape. It looks just like the head of an Earth animal called a horse."

"That is correct. And galactically speaking, it is not far from where we are heading," Jeaves said. "But the animal it actually represents is not a horse, it is an animal from another world altogether, called a *n'kelk*. And that nebula is not a natural formation, it is a sculpture."

Bandicut opened his mouth, and closed it.

"That, at any rate, is the legend," said Jeaves. "Very few reliable records remain. But . . . we know that not all of the works of this civilization were so creative. Some were terribly destructive. And some apparently still exist, and remain dangerous. That was probably one such artifact that Deep saved us from."

"Rrrl, how can you be certain?" Ik asked.

"I am far from certain. But there are stories with common elements, themes that have appeared on many widely separated worlds throughout the Sagittarius and Perseus spiral arms. Sometimes the stories take the form of old legends, or songs, or ancient scriptures. Tales of otherworldly peoples, sometimes called by names plausibly similar to Alenora, Coreselia, Lo-ko-hin, or K'nent. Also tales—much darker tales—of *void eaters, twisters,* and *angels of death*—all telling of entire worlds, even groups of worlds, being destroyed by marauders from the stars."

Li-Jared made a clicking sound. "That narrows it down."

Jeaves ignored the sarcasm. "Some of the records are true-memories, passed down telepathically through eons of generations. Those are considered most reliable. Others come through writing, art, or cybernetic storage. More than a few include images of attacks that are consistent with space itself collapsing, or somehow being twisted destructively. Images consistent with what *we* felt as that object approached a short time ago, before Deep intervened."

Ik stroked the side of his bony, pale blue-white face.

"Okay," said Bandicut, "but isn't it kind of a leap to assume that stories from a bunch of different worlds all over the galaxy all point to the same thing?"

"It is. Some of these conclusions are speculative. But there is further evidence—a historical basis, which I would like to share with you. Please . . . eat. You might as well relax while you can."

Bandicut realized he had been holding a piece of bread the entire time and had not eaten a bite. He tore off a small piece and chewed, as Jeaves continued.

"We—that is, the ship's AI, Delilah, and I—believe that object may have been part of a cluster, because they are thought to have traveled in clusters—that came from an ancient war zone.

Whether it has a new mission, or is still trying to carry out a war-related mission, we cannot say."

"Hrrm, like the Maw of the Abyss," Ik muttered.

Bandicut had exactly the same thought. The Maw of the Abyss, in the undersea world of the Neri, had nearly killed them, along with the Neri and Astari civilizations. It was a relic of an ancient civilization, still trying to carry out a long-since irrelevant mission.

Jeaves had cocked his head at Ik's words. "From your description of the Maw, I wonder if it could be from the same complex of civilizations. It is surprising how many places in the galaxy such remnants turn up."

Bandicut was chilled by a sudden thought. "You don't suppose our *translator* is related to those things, do you?"

"I would be very surprised," said Jeaves. "I do not know the story of the origin of the translator. However, I believe that its actions are more likely to be directed toward remediation of the war influence than in concert with it."

Correct, if an understatement, the translator-stones muttered quietly in the back of his mind.

"We do not know too much of the history of those ancient civilizations," Jeaves said. "But we *do* know there was a war so devastating it severely diminished a major galactic culture, millions of years before any of *our* peoples were even a twinkle in the genome. It took place in a region of the galaxy that spanned thousands of light-years." As the robot spoke, a holo-image of the galaxy appeared, floating above the table. A red glow highlighted a coin-sized region, a modest distance from the center of the galaxy. "The region is dense with stars, so the war zone probably encompassed hundreds of thousands of star systems."

Antares's breath went out in a hiss, and Bandicut felt her heartache wash over him. Ik stirred. "So many?"

"Yes. And the effects of the war rippled outward beyond the actual war zone." As Jeaves spoke, a pale orange ring expanded from the red area. "Refugees fled, seeking to escape the conflict, sometimes in the process overrunning innocent inhabited worlds." Now a violet ring expanded slowly outside the orange ring. "An even wider space was affected by wandering remnants of the robotic fighting forces, as well as by star-system-altering devices whose intended function we do not know. Construction, perhaps."

"Hrrm, construction for what purpose, I wonder," Ik muttered, reaching for another Hraachee'an-style food bar.

"We do not know," said Jeaves.

"Rrr, how *do* you know the things that you know, then?" Ik asked, before biting down with a clack.

Jeaves seemed to *hmm* to himself for a few moments. "The details have been gathered across the ages by the Shipworld masters and others, from a large variety of sources. Some of the civilizations that have been seeded on Shipworld are survivors of the great war, and they have brought their own stories with them." Jeaves raised his hand in a cautionary gesture. "Of course, stories change over time, and some are made up to begin with, so there is much that is uncertain. Many conflicting tales have been mingled as the stories were gathered. And yet . . ."

Li-Jared's eyes flashed. "How do we know which parts of your story are real, then?"

"Partly by the common threads. On rare occasions, actual artifacts of the war have been gathered, and information extracted from their memory stores."

"So," Bandicut said, "things like that device Deep destroyed have been captured and studied?"

"Nothing so large. If we have an opportunity to capture such a device without endangering our mission, we might consider it. It could provide valuable information."

Bandicut shivered as Ik asked, "What details about this war do we *know*?"

Jeaves paused and looked around at each of them as though they'd finally gotten to the heart of it. "Let us consider one story that has come down to us in many versions. Quite a number of the details are chillingly consistent among the versions, and for some events, we have additional persuasive evidence. I'm going to ask Delilah to assist. I suggest you put down your food and drink. Parts of this might be disturbing."

Delilah dropped from the ceiling with a single harp-strum.

Before Bandicut could so much as blink, he felt the room twist, as he slipped into the halo's learning trance . . .

✶

How many thousands of years into the war this happened—or how many millions of years in the past—no one knew. The planet, possibly called Thanatolla, had repeatedly been the focus of bitter fighting. It was the nerve center of the most efficiently ruthless robotic killing machines in the war, and its very existence instilled terror.

(A holo-window opened, revealing images of a world devoted exclusively to military might, most of it machines under the control of machines. Nanomachines tore down and built up, and nanomachines swarmed and fought . . .)

Despite many attempts to destroy it, Thanatolla survived, as the tides of strategic balance shifted hundreds of light-years this way and hundreds of light-years that way. Several times bombardment from space had sent it to the brink of biological and technological collapse, and each time it had returned—struggling for centuries just to survive, then rebuilding to greater power than ever.

Some viewed its potential for power as useful and malleable, and fought not to destroy it but to turn it to their own purposes. To others, its artificial lifeforms were so virulent as to defy any justification for its survival. It was nothing less than a disease afflicting all of civilization. Indeed, Thanatolla may have been the ignition point of the whole war.

In the end a coalition of forces undertook a desperate mission: a years-long thermonuclear bombardment, to cease only when the threat was utterly eradicated, the planet Thanatolla sterilized, biologically and cybernetically.

(Another window revealed the planet from orbit, *flash, flash, flash,* turning the atmosphere into a poisonous, ruinous blanket . . .)

History did not record the identity of the attacking force, but so determined were they that they placed telepaths in orbit, telepaths whose job it was to monitor life on the planet's surface as nuclear fire rained down on it.

(Another window: glimpses of beings in elaborate installations, isolated as they opened their minds to the telepathic choir, the death-agonies of millions, as the unceasing rain of war-heads fell . . .)

Most of the telepaths were insane by the end, but it was they who provided final assurance that the job was done, that no sentient life survived, and so far as they could tell, no life of any kind. What was left was a radioactive wasteland, utterly uninhabitable. Even so, monitoring forces remained in orbit until, with the passing of time, the tides of the fading war swept them away, too.

(The windows closed; all that followed was reconstruction and supposition.)

Only robotic monitors, long forgotten, noted the reemergence of life a half-million years later—cyber-life, remnants of shattered nanomachines that had survived in some form, in some minimal way. In the radioactivity, the reemerging life mutated and evolved and grew, with only trace memories of what had gone before. And yet, buried perhaps in a collective unconscious composed of a billion individually meaningless fragments were shadows of memory—of the war that had destroyed them.

Perhaps they learned from the memories, but *what* they learned was unknown. Over the eons the surviving lifeforms grew, unwatched and forgotten. If a few surviving probes noted the reappearance, they had no one left to report to. In time the survivors' descendants migrated off their world.

And what became of them?

Were they related to the machines that now threatened Star-maker?

No one knew.

"But we know this," Jeaves said as the trance fell away and the company again faced each other over the table. "There are powerful adversaries in the galaxy today. And if there were no connection with the ancient wars, we would be surprised . . ."

✶

Back in their quarters, Bandicut and Antares sat quietly on the bed, their backs to the wall, leaning shoulder to shoulder. Neither of them felt much like talking. After a time, Antares took Bandicut's hand. "No new Charlie?" she whispered.

He shook his head.

Antares rested her head against his shoulder. He sighed softly and pressed his cheek to her hair, and tried to blink the mist from his eyes. Finally he closed his eyes and smelled the rich piney scent of Antares's hair, and let his thoughts slip away to wherever they might go . . .

Deadly peril from the stars.

Fear.

Charlie. (Will she return?)

Antares.

Earth. Home. The Sun.

Ed the hypercone, and his strange, imperiled world.

Julie Stone. *Julie, I miss you.*

Antares . . . the smell of her hair, the soft movement of her breathing . . .

Making love with her on the world of the Neri . . .

Awkward, exciting.

Feeling her touching him with her thoughts, feelings; joining her emotions to his.

Wanting to know her, to share his pain, thoughts, needs.

Becoming slowly aroused . . .

Wanting her.

✶

Antares felt a great weight of grief for John and his loss. Still, she was comforted by his solid presence against her, his shoulder under her head. His warmth radiated into her, his breathing lifted her head and let it down again. His sadness and fear surged around her like sea foam; but even in his fear, he was a solid and comforting presence.

With time, though, she felt an itching arousal, a tightness in her midsection; and she wondered, can it be right to feel such arousal now, in a time of such danger and grief? Her first instinct was to hide her feelings from him; but these feelings arose from echoes of *his* emotions. And wasn't that precisely as it should be? Wasn't it a proper condition for Thespi arousal—as a Thespi Third, if her role was to assist in joining—or even for true joining, since there was no one else here to join with John Bandicut?

She felt uncertain. She felt his emotions shifting from dread to moving memories to hungry desire, all uncontrolled. She sought to calm his rush of feelings, to soothe him. She realized she was pressing both of her left breasts against him in invitation, and wanting to. Memories bubbled up: of their union before, among the Neri. Desire surged through her to feel that again.

He turned and whispered something to her, and she whispered back, not really hearing his words or even her own. His lips found hers, and she experienced a moment's hesitation; and then the pleasure of the memories of that human gesture came back, and she returned the kiss, feeling his desire and solace, and sharing it. His tongue touched her lips, and she shivered with their joined pleasure.

His emotions still churned; but as his arms encircled her, and she pressed a hand to his stomach, and then lower, she *remembered,* and knew what she wanted. She felt him rising physically toward her, and she closed her hand around him through his clothing, and echoed his sigh of release and pleasure. *He feels comforted . . . this is right . . .*

And her full Thespi powers awakened and unfolded, touching one strand of soul to another as she shivered and gave herself to him with growing passion.

10

PACKING FOR DEPARTURE

 The mental transition took Julie Stone the better part of the night. *The translator wants to go to Earth.* Well, okay. /You could have told me that before, and it would have saved me a lot of trouble in the meeting,/ she muttered, trying to sleep.

We had not heard. The translator has now gathered the data it needs.

/Data about—?/

Status update following the elimination of the comet. As-tronomical data.

/Oh . . . / And with that, she was asleep.

✳

She didn't wait for the meeting the next day, but sent a message to Lamarr, Jackson, and Takashi, saying that she had received word: *The translator is ready to travel.*

Her appearance at the meeting was canceled, and she was instead told to report to Cole Jackson, the Survey Operations director.

"This is good news for you," Jackson said, adjusting his eyeglasses as she stood before his desk studying her new written orders. "You'll get to ride to Earth with the thing. It's bad for *me,* because I have to stay here and face the Coalition team when they arrive. And let me tell you, they're going to be some pissed."

"Yeah," Julie said, reading the proposed schedule. "I imagine they are. Wouldn't be surprised if they considered it an act of war." Her eyes widened. "You want me out there *tomorrow,* crating it? Have you been preparing for this all along, without telling me?"

Jackson shrugged. "There was a general belief that you might object. Anyway, you've got four days to get it crated, lifted to orbit, and aboard the *Park Avenue* for departure. Lamarr and the MINEXFO group want to be on their way as soon as possible before the Coalition gets here. It's all been worked out."

Julie glanced up. "They all know, right, that it's not like people from the other groups won't be waiting for us when we get to Earth?" She shuddered at the welcome they would receive, if they were perceived as absconding with the only alien artifact ever found.

Jackson shrugged. "Maybe. But you'll have three months to pick its brains in the meantime. And maybe get it on MINEXFO's side." Jackson took off his glasses and smiled. "Anyway, it already likes *you.* Now, shouldn't you be down in the ready room? The excavation-prep team is scheduled to roll in an hour."

"*Excavation* prep? An *hour?* Was anyone planning to give me a heads-up before a bunch of people blundered out there again?"

"I just did. You're to go ask the thing nicely if we can put it in a box for the ride." Jackson stood, hitching up his trousers. "Now, shouldn't you be going?"

She was already running out the door.

*

"Julie, we're all set back here. You can go ahead and make contact when you're ready." The voice in her spacesuit helmet belonged to Kim, her supervisor. She turned to look behind her in the floodlit ice cavern, where Kim and an assistant were waiting to record the meeting. Fifty feet over their heads, on the frozen surface of Triton, the prep crew were bringing in the first pieces of drilling and hoisting equipment. Tipping her head back to look up, she thought, If this were Earth gravity, I'd be waiting for that stuff to land on top of me.

Shuffle-walking forward on the translucent ice surface, she approached the translator. It was standing right where it had been the first time she had seen it, and probably where it had been when John first fell through the ice to land beside it. The device was a little taller than she was: shaped like a top, but consisting of a squirming collection of black and iridescent spheres, all moving in what looked like continuous Brownian motion. As she stood before it, she had the feeling that it was busy thinking deep thoughts. She hoped it would spare a few ergs of its concentration for her questions.

"Hello," she said.

For a moment, there was no indication that the translator was even aware of her presence. Then she heard the reply in her mind, with a sound ever so slightly deeper than the stones: *We are prepared for the journey.*

Julie nodded slowly, not wanting there to be any mistake. "I just want to be clear. The last time we tried to move you, it was not . . . very successful."

We were not prepared then.

She hesitated, suddenly conscious of the fact that *her* words were being recorded, but the words of the translator were in her mind, and nowhere else. "Then I can confirm you are . . . prepared?"

Yes. But we require that you, Julie Stone, accompany us.

Julie cleared her throat and repeated, for the recording, what the translator had just told her. "Then may I report to the crews up on the surface that you're ready for excavation? We would like to pack you into a protective crate, for shipment aboard one of our spacecraft. Will that be satisfactory?"

Yes.

Julie felt as if her world were spinning.

★

The prep crew took careful measurements, and the next day they were all out there again, with a complete arsenal of hoists and excavators. Julie stood to one side, watching the crews jockey the vertical boring machinery into position. The plan was to drill a wider shaft on the side of the cavern farthest from the translator, where the operation would pose the least danger in the event of a cave-in.

Standing on the gray-white Triton surface of frozen nitrogen, methane, and assorted oxides, barely illuminated by the wan sunlight, Julie found her thoughts gravitating toward feelings of cold. There were at least thirty people out here with her, and only about ten of them actually had a job to do at the moment. She peered up into the star-pricked blackness, where the ghostly planet Neptune, cerulean with white swirls, floated like a moody goddess. A point of light moving slowly across the sky was undoubtedly Triton Orbital, where the interplanetary transport *Park Avenue* was docked, awaiting its precious cargo. That station was where John Bandicut had boarded and hijacked *Neptune Explorer*, before flying it halfway across the solar system to stop a comet.

She felt a slight vibration under her feet, and jerked back to the present.

"Hey! Who the hell did that?" someone shouted on the comm.

"What? Did what?"

"Look! Right there! It just appeared!"

Julie turned around, trying to find the source of the commotion.

"Things like that don't just mokin' 'appear'!" the first voice hollered. *"I coulda' driven right off the edge!"*

"Yeah, but—"

"Would someone report?" shouted an annoyed supervisor. *"What the bloody hell's going on?"*

Julie joined the crowd near the boring rig, and was stunned to see what everyone was yelling about. A perfect, four-meter-wide ice ramp now sloped in a straight line from the surface down into the cavern. The roof had vanished from the cavern altogether. The translator was visible at the bottom, standing alone in a pool of light under the starry sky.

/How the—?/ Julie began, then shook her head and looked around to see that pretty much everyone was either turning in circles, looking to discover what supermachine had done this, or staring dumbfounded down the long ramp.

It was a simple translation of the ice molecules, said the stones, in her head.

Julie blinked. /You mean you *moved* the ice? Is there a big ramp-sized pile somewhere?/ She swung around, searching the landscape.

The molecules were translated into the surrounding and underlying ice. The ground you're standing on is a little denser now.

/Oh./ She absorbed that for a moment, then made her way to the top of the ramp where it cut into the surface. Nudging a few of the spacesuited gawkers out of the way, she started walking down the long ramp toward the translator. As the comm-chatter died down, she could hear the excavation supervisor hollering, *"Julie Stone! Where's Stone?"*

She waved a space-gloved hand, but kept walking. "On my way down, Paul."

"Find out if the translator did this, will you?"

Julie waved again, without answering.

At the bottom, she found most of the floodlights that Kim's team had set up still working. It was an eerie sight, like approaching a sunken stage, with the translator standing alone at its center. It was poised like a top, as always. But it seemed to her that the churning inner movement of the spheres had slowed. "Are you all right?" she asked. "This—" and she paused to gesture back toward the ramp she'd just descended "—was pretty impressive."

It was a simple shifting of molecules. You may bring your equipment down now.

For a moment, Julie just stared at the translator through the reflections on her faceplate, and listened to the rasp of her own breathing. Then she said, "Okay. They are intending to install a protective crate around you first, then move you from this location. You will be placed aboard a spacecraft."

Yes.

"We may go ahead and do that?"

Yes.

Julie turned around and peered up the long incline, where several spacesuited figures were trudging after her. "Gentlemen," she said, raising her voice as if she needed to shout up to the others, "your hole has been bored. You may begin crating the translator."

✳

Once the necessary equipment was in place at the bottom of the incline, the foreman turned to Julie for advice. It took her a moment to understand the problem. The men were unloading the pieces of a large shipping crate from one of the tine-lifts. But how were they going to get the bottom panel of the crate under the translator? Two other men were stretching out cables and hooks, with the apparent intent of grappling the translator and lifting it with a hoist. She had a feeling those would not be welcomed by the translator. /Do you have any suggestions?/ she asked the stones, or the translator, whichever was listening.

Allow the translator to handle it, the stones replied.

Julie frowned. /How—?/ she began, then caught herself. The translator had begun to glow more brightly. Now it was floating, with a space of about ten centimeters visible between it and the cavern floor. Julie cleared her throat and said aloud, "Is anyone else seeing what I'm seeing?"

"What's that?" the foreman asked. He had turned his back, watching the crew set out the pieces. No one except Julie was actually looking at the translator.

"Would everyone please turn around and look?" she asked quietly.

The work crew all shuffled to turn in their spacesuits, helmet lights flashing in every direction. For a moment, no one spoke. Then the foreman said, *"Was it like that before?"*

Julie chuckled. "No, it was not."

"Then what—?"

"How is it doing that?"

"Does someone have a magnetometer—"

Julie broke in. "Hey, guys? It's waiting nicely for you to slide the bottom of the crate under it. Are you going to keep it waiting?"

The foreman stirred himself to action. "Let's bring it under with the lift. Tommy?"

"Ready, boss," answered the driver. Tommy edged the lift forward, with the bottom of the crate balanced on the tines. Julie could see the concentration in his eyes, even through his helmet visor. He was no doubt remembering melted equipment.

As Tommy slid the piece under, the churning spheres of the translator looked as if they might at any moment come crashing apart like a hundred bowling balls. The front of the tine-lift reflected the weird glow; it looked as if it were on fire.

"Stop," Julie said. "You've got it." The translator was floating about one centimeter above the bottom of the crate. /Is that okay?/

∗*Affirmative.*∗

"All right," she said, "you can put the rest of it together."

The men worked with deliberate speed. When they were finished, the translator pulsed and glowed from within what looked like an enormous archival display case, held securely with impressively large bolts and fittings. Julie checked it over and gave it her approval, though she secretly wondered if the translator actually *needed* the protection. "That's it," she announced. "Let's load it up."

The box was lifted onto the back of a flat carrier, and the transport started the long, slow crawl up the ice ramp. Julie rode on the back with the translator, hanging on to the grill that separated the cab from the cargo bed. She tried to beam thoughts at it, such as /Are you okay?/, but the translator had fallen silent. It floated impassively in the case, its spheres moving like soap bubbles. It remained silent all the way up the ramp, and for the entire trip back over the Triton landscape to the station.

✶

Inside the hangar, Julie hopped down and looked around for Kim. She found him stepping out of one of the buggies. "Where are we taking it?" she asked. She'd been so focused on getting the translator out of its underground cavern that it was only on the ride back that she'd started to think about where they were going to put it.

"Into the secure-lab for the night," Kim said. "First thing tomorrow morning it's going onto the shuttle for Triton Orbital. That gives us the night to take every kind of measurement we can get."

"Just don't annoy it," Julie said, though what would constitute annoyance, she could not have told him.

"We'll try not to." Kim smiled inside his space helmet. "But I suspect a lot of people are going to find reasons to come to the lab tonight, to get a firsthand look. That'll probably be more annoying to it than anything."

Julie pictured the parade. "You want me there?" she asked, not sure whether she even wanted to be part of it.

Kim put a thick-gloved hand on her arm. "You've been out there all day, *and* you're leaving for Earth first thing in the morning. Your assignment is to have a good meal, get some rest, and pack." He paused. "But stay on call for us, okay?"

"Okay," she agreed, realizing suddenly just how tired she was. She looked up at the translator, on top of the carrier. /You going to be okay there?/ she asked silently.

There was no reply.

✶

Over one last dinner with Georgia, Julie tried not to dwell on the fact that she was about to uproot herself to fly across the solar system to an entirely new life. Once they had the translator stowed aboard the *Park Avenue,* they would light the fusion rockets and head inbound toward the sun, and Earth. She found herself not wanting to think about that, nor did she want to think about the translator being treated like a specimen and a curiosity for everyone who felt important enough to invite himself down to the lab.

"Jules," Georgia said, leaning across the table to grab her forearm. "Have you heard a word I've been saying to you?"

"Hmm?" She blinked. "That depends. What did you say?"

Georgia rolled her eyes. "That's what I thought. Look, they're not down there torturing your friend. Kim is in charge, and you trust Kim, don't you?"

"What—Kim? Yes," Julie said, her head swimming.

"All right, then. Have a drink with me, and let's celebrate, okay?" Georgia hoisted a glass of ersatz merlot for a toast. "Here's to your return home, with the goods."

"Fair enough!" she said, raising her beer stein with as much enthusiasm as she could. She took a deep draught, then said, "Maybe it is okay, after all. I'll have three months on the ship to get to know it. Three months to create my empire!"

"There you go, girl!" Georgia said cheerfully. "Don't forget your friends when you're on top of the world, okay?"

Julie half laughed, and then broke into her first full smile of the day. "I promise. When I am emperor, I will remember you all . . ."

11

DREAMS AWAKEN

 Bandicut's dreams seemed to be growing in intensity. He was in the field again—so real, he could smell the earth and feel the stubble poking into the soles of his sneakers. Wheat stalks rustled against his legs, and the ripe heads brushed his upper arms as he trotted along the wheat rows, trying to keep up with his dog Blackie. He was a small boy.

The storm clouds on the western horizon were glowering. So were the farm's automated combines bearing down from the far end of the field, cutting and threshing the wheat in wide swaths. The combines were running at top speed, his grandfather trying to get the wheat in before the storm arrived. The young John Bandicut halted, watching the machines churn toward him, great clouds of dust rising in their wake. Something was nagging at him; something felt wrong. He felt a cold, sweating apprehension. "Blackie?" he called. "Blackie, where are you? Come here, boy."

And then he remembered why he was scared. His grandfather Anthony had been having trouble with the ranging pilots on those combines, and hadn't been able to get them fixed before the harvest. That was why he, John, had been severely admonished to stay out of the fields until the harvest was done—because the combines' autopilots might or might not sense a young boy in the field in front of them, or a dog.

His heart was pounding as he called out again to Blackie. The sky was darkening rapidly, the roar of the combines building in his ears. The great machines loomed . . . he heard a piercing howl . . .

"BLACKIE!" he screamed, and with that, silence-fugue swept over him. The terror of the dream rose up like a gargoyle face, leering at him, eyes grinning with hideous laughter, mouth agape echoing his scream and amplifying it until the sound reverberated around him.

He was no longer asleep, but he was as helpless before the silence-fugue as he'd been before the dream. *Blackie! Blackie! Don't let yourself be run over by the machines! You did, didn't you? You're gone now!* He was trying to scream out loud, but if anything escaped his lips, it was tortured and incomprehensible. He was being swept away on the winds of silence-fugue . . .

*

Antares awoke with a riveting stab of night terror. She rocked up to a sitting position in bed, breathing hard, peering around in the gloom. She heard a muffled, distorted moan from John Bandicut, and only then did she realize that the stab of fear was his. "John!" she cried, reaching out.

His eyes were wide open, and he was turning left and right, not quite thrashing. He was trying to speak—but he seemed unable to get words out. He needed help, and quickly. She shook him; then, gripping his arm tightly, she bowed her head and closed her eyes. (John? *John?* Can you feel me here?)

She felt wave after wave of pain and fear. Churning beneath it all was grief over Charlene. What was happening to him? Was this one of his hallucinatory silence-fugue episodes? *Please no.* The fugues had something to do with the loss of his neurolink connectors in an accident long before she knew him. As a pilot, he had flown by direct mind-computer link, until a malfunction destroyed his connections, leaving him vulnerable to a strange kind of mental dissociation. Silence-fugue, he called it. It still came over him at times—especially during periods of emotional stress. Charlie's death must have triggered it this time.

Once before, in a crisis, she had managed to help him; she would have to do it again. (You aren't alone. I am with you. I am here with you.) She didn't expect him to understand her words, but hoped the emotions would get through.

It wasn't enough; it wasn't working. She had to dampen the emotional waves somehow. Step into them and deflect them. It was going to be like stepping into an ocean breaker and trying to change its course.

You can do it. You have to.

✳

Bandicut was dimly aware of Antares trying to help. *No use, no use! Blackie has gotten himself run over, and I can't do anything to stop the machines! He's gone, he's gone!* Bandicut fought to cast off the terrors, but he couldn't. He felt someone shaking him.

No use.

He was alone against the terror, alone. Alone on a sea of fear, drowning. He had to claw . . . fight . . . stay on the surface.

A wave of fear rose and washed over him, choking him, pulling him down. Then another. But something seemed to catch this last wave and turn it a little, deflecting its power. He gasped and caught half a breath, enough to carry him a few more seconds. He was sinking, but he'd snatched a gasp of hope. He clung to it, clung for his life.

The next wave came, not quite as large, not quite as terrible. He caught another breath, a bigger one this time. He felt something touching him, buoying him up in the waves. What was it? When the next wave hit, he managed to rise up over it, still choking but breathing. He felt her touch now, Antares's presence. There was an opening in the madness. He felt Antares touch him in places he had forgotten; and some of the waves passed him by, and overhead in the sky, the black clouds began to disperse.

He caught a deeper breath, slower. He no longer quite needed to scream. (John,) he heard somewhere.

But he heard something else, too, another voice altogether, struggling to be heard. What was this?

"Hell-lo . . . hear-r m-me?"

Still panting, not fully out of the fugue yet, he swung around, trying to locate the source. A familiar voice. *Charlie?* No—no Charlie. Then who?

Something was moving on the wall, something shadowy. It reminded him of the hyperdimensional creature they'd met back on the waystation. *"Ed?"* he whispered. "Is that you?"

"Can-n you . . . ?"

He saw a glimmer of light. "Ed? Is that you?" His head was buzzing, trying to sort out real from the imagined.

He felt a movement beside him and turned his head. Antares was gripping his arm, her thoughts somehow intertwining with his, interceding in the fugue. He felt the bands of fear loosen, and finally fall away.

He drew a deep breath and collected himself. He was sitting on the bed with Antares. His chest was thumping. He thought . . . *I can think and reason. I am no longer in silence-fugue.* But his mind was flooded with memories. A dream, a terrifying onslaught of machines. Was it a dream—or a real memory?

He gazed at Antares and remembered their urgent lovemaking. It had been intense, driven by profound grief for Charlene, and a need to connect with Antares. The memory dizzied him, the feel of her body against his, her open rushing emotions flowing over him.

But it was not just Antares with him now. "Ed!" he whispered. "Ed was here!"

"He's here now. I can feel him." Antares closed her eyes and pointed. "There."

"I don't—wait, yes I do." Bandicut rose unsteadily and approached the wall. He felt vulnerable without clothes on, but dared not take his eyes off the spot. "A little shimmer, right here. Ed?"

The shimmer turned into a lozenge-shaped outline of watery light. *"T-trying-ng . . ."* The light suddenly gave way to a three-dimensional distortion of the wall itself, a sharply layered bas-relief. It was hard to look at; the individual layers seemed to curl away into eye-twisting dimensions. He blinked and looked away.

"Bet-t-ter," Ed managed. *"It has been hard-d to reach you . . . since you s-sealed yourselves into—*rasp*—bubbles of—*rasp*—multispace."*

"We need this bubble to live," Antares said.

"Yes-sssss. But hard to reach through. Just-t now it-t was easier-r."

Easier? Because of the silence-fugue?

Ed's voice grew a little stronger. *"I came to warn-n you . . . adversaries-ss ahead-d."*

Bandicut felt a chill run down his bare back. "Jeaves!" he hollered. "Are you listening to this?" He glanced at Antares, who was wrapping herself in a blanket, then back at Ed. "Do you mean, like that thing we just encountered, Ed? You don't mean *Deep,* do you?"

"No, n-no. Not-t the strange, quavering-ng one. But the other-r, the one it destroyed-d. Know its kind-d, be war-r-ry. There are others-ss."

Bandicut pressed his lips together. "We really . . . don't know what we're facing, you know. If there's anything you can tell us—"

"Ssss, you must find . . . a great fire . . . sss-sun-n. Must find it . . . speak-k with it . . . learn from it."

"A sun? You mean *your* sun? Speak with your sun? Or one of the other stars?"

"Man-ny ss-suns. S-sun called N-n-ck-k-k-k . . . in grave peril . . . mussst save N-n-ck-k-k-k . . ."

"But we don't—how can we—?"

"All connected-d. The worldsssss, breaking up-p-p . . ." As Ed spoke, the bas-relief protrusion on the wall slowly changed shape, as though he were struggling physically with the walls to get the words out. *"There is a-nother . . . ss-sun . . . who knowsss. ∗Bright-burn-n∗. Speak to ∗Brightburn∗."*

Bandicut leaned forward, trying to follow Ed's words. "How do we speak . . . to a star?"

"Must . . . listen-n . . . carefully. May need help-p."

May need help? There was an understatement. Bandicut glanced around, feeling eyes behind him. Ik and Li-Jared were standing in the doorway, staring at the Ed manifestation. Bandicut suddenly felt a lot more naked. He grabbed his shorts and pulled them on. "Jeaves called us," Ik said.

Bandicut nodded and turned back to the hypercone. "Ed— your world. Is it getting worse?"

"Sss . . . yes . . . breaking up-p . . . may be too late."

"We'll do what we can," Bandicut said. But his words felt hollow.

Antares spoke. "Ed? The one John spoke of, the one called Deep, the, uhhll, *cloud?*" She hesitated. "Can you speak to it? It helped us, we think."

Ed squirmed, seemed to be struggling. *"Ssss . . . very difficult-t for me . . ."*

"We may need to work with Deep. Can you help us communicate?"

The bas-relief Ed suddenly collapsed into the wall, and turned into a series of glowing concentric ellipses, extending out into space in an infinite regression. *"Ssss . . . difficult . . . out of phase . . ."*

"Please try."

"Trying, but . . . I doubt-t . . ." The regression of ellipses irised down to a point, then vanished.

"Uhhll," said Antares, "he is gone."

*

Though day and night were purely arbitrary aboard *The Long View,* it felt to Bandicut like a predawn meeting when Jeaves and Delilah joined them all in the dining lounge. Antares called for hot water for tea, and Bandicut called for coffee.

"All that stuff you told us about these weapons we might be facing?" he said to Jeaves, once he had a steaming cup in his hands. "Ed didn't say weapons, but he said there were adversaries ahead. He said we needed to know about them. How are we going to do that?"

"Hrrm. Ed said we must speak to stars," Ik said gravely.

"Yes, that too. Speak to stars." Bandicut took a deep breath and exhaled noisily. "So something I'm wondering is, if we're going to be facing some kind of ancient, planet-killer weapons, do we have any *modern* weapons to fight them with?"

Li-Jared flicked his fingers in vigorous agreement.

Jeaves took a few moments before answering. "We are not going in unprepared. We have powerful n-space field generators, which offer both protection and—"

"*Weapons,* Jeaves. I asked if we have *weapons.*"

"I understand your question. Our n-space fields really are both our first line of defense and our first line of offense."

"Are you saying we *don't* have weapons?"

"If you mean missiles or ship-to-ship energy beams, or devices of mass destruction, no. We do have some smaller, hand-carried devices." Jeaves rotated to look at each of them. "This is not a military ship, and it is not our intent to go into battle. We hope to find other ways of dealing with the adversaries."

Li-Jared made a strangled sound. Bandicut massaged his temples. Ancient killing machines. No weapons.

"By the way, in case you're wondering," Jeaves continued, "we are drawing nearer to our general destination. We are now in the outermost fringes of the gas envelope surrounding the Starmaker Nebula." The wall of the lounge collapsed into a holo. "This is a condensed view of our progress."

The ship was plowing through palely glowing nebular veils like an airplane through cirrus clouds. Here and there, small nubs shone through the veils—eggs, or Bok globules, where star formation was in its early stages even as they watched. "Understand," Jeaves said, "this is a highly processed image. We're still in n-space, moving fast, and if you *could* look out the window, what you'd see would be very different." As the image zoomed in and panned, it revealed more and more detail of dust and gas clouds, and here and there the fiery cauldron of a mini star-factory.

"So," Bandicut said, noting how adroitly Jeaves had moved the subject away from their lack of weapons, "we're closing in on this nebula where ancient weapons are lurking. And meanwhile, there's a star in particular danger, which we need to somehow save and maybe even *speak to,* and it's even got a name. What was it?"

"N-k-k-k-k," Antares said, struggling to mimic the sound of the hypercone.

"I may have picked up a more detailed reading of Ed's vocalization," Jeaves said. "It sounded like 'Nikk-kehh-keh-keh' and something I couldn't quite hear after that. I surmise that it is an attempt to reproduce or signify certain distinctive vibrations within the star. I have heard of stars being named in such a fashion."

"Distinctive vibrations?" Bandicut asked.

"Yes. Stars, you know, ring like bells from internal shock waves. Including your own sun."

"Yes, yes," said Li-Jared impatiently. "We all know that, I'm sure."

Bandicut glanced at him in annoyance.

"But," continued the Karellian, "since we can barely pronounce the name Ed gave us, let's call it—what?— *Nick*?" Imitating Ed in his own way, he pronounced the name as if biting something off.

"Okay," Bandicut said, with a sudden pang from an old memory. "Yes. We'll call it *Nick*." It was the first time in a long while that he had thought of his school friend Nick, who had died as a teenager. The memory came with a stab of regret, which caused Antares to turn her head to gaze at him. He didn't meet her eyes. Nick's death in a fire, now that he was reminded of it, was still very much with him. Probably always would be.

"*Nick*, then," Li-Jared said. "That okay with everyone?"

Antares nodded her head. "Maybe eventually we'll get a chance to ask the star itself. Although if any of you knows how to speak to a star, I'd like to hear how it's done."

"That time may come soon," Jeaves said.

"Do *you* know how to speak to a star?" Antares asked.

"Not precisely, but . . . I *heard* a star speak once. It was long ago, and I don't think we would want to reproduce the conditions that led to it, since they involved a supernova—but perhaps there is some useful information I can recall from the event. I will think on it."

"Ed said we should speak to one called . . . *Bright*-something," Bandicut said.

"He said *Brightburn*," Jeaves said, giving his own spiking intonation to the name.

"Well, do we know which one is ✻Brightburn✻? Is there any way to know which star is which?" Bandicut poured himself another cup of coffee, waiting for Jeaves's answer. Ik cocked his bony head to one side, murmuring his own puzzlement.

Jeaves's sparkle-cluster eyes seemed to gleam with concentration. "I think we can only find out by asking."

"Asking?"

"It may be fortunate that Deep is here. I don't know all that Deep can do. But if he has spoken to stars, as the shadow-people said, it is possible he might be able to help us."

"Um . . . how?" Bandicut asked.

Jeaves made a gesture not unlike a shrug. "There are so many things that could make talking to a star difficult. The problem of getting close. The problem of how you would actually make contact. And of course, the problem of time—"

"Time?" Antares asked.

"I'm speculating. But don't you imagine that a being whose lifespan is measured in millions of years must experience the passage of time rather differently from you?"

"Hrrm," Ik said as Li-Jared paused in his pacing.

Jeaves continued, "How long does it take a star to complete a full thought? An instant? A thousand years? I don't know. The event I mentioned, when I briefly experienced contact with a star in the moment of its death—I had a distinct sense that its experience of time was . . . well, I can only say . . . *different*."

"So from this we draw the conclusion—?" Bandicut began.

"That it was different," Jeaves said. "Figuring out what that means is a problem we'll have to solve when we get to it."

Bandicut moved his jaw from side to side, thinking. "So what you're saying is, we're going to need . . . a bridge . . . if we're going to communicate with stars. And you think Deep might be the one to do that?"

"That's where my money is," said the robot.

Bandicut sighed softly. Seeing Deep up close last time had cost Charlie his life. Bandicut wasn't eager to try that again. And yet, his head was full of images that Charlie had given him, right

before the end. Tantalizing images of what Deep saw, or maybe
felt. But was it possible to touch Deep without killing or hurting
someone else? "I don't know, Jeaves," he whispered finally. "I
don't know how we could do it."

Antares stirred. "I could try again." Seeing Bandicut's alarmed
reaction, she added, "Perhaps this time, with the benefit of my
past experience, and some time to prepare, it will not be so
hard?"

★

They were still finishing their breakfast when Jeaves interrupted
to say, "I think we'd better get to the bridge. Deep has changed
course." Antares felt a sudden band of tightness in her chest as
she hurried with Bandicut and the others.

Deep was now clearly in view, ahead and to the left of their
course. There was something else visible as well—a very bright,
red star ahead, shining from within a thin veil of dust and gas. It
lay between them and the distant nebula, though Antares could
not tell how far in front of the nebula it was. It had already grown
from a pinpoint of light to a tiny, round shape, peeking out past
the local nebular material. Antares thought it was beautiful.

"Is this it?" Bandicut asked Jeaves. "Is that the star we're
headed for?"

"I'm not sure," Jeaves admitted. "That star does not seem to
be connected to any of the disturbances, but Deep has turned
toward it."

"Do you have any idea why?" Bandicut asked. "Or how we
might find out?"

Antares closed her eyes. *Don't we already know how to find
out? We have to talk to Deep.*

Jeaves said something she missed, but when she opened her
eyes, everyone was looking at her. Drawing a slow, centering
breath, she said, "Uhhl, yes." *Not exactly the preparation time I
was hoping for.* Exhaling with deliberation, she stepped forward
onto the balcony and knelt, surrounded by the stars, as she
would have for a Thespi joining. John Bandicut came up behind
her, and rested his hands lightly on her shoulders. She shook her
head and gently removed them. "Just stay close," she whispered.
She closed her eyes, bowed her head, and reached out.

She was stunned by how much she found immediately.

The path in front of the ship was filled with shimmering, indistinct presences. Deep was the closest, but too far away for real contact. The star was in her field of awareness, too—even farther away, but still a potent presence. It was distinctly more than an inert physical object, though what beyond that she could not say. *Alive? Intelligent?* The sensation was unlike anything she had felt before. Beyond the star, elsewhere in the nebula, she felt vaguer and more distant, but similar sensations.

Drawing another centering breath, she pulled back from the extreme distance and focused again on Deep. Did it want contact? Something *changed* in the space around her, and she felt a sudden closeness to the mysterious cloud, an opening that hadn't been there a moment ago. Did Deep do that? She reached farther. She felt something shifting, fluid, dangerous. Deep was opening and closing in swirls, revealing momentary glimpses of feelings and images—but only for a heartbeat at a time.

A familiar touch . . .

Now it was gone.

The details blurred. Was she trying too hard, hoping to find things? Or afraid to? She imagined herself on Thespi Prime, and calmed herself and extended the wave of quiet outward, not knowing how Deep would respond to it.

At first, no change. Then a curtain whispered open, just for a moment, revealing a glimpse of . . . *something* . . . a shivering sense of longing, and loneliness. The curtain closed. A moment later it rustled open again; another glimpse, a brief sensation of staring down endless, echoing corridors of time and space. She reeled with dizziness. The curtain closed; but when it opened a third time, she felt a wrenching pang of *loss*, incomprehensible loss, followed an instant later by a great tide of joy, as some astounding barrier gave way, a barrier at the very edge of reality.

Antares's mind swam. No joining had ever been like this. But she was submerged now; she doubted she could pull free even if she wanted to. There was more:

Glimpse of a brief, bitter fight to the death with an entity, a *machine* that threatened some approaching beings, ephemeral life. The fight ended with a tang of victory and the acrid dust of destruction. Antares was left trembling. She and the others on *The Long View* were the ones approaching, the ephemerals.

Then the curtain shifted, and this time lingered open.

Familiar presence . . .

It took her a heartbeat or two. *Charlene?* She was jolted back into herself for an instant, reliving her own feelings of loss, a shadow of John's. She gulped and eased herself back outward. It seemed impossible; she had felt the quarx being torn away from Deep and restored to John, just before she died. And yet . . .

(Charlene, is that you?)

★

Bandicut had been feeling twinges of *something* ever since they had come to the bridge. But he hadn't been able to identify it— and until now he had assumed it was nervous fatigue, after the fugue. He was trying to keep his apprehension at bay as he watched Antares reach out toward Deep. He forced himself to breathe slowly and deeply. If he could lend any kind of calming influence in the presence of the unknown and dangerous, surely it might help.

Each time he tried to calm his own thoughts, he almost immediately felt the twinge again.

What am I feeling? Is it Antares, remembering Charlie?

No. It was someone else. Stirring in his mind.

A tiny voice, deep in his thoughts.

His heart rate spiked. He breathed deeply and raggedly, struggling to calm himself. /Charlie?/ He had not expected this. He'd really thought she was gone for good this time. /Charlie, is that you?/

/// Confused . . . ///

/Charlie! *My God!*/

/// Help . . . me . . . ? ///

The voice was very faint. /Can you hear me? Are you Charlie?/

/// Who? Charlie? ///

/Quarx./ Bandicut shut his eyes, tried to shut everything else out, tried to focus on this one thing that was happening in his mind. As he did so, he felt Antares struggling, too—and somehow it felt similar.

The voice came back a little stronger. It seemed more female than male.

/// Quarx. I am quarx. ///

/Yes. *Yes!*/

/// Who are you? Are you quarx? ///

/No. *No!* I am human. I am John Bandicut./ He felt a rushing urge to shout aloud with joy, and also to cry with grief for the Charlie he'd lost. But this new presence felt very tentative, and frightened, so he tried to subdue all that.

/// You called me—///

/Charlie. I called you *Charlie,* because all the quarx before you were called Charlie./ He would get to the *Charlene* part later. /Is that all right?/

/// I . . . not sure. ///

Bandicut forced himself to take it slowly. So much to convey, and learn. He so desperately wanted Charlene back. /I know it is confusing. Please—try to search your thoughts, and see if you re-member me. Or any of your predecessors. You are quarx. You have many lives./

/// Yes, many. Very many . . . ///

Bandicut waited, heart pounding.

/// I remember something large . . .
dark . . . powerful . . . ///

Bandicut drew a sharp breath. What was she remembering? Deep? The Maw of the Abyss? The boojum?

/// I remember a destroyer of worlds . . . ///

Bandicut held his breath, frozen.

/// Long ago, it . . . I think it . . .
destroyed my own world. ///

He found himself wordless. There was an inexpressible sad-ness in the quarx's voice. Not for her own past lives, but for her lost home, millions of years ago.

/// I feel something else . . . here.
Large, powerful. It is very close. ///

/Yes,/ Bandicut whispered.

/// Is it the same as . . . the destroyer? ///

A hundred shouts tried to get out at once. *I don't know. It killed the Charlie before you.* /I don't think so, no./

/// And I?
Am I the only . . . quarx? ///
Bandicut trembled. /Yes,/ he whispered.
/// Then I . . . must act. ///
/Uh?/ He didn't know what to say. He felt as if he were tee-
tering on the brink of something large and uncontrollable. This
new Charlie was different; he could sense it already. Her initial
tentativeness was disappearing; he could feel an emerging quick-
ness and impulsiveness. She was boiling over with an agitated
need to learn, and quickly. Too fast! She was rippling through arrays of memory in his head. Dissatisfied with that, she strained
to see what lay beyond. She was like a bird hatchling, flapping
its wings before it was ready. She noticed Antares, but slipped
past her, trying to catch a glimpse of Deep. Not a good idea!
/Charlie, wait—be careful! It's dangerous to approach!/
The quarx responded with surprising forcefulness.
/// I must know what that is—
that thing out there! ///
/I know! I know you need to learn these things. But give
yourself time! Get acclimated. Get to know me. Find out what
the dangers are before you—/
/// But I feel time is—I feel it fleeing! ///
There was a sudden wiry strength in the quarx's voice, and
an urgency that startled him.
/// I feel the peril.
I must seek out and learn . . . ///
/Charlie, wait!/
But before he could think of anything—indeed, there *was*
nothing he could do—the quarx hurled herself outward to make
contact with Deep. He was stunned to feel her pull the physical
strength from his own body—too much, too fast! Two heartbeats later, he crumpled to the deck as the quarx stretched out
to do the very thing that had cost the life of Charlene before it.

★

Charlie, is that you? What Antares felt in response to her question was a wordless reply that *felt* like the quarx—and yet wasn't
quite the same: more like an echo, several times removed. How
strange.

As Deep drew closer, the opening that felt like Charlene swirled closed; but other openings appeared, revealing glimpses of stranger things, twists and turns in space, and great balances of power and energy, all churning turbulently beneath the surface of Deep. Antares reeled at the sensation. She felt as if she had taken the forbidden *kasa* hallucinogen during a Thespi meditation, and her mind was spinning out of control. Then the opening closed and the feeling passed.

Behind her, John Bandicut was stirring. She sensed powerful emotions. She didn't dare pause to ask what he was feeling. She forced herself to focus on the being she had come to meet. *Deep, if you can . . . we must try to exchange thoughts . . . but slowly, please! Slowly . . .*

Another breath of air gusted through an opening, and suddenly she again felt something very much like the presence of the quarx. *Charlene?* Her voice reflected outward, and back, and in its own peculiar echo, she felt somehow that the answer was yes, and no . . .

Deep suddenly seemed much closer, surrounding and engulfing her. Once more she felt her control slip away, and with a hot flash of fear, she plummeted into a realm where knowing and unknowing became indistinguishable.

12

TWO MINDS

 Ik sprang forward in consternation as first Bandicut and then Antares collapsed to the deck of the bridge. "Hrahh!" he barked, kneeling between the Thespi and the human and placing a hand on each. "Jeaves! What is it doing to my friends? Is this going to happen every time they approach this creature?" He glared up at the growing image of Deep.

"I am not certain," Jeaves replied. "But ship's monitors indicate that their life signs are strong. I recommend against interfering. However, I am asking Delilah to investigate."

Ik bent to examine Bandicut and Antares. Both were breathing, and neither was changing color. Beyond that, what else could he do?

They are both physically unharmed.

Ik started. His stones had been so quiet of late, it had not occurred to him to look to them for assistance. /What about their mental state?/

More difficult to assess. But they should be aided by their stones.

Ik grunted, and looked up as Delilah descended toward them. He rocked back on his haunches to give the halo room to work. Delilah's glowing ring expanded slowly, until it encircled both Antares and Bandicut. It began to produce a soft sound, like the wind whistling through stone passages in a high place. Ik felt a momentary dizziness. "What is it doing?"

"Learning," Jeaves said. "If your companions are injured or do not survive, we will want to know why. I suggest you move back."

"Hrrm. I suggest you worry more about how to keep these two people safe, and ask Delilah what she can do about *that*," Ik growled. He had no intention of moving from his friends' side.

Li-Jared, behind him, was pacing around the bridge, muttering to himself. He cast an occasional, worried glance in Ik's direction. Ik didn't know what Li-Jared was thinking, but if that cloud out there made a threatening move, Ik was pretty sure he could count on a yell from the Karellian.

*

For the quarx, it all seemed to make a terrifying kind of sense. She had come back to life with a startling degree of clarity about previous incarnations, clear enough memory—once she'd gotten over her initial shock—to know that having this much memory was unusual. Was it just coincidence, or had the manner of her last death yanked her back for some unusual need or purpose? Maybe it had something to do with that terrible dark thing hovering at the edges of her awareness. Was she here to confront the monster that had destroyed her world? Or for something altogether different?

She had a mental snapshot of that scene, but also many

others reverberating in her memory. Hosts and friends ranging down through the timeline—the Fffff'tink, and the Rohengen, and the Osos, and the ones whose name sounded like a vibrating guitar string, and the human, who actually would have understood a guitar string. And so many more. The memories reverberated like voices in a crowded room. She could hardly sort one from another, or even be sure she could distinguish her own memories from those of her host.

Did every life start this way?

So many relationships . . . she desperately wished she could take time now to look back at them all, and understand who had meant what to her. But that wasn't possible; there was a deadly dark thing waiting out there, and she needed to confront it.

But . . . was this being called *Deep* that thing? She didn't think so, although Bandicut feared it. Indeed, he felt it had cost her her last life. Nevertheless, Deep might have some knowledge of the terrible thing, and it now also had knowledge of quarx.

All these thoughts took approximately as long as ten of John Bandicut's heartbeats.

And then she suddenly *remembered* Deep, really remembered it, not from Bandicut's memories but from her own. She remembered *visiting* Deep, and being caught up in a fantastic tangle of images—memories reaching as far back in time as her own—glimpses of places that were, she realized with startlement, possibly not of this universe at all. There was a gap following that—but she remembered flying back to rejoin with Bandicut. And she remembered dying.

All *that* took several more of Bandicut's heartbeats.

It left her reeling, and she retreated for a while to speak with John and get to know him again. *Charli,* he called her, or so she chose to hear it. He had known several Charlies; she could be a Charli.

Her initial tentativeness and fear were not feigned; she really did feel shy in the presence of this person to whom she was instantly, intimately connected. But she was also determined. She sped through Bandicut's thoughts and memories, learning, even as he was inviting her to take a look. *I was brought here for a reason. I am sure of it. I must not let my fears deter me.* The look through John's memories was fascinating, and she vowed to return. But right now, it wasn't what she needed to learn. *That* was over there in the one called Deep. It had killed her, touching Deep before, but maybe it wouldn't this time. Deep had touched the dark one, or some agent of it. Deep knew things she needed to know.

John Bandicut already sensed her intention, and wanted to stop her launch outward to Deep. *I'm sorry, but I can't stop. There's too much at stake.*

She took a quick look around to take in her surroundings, the ship and the friends gathered here. Then—afraid, but determined not to fail—she leaped out into space. She touched the outer fringes of the dark cloud, and then, with a shiver, the real presence of the thing. She was startled by the mood she sensed: curiosity and urgency, but no hostility, no intention to destroy.

She reached out again: diverse strands of thought. There was the part that had destroyed the dark agent, one strand among many. She could find no language. She continued looking. To her surprise, she felt the presence of someone who, like herself, was trying to find her way into Deep from the outside. *Who is this?* She seemed rather like the human—different, but familiar. *Thespi?*

So many strands. Here was one rooted in the very fabric of space and time, and apparently able to exert influence over both. And here was one that stretched out in many different directions, to make contact with others. And here was one that was almost . . . *quarxlike.*

She felt a ripple of surprise. *Quarx?* Her prior incarnation had died. So what was this? Another quarx inhabiting Deep?

Cautiously, she reached out to the presence. She had no memories of any contact with another quarx since the death of the homeworld. It felt very strange even to think of it.

/// Hello? Can you hear me? ///

The other presence stirred. Its response sounded a little like her own voice, an echo.

<<< Hello? >>>

She waited for more, then tried:

/// Are you quarx? ///

The pause swelled to a bursting point. Then:

<<< I... think so. I'm not certain.

Who are you? >>>

Feeling a combination of disbelief and excitement, she answered,

/// I am known to my host as ... Charli.

But my real name is—///

She released a series of wails—ending in a long, shuddering shriek.

The other sounded puzzled.

<<< I am known as Charlie also.

And this is my real name— >>>

The sound reverberated from a greater distance, but was otherwise identical to the name she had given.

A stunned silence followed. Finally she said, softly so as to ensure that she was not actually producing an echo:

/// Do you know John Bandicut? ///

And the voice that could not be an echo, but sounded like one, came back:

<<< Of course.

He knows me as Charlene. >>>

That sent the stars reeling around her, and she had to resist the impulse to pull away in shock.

/// You are Charlene?

John Bandicut believes you died.

I believed you died.

You must have, because I am the one

who followed. ///

The echolike voice hesitated, before answering:

<<< I did ...

At least, I felt that I was dying.

Even now, I don't feel quite ... alive.

I don't know why I am here. >>>

Another pause.

<<< Did he mourn me when I died? >>>

The new Charli reflected on the memories she had viewed and said softly:

/// Yes, be did. ///

A soft acknowledgment came in answer, and for a few moments silence filled the space around them. Charli drew Charlene's memories to herself, trying to understand and find a place for her. The moment of Charlene's death was clear, and yet not. There was a sharp break—no, more like a *rent*—in Charlene's memory. But instead of ending there, it was followed by a blur. And then, somehow, this Charlene-*echo* was caught up in Deep's web of consciousness.

The Charlene-echo seemed to sense her struggle to understand.

<<< I came to Deep to learn,
but I went too far.
The visions . . . overwhelming.
I tried to bring them back to John Bandicut.
But it hurt, terribly, and he was suffering.
I'd been torn away. >>>

Charli glimpsed the memory, the agony of John Bandicut at the loss of his quarx. Something in Charlene had been hurt beyond healing. Death was upon her; she felt herself dying even as she tried to return. And then?

A blur.

/// Why are you here?
Are you . . . really Charlene? ///

Silence hung between them, until the other said,

<<< I'm not certain.
I have memories, but . . . >>>

Charli listened carefully, trying to hear the nuances, and feel the thoughts of the other. It felt different from the Charlene she thought she should feel. Was this really just a ghost, an echo of the real Charlene? Maybe the distinction didn't matter.

/// Can you communicate with Deep now?
Can you speak, and be understood? ///

The answer came in a strained whisper, as if her question had pushed the other back into a place of darkness and uncertainty.

<<< *A little. Yes.* >>>

Charli pressed.

/// *Then will you help me?* ///

And the answer seemed to whisper from a great distance:

<<< *I will try.* >>>

∗

It was the strangest thing Delilah had ever encountered, and she scarcely knew what to make of it. As a fractal being, and kin of the shadow-people, she sometimes thought of matter-life as a kind of flat projection—intelligent, to be sure, and fully sentient, but frustratingly limited. But the matter-life on this ship seemed capable of far more interactions outside of their dimensions than Delilah would have imagined.

She had helped a little, adjusting the fields just so, to make a stronger connection with the spacetime disturbance known as Deep. The matter-life called Antares had not asked, but it was clear she wanted to make contact. And without taking risks, how could they learn anything?

The risk had paid off, with powerful emotional crosscurrents. But the reappearance of the quarx in the Bandicut had made it all blossom, maybe too fast. Now both the Antares and the Bandicut lay motionless, in states that left the other matter-life in dismay. Delilah, looking closely, could see that they were not dead or dying—and that they remained, in some fashion, in contact with Deep.

Delilah was uncertain what to do. She was supposed to help, and she certainly wanted to do no harm. Perhaps it would be best if she just closed off that spacetime channel, and let the connection fade.

∗

"John Bandicut! John Bandicut! Can you hear me?"

That was Ik's voice. Bandicut's return to awareness was accompanied by a shuddering sensation. Was it the ship, in trouble? He blinked his eyes open painfully. Ik was bent over him, fingers digging urgently into his arms, shaking him. A halo was encircling him with a pulsing light, chiming.

Bandicut's mind soared out, looking for Charlie, then sprang back to make sense of Ik. "Stop shaking me!" he croaked.

"Hrahh, you are all right?" Ik breathed, letting him go.

Wincing, Bandicut pushed himself up to a sitting position. The halo seemed to take this as a cue, and rose back toward the ceiling, its sound dying away. Bandicut closed his eyes and took a deep breath. /Charlie? Are you there?/

In response, he heard a sound like something sliding quickly down a wire. And then:

/// My God. ///

The quarx was struggling to reestablish itself in its quarters. /Are you hurt? Did you touch Deep, did you touch that thing out there?/ Bandicut asked, trying to be still enough to let the quarx recover.

/// I don't . . . yes. Yes, I touched it.

But I don't—///

The quarx hesitated.

/// It was as if I touched a part of myself.

Except it wasn't. ///

/Part of yourself?/ Bandicut asked, puzzled. But before he could pursue the question, he saw Antares sitting up. He reached over and touched her arm, and felt in her gaze a kind of shell-shocked wonder.

"John Bandicut," she whispered. "I felt something astonishing. It was as though I felt . . ." She seemed unable to finish her sentence, but her eyes would not release him.

Bandicut felt a burning in his eyes. "Was it Charlie?"

Ik's bony, bluish face appeared beside them both. "My friends—"

Antares sighed with a whistle. "Thank you, Ik. I am shaken. But unharmed. John Bandicut—?"

Letting his own breath out slowly, Bandicut said, "It was very strange." He put a hand to his temple. "I have a new Charlie now."

/// Charli. ///

He blinked, startled—but nodded to himself.

Antares looked at him with a wide gaze. "Then was that what I felt?"

"I don't think so. Because my new . . . Charli . . . encountered something, someone." He held out his hands. "Can you feel?"

Antares touched his wrist, then his forehead. "Uhhl, indeed

yes! I sense your new quarx! But I do not think this is the one I met."

"No."

"Then—"

/Can you explain it, Charli?/

The quarx seemed uncertain.

/// It was like an echo.
An echo of the one I used to be. ///

Bandicut hesitated, then relayed the words to Antares.

Antares touched her temple, as though trying to find her own memory. "Strange, that is what I felt, also. As if Charlene had become *imprinted* on Deep, so that a part of her remained, even after death."

Sitting back, Bandicut glanced up at Ik and Li-Jared and Jeaves. "Are you following any of this?"

Ik and Li-Jared looked uncertain. Jeaves answered by asking, "Were you able to make any contact with Deep?"

Antares stirred. "I could *sense* Deep, and I felt an empathy, and I think a desire to help. But more than that—no."

Bandicut squinted in concentration as Charli spoke to him, then said, "Charli tells me she did make contact, through Charlene."

/// I would prefer to say, Charlene-echo. ///

"Charlene-echo," Bandicut corrected, his voice faltering a little. "Charlene is gone. But some part of her remains, and it can apparently function as a go-between."

"And did Deep say anything meaningful to us, through Charlene-echo?" Li-Jared asked impatiently.

Bandicut focused inward again. "Yes," he said. "Deep has changed course. He is now headed for the star we noticed earlier. That is *Brightburn*. That's where we need to go."

13

JEAVES PROCEDURAL DIARY: 384.14.9.4

Another day or two in transit, following Deep, should bring us to the star we called *Brightburn*. During that time, the company must prepare for contact with the star. None of us really knows how to prepare for contact with a star, of course, though I have more information than the rest, having once experienced communication with a star. I know this: spacetime itself must be stressed for such a contact to work. For that reason, I hope Deep will be able to help us.

Another matter on the minds of the company is what they can expect from The Long View, should we confront another adversary device without Deep to defend us. They reasonably suspect that conversation alone may be insufficient, and we may desire to wield more persuasive power. I do regret the Shipworld mission designer's decision to limit our fighting options. Not that we would choose to undertake combat; indeed, none of us is trained for it. Nonetheless, I sensed the company's palpable dismay upon learning of our lack of weapons, even for self-defense. They were scarcely reassured by the protection of our n-space generators.

Clearly they are uncomfortable with the mission being controlled by the shipboard AI, which they don't trust, and by Delilah and me, whom they trust little more. They feel undervalued—despite the explicit value we place on their experience in solving difficult, world-threatening problems. I have no doubt, as their knowledge grows, so will their ability to take control of the mission.

How can I persuade them of this? Even after my own travels up and down the timestream, and personal glimpses of some of the terrible events I showed them (I spoke of persuasive evidence, but did not mention that I glimpsed some of the events as an eyewitness)—even after all that, I barely feel that I have the necessary knowledge. For the sake of crew confidence, I have tried to act as if I have a clear grasp; but the truth is, I am far from understanding these matters in their entirety.

My relations with the crew concern me most of all. The transmission of my personality components to the waystation was not altogether error-free, and I worry that my personal relations capabilities may be incomplete. How have I been performing as de facto commander of the ship? Do I need to relearn how to work with humans and their friends?

If so, I had better learn quickly.

∗

Bandicut, while trying to get to know Charli, was still shakily absorbing the revelation that there were now *two* quarx in existence. Maybe one was only an echo of the real Charlene, an imprint on Deep's mind. But echo or imprint or *whatever* she was, she was still out there, still communicating and—he guessed—thinking. Was she still *feeling*? Could an echo feel? His robots seemed to feel, and who knew about Jeaves? If AIs could, why not an imprint of a quarx? Was this Charlene-echo still capable of grief, and hope, and caring? Was her *soul* still there? He brooded a long time on these questions.

The new quarx felt very much like Charlene in her personable nature and sharp intelligence, and different in other ways. She seemed at times timid, and yet almost aggressively curious, exploring memories and deeper matters. The way she'd launched herself out to encounter Deep, barely minutes after coming shyly into the world—how soon would she do something like that again? Afterward, she'd seemed concerned for the alarm she'd caused him. She spent a long time perusing his memories. He had a feeling something was happening back there in the library stacks of his mind, but she couldn't tell him what it was. She was extremely interested in the subject of the galactic war survivors, though; maybe she was searching for clues.

That night, Antares reached out to him with quiet urgency. She wanted to draw close to him, to make love; he could feel it as clearly as his own desires. But—unsettlingly—she also wanted to seek out and touch the new quarx. For a while, he felt weirdly left out of the exchange as Antares probed, *through* him, at Charli's feelings and thoughts. Even as she enveloped him both physically and emotionally, he could feel the intense mutual touching of Thespi and quarx. He felt a twinge of jealousy as the two explored each other. Antares at last responded to his need and drew him closer, bringing him to a pitch of arousal. As he climaxed, shuddering, he was aware of the quarx watching with keen interest. Afterward, he folded his arms around Antares and hugged her close, feeling satisfied and embarrassed all at once.

The quarx was quiet for a time, before murmuring,

/// That was . . . extremely moving.
If that is a normal part of your
relationship with your friend . . . ///

/What?/

/// I have much to think about. ///

Bandicut grunted wordlessly.

Sleep that night brought dreams of a different sort. Charli was all tangled up in his thoughts, and seemed to speak to him as he slept, and he spoke back to her, only half aware. They talked of lives, and loves, and relationships lost in time, and finally of Deep. Charli hoped that if she could engage in further dialogue with the Charlene-echo, she might be able to open up a comprehensible dialogue with Deep.

If you think you can, he murmured in his sleep. But Deep is a long way away now.

He'll be back, she seemed to say. He'll be back.

*

Li-Jared couldn't make himself relax. He slipped out of his quarters after an unsuccessful attempt at sleep. Damn it, he thought— the others seemed able to take these bizarre events in stride, but he just couldn't. It was crazy, what was happening: John Bandicut and Antares keeling over every time they encountered that damn cloud; Jeaves and the ship's AI making decisions that left the rest of them completely out of control. *By the blazing heavens, we should be in charge of this mission, not some faceless AI!*

Li-Jared understood that there was a danger they had to face, and that worlds might be at stake. He could accept that. But in no way did that excuse the way they were being pushed around.

Hadn't they managed to make their own decisions during several major crises, and hadn't that worked out? If they were going to put their lives in jeopardy, why couldn't they be given the authority they needed?

And now—without anyone asking his opinion—they were detouring to talk to a *star*?

It was infuriating. It was not that he objected in principle to communicating with a star—far from it, if such a thing were *possible,* and *comprehensible,* and if anyone had included him in the decision-making. But this was all about control. The AIs were controlling *him,* and it should be the other way around. And as far as he could tell, his companions were simply going along with it.

Well, he wasn't.

Li-Jared paced back and forth in the corridor for a few minutes, then looked in on Ik, because if anybody would listen to him, it was Ik. But Ik was sitting perfectly still on his round sleep pad, deep in meditation, the nearest he ever came to sleep as Li-Jared knew it. Rubbing his chest in frustration, Li-Jared stepped back into the corridor. He wasn't even going to try Bandicut and Antares, because if they weren't busy mating like Karellian lemitars, then it was probably only because Bandicut was in silence-fugue or maybe trying not to go crazy again with a new quarx in his head. No, no point in going there; for now at least, Li-Jared was on his own.

So he thought he would explore the ship a little more. He'd been wondering, with more than casual interest, where the ship's nerve center was. Not what they called the bridge, which as far as he could tell was nothing more than an observation deck, but the *nerve* center—wherever the hell the ship was *controlled* from. It had a built-in AI; surely there was an interface where he and the AI could have a chat! He was going to see if he could find it.

The corridors continued to be strangely glowing passageways, but at least they were staying put now, and were redder in the living area. Li-Jared strolled into the bright orange sections they had explored briefly. He passed several compartments that he had already seen, and poked his head into each just long enough to reassure himself that they hadn't changed much. Then he slipped into the hangar deck to take a look at the little shuttle that was docked there. It was shaped like a flattened, elongated egg. It was also sealed shut, so he gave up on trying to get a look inside. He exited the hangar, determined to push on to the yellow-glowing section of the ship.

Pausing at an intersection, he heard a familiar ticking sound. "Copernicus?" he called. A moment later, the robot rounded a bend in the corridor and wheeled up to him. "Good evening, sir," Copernicus said, bobbing his forward end in greeting.

Li-Jared cocked his head, peering at the robot. "What are you up to at this hour, my friend?" He continued to feel a fondness for John Bandicut's robots, though he also had doubts about their newfound predilection for romance fiction. He thought it might be leading them to some strange notions about human and other sentient behavior.

"I am merely patrolling the corridors, checking to see that nothing is amiss," Copernicus said. "Are you aware of any problems?"

"I guess not," the Karellian said. He rubbed his chest thoughtfully. "Tell me, how is your reading going? Are you learning a lot about the behavior of organics?"

"To be sure," answered the robot. "It seems that humans are prone to extremely impulsive and unpredictable behavior, when driven by love. Wouldn't you say?"

"I'm sure I wouldn't know," Li-Jared said, quickly losing interest in the subject. He paused, and on a sudden impulse added, "Say, Copernicus, would you be willing to help me find something?"

"That would depend, I suppose, on what you hope to find," answered the robot, blinking a single diode.

"Nothing big. Just an input to the shipboard AI."

"There are many such places," Copernicus said.

"Good. Would you be willing to show me?"

"Why not?" said the robot. "I presume you would like a voice or keypad interface, rather than a straight jack-in?"

"I suppose," Li-Jared said, and together they continued down the glowing corridor. "How are you doing with the library research we asked you about? Have you found anything about the survivors of that ancient war?"

"Nothing conclusive," Copernicus said, rolling along beside him. "We did find some very old narratives from a nomadic race called the Fffff'tink, about a dreadful, invasive inorganic lifeform called the Mindaru. We are examining the texts now to see if the Mindaru might be connected to the ancient survivors."

Li-Jared looked at him in interest. "You think these Mindaru might *be* the survivors?"

"Time and research will tell, we hope." The robot stopped and turned to face a small recess in the wall. "Here, I believe, you should be able to converse with the shipboard AI. Shall I establish a link?"

Li-Jared's hearts quickened. "Please do . . ."

*

The next morning, Bandicut came out of his quarters rubbing his eyes. Antares was still sound asleep. But Bandicut had not slept well: too much thought expended coming to terms with the new Charli. The first thing he saw was Napoleon coming down the corridor. "Good morning, Cap'n. Are you ready for the coming encounter? We should be arriving by late tonight or early tomorrow."

Bandicut scratched his head. "I don't know about *ready*. How about you? Have you and Coppy come up with anything?"

Click. "We have been extending our knowledge of the ship, and of the mission profile, mostly."

"That's a pretty vague answer, Napoleon."

Click click. "I will try to be more specific, Cap'n. Copernicus and I have been searching the ship's libraries for information concerning the adversarial beings known as the Survivors, or possibly the Mindaru."

"Do you hope to find information Jeaves hasn't given us?"

"Not so much that, Cap'n, as hoping we'll find some correlation with things we learned about the Maw, and about the boojum, and so on. We thought we might find patterns that others, without the same knowledge, might miss."

"That makes sense, I guess."

The robot bobbed his head slightly, raising himself to a

greater height. "Thank you, Cap'n. Also, we have been interacting with some of the shipboard AI interfaces, seeking to improve our capabilities. We may be called upon to assist in operating the ship at some later time, when the AI gives over more of the decision-making to you."

"I see. So we can come to you if we have questions about the ship?"

"Indeed. Li-Jared has already—"

Bandicut frowned. "Already what?"

Click click. Napoleon jerked his head a little to one side, then back. "He was exploring some of the AI interfaces. It was within the permissible guidelines." *Click.* "Perhaps it would be better if he told you himself."

Bandicut stared at Napoleon, wondering what the robot was *not* saying. "Perhaps it would."

"Yes. Now, I see m'lady is waiting, Cap'n. So perhaps I should remove myself and allow you to carry on your affairs of the heart." Napoleon nodded pointedly toward Antares, who was just emerging from the room behind Bandicut. She caught his arm, and he drew her close to kiss her lightly. By the time he turned back to Napoleon, the robot was sauntering away down the hall.

"What was all that?" Antares asked.

Bandicut shook his head. "I'm not sure, really. But I think we might want to ask Li-Jared when we see him."

✶

There was no chance to speak with Li-Jared before they were called to the bridge. Deep had disappeared into the growing glare of the star ahead. They were already flying through the star's particle wind and gravitational influence, and they had begun to slow their high-speed passage through n-space as they entered what could be a planetary system. Bandicut was starting to feel a knot in his stomach, where his feelings of anticipation were colliding with a rising uneasiness.

They were going to approach this star—how closely, he wasn't sure—for a purpose that didn't quite compute, from his point of view. They were going to attempt communication with a star. They hadn't even mastered communication with Deep yet.

What had been a dazzling point of light was now growing to a ball of fire. They were watching on the bridge through a series of adjustable "filters," which were really just modifications in the way the image was brought in through the n-space fields. In some of the views, the corona could be seen flaming like a magnificent halo around the sun; in other views, they could see tiny granulations on the star's surface, and what looked like the black volcanic openings of sunspots, but were really just slightly less incandescent regions on the surface. Other views showed them the looping whorls of the star's magnetic fields, and an occasional fiery arc of gases following the field lines out into space.

That was all very scenic, and not too alarming, since they were still at a good distance, perhaps the distance of Jupiter from Earth's sun. On the other hand, it was a larger star than the Sun, and Bandicut started to sweat a little when Jeaves switched to a higher magnification that swelled the image to a size that took up much of the viewspace. Switching filters, Jeaves advised, "Here is a neutrino view of the interior of the star." Bandicut stared with a mixture of wonder and fear at the fires in the star's core. It looked like the magnified pulsations of nuclear reactions. It looked insanely hot, dangerous, and otherworldly. He was certain it could vaporize their ship in an instant. It reminded him of a glimpse Charlie had once given him of his true appearance—a glimpse of powers and energies different from anything he could ever imagine.

Shaking his head, Bandicut looked away from the view. He was surprised to see Antares supporting Ik, who was visibly upset by the sight. With what appeared to be considerable effort, Ik spoke to the Jeaves-holo. "*Hrahh.* Can we change that view, please?" His voice was strained, with an unusual urgency. *Fear?*

"Certainly," said the robot. "I'm sorry if that is . . . well, I intended it to be informative. Is this better?"

The image shrank by half, and the pulsing bursts of energy subsided, replaced by a field of ghostly light, not so much from within the star as surrounding and enveloping it. Bandicut could faintly perceive an outward streaming movement in the light.

"What is that?" Ik said, his voice as tight as before.

"That," said Jeaves, "is a display of the star's solar wind, all of the high-energy particles streaming outward into space. As you can see, we're passing through it now. It is very tenuous here, but will become steadily stronger as we move inward."

Ik nodded stiffly. "How close are we going?"

As Ik spoke, Li-Jared strode onto the bridge, looking distraught. "Yes, how close *are* we going?" he cried.

Ik shifted just his eyes. "Hrah. We wondered where you had gotten to."

"I've been talking to the shipboard AI," Li-Jared said. "And you know what it told me? It told me we may be flying *right into* that star." *Bong.* "What about that, Jeaves?"

"Well, it depends," Jeaves answered. "We don't really know how close we might have to get to establish communication, assuming we *can* do that. But be reassured—the ship *is* capable of flying into the body of the star, if it proves necessary."

"Great," Bandicut muttered softly, with a glance at Antares.

"It only depends on our n-space bubble remaining intact."

"*Excuse* me?" Bandicut said, not knowing whether to laugh or shout.

"You understand, yes?" Jeaves said. "Our survival is *always* dependent on the integrity of the n-space bubble—whether we're in deep space or making a close approach to a star. We can't go two kilometers, or two minutes, without the n-space fields."

"Are we supposed to find that reassuring?" Antares asked.

Jeaves looked vaguely put out. "The field generators are very reliable, and have backups."

"No doubt," Bandicut said. "But are you telling me that going into the body of a star wouldn't put unusual stresses on the n-space bubble?"

"Possibly," the robot said. "But not as much as you might think. The n-space bubble by definition removes us from the region of greatest stresses."

"What about all the heat? Wouldn't it build up? How does the ship get rid of that?"

"It doesn't have to, because the heat simply passes us by. The only component that's really at risk is the probe that might be extended into normal-space. It *does* pick up heat, but it's piped away into a cold layer of n-space, so there's no violation of thermodynamics."

"Has anyone ever actually tried it?"

"Indeed, yes. There have been cases in which beings very much like yourselves have used far more primitive n-space fields as protection while penetrating the interiors of stars. In one case, the fields even survived pre-supernova conditions."

Bandicut blanched. *"Supernova?"*

"Pre-supernova."

"I'm so sorry. So you're saying they got out before the star blew?"

Jeaves twitched slightly. "Well . . . no. But we're not expecting supernova conditions."

"Then *what?*"

"My friends," Jeaves said heavily. Was that impatience creeping into his voice? "Our mission depends in many ways on the versatility of this ship. Please don't sell it short."

"Hrah." Ik, looking paler than usual, pointed ahead toward the star. "I hope you are correct. Because we're flying toward this star *very fast.*"

Ik was right. The disk of the star was growing perceptibly as they stood watching. Perhaps they had not slowed as much from interstellar speed as Bandicut had thought. It looked as if it would be just a matter of minutes before they plunged into the star. Surely that was an illusion. Still . . . "Jeaves, how long before we reach the star—and who is in control right now?" Bandicut asked.

Was that another hesitation? "At our present speed," Jeaves said, "we could theoretically enter the star's atmosphere in about two hours. Whether we *will* or not depends on what we learn as we get closer."

"So who—?"

"And the shipboard AI is running the vessel, with input from Delilah and me."

Bandicut and the others looked at each other. Ik seemed frightened in a way that Bandicut had never seen before, Antares appeared alarmed, and Li-Jared looked mutinous. Bandicut cleared his throat. "Let me rephrase. Who makes the decision whether or not we actually *fly into the sun?*"

The hesitation was longer this time. "Delilah is right now probing for ways to make contact with the star-consciousness," Jeaves said at last. As he spoke, the view changed to a ghostly image that reminded Bandicut of an X-ray holo of the sun. At the fringe of the glowing sphere, a shadowy fleck was visible, very close to the surface, or possibly just beneath it. "Our plan," Jeaves continued, "is to follow Deep as close to the star as necessary."

Li-Jared growled, "Do you hear that, everyone? You'd better get your sun shades ready—because we're going in. You might also say your prayers." Bristling with indignation, he said to Jeaves, "You're evading the question. You aren't going to let *us* make the decision, are you?"

They all glared together at the robot. Finally Jeaves answered, "It will be the shipboard AI. But it pays very close attention to my suggestions. Is that . . . satisfactory to you?"

Li-Jared practically snarled, "*No,* it's not satisfactory! You're telling us a *machine* is going to decide whether or not *we* fly into a sun?"

"We will definitely take your opinions into account—"

"Why can't *we* talk to the AI, here from the bridge?" Li-Jared snapped.

"I'm afraid the AI's current programming enables it to respond only to haloes, shadow-people, and . . . me."

Brrr-d-d-dang. "Is that so? Well, it was happy enough to talk to me a little while ago."

"Yes," Jeaves acknowledged. "That was a conversation, though—not a chain of command. A more fundamental change would be required before it would accept instructions from you. I am sorry, but—"

"Sorry that you're scaring my friend Ik out of his wits?" Li-Jared turned toward the Hraachee'an, who stood staring fixedly at the ghostly image of the growing sun, seemingly oblivious to everything else.

Antares had a hand on his long, angular arm, apparently trying to reassure him. Ik's breath hissed loudly in and out. Bandicut joined her and peered worriedly at Ik's strained face. "He is in great distress," Antares said. "Ik, what is it? Is it the sun? Are you feeling its presence?"

Ik whispered, "It is the memories." He raised his long-fingered hands and held them up in front of the sun.

And then Bandicut remembered: Ik's homeworld of Hraachee'a had been destroyed when its blue sun had exploded. And Ik had survived by . . .

"He fell into his own sun," Li-Jared said suddenly. "And the star-spanner, or something like it, took him to Shipworld. Isn't that right, Ik?"

The viewspace was now almost entirely filled by the image of the sun. Jeaves spoke in the silence that followed Li-Jared's voice. "Delilah says we must move closer to Deep if we are to make contact."

"Closer?"

"I am sorry. Deep is at the outer edge of the star's atmosphere now. If we are to learn what we can from the star, there is no choice. We must follow."

14

★BRIGHTBURN★

 Ik could not turn from the image of the swelling red sun. It bathed his thoughts like the flame of a torch, searing together memory and the incomprehensible present. His eyes were filled with the memory of his homeworld, Hraachee'a, enveloped in the flames of an erupting sun. Everything he had known in his life, consumed by fire. And everyone: his lifebond partner, Onaka, and his heirs, the offspring of his egg-brother Aon, consumed by fire. His heart was broken, broken forever.

Escaping spaceships fled like spores into space, but most of them flared like tiny bits of combusting dust as the sun expanded and consumed them. His own ship, a work boat from the polar orbit station, had lost power—but only after the drive unit had stuck at full thrust, burning up all of its fuel, sending him on a trajectory toward the sun. He was coasting, helpless. It was only a matter of moments before he, too, would flare and be snuffed out in the final fire. The strange new voice-stones in his head seemed to be saying something, but he couldn't follow what it was.

Here and there he thought he saw things that could not really be—tiny flickers of something different—*not* spaceships burning up, but something like tiny openings or windows, and spaceships disappearing into them. Perhaps he only imagined it; perhaps he only *wished* for something. Wouldn't it be wonderful if some miraculous force appeared and whisked, not just him, but those he loved, to safety?

But that was impossible. Because who or what would come to save them now?

And then a curtain of light billowed open directly in front of him—and in an instant, everything that had been burning around him was gone. He seemed suspended in space and time, and felt as if his ship were being flung down some endless, invisible tunnel. After an achingly long period, he was wrenched back into space as he knew it. But gone was the swath of stars that was the galaxy, replaced by an astounding sight—a necklace of enormous linked space habitats, floating in extragalactic space: Shipworld.

It was unbelievable, and terribly disorienting. He *had* been saved. But what about those he loved? Or *any* of his fellow Hraachee'ans? Had anyone else escaped?

He didn't know, even now. Any more than he knew what was happening to him on *The Long View.*

He was flying into a sun. Once more a sun was engulfing him and he didn't know why. He felt a desperate knot in his chest; it threatened to squeeze off all his hearts. He didn't think he was going to escape this time.

He could not bear it. Could not face it, could not turn away from it.

But he *had* to turn away from it.

Had to make them see.

The robot.

The halo.

Make them see how he was dying.

*

Deeaab had just one real goal as he streaked from the outer fringes of the star toward the hotter, denser regions. That was to find a way to bring these interesting ones together. No, it was more urgent than that; they *needed* to find each other. That was why he was pursuing the goal so relentlessly. It was a clearer need than any Deeaab had felt since his escape from the dying universe of his origin.

The new one who was now part of Deeaab, the one who was able to speak and listen to the small ones, the one called Charlene-echo . . . that one drove him with a sense of urgency. If Deeaab did not help make these connections, the others would not find the source of the deadly troubles in this area—both the dying stars and the shock waves that rippled and caromed through space. And to help them connect, Deeaab needed to reach out and seize the very *stuff* of space, and the threads of time, and twist and bend them in a way that would make communication possible.

That was something Deeaab could do. But could he do it delicately enough for all of them to follow? The small ones seemed alarmingly fragile. But the large one . . . Deeaab could feel its distress, its failing energies. It was possible that it was on the verge of explosive stardeath.

Could he do this without harming either?

There was really just one way to find out.

*

"We are entering the sun's corona," Jeaves reported. "This star is a helium-burning red giant with not much life left in it. Once the helium at its core has all fused to carbon, the core will stop burning, and its outer shell will swell up to a much larger size, to a supergiant. That may happen anytime in the next few thousand years."

"Uhhl, you mean a—" *rasp* "—supernova?" Antares asked.

"It's not massive enough for that. But as it balloons outward, it will engulf its entire planetary system."

Bandicut swallowed hard. That would be the eventual fate of Earth's sun, he knew; but Earth's sun wasn't scheduled to blow up for another five billion or so years. "And how many of those planets are inhabited?" he murmured.

"Unknown," Jeaves answered. "From the spectro readings on one of the planets, I'd guess there's life—but how evolved, it's hard to say. It may be primitive life only. I don't think it's in immediate danger."

Bandicut grunted. "No, it's just going to be incinerated in a thousand years or so."

"I'm sorry. There's nothing we can do about that. Everyone please note: while the temperature outside our ship is relatively high, that is in normal-, not n-space. Also, even in normal-space, the gases are extremely tenuous and much cooler than they would be in a main-sequence star, a blue or a white or a yellow. This is a red giant, and cooler. We are well within safety margins."

Ik stood with his eyes closed, trembling.

"We will soon be approaching the outer edge of the photosphere," Jeaves continued. "There we must make a decision on entering the body of the star—still in n-space, of course. Please tell me at once if you feel any contact with the star's consciousness. I don't necessarily *expect* you to feel anything, but—"

"I feel it now," Antares said.

Delilah sprang into view overhead, pulsing. Was she watching Antares? Bandicut had the distinct impression that the halo was watching both Antares *and* the sun outside with feverish interest. Jeaves spoke quickly. "What do you feel? Can you describe it?"

"No. Yes. It's a great presence. As great as Deep, but very different. More ponderous. *Slower.* So slow I can hardly feel the movement of thought." Antares had both hands to her throat now, touching her stones. Her eyes were wide with expectation. "I feel . . . *Deep* . . . and something happening. *Something is happening.* I don't know what. But something is *changing.* It—" She threw her head back suddenly, her mane of hair cascading from head and neck, her eyes narrowing and sharpening to a squint, and her mouth twisting in a grimace. *"Uhhlll,"* she whispered.

Bandicut reached out, then hesitated. Should he break her concentration? He didn't want to leave her in pain. He saw Li-Jared peering at the two of them, as if wondering if the madness was returning.

/// I think . . .
it is not so much pain she feels,
as things shifting and coming apart . . . ///
/Can I help her?/
/// I think she is managing . . . ///

★

What Antares felt was so utterly different from anything she'd known before that she was frozen with astonishment. At first she felt pain, staggering pain. And then it changed, and it was no longer pain, but something at once frightening and thrilling; space and time shifting and wrenching apart *(Is Deep doing this?),* and then coming back together, and she no longer knew *what* she was feeling, except that she felt herself suddenly surrounded, then engulfed by the thoughts and feelings of the star.

Past and future wrapped themselves around her like a coiled wire, enveloping the present. It was difficult to follow; thoughts from the star were drifting around her, and some of them she could understand. Images, names, fears and hopes intertwined.

And now something was coming: waves of overwhelming energy . . .

★

For Li-Jared, it was too much to bear. His friend Ik was racked by pain and fear; Antares too, but differently. This madness had to end. The robot was going to kill them all unless he did something to stop it. He waved his hands in the air, shouting at Jeaves, "Get us out of here! Don't you see what you're doing? The *ship* may survive, but look at Ik and Antares!"

Jeaves was unmoved. "I understand your concern—but we're getting contact with the star. Just a little farther, my friends. Antares, have you established any link?"

The Thespi cried out in frustration, "*Yes!* I'm feeling *something*—but I can't understand it!"

"That's why we must be patient," Jeaves said. "Please, everyone! Keep courage!"

Snarling, Li-Jared picked up a mug and hurled it at Jeaves. As it flew through the robot's holo-image and bounced off the deck, Li-Jared swung around in despair. "John Bandicut!" Maybe the human could get through to Deep and tell *him* to stop, to turn away . . .

*

It all seemed to Bandicut to be happening at once: Antares reaching out to the star swelling around them, and crying out in words he couldn't understand. Li-Jared clamoring for his attention. Ik clearly in distress. And Charli saying just a minute, just a minute . . .

/Charli, talk to me!/

> */// Antares is getting something from the star.*
> *I can't tell what it is,*
> *but I don't think it can last.*
> *Ik and Antares, they're—///*

/In trouble. Charli, this is a suicide dive! Deep could stop it. If Deep turns away, I'm sure we'll follow. Can you reach Deep? Can you reach what's left of Charlene?/

> */// I'm not sure . . .*
> *I'm trying now . . . ///*

*

"*Must leave! Must leave! Hraahhhhh!*" Ik's voice tore from his throat with a rasp of pain. He could not survive this a second time. He could feel the star swollen around him—not just physically, but its *presence* as a living thing in pain. They could die in the grip of this star, and it would never know what it had crushed.

"*We cannot do this!*" he cried, lurching backward from where he had been standing. He backed into a wall and staggered.

"Just a little farther," Jeaves replied, turning again to Antares to see if she had made contact.

Ik looked around wildly for someone else who might help.

Li-Jared was shouting at Jeaves. But Bandicut was bending over, hands to the sides of his head, murmuring madly.

✳

The life-fire called ✳Brightburn✳ was aware of the tiny, quick visitors, and of another that was different. It felt very strange, this presence of the others. It was hard to know who or what they all were. And yet there was something about the presence that felt good and true, that gave ✳Brightburn✳ a desire to make its acquaintance. And so, not knowing how to speak, she began reviewing her life, which would soon end, for her fires were burning low.

✳Brightburn✳ began singing and remembering.

✳Brightburn✳ had been here long . . . very long. She was not the oldest, not by far—because the Firstborn had come before. But the Firstborn were all a memory now, lifedust scattered throughout space. ✳Brightburn✳ was of the Secondborn, and one of the oldest of the life-fires still living in Starmaker. Long before the trouble had begun, ✳Brightburn✳ had been here. She had watched the clouds and storms of creation issue forth new life-fires, sister suns flaring into being. And among them, she looked for the ones that were true-life, like her.

For although some did not speak, many did. And together, they became a clan of life-fires.

With light they spoke
    with heat
        with coiling arcs of fire
Space itself quivered
        with their shaking and their thunder.

Though ✳Brightburn✳ was not the first of the Secondborn to sing, or to tell stories, she may have been the first to tell stories *as* songs, to spin tales and memories in word and thought and song.

She had passed on stories from the Firstborn, stories of the Earliest—who came even before the Firstborn, out of some other crucible altogether, who were already here when Starmaker was coalescing out of the gases and dusts of time. The Earliest had watched Starmaker form, and some even claimed to be the nucleus that drew Starmaker together.

But those memories, handed down in fragments, were never quite clear. Perhaps it was a failure of the memories, or perhaps

the Early Fires had not been as adept at setting thought to words.
∗Brightburn∗ rather thought of the Early Fires as being perhaps

    Stronger but

      less wise

        barely aware

And yet, they had been here and seen it all begin. How often
∗Brightburn∗ had wished they had handed down their stories as
∗Brightburn∗ was trying to do now—before her end.

    Death approaches

      thoughts grow confused

        can the stories be told in time ?

Foremost were the stories of her own birth into life—her
vivid, if splintered, recollection of her emergence into being,
into thought.

She remembered the first billowing burn.

Remembered blossoming and burning hot.

Remembered changing as she grew larger, hotter, yellow and
white. (This was long before the swollen redness came over her,
before the inner fires changed, before she grew cooler and larger.)

She remembered the appearance of others like her, life-fires
with intelligence and wit and song in their souls. Sometimes
they sang together, especially when stories abounded of new
births, new fires erupting from the glowing cloud. It was a time
of joy and hope.

There were stories of ∗Dazzle∗ and ∗Blaze∗ and ∗Deepburn∗.
Stories of the clan and the sisterhood, growing out of the many
individuals. It was a time when so many of them thought to the
future, dreaming and wondering what to expect from the cloud
of light.

And then, in a fraction of a lifetime, it all changed. A dark
new presence came to Starmaker.

    Something dark

      and difficult

        with rippling waves

          that tore at Starmaker herself

        destroying

      Why ?

Where it had come from, ∗Brightburn∗ didn't know.

What had brought it here, ∗Brightburn∗ didn't know.

But its presence was unmistakable.

It brought uncertainty, and fear. And in time

> **insanity**
>> **and death**

∗Brightburn∗ did not know, could not fathom why. She herself was not struck in the beginning.

But ∗Deepburn∗ died shockingly young, flaring brightly and then sputtering down.

∗Crimson∗ lost her memory, then her ability to speak.

Then ∗Crimson∗ died.

And ∗Raybright∗ stopped speaking, but did not die.

And they all shook at times with the waves that came over them, waves that troubled them and made them feel unwell.

> **Why ?**
>> **Why ?**

This thing that had invaded Starmaker did not make itself visible or present for anyone to see. But it tugged at the very fabric of space, hurt the life-fires in the belly, made them cry out with their thoughts.

It never spoke.

Never explained.

Only killed, or changed.

Or crippled the newborn, who had not yet learned to speak.

> **Wrong**
>> **it was wrong**

∗Brightburn∗ could feel its presence even now. It knew where the Other was: up in the valley. In the rift, among the powerfully bright fires at the heart of Starmaker. There where ∗N-n-ck-k-k∗'s belly was growing hard and tight and swollen with whatever the Other was doing to it.

There the Other was preparing the greatest cataclysm ever, the one that might destroy all of Starmaker, though ∗Brightburn∗ herself might no longer be here to suffer it.

∗Brightburn∗ wished she could warn the others, the tiny ones.

> **For all the good**
>> **knowing would do . . .**

O small ones
   and strange one,
hear me
   somehow
      hear

✳

Charlene-echo was no longer the same being who had once lived in the mind of a human. But the old instinct remained, to protect the ones it loved. When she heard the cry for help, she felt a pang for Bandicut, and for Charli, the one who reached out and spoke to her.

<<< *Is it bad, what is happening?* >>>
Charlene-echo asked.

Charli answered,

/// Frightening, terrifying.
We are being pushed into something
we are not prepared for, not made for.
Please help! ///

Charlene-echo tried to understand. She felt that they/she /Deeaab were hearing something from the fiery one. It was not yet clear. Perhaps if time could be squeezed together a little more here, and stretched a little more there . . .

And yet, if it was hurting those they were trying to help . . .

<<< *Antares and Ik?*
Are they the ones? >>>

she asked. And she was answered by Charli, who was herself stretched to the limit even to have this conversation.

/// They hurt most.
But Li-Jared and John Bandicut, too. ///

Charlene-echo urgently conveyed the need to Deeaab. And Deeaab, who was no longer just a host, but a part of her now, heard the cry.

But before he could respond, they felt something new: a rumbling in spacetime, a shock wave. It was another of those periodic disturbances that shook everything they touched. And now it was shaking the star, unexpectedly and hard. And through the condensed bubble of time Deeaab had created around the star, he immediately saw the danger. This star was on the verge of collapse, and Deeaab's time bubble was squeezing years' worth of energy into minutes.

Deeaab turned, changing course. He could do nothing about the shock waves; he could do nothing about the fragile condition of the star; and it was too late to remove the time bubble. But he would do what he could to lead the smaller ones away, before it was too late for them.

✷

Bandicut felt Charli snap back into his mind like a rubber band. He gasped and blinked up into the view of space. It was shaking. Or *he* was shaking; the entire ship was shaking. "Jeaves, what's happening to us?" he yelled. There in the viewspace, where the large granulations on the red surface of the star seemed about to swallow them, he saw a barely visible shadow, but way down in the star's photosphere. It was Deep, making a sweeping turn.

Jeaves called in a crackling voice, "Hypergrav waves! We're trying to stabilize . . ." Bandicut held his breath, watching Deep. It took a few moments to be sure: Deep was leaving the star.

Jeaves spoke again. "The shock waves are reverberating throughout the star. This could present unexpected danger, given its fragile state. Please stand by while I attempt to determine how we should respond."

Bwang. "Respond by *getting us out of here!*" Li-Jared shouted.

"Deep is leaving!" Bandicut called. "Look!" He pointed to the moving shadow.

"Yes," Jeaves said. "But if we are getting information . . ."

"*What* information?" Bandicut yelled.

Jeaves was in motion across the bridge. "Antares, can you report?"

Antares was breathing hard, holding her hands to her head. She didn't speak, didn't seem *able* to speak. Bandicut, forcing himself to be calm, touched her shoulder. He could feel her struggle, but couldn't tell what she was struggling *with*. He looked up and glared at Jeaves. "She can't report! Get us out of here before you kill both of them! Before you destroy the ship!"

Jeaves cocked his robot head for a moment, then said softly,

"Hold tight." As he spoke, Delilah spun away and vanished. Bandicut thought he saw a flicker of change in the view of the sun. The granulations on the surface began to shift sideways in the view, as though the ship were altering course. The sun began to grow smaller.

Still touching Antares, Bandicut looked across at Li-Jared and Ik. "We're leaving. Hold on. We're leaving the star. Hold on . . ."

✳

✳Brightburn✳ had never felt such pain. These waves were much worse than any that had come before. There was something *wrong* in the way it was all happening, as though it were all too fast, as though the ending of life were somehow being crushed together, compressed into too short a time.

The death blow
> **too soon**
>> **too soon**

Not ready

It was hitting ✳Brightburn✳ in the belly. She felt the pain and weakness there the most.

> **Is this the time ?**
>> **the end ?**

I must try at the last
> **must share**

The small ones and the strange one were all turning and fleeing, and she did not blame them.

But she must try one last time to tell them. Show them.

15

OUT OF THE STAR

 Antares was in pain, and struggling, and she didn't know why. Everything was coming apart around her, all of space and time, and was *she* supposed to hold it together? Her mind was spinning with forces and threads of life she could not understand. Deep was doing something, and the star was doing something . . . there were *voices*, all verging on comprehensibility. She felt Ik struggling beside her.

Voices . . . who are they speaking to? /Stones, help me!/ But the stones could not.

She felt intensely alone.

I must hear this star . . . something it is trying to tell me . . .

But they were moving away now.

"John Bandicut?" she whispered. Was the sun getting smaller? She closed her eyes, breathing deeply, then looked again. Yes, definitely smaller.

"Antares? Can you hear me?" John's voice was close; he wanted her to turn. She was afraid to, afraid she would lose the last remaining connection with the star.

But it was too late; it was vanishing, like a fog burning away. Except she thought she *understood* something now, some understanding from the star. She stared at the fiery orb, trying to grasp the thought before it could slip away. Something about Deep. But then it was gone, like a memory of a dream.

She fell into John's arms with a gasp and pressed her face to his shoulder, unable to talk, as John murmured over and over, "We're moving away now, we're moving away . . ."

*

Deeaab could feel the instability growing, and he shifted course to move as quickly as possible out of the body of the sun. At the same time, he felt something else—an upwelling that was not physical, but coming rather from the star's mind or spirit, as if it were trying consciously to reach out, to convey something. Deeaab had not sensed this particular star's thoughts directly before, though he had felt the unmistakable *presence,* as they'd passed into it. This star had felt mute, but now shadowy images were rising from it. Was *Brightburn* trying to speak?

<<< *Look, do you see it?* >>>

See what?

<<< *I see a shape. It's communicating.*

It looks like . . . the shape reminds me of Starmaker. >>>

The cloud?

<<< *Do you not see the shape of the nebula?*

And in the center, past the four bright stars

that Bandicut calls the Trapezium,
I see a knot of turbulence.
And that is— >>>
Where the trouble is located? Where we are to go?
<<< *Where the one called N-ck-ck-ck-ck lives,*
and perhaps the thing that is attacking Ed's world. >>>

Deeaab could only just make out the shadowy impression of images, but he could see what the Charlene-echo part was saying, and was willing to trust that part of himself to interpret.

But in the meantime, he could feel something else happening inside the bubble of time that surrounded the star. It was another series of shock waves from the distant disturbance. They were hitting the star, hitting the region of time-fusion, where Deeaab had compressed the star's time to allow communication with the ephemerals. As the shock waves entered the time-bubble, they were concentrated and amplified—and to Deeaab's horror, they were extinguishing the star's inner fires. ✴Brightburn✴ was dying.

The Charlene-echo part of Deeaab was momentarily confused.

<<< *Why is it happening so fast?*
Because of the change to the time-stream? >>>

Yes. ✴Brightburn✴ was beginning to swell outward at an accelerated rate. And the tiny ship carrying the ephemerals was only beginning to turn away.

✴

Bandicut was immensely relieved to see the star receding. It felt far less threatening as a glowing basketball than it had as a wall of fire. He and Li-Jared had managed to get both Ik and Antares sitting down, and were now trying to calm them enough to talk.

Ik was the most shaken, but he was starting to find his voice, a bare rasp. "I don't—*hrah*—don't know what happened to me. I don't know *why*—" He brought his hands up, pressing his opposing pairs of thumbs together, then suddenly jammed a knuckled fist to each side of his head. He drew a hissing breath. "I'll be . . . fine. Give me . . . a moment."

"All right," Bandicut said softly, and turned back to Antares. "How are you doing?" he asked, bending to see her face.

"I'm not sure," she whispered. She seized his hand and squeezed it. "John, I . . . *felt* . . . the mind of the star. *I felt it.*" Her eyes, bright gold and black, met his—and for a moment, he felt a fierce, electric connection. Then her focus shifted, and she was suddenly far away. But the emotion of her encounter with the star continued to reverberate through him like the sound of a bell. She was awestruck, terrified, and moved by what she had felt.

/// Find out what she learned! ///

/I'm trying./ Bandicut leaned closer to Antares. "Can you tell me *what* you felt? Or heard? Was there *communication*?"

Antares ran her hands through her thick hair. "Not precisely. But *voices.* I heard voices. I don't know exactly what they were saying. But it . . . the star sensed *me,* John. I know it did. And it was trying to say something to me."

"What about Deep? Was Deep part of the communication?"

Antares's eyes seemed to haze over. "Deep was there, doing something that made it all possible. Stretching *time,* somehow, I think. I couldn't feel Deep's thoughts, exactly. But I'm sure Deep and the star, Deep and *Brightburn*, exchanged some knowledge."

Bandicut's hand tightened on her. "Do you know what kind of knowledge?"

"No, I—" She struggled for a moment. "Wait. *Yes.* There were images. I believe Deep knows the way to *Nick* now. I'm almost certain *Brightburn* showed him the way."

For a moment, everyone was silent, looking at Antares—even Delilah, who'd dropped down from the ceiling to hover nearby. The deck continued to shake beneath them, but it was becoming an almost familiar sensation, like the engine of a boat. Jeaves spoke over it, to make an announcement. "Deep has left the star's atmosphere, and is accelerating on a course very close to ours, heading toward—*wait a moment!*"

Everyone stiffened, waiting for him to continue.

The next thing they saw was the viewspace blossoming with crimson light, and *Brightburn* swelling rapidly from a distant ball of fire to a sphere of glowing gas that once more filled the view. "Are we falling back in?" Bandicut asked, trying not to shout.

"No," Jeaves said in a tight, quiet voice. "*Brightburn* is undergoing rapid expansion to supergiant phase."

★

Antares felt two distinct, but simultaneous, waves of fear. One was her own at the sun that was exploding right behind them. The other was *Brightburn*'s presence suddenly in her mind again— *Brightburn*, in shock and fear at what was happening. *Brightburn* was dying, and in rapidly advancing stages. The star's fear and sadness were far clearer now than the feeling she'd had before; the emotions were stark in her mind. Whatever Deep had done to enable their connection was not over; it had rejoined with greater strength.

Brightburn *knows she is dying, and she doesn't want to, not yet.*

Antares's own fear was insignificant in comparison. Her thoughts quaked with the star's outcry:

Waves

> **waves**

>> **waves**

> **cannot resist**

> **longer**

The words were a bewildering orchestration in her thoughts. Most of it she couldn't understand. But an unmistakable fact came through: this star was being overwhelmed by a force too great even for its massive size and power.

Antares's thoughts ballooned with images and thoughts. She felt plunging pain in her core, where the last of the fires were guttering, snuffed by the hypergrav shock waves. She felt a searing pain just below her skin, where the fusion-fires still burned, and were now pushing the outer shells of the sun farther out still; she felt the heat of those fires expanding to incinerate anything in their path. She felt a warm, cottony breath exhaling from her skin, blowing into space, puffing out an enormous shell of gas, an exhalation of surrender—not to death just yet, but to time and inevitability.

Antares watched the staggering energy billow from the dying star's core, time clearly distorting as she followed the progress of the star's death-explosion. Its dying cry reverberated . . .

Why-y-y
      y-y-y-y
          y-y-y-y-y ?

And then it could no longer speak.

Antares felt a sadness such as she had never felt before. She wept for the star, for the life taken too soon. And she burned with anger at the cruelty of its being taken by a distant and cold interloper, its name and purpose unknown.

Not all of the life was gone yet; she felt other images flickering out of the star's failing consciousness: the flares of thought of other suns, the memory of stars bursting forth into life, and of some of them sputtering into an early death. She saw, through a sight very different from her own, the contours of Star Home stretching away into the distance, its great glowing clouds, and its clusters and chambers of stars; and deep within that place where even now new stars were coming into being, she was aware of the deadly pull of the star-killer. She knew little of it; but she *felt* it, like a cancer eating at the heart of this place that was her home.

All of this wheeled around Antares's head like a landscape out of control; she felt as if she were falling, spinning. And then it all began to go out of focus, and to fade. She tried to hold on to the images, to see more—but it was no use. ∗Brightburn∗ was finally, irrevocably, fading from her reach.

∗

Bandicut saw Antares's eyes blink and move about rapidly, like a human in REM sleep, and then flick open to stare at him. "I—" she began, and then immediately sank, as her knees weakened.

Bandicut supported her. "What is it? What happened?" he asked, steadying her as another tremor passed through the ship. "Was it ∗Brightburn∗ again?" As he said it, his gaze shifted to the swollen sun. It wasn't getting visibly larger, but that, he thought, was because they were hurtling away from it at reckless speed, through n-space.

"Yes," Antares whispered. "∗Brightburn∗ is dying, but I felt her much more closely this time. And I saw images in her thoughts."

Bandicut listened, stunned, to her description. *My God.* Shakily, he drew a breath. "Well, I . . . right now, I'm wondering if we're going to be swallowed up in that fireball—or are we going to get out of here so all that information can do some good.

For a moment, that question hung in the air. Then Jeaves spoke. "We will not be engulfed," he said. "We are accelerating rapidly through n-space as we speak, and we can outrun any expansion of the star, barring unexpected problems."

That stopped Bandicut. "Barring—what? What kinds of problems?"

"*Unexpected* problems," Jeaves said impatiently. "Which means, I don't expect them."

"Well, then—"

"But look here—look at *Brightburn* now. Watch it for a minute."

Bandicut shifted his gaze again. It looked as though the star had grown *smaller*. "Why? What's it—holy shit, Jeaves. What's happening? Is it *shrinking*? Are we moving away from it that fast?"

"Yes, it's shrinking," the robot answered. "And no, it's not just because we're moving away so fast—although we are."

"Then *why?*"

"We believe it's because Deep—well, because Deep is no longer creating the fusion of *time* that made all this possible."

Bandicut shook his head. "I'm not sure I—"

"You understand that Deep squeezed months, maybe even years, of *Brightburn*'s time together into an interval that would match your visit, so that you could converse. Yes?"

"Um . . . sort of. But I don't understand *how*—"

"I don't, either. But the point is, we were watching *Brightburn*'s death *in compressed time.*"

Bandicut stared back out at the shrinking sun. "And now?"

"The time-fusion is relaxing, and the events that were squeezed from your future into the present are returning to the future. *Brightburn* is indeed going through an end-of-life expansion, but you might watch it over the next few years, or few hundred years. We are not in danger of being caught in its shock wave." Jeaves gave a dry chuckle. "We have plenty of other worries. But not that one."

Bandicut blinked at him. "That," he said, "is very . . . very . . .

weird." As he slowly caught his breath, he added, "So then, where exactly are we heading now?"

"Out of this star system and on course for the heart of Star-maker Nebula," Jeaves said. "Following Deep, who we *believe*—" and the robot paused to nod to Antares "—knows where he's going."

16

EARTHWARD BOUND

The boosters felt like outstretched hands beneath Julie, lifting the small shuttle toward Triton orbit. The launch was gentler than she'd expected. She turned her head against the cushion and peered out the window as Triton's frozen surface of nitrogen and methane fell away beneath her. The landscape began to slant away as the shuttle rolled into flight attitude. Her last sight of Triton was a puff of a nitrogen eruption against the horizon. Then all she saw was blackness, and stars.

The acceleration increased gradually as they climbed toward orbit around Neptune's largest moon. She sighed back against the headrest and closed her eyes. Though the shuttle carried a handful of passengers, she'd avoided conversation, preferring the silence of her own thoughts. Her thoughts were dominated by the enigmatic translator, riding in the cargo hold beneath her. Julie would oversee its transfer into the hold of MINEXFO's interplanetary transport, *Park Avenue.* And before the day was out, the transport's engines would light, sending them on their way home to Earth.

It occurred to Julie that the liftoff of this little shuttle was like the closing of a knife blade, neatly dividing her life; she was leaving Triton, probably forever. She didn't know why this moment should feel so singularly irrevocable. But at least she was on her way back to where the sun could warm her face; she sometimes forgot how much she missed the sun. She wondered if being out here in perpetual night led to skewed ways of thinking.

She recalled Georgia's final words as they'd hugged at the airlock. *"Don't be a stranger. Stay in touch, okay?"*

She'd murmured back a feeble reassurance: *Of course I will. I'll let you know everything that happens. Look for my holos.*

But the truth was, she already felt like a stranger. Not to Georgia, but to herself. She felt, as she set out with this unknown alien power, as if she were taking the first steps down a strange and slippery slope.

Don't be a stranger . . .

She was traveling with a most remarkable stranger. Gazing out the window at the curving horizon of the majestic blue planet that dominated the Triton sky, she wondered if the translator, in its crate, was aware of Neptune, or of the greater solar system around them.

She wondered what the translator was thinking right now.

What it was planning.

✳

Julie had little time to enjoy the change of pace of the Triton Orbital Station and take in the views from its observation ports. From the moment of docking in orbit, she was busy overseeing the moving and securing of the translator in the hold of the ship that would take them to Earth. The *Park Avenue* was a modest-sized interplanetary transport, but it was so much larger than anything that ever descended to Triton's surface that it seemed like a luxury liner. On the outside, it was shaped like something an imaginative child might have assembled from moldable silver play pieces. On the inside, it had cabins and common space and corridors, and most of all, a decent-sized cargo hold.

She was in the corridor outside the hold now, gripping the handrail to keep from floating away, as she watched the ship's crew move pallets around and fiddle with the securing of the translator's crate.

"Is everything satisfactory, Ms. Stone?"

Julie pushed back from the window and rotated to face the navy-blue-uniformed officer who had spoken: Lieutenant Henry Cohn, if she remembered correctly. "Hard to say," she said. "Will the compartment be pressurized in time for me to check on the translator before we leave orbit?" The loading had taken much longer than she'd expected.

Lieutenant Cohn shook his head. "I'm afraid not. We're on a tight schedule. We'll be calling all the passengers to their cabins for departure in just a few minutes." He peered at her curiously for a moment. "May I ask—are you in contact with the translator now?"

Julie shook her head and felt her body twisting slightly with the movement. She was still getting used to zero gee. "It's not like that. I have to be a lot closer—and *it* has to make the contact. I'm not even sure what it's aware of through this wall."

"Is it important that you make contact before we depart?" Cohn asked.

Julie shrugged. Truthfully, she had no idea. But if the translator didn't like the way it was being secured aboard the ship, she'd rather know sooner than later. The spacesuited workers were now clamping its crate to large mounting brackets on the floor of the cargo bay where a space had been reserved for it. If it had any special requirements, she didn't know about them.

Not necessary.

She started at the voice in her head. The stones had been silent since before her departure from the mining base.

The arrangement is satisfactory, as long as there is access in flight.

Julie cleared her throat and said to the officer, "As long as I can have access once we're under way . . ."

"As soon as we're clear of orbit, and under steady boost," Cohn assured her. "With the permission of Dr. Lamarr, of course. He has final authority over everything having to do with the translator."

Of course he does, Julie thought with a sigh. *Or thinks he does.* She forced a smile. "Thank you."

✳

She finally went to find her berth. Though the ship was large compared to anything local, room was still at a premium. Her cabin was a third the size of her compartment on Triton station, and it was not hers alone. As she was sorting through her bags, a young woman floated in the doorway and nearly landed on top of her. The energetic-looking brunette reminded Julie of herself, a few years ago.

"Whoa," the woman said, pulling herself to a stop. "Hi. I'm Arlene—your roommate. You're Julie Stone."

"That's right." Shaking hands, Julie tried to back into one end of the compartment to make room. "Arlene, you said? What department are you in?"

"Language analysis." Arlene rotated in midair and pointed to the left-hand row of drawers in the built-in cabinet. "Those are yours. I already put my things in the other side."

"Ah. Thanks."

"I came in from Earth on the *Park Ave.* with Dr. Lamarr. I've been working here in orbit, studying the recordings of your interactions with the translator." Arlene hooked her wrist into a restraint to stay out of Julie's way. The zero-gee trick seemed perfectly natural to the woman, as though she were resting in an easy chair. "It's been absolutely fascinating—the recordings, I mean. I have a hundred questions for you."

Julie felt herself stiffening, as the meaning of Arlene's words sank in. "You've been . . . studying . . ."

"All the holos, all the sound recordings." Arlene had a look of excitement on her face, and a complete absence of guile. "I've been analyzing for patterns of various sorts, and trying to correlate your descriptions of what you've heard and felt with all the readings we have on your biometrics—breath rate, synaptic rate, various kinds of brainwave functions—everything we've recorded."

Julie felt her head spinning. "Which you got—?"

"Excuse me?"

"How did you *get* all of that data?"

Arlene looked puzzled. "Well, it was all recorded from the sensors in your suit when you communicated with the translator. You know about that, right?"

Julie shook her head. "*Brainwave* sensors? There were no brainwave recorders in my suit that I know of."

"Um . . . they were put in after your first encounter, when you lost consciousness." A frown grew on Arlene's face. "You didn't know?" Obviously Julie's dismay was showing, because

Arlene winced. "Oh dear. They must have forgotten to tell you."
She bit her lip in embarrassment. "Or maybe they didn't want to
make you self-conscious and—you know—skew the readings."

"Yes, I suppose that must have been it." Julie cleared her
throat noisily. "So—did you learn anything interesting about
me—or the translator?"

Arlene shrugged. "Nothing definitive. But there's a lot I want
to get your viewpoint on. You know, having just the biometric
readings leaves it all pretty abstract and—cold, I guess."

"I imagine it would, yes," Julie said, trying not to feel cold herself, as she envisioned a stranger poring in secret over her biometric readings. What embarrassing thoughts or urges had she
had while hooked up to Lamarr's spy sensors?

Arlene's frown deepened. "I get the feeling I've just made
you really uncomfortable."

"No, it's fine." The lie was obviously transparent. "Really." She
was no more convincing the second time.

"I'm sorry," Arlene said. "I never meant to pry. I was just sitting in a room at Triton Orbital, analyzing the information they
gave me. I never imagined they'd take readings without telling
you."

I'm sure you didn't. Julie immediately felt guilty for the
thought. *Okay, you probably didn't. Why would they tell you?*
"Listen, I'd better get my stuff stowed for departure."

"Okay," said Arlene. "I have to go check on something, real
quick. I'll be right back."

As Arlene disappeared, Julie took stock of storage in the
cabin. It was pretty tight, but since she was going to be living
here for several months, she'd better settle in as best she could.
She quickly unpacked her most comfortable clothes and crammed
them into the little built-in drawers, and stowed her toiletries,
books, and other personal items into a small set of closable
cubbies. She had to chase a few items that began to float away
across the room. She'd forgotten the little tricks of weightless-
ness she'd learned on the trip out. As she turned to close her
duffel, which was still half full, she saw a message scrolling on
the comm panel:

"Welcome to the MINEXFO shuttle Park Avenue. Please click the acknowledgment icon beside your name to notify our staff when you have stowed your belongings and are ready for departure. All luggage items should be stowed in the under-bunk compartments."

Julie wrestled her duffel into the tight compartment under her bunk, then turned and clicked the acknowledgment key.

"Thank you," said a male voice from the panel. "Departure will be in *nine* minutes. For your safety, regulations require that you strap yourself into your bunk for ignition and initial acceleration. Observe the signs on the walls to determine the correct ship-vertical attitude. Acceleration will reach one-fourth gee approximately ten seconds after ignition. Please remain in your bunk until the restraints sign has gone out, and use caution in moving about until you have adapted to the new gravitational conditions. For your own safety, all passengers will be monitored by remote cam for the first half hour of flight. If you have any questions, press the call button without delay."

So don't pick your nose or scratch in any embarrassing places . . .

*

Arlene returned about thirty seconds before the first warning horn. She and Julie strapped in, Arlene on the bottom bunk, Julie on the top. They talked little, except for Arlene's voicing a wish for windows so they could watch the departure. Julie, preoccupied by other thoughts, didn't answer.

When the departure boost finally came, it seemed almost anticlimactic—a gentle pressure pushing her back into the memory-foam of the bunk. Julie couldn't wait to get up and move around. The one-quarter Earth gravity produced by the ship's acceleration made her feel heavy, after the one-thirteenth gee of Triton, but it was mild compared to her exercise periods on the centrifuge track. It was just going to last a little longer—something close to this all the way to Earth.

When the bunk light went out at last, she cautiously climbed down. She felt an enormous and unaccountable sense of relief, being under way at last. Arlene pulled herself up from her lower bunk, but looked more wobbly and disoriented than Julie. "I've been in zero gee too long," she confessed.

"Better take it easy, then," Julie advised. "Are you going to be okay? I need to go see someone, but I won't leave if—"

"No, no—I'm fine," Arlene said in a tremulous voice. "But I think I'm going to lie here a few more minutes. Go ahead, I'll be all right."

"Okay." Julie closed the door behind her and strode down the passageway that a few minutes ago she had floated through. She searched until she found a small work area just aft of the bridge. "Lieutenant Cohn?"

The officer looked up with a grin. "Call me Henry. I'll be right with you, as soon as I check in with all the passengers and make sure everyone's all right. Some people get off to a queasy start."

"I think my roommate's one of them," Julie said. There was an outside window nearby, so she went over and peered out at the curving twilight blue horizon of Neptune, which had not yet diminished at all.

"Pretty sight, isn't it?" Cohn said a minute later.

"Hard to believe I'm leaving it behind. It feels like a natural part of the sky."

"I guess I haven't been here long enough for that. What can I do for you, Ms. Stone?"

"Julie. I'd like to check on the translator."

"Ah yes. Have you gotten permission from Dr. Lamarr?"

"Oh, hell." Could it be she didn't *want* to ask Dr. Lamarr? Cohn grinned. "Shall I call him for you?"

"Yes, please," she muttered. Pressing her lips together, she stared out the window again until Cohn returned from his console.

"He'll meet us at the cargo deck. Follow me?"

She pushed back from the window at once.

Lamarr beat them to the cargo deck. He was standing outside at the observation port, giving orders through the intercom. The translator's corner of the cargo area had not been kept as isolated as promised, and a number of standard shipping containers, apparently secured at the last minute, blocked access to the much larger crate holding the translator. After a moment, Lamarr noticed Julie. "Miss Stone. Are you ready to look in on our charge?"

Nodding, Julie surveyed the scene. "It looks like we have to do some rearranging."

That provoked a jerk of the head from Lamarr toward the crewmen inside the compartment. "They were supposed to keep that area clear."

A crewman in the passageway explained, "Departure time was moved up, and we were informed we had exactly one hour to get everything secured. We *could* have kept that area clear, if we'd been given a little more time."

Lamarr still looked irritated. "How long will it take to move that stuff out of the way?"

The crewman shrugged. "We need an hour or two to find a place to secure everything else. Are you planning to open up the artifact container?"

Lamarr turned to Julie. "What do you need, to make contact? Do we have to open it? It might be safer to leave it closed."

"I won't know until I try," Julie answered. "But if you want a more open communication—if you want it, for example, to recognize *you* and respond to *your* questions—"

"That is certainly a goal."

"Then I think we should remove at least the front of the crate, so it can see us." *If it even has vision. I wonder how it actually sees.*

Lamarr turned to the crewman. "You heard her. We want to open the crate. The sooner the better."

The crewman's eyebrows twitched. "We've got a long trip ahead of us, Dr. Lamarr."

"Yes," Lamarr answered. "And a great deal of work to do."

The crewman shrugged and turned away. Lamarr glanced at Julie and Lieutenant Cohn. "That's settled, then. Officer Cohn, I'll call you if we need you again. Miss Stone, if you will come with me, we must discuss what you will do when you reestablish contact. What you will say, and so forth."

What I will say? Julie thought, trying to imagine what instructions Lamarr might issue. *Or what I won't say.*

Lamarr had never been present for her visits with the translator. She had heard, however, that he had been among those
who had gone to see the artifact last night. Reportedly, it had
ignored his attempts to communicate.

This could be interesting.

*

"Dr. Lamarr, you're asking me to promise things that are beyond
my control." Rocking forward on the crate she'd found to sit on,
Julie spread her hands in exasperation.

"I'm not asking you to promise. I'm asking you to do what it
takes to establish communication. Is it unreasonable to ask that
you push a little bit?"

Was it? The translator would decide for itself how to respond
to Lamarr. Her own feelings, she supposed, were irrelevant. She
shrugged and changed the subject. "Were you ever going to tell
me that you'd bugged my spacesuit with all kinds of biosensors,
back on Triton? I just learned about it, from my roommate."

Lamarr's gaze met hers for a moment, then moved away dis-
missively. "There were experimental considerations during that
phase. It's nothing for you to be concerned about."

She suppressed a snort.

His gaze darkened very slightly. "I understand your discom-
fort. But let me caution you, Ms. Stone, not to fall into the trap of
thinking of this artifact as yours. It may have chosen you as its
medium of communication for now, but that does not make you
its only keeper."

Julie bit back the first reply that came to mind and said carefully, "I am aware of that. But it's part of my responsibility to *protect* the translator to the extent I can, while I work at establishing
communication."

"Of course," Lamarr said, "though the translator seems capable of protecting itself." Julie felt herself redden as he continued,
"Ms. Stone, you do not hold me, or MINEXFO, in particularly
high esteem—I know that. You think we're in this just for the
money, or the power. You think we want to exploit the translator
for our own gain."

With an effort of will, Julie kept a neutral expression.

"Well, I don't deny that we hope to gain from our position regarding the artifact. As I've said, we would not have come three billion miles to Triton if we hadn't hoped to find a profit." Lamarr paused, tapping his pen on a notepad. "We haven't yet made a profit, you know, in spite of the interesting metals we've mined. And now we have the *potential* for a return on all of those trillions of dollars that were spent by investors and taxpayers, building an outpost at the edge of the solar system."

Julie answered as evenly as she could. "I understand the need for profit. I'm not opposed to profit."

"I'm glad to hear you say that."

"But—" she paused "—profit isn't the only thing that matters, either."

"No, it's not. This . . . *artifact* . . . could be of significant benefit to all of mankind."

"Exactly."

"Or, to view it from the other extreme, it could pose a significant threat."

Julie flushed. *It already saved the Earth once. What more can it do to prove itself?*

"Now, I don't really believe that," Lamarr continued. "If we thought it posed a threat, we wouldn't be taking it anywhere near Earth."

She relaxed slightly.

"But I say this to point out that since we don't *know* what the end result of its presence is going to be, someone needs to be in charge of it. And that someone—"

She tensed again.

"—is not you. Or even me, personally." Lamarr paused, to let his words sink in. "It is the organization that made the discovery of the translator possible—the Mining Expeditionary Force—at least until some greater body decides differently. However, since MINEXFO is a multinational and multiworld consortium, there aren't too many greater bodies out here."

"I understand that, but—"

"And I am, currently, the chief representative of MINEXFO in the vicinity. That means I'm in charge until someone more senior arrives on the scene. And since we're now on a three-month journey from Neptune to Earth, it would seem I'm going to have this job for a while."

Julie stared back at him. *Especially since you timed our departure to make it impossible for a competing team to join us. Yes.*

Lamarr nodded, then rose and peered through the window into the cargo hold. The crew were just moving the last of the cargo away from the translator's crate. An olive-complexioned man, who seemed to be in charge, saw Lamarr and thumbed the intercom. "Do you want us to begin opening the artifact crate?"

"Not yet," said Lamarr. "We need to get our instruments and recording equipment in place." He turned. "Ms. Stone, will you please oversee the setup of equipment?"

"Of course. Do we know where the equipment is?"

Lamarr asked the crewman, who pointed to three shipping pods stacked beside the translator's container. "We were told to keep those boxes with the artifact. I don't know what's in them."

"May I come in?" Julie asked.

The crewman gestured toward the pressure hatch. There was a loud click, and the door slid open. She stepped into the cargo bay. Lamarr called after her, "I'll send some people to help you. Call me when you're set up. But don't open the artifact until I'm back. Understood?"

Julie nodded and turned her attention to the cargo. The olive-skinned crewman followed Lamarr with his gaze, then said to Julie, "Would you like a hand with that stuff? I'm Ashmar, and this is Jose."

She shook hands with both. "Can we clear some more space around the translator to set up equipment?"

"Well," said Ashmar, "I guess we could stack some of this stuff on the other side of the bay. But do you mind if I ask you something first?"

"What's that?"

Ashmar hooked a thumb toward the translator. "What's in that thing? We've heard a lot of rumors, but no one seems to know. Do you?"

Julie pondered how best to answer. "Let's just say—it's extra-terrestrial, it's intelligent, and sometimes it communicates. As to *what* it is, no, we don't have a clue." As she spoke, she saw Ashmar's eyes shift downward to the stone glinting in her right wrist. It was no secret back at the station how she had gotten the stones. How could it seem anything but weird to him? Did he wonder if she was being controlled by the device?

Sometimes I wonder myself.

Clearing her throat, she said, "Maybe we'll get some answers. Shall we get started?"

*

By the time they'd cleared the area, the extra help had arrived in the person of her roommate. "Feeling better?"

"Yah." Arlene flashed an unsteady grin. "I just needed a little time to get my feet under me again. What do you want me to do?"

Julie pointed to a set of three black, heavy-duty shipping cases. "Let's get the lights set up, for starters." She turned in place, surveying the area. "We need to space them as evenly as possible. The translator throws light in unusual ways. You've seen that in the holos, right?"

"I saw *something* in the holos," Arlene said, lifting a bar lamp out of the first case. "I couldn't really tell *what* I was seeing. So . . . what do you think it'll do when you open the container?"

"I have no idea. I just know we want it on holo."

Jose set another case in front of them. He seemed nervous working around the crate. "Relax," Julie said. "Can you set this light stand up over there?"

Jose nodded, but shifted his eyes toward the crate. "What if this thing doesn't like Mr. Lamarr bossing it around?"

Julie saw Arlene's eyebrows twitch at the question and stifled a laugh. "I guess that's a risk we'll have to take." She heard the clearing of a throat behind her, and turned to see Henry Cohn. "Hi. Here to help?"

"Actually," Henry said, "I'm here to ask what your plans are for opening the container. The captain wants to know. You know, in case it—" He coughed discreetly.

"What? Blows up? Or decides to take over the ship?"

"Well . . . yes."

"My plan," Julie said, tightening a holocam onto its tripod, "is to open the container very carefully. If the translator wanted to blow up or take over the ship, I suspect it could do that anytime it wanted."

"Then why take it out of the crate at all?"

Julie glanced quizzically at him. "Doesn't it seem more courteous? I suppose it *could* talk to us from in there, but it is, after all, a fellow sentient. Plus, we want to study it."

Henry rubbed his jaw thoughtfully as he walked away.

★

They broke for dinner, sending word to Lamarr that they were nearly ready. Julie sat at a long table in the dining room with Arlene, Henry, Ashmar, Jose, her chicken teriyaki and rice, and her own thoughts. She barely noticed the conversation, until Arlene said, *"Julie?"* She looked up and blinked. "I was afraid we'd lost you," Arlene said with a chuckle.

Julie forced a smile. "No, I'm just . . . preoccupied." Which was putting it mildly. Her stomach was in knots as she contemplated opening the translator—not for another meeting with *her*, but to introduce it to Lamarr. Was he right? Was she afraid of losing what leverage she had over the translator's fate? Things were going to change, that seemed certain.

Lamarr appeared in the doorway. "Everyone ready to go?"

Julie had just taken a large mouthful, so Henry answered. "It's all set up, Dr. Lamarr. As soon as we finish eating, I think we can start. Is that right, Ms. Stone?"

Lamarr looked sharply at both of them. "You can eat later. What are we waiting for?"

Julie sighed, drained her soymilk, and stood up. "All right. If we're in a hurry, let's go see if it's in a mood to talk." Lamarr's eyes seemed to narrow, but he said nothing as Julie excused herself past him.

Five minutes later Julie, Lamarr, Henry, and Arlene stood together in front of the translator's crate. The recorders were running. Jose and Ashmar kept their distance, ready to assist if needed. Even before anyone touched the crate, Julie felt the tickle of the translator in her mind.

∗We are glad you have come.∗

Julie relaxed a little. /There are others with me. Are you aware of them?/

∗Yes. It is time we spoke. All of us. Can we trust the others?∗

Julie blinked in surprise and tried to maintain her composure. /I . . . think so. I think you have to try./

∗Very well. Then we will try. There is much for us to discuss.∗

She must have reacted visibly, because out of the corner of her eye, she saw Lamarr glance at her questioningly. She nodded as she gathered her thoughts, and finally said, "It seems . . . the translator is eager to speak to us. To *all* of us." She faced the sealed crate again. She felt a more expansive presence in her thoughts, then heard in a well-modulated voice:

"Greetings to all of you. Thank you for providing transport. Is it possible to open this container, so that we may see each other?"

Had that sound come from her stones? Julie glanced around. "My God!" Arlene said. Behind her, Jose was crossing himself, and Ashmar's mouth was open in wonder. Henry looked as if he were debating whether he'd actually heard something.

Even Lamarr couldn't conceal his surprise. "All right," he said, "let's get the crate open." Henry and Julie stepped up to remove the outer cover. It was secured by three large clamps on either side. They each took a side and released the clamps, then lifted off the protective front panel and set it aside. The translator was now visible, pulsing, behind the archival glass of the primary case.

"Would you like us to open the inner case?" Julie asked the translator.

"Yes, please."

Julie turned to find the toolbox carrying the wrenches that would loosen the large bolts on the front of the case. She heard a gasp from Arlene, and looked back. The bolts were slowly turning, backing out of the threaded holes on their own. They dropped with a *clink* to the deck, and Julie and Henry—exchanging glances—lifted the heavy glass front from the case. Now there was nothing between them and the alien device.

To her surprise, Julie found the translator less overwhelming here, in a crate, than it had been in the ice cavern on Triton. And yet, as she stared at the revolving, iridescent and black spheres, she felt herself drawn, more than ever, by its presence. She felt a sudden *personal* connection that had been impossible in a large, frozen cavern where she had been encased in a heavy spacesuit. She had to remind herself to breathe. She stepped back slightly, so that they were all gathered in a semicircle in front of the translator.

"It's *different* in person," Arlene breathed. "It doesn't look solid, exactly, does it?"

Julie shook her head. "It seemed to mass about five hundred kilograms when we measured it in the cavern. But in flight, I was told, it barely registered any inertial mass at all. Is that still true?"

"That's right," said Henry. "We measured it three times for the mass calculations for the ship's acceleration."

Lamarr spoke finally, in a gravelly voice that only just betrayed uncertainty. "These are questions," he said, "to which we may find answers soon. Ms. Stone, does the artifact appear here as it did on Triton?"

"As far as I can tell." Without taking her eyes off the alien device, she said, "May we speak to you now?"

The answer was startlingly resonant. *"We sense a variety of thoughts. Could we know the identities of those who stand before us?"*

"Of course." Julie hesitated, wondering if she should introduce Lamarr first, or last. She decided to simply go in order, around the semicircle. "This is Lieutenant Henry Cohn, whose job is to help run things aboard the ship. Next is Dr. Keith Lamarr, Special Envoy of MINEXFO, the organization that is . . . currently responsible for your safe transport."

∗*And you answer to Dr. Lamarr?*∗

"Y—" she began, then realized that last question had come inside her head. /Yes,/ she said silently. /I answer to him./ Speaking aloud again, she introduced Arlene, then turned to include the cargo-hold workers, in the background.

Lamarr stepped forward as though to cut off the last introductions, but she pretended not to notice and finished naming

Jose and Ashmar. "I think Dr. Lamarr would like to speak to you directly. Is that all right?"

"Of course. Dr. Lamarr?"

Lamarr spoke in a gravelly voice. "Welcome to our ship, the *Park Avenue*. And greetings, on behalf of Humanity. I confess— there are many things we're hoping to ask you."

"We are eager to exchange knowledge," the translator said, its black and iridescent balls squirming hypnotically in the light of the holocams.

"Excellent!" Lamarr said, tapping his notepad. "May I proceed with some questions now?"

There was a momentary silence. Then: *"We will try to an- swer your questions. But first we must advise you—there is urgent business we must discuss."*

"Urgent business? What sort of business?"

The translator seemed to spin faster. *"Your homeworld is in danger. Grave danger. It is beyond your technology to pro- tect it—but if you will work with us, we can help. Will you do this?"*

Lamarr's expression of triumph vanished, replaced by aston- ishment and dismay.

The knot hit Julie's stomach again as she remembered the translator's words to her, months ago. And she found herself holding her breath again, waiting for the translator to explain itself at last.

17

AFTERSHOCKS

 In the two days since the encounter with the dying star, Bandicut and his companions on *The Long View/One Way Trip* had spent most of their time re- covering, sorting things out mentally and emotion- ally, and trying to understand what they were going to be doing next. It was clear that Jeaves didn't really know what to expect. From ✴Brightburn✴ they had learned—or they hoped

Deep had learned—the location of ✱Nick✱, the star that was in most immediate danger. But they still had no idea what to do when they got there.

Ik had talked little since the encounter, and Antares was visibly worried, sitting with him for extended periods. "I feel a great sadness in him," she murmured to Bandicut as she touched Ik's wrist. The three of them had been in the common room for an hour, but Bandicut, hungrily consuming a grilled cheese sandwich, was the only one eating. The Hraachee'an was staring down at the table, lost in either pain or meditation. If it weren't for the fact that he answered—briefly—when spoken to, Bandicut would have worried that he'd gone into some kind of autistic state. "I think he's trying to find his way through the star's trauma," Antares said. "I think it may have taken him back to his own star's death."

Bandicut stopped eating for a moment and gazed at his friend. "Is there anything we can do for him?"

Antares sighed softly. "I wish I knew."

✱

To Ik, the explosion of ✱Brightburn✱ had been like a flash of fire across the soul, an eruption of the past into the present. Hraachee'a, too, burned in his mind, his own sun incinerating his homeworld.

It was a mad, terrible dive into the exploding blue sun, urged on by two fiery gems in his head. He had no idea what the things were. But moments after his ship had tumbled through a debris cloud, he'd felt a sudden electric twinge in his temples. Removing his helmet, he tried to inspect for injury by studying his reflection on the inside of the cockpit canopy. He saw two glowing stones, one embedded on each side of his head. The stinging ceased, but when he rubbed and picked at them, he felt a wordless rebuke.

Shortly after, they began talking to him, telling him his only hope of escaping death was to fly his ship into the fury of the billowing sun. He thought he had lost his mind. It was terrible. *Terrible!* But he had little choice, since his ship was tumbling out of control. Had he seen other Hraachee'ans do the same?

Had they somehow survived? If so, where were they? Where was his world? *A glowing cinder now. Nothing but a cinder.*

And now another dying star. Did this one have planets? Did it have people, too? He thought a long time about those who might have lived on planets circling ✶Brightburn✶, and he wept for them.

Ik was aware of John Bandicut at his side, and Antares. He heard Bandicut saying, "Does anyone know where Li-Jared has gotten to?"

Without knowing why, Ik suddenly found his voice, and focus in his eyes. He clacked his mouth, once. "I believe, hrrm, that Li-Jared has gone to speak with the AI."

"Oh, hell," said Bandicut.

✶

Somewhere in the rafters of *The Long View,* in the interstices between the various dimensions of n-space that constituted the structure of the ship, Delilah the halo was resting and thinking . . . and *frustrated.* Frustrated and a little angry. They had just fled from a situation that might have brought useful knowledge, if they had just stayed a little longer. The matter-beings on this ship were too afraid of taking risks. What was the point of undertaking the mission, if they were going to flee every time things got a little dangerous?

Granted, matter-life was more vulnerable than she was. And she, in her halo-phase, was less able to slip through the fractional dimensions spying out information than she might have in her shadow-phase. Despite all that, she *knew* they could have spent more time with that star, and learned not just about the star but about the strange forces acting on it. And the more they knew about *that,* the better their chances of intelligently carrying out the mission. It was all embedded in the star's memories; Delilah could *feel* it. But she hadn't had time to do anything about it, before Jeaves and the AI decided to flee to safety out of deference to the matter-life.

So what now? After all that, the matter-life seemed fractured and disjointed, trying to put pieces of themselves back together. But the robots, now—they appeared to be on to something. Delilah was watching them with interest. And meanwhile, she was scanning forward along the path through n-space. There was something interesting ahead, though she couldn't tell yet exactly what. But surely there would come a chance to find out.

⋆

Li-Jared, picking his way through obscure corridors of the ship, could not stop muttering to himself as he walked. How much longer could they continue with Jeaves and the AI in control? It was ridiculous. Their present course seemed certain to lead to disaster. Look at what had happened. They'd nearly been toasted in the explosion of a star, and Ik still hadn't recovered. It looked as if it was up to him to find a way to wrest control of the mission from the AIs. He might not be ready for full mutiny yet, but he was damn well going to lay the groundwork in case it came to that.

Now, if he could just locate that input node again, the one Copernicus had led him to before. He hadn't been able to find either of the robots; they seemed totally absorbed in some kind of research with the ship's library, and never seemed available when he needed them.

Rounding a bend, Li-Jared came to a yellow-glowing, three-way intersection. This didn't look familiar at all. He looked right, left. He turned left. The passage began curving sharply, as though it were going to loop back to the other side of the intersection. *So where are we?* After following the curve for what felt like two full circles he arrived, not back at the intersection, but at the entrance to a chamber. *Control station?* Drawing a breath, he ducked through the entrance and peered around.

Well, it *looked* like a control station. He was in a small room, surrounded by surfaces that glimmered with patches of variously colored light. There were some recesses that resembled the recessed contacts he'd put his hands into, the last time he connected with the shipboard AI. Were they the same? He scratched his chest for a moment, before deciding that there was only one way to find out. He felt a moment of doubt, because he had told no one of his intentions.

The hell with it. He inserted his hands and felt an immediate, tingling surge of power. It took his breath away as he felt the AI draw close.

"Ship," he said.

Li-Jared, he heard, once more in the voice of his stones, slightly raised in pitch. It sounded a little different this time.

"This is the shipboard AI, isn't it?"

This is the scout craft AI. You are in the control center for Auxiliary Scout Module One.

"Oh."

We are prepared for flight. Do you have need to separate from the main ship?

"What? No! Moon and stars, *no!*" Li-Jared's hearts beat wildly in horror. "No separation. *Please.*" The AI acknowledged, and he slowly calmed down. This was very strange. He had encountered the scout from the outside on a previous exploration. How had he managed to enter it without even seeing the vessel? Finally he said, "I *don't* want to go anywhere. I need to talk to the main shipboard AI. Can you do that?"

One moment. Then, *Li-Jared.*

"Yes! Is this the ship?"

It is.

"Thank heaven!" he gasped.

How may we help?

"Do you remember you told me to come back if there was need, uh . . ." He stammered to a halt, because he had not prepared how to say this.

Need of what?

He struggled to control his out-of-synch heartbeats. "You said . . . you would consider changing the command structure—" he struggled to fit the words together "—if it was necessary to take control of the mission away from Jeaves." He rubbed his fingertips together nervously. "You said it might be possible. Well, I just want to know more about how that might happen. If it proves necessary. What the protocols are, and so on. Because I think Jeaves is going to get us all killed."

Please specify.

Li-Jared felt his hands spasm into fists. "In case you hadn't noticed, we just almost got caught in a star exploding."

Jeaves indicates that we have safely transitioned through the current emergency.

Li-Jared tried to control his temper. He forced his voice to go low. "Jeaves doesn't know what he's doing."

We are presenting that assertion to Jeaves, and requesting a response.

"Wait! I didn't mean—"

But Jeaves is not the only command authority. He shares authority with us, and with others.

Clouds above. Li-Jared's thoughts were starting to spin.

"Ship," he said, in a tone that he hoped would sound earnest and potentially commanding. "Does that shared authority include *us*?"

Please clarify: meaning of "us."

"I mean me. Ik. John Bandicut. Antares." He thought a moment. "I suppose I even mean Copernicus and Napoleon."

The status of the robots is in flux. The status of the others, the group we refer to as the Company, is advisory.

Li-Jared almost snarled, "Define 'advisory.' "

We take your expressed opinions into consideration.

"That's *it*? You take our opinions into *consideration*?" Li-Jared was having trouble standing still. "And the robots—are they even lower on the ladder?"

The robots are part of your Company. However, in addition, they hold subsidiary command authority.

Lightning fire from above. The robots had more say on this ship than *they* did! Li-Jared closed his eyes, his mind a blur of anger and exasperation. He forced himself to breathe, to think carefully. "Let me ask this, then. Could Copernicus or Napoleon order a course change, if they believed it was required by circumstances?"

They could input such an order for our review.

"And then you would—?"

Review it.

Li-Jared clamped his eyes shut. *Hardware bureaucrat!* It was hopeless. He was better off trying to work through Bandicut's robots. "I see," he said finally. His breath hissed out. "Thank you." *Bwang.* "Can you give me directions out of here?"

"Of course," said the AI. "Just follow the lighted arrows."

★

Bandicut and Antares were back on the bridge—Ik having returned to his quarters for meditation—when Napoleon trotted in with an unusually springy gait. He was followed a moment later by Copernicus, humming smoothly on his four wheels. "Lord Captain and Milady," Napoleon said, coming to a stop and bowing.

Bandicut rolled his eyes. "Nappy, please—"

The robot ignored him and continued. "Cap'n, we believe we have served you by assembling some potentially useful information regarding the Mindaru."

Bandicut glanced at Antares. "Regarding the what?"

"The *Mindaru.* We believe that is the real name of the adversary we are flying to meet."

/// The Mindaru! ///

/That name mean something to you?/

/// It was the name given by the Fffff'tink
to the invisible enemy that was afflicting them.
And I have a suspicion that it was
also the destroyer of my own homeworld. ///

Bandicut swallowed hard. /That's . . . alarming. So you're saying all of these legends Jeaves talked about really referred to one adversary? And it's one that seems to win all of its wars?/

/// Maybe. A lot of them, anyway. ///

Copernicus was speaking now. "We found some correlations in the library that cast light—"

"You mean the ship's library—which Jeaves should know by heart?" Bandicut interrupted with a glance at the Jeaves-holo.

"Yes," Copernicus answered. "But Jeaves and the library did not have the benefit of knowledge we gained on the Neri world, or even on Shipworld—with respect to the boojum, for example."

Bandicut shuddered at the reminder of the boojum, the bodiless, malicious intelligence they'd faced down on Shipworld. "Okay. The boojum I can see. What knowledge did we gain on the Neri world?"

"Cap'n, sir, we had contact with the Maw of the Abyss during

our passage through it, on our way off the Neri world," Copernicus said. "We picked up some information."

"Some information? And you never thought to mention this
before?"

"It did not seem relevant. It was more like random pieces of
history and writing from a fractured collection. But the Maw—"

"Uhhl," Antares broke in, "are you saying that the Maw of the
Abyss is part of this . . . *enemy* . . . we're fighting now?" She
stretched her arms wide as if to enclose the galaxy.

Napoleon flexed his knees for a moment, then cocked his
metal head before answering. "Not necessarily *part* of the enemy,
no. But it had some knowledge, not well organized, of a wide-
spread pattern of threats to inhabited worlds. It is a pattern that
fits well with similar patterns described in our ship's library. The
Maw called the force behind these threats the *Mindaru*. And
variations on that name appear repeatedly among widely separated legends mentioned in old historical writings in the library
here."

Bandicut cleared his throat. "It also seems to have appeared
in certain histories reported to *me* two minutes ago by Charli.
So I'd say we've got a pattern. And does the boojum fit in?"

Napoleon dipped his head. "The boojum, now—"

Napoleon was interrupted by Jeaves's sharp voice. "Excuse
me, but I think we'd all better take a look forward out the window." Jeaves rotated and pointed into the distance.

Antares strode into the viewspace, peering forward. "What's
happening to Deep?" she said, pointing to the dark cloud currently just visible against the glow of the growing Starmaker
Nebula.

Bandicut came alongside her, squinting hard. It looked like . . .
"Are there *two* dark clouds that look like Deep out there?"

/// Ah, so that's what it meant. ///

/That's what *what* meant?/

/// A feeling I didn't understand before.

A sense that we would be meeting another. ///

/Another *Deep?* Dear God. Is there a family of these things
out here? Did Deep divide?/

/// My sense was of something different.
Perhaps that's why I didn't understand. ///
"I do feel the presence of two beings out there now," Antares
said. "And I believe they are turning to meet us."

Does anyone else have something to share that they haven't
mentioned? Bandicut wondered. He drew a long, slow breath as
he awaited the newest arrival.

18

TRAVELING IN THE DARK

JEAVES SITUATIONAL DIARY: 384.15.7.8

I find myself unexpectedly at a decision point. With a new unknown approaching, the timing is particularly—how would the
humans who created me put it?—dicey.

Li-Jared twice has gone off to speak privately with the shipboard AI. He is clearly testing the waters for a change of command authority, by charging me with incompetence.

Perhaps I should have foreseen this.

And perhaps Li-Jared has a point.

What have my decisions yielded us so far?

Answer: Ik traumatized, a dying star left behind, limited knowledge gained, and members of the team in various stages of dissatisfaction.

Do I know what I'm doing? It's not entirely a rhetorical question.

I'm clear on the goal. To find the source of hypergrav disturbances, and put a stop to them—and to whatever other havoc is
involved in their creation. I'm clear on some of the steps that must
be taken. But perhaps I know less than I should know to continue
in command. Is it time to put the company in control?

Delilah will disagree. But Delilah's interpersonal skills make my
own look polished.

It has been my hope to gradually encourage in the company a
greater sense of ownership of the mission. With this new unknown

approaching, do I dare take the step of granting them greater autonomy?

Do I dare not?

✶

To Deeaab, the way ahead was unclear, a series of skips through murky realms of n-space. He understood well enough the general direction the dying star had indicated to reach N-ck-ck-ck-ck, but the path led through much of the body of Starmaker. The path was strewn with stars being born, the dust of stars not yet born, and ferocious winds of radiation from stars erupting in the full bloom of life. Deeaab had considerable facility in moving through space and time, but all that concentrated matter and energy obscured his view. And the periodic gravitational shock waves, like a kind of sickness, just made matters worse.

Often, he wished that another he knew might come to help: one whose origins were like his, who could shape energy just as he could shape time. He thought of her songs, the one who traveled as a dark cloud, whose haunting, reverberating name recalled the quality of dark that she loved. They had traveled together at times, but Deeaab did not know where Daarooaack was now, and had no way to call her.

He was therefore surprised when he heard Daarooaack's low, keening whistle out of nowhere, and felt her approach. How could she have known? Perhaps she had felt the throes of the star's disturbance in spacetime, or maybe Deeaab's own manipulations, and had come to investigate. Whatever the reason, Deeaab called joyfully across space, *"Daarooaack? Join me! Much is happening!"*

He sensed her darkness skidding across the star-cloud as she called back, *"Much that is strange! You are not alone."*

"New visitors," answered Deeaab. *"They have come to battle the sickness. Come and meet them . . ."*

Daarooaack answered with a rising note, circling to join him.

✶

Deep and his new companion were drawing close now. Bandicut waited quietly for Charli to connect with Charlene-echo, and beside him, Antares was poised to gather her own sense of the approaching clouds. Li-Jared had joined them on the bridge, but hadn't said much, except to gulp with surprise at the second approaching cloud.

Deep and the new one were flying a little apart from each other, approaching *The Long View/One Way Trip* from eleven o'clock and one o'clock respectively. Jeaves noted aloud that they appeared different from each other in electromagnetic readings, but he couldn't say what that meant.

/// *Perhaps it's time I made contact.* ///

Bandicut sat on the padded bench, steadying himself. /Go./

The transition this time felt smoother, with Charli following a now-familiar route into the mind of the entity. The quarx and Charlene-Deep began to speak. For a time it was indecipherable to Bandicut—like distant bell buoys clanging to each other on a foggy night. But gradually words began to emerge, and fragments of conversation drifted across . . .

/// *. . . know where we are going?* ///

<<< *Daarooaack will lead.*

Daarooaack can see paths that are obscure to us. >>>

/// *Daarooaack. What is Daarooaack?*

A part of you . . . of Deep? ///

/Daarooaack?/ Bandicut blinked. /Forget it. *Dark.* We're calling her Dark./

<<< *Yes? Dark, then.*

Dark is another . . . different . . .

can do things we cannot.

We . . . things Dark cannot. >>>

/// *But where did Dark come from?* ///

<<< *Like us . . . another place and time . . .*

place-time . . . >>>

/// *Universe?* ///

<<< *Yes.* >>>

/// *Both of you?*

From the same place? ///

There was a perceptible pause before Deep answered, in the quarx-echo's voice.

<<< *We think so, yes.* >>>

Bandicut felt the quarx's empathy. But while he was interested in what these clouds were and where they came from, right now he had other things on his mind. /Charli, can you find out where we're going, how we're supposed to find our way there?/

Charli responded smoothly:

/// Where will Dark lead us? ///
<<< Between ridges, and down rivers.
Dark can find the way. >>>
/// Are you saying that Dark can . . . ///
<<< See the paths through n-space, yes.
You could say it is a gift. >>>

The echo of Charlene reverberated softly, almost as though with laughter.

<<< And as to where . . .
we go to where stars are being born,
at the end of the river.
To where starlife is aflame.
To where the trouble lies.
We cannot defeat the sickness without going
to where the trouble lies. >>>

/Dark can get us to the Trapezium, is that what she's saying?/ Bandicut asked.

/// Dark's the one to follow, yes . . . ///

★

Antares, clearly puzzled by the new entity, wondered aloud just what Deep and Dark *were.* "They feel so similar in some ways— but in other ways feel very different."

"I can tell you this much," Jeaves said. "They seem to create, or maybe even are made of, moving quantum disturbances."

"Uhhlll . . ."

Charli spoke slowly.

/// I perhaps think I know what these clouds are.
I think they're diffuse singularities. ///

Startled, Bandicut turned his attention back inward. /Aren't singularities points, like in a black hole?/

/// That's how we ordinarily think of them.
But this is something different.
You know how a singularity can be thought of
as an opening in spacetime,

where the rules of physics cease? ///

Bandicut nodded, aware of the others in the room watching him.

/// Well, Deep and Dark say
they have come to this universe
from another. ///

/Another universe?/

/// Yes.
And whatever they were in their own universe,
here they took the form of
singularities distributed over measurable space.
That's why they can affect
spacetime in ways that might otherwise
seem unlikely. ///

Bandicut exhaled softly. /The whole thing seems plenty unlikely to me./

/// And yet it happens.
That's my belief, anyway. ///

<<< *Yes.* >>>

That last was a whisper from afar. Bandicut hadn't realized that Charlene-echo was still with them.

"John? *John,* have you gone away again?"

He brought his eyes back into focus. Antares was peering at him. "Uh," he managed.

Bwang. "Silence-fugue?"

Antares's hand was on his arm. "No, not silence-fugue. But he had that lost look on his face again. John, was it Charli?"

Bandicut nodded, searching for his voice. Finally he was able to say, "I was just . . . learning about our friends." He tried to convey what the quarx had just told him. The others looked puzzled. "It's not like I understand it exactly."

"Understand what?" Ik said, striding onto the bridge.

Bandicut turned, startled. "Ik! Are you all right?"

"I am fine," Ik said—a little shakily, Bandicut thought. "What have I missed?" The bony-faced Hraachee'an looked from one person to another with his deep-set eyes.

Bandicut opened his mouth and closed it.

"Perhaps," Jeaves interrupted, "I should start. I have been

thinking, it is time I turned some of the control of this mission over to the four of you."

This time everyone turned and opened their mouths. Li-Jared bonged softly. Bandicut stammered, searching for a reply. Finally he managed, "Do you mean you are asking our opinions?"

Jeaves regarded him in apparent thought. "I have always intended to do so. I have not always, I'm afraid, set you at ease in the *manner* in which I accept your input. I suspect I have seemed at times . . . *autocratic,* in my approach."

Bandicut coughed.

"I apologize. My preparation—my experiences leading up to meeting you—did not prepare me well for dealing with relationships. I used to be better at it. But I have had far more practice, of late, in working with other AIs. And with beings such as the haloes, with whom the dynamics are rather different." Jeaves inclined his holographic head slightly.

Bwang. "That all sounds wonderful and moving," said Li-Jared. "What, exactly, are you offering?"

"I am offering to step down, on a trial basis, from what we will for the sake of argument call *command,*" said the robot, "and function instead as your advisor and executive officer. The four of you will make the decisions, and I will help you carry them out."

"Rrrm, that sounds . . . well . . ." Ik rubbed the opposing thumbs of both hands together for a moment, studying them. Then he looked up. "What do you mean, *trial basis?*"

Jeaves shifted his gaze to take each of them in. "It means, if it doesn't work out—if, for example, you squabble among yourselves, because I have no basis on which to assign command to just one of you—or if you make decisions that are clearly antithetical to the mission—then my transfer of authority will expire. And the shipboard AI will once more recognize my command authority."

"So-o-o," Bandicut said, "it's more of a *pretend* change of authority. You're going to let us play-act, and see how you like our acting. And if we're good, we get to keep play-acting. Is that it?"

"No—no—you will make the decisions. And if it works out, you will stay in command. I really am hopeful that your command will work out better than . . . mine."

Bong. "I see," said Li-Jared. "Then—if we were to decide to abandon the mission and turn around and get out of here while we're still breathing, you would—what did you say—help us carry that out?"

"I—" Jeaves paused, and for a long moment, seemed as if he had frozen.

"Yes?" Li-Jared prompted.

Finally, Jeaves twitched. "I don't know," he said finally. "I really just don't know."

Li-Jared snorted and turned away, but Bandicut stared at the robot thoughtfully. He wondered just how serious Li-Jared was in his hypothetical proposal. "At least he's telling the truth," Antares said, speaking before Bandicut could think what to say. "Uhhl, Li-Jared, is that what you want to do? Abandon the mission?"

This time it was Li-Jared who took a long time to reply. He studied the robot out of the corner of his eye as he was thinking. "No," he said finally. "Not really. But I wanted to know if Tinman here would tell us the truth. I didn't believe for a second that he'd let us get away with something like that." He bowed slightly toward the robot. "Thank you for being honest."

Bandicut could have sworn he saw Jeaves sigh in relief.

"But there is something I want right now," Li-Jared continued.

"Yes?" asked the robot.

"Input controls to the AI, here on the bridge." Li-Jared pressed his mouth tightly closed, thinking. "And . . ."

"And flight controls," Bandicut interjected. "It's about time you taught us to fly this damn thing. Is that what you were thinking, Li-Jared?"

"That's it. Flying lessons. When do we start?"

★

The changes, Jeaves said, would take a little time; they should get some lunch. They did. And when they returned, they found the walls glowing red, and flashing violently like a malfunctioning lighting panel. Jeaves asked them to wait a moment. The red lights gradually faded. A soft, white light appeared in its place, and a panel of instruments slowly extruded from the wall on the left. Another panel extruded on the right. The left one, however, detached from the wall and floated slowly to the center of the bridge, where it came to rest, still floating, in front of the balcony viewspace.

"John Bandicut," said Ik. "Are those your flight controls? Can you fly with that?"

Bandicut stepped up to see. He peered over the instruments, which were largely incomprehensible. But in the center, there was a knobby thing like a joystick. He closed his hand over it. "I don't see why not. Jeaves? Are you giving the lessons?"

In answer, Delilah descended from the ceiling and circled around him, chiming.

∗

While Bandicut was learning to fly, trading off from time to time with Li-Jared, Antares kept a silent watch, senses alert, trying to gain some understanding of Dark, and of the region they were flying through. Dark and Deep were now leading the ship together, but while Deep stayed relatively close, Dark ranged out ahead, scanning the territory, and then circled back for a periodic rendezvous. Dark didn't seem to like to stay in one place, or even to move slowly. And, she liked to sing.

It sounded to Antares like three or four, or perhaps many more, songs being sung around her at once, echoing back from space like sounds from distant bodies. Antares felt herself in the center of something noisy and confusing, and perhaps wonderful, and perhaps perilous. Songs.

(Who is singing?)

(Who is here?)

Besides Dark, she felt the presence of Deep, and of her friends, but this wasn't any of them. *(Who is here?)* Was it really just Dark, whose strains echoed across the seeming emptiness of space? She didn't think so. There was a certain lyrical quality to the sounds, which she thought Deep and maybe Dark were enabling her to hear.

But were they cries? Cries for help? She was starting to hear, or imagine she heard, words.

Can we not ?

Do we feel ?

Do we know ?

together we

Torn
> **we are torn**
> > **Great wave coming**
> > > **cannot be stopped**

It came as a slow realization, that she was hearing the *stars,* in a confusing choir of voices. The voices were coming to her through Deep, and maybe Dark—but reverberating like widely separated voices echoing together in a ravine.

But she felt among them a sense of growing urgency.

*

For Delilah, change was certainly in the air. Jeaves's passing of control over to the organics was unsettling, not that she necessarily believed he meant it completely; but the AI was treating it that way, so she needed to, as well. The flying was different, too, with Dark scouting ahead to find the best n-space route to the heart of Starmaker, and Delilah herself teaching the organics to fly. While they were resting, though, she could focus on the closer details and keep her senses attuned to matters of interest, or danger, as they passed.

Indeed, there was something coming into range now, just over the horizon of the n-space lines, something she'd like to take a look at if it didn't mean deviating too much from their path. What *was* that? she wondered.

Distortions in the background patterns, almost like a lensing effect. Was there something out there they should know about? Better to know than not know.

Ever so gently, Delilah shifted their course to see.

19

A DEADLY DETOUR

Li-Jared was the first to notice that the ship seemed to be veering somewhat to the right. He stood, hands on hips, glaring at the view ahead. "Why are we—" *b-dangg* "—changing course?" he asked loudly, of no one in particular.

"Rrmm, what do you mean?" asked Ik.

"Take a look." Li-Jared pointed impatiently to the left of center. "We used to be headed straight for *that* star cluster. The bright clump. Now we're aimed for that dark section to the right. In fact, that looks just a little *weird* there, don't you think?" There were some faint arcs of light, almost as if some kind of gravitational lensing were occurring. He saw the confused look on Antares's face. "You know—light rays bending as they pass a strong gravity source?" He spun around. *"Jeaves?"*

"I'm here. No need to shout," the robot said, shimmering into place in front of Li-Jared.

"We're turning. Why are we turning?"

"I'm not sure, actually," Jeaves said. "Wait a moment."

Li-Jared waited, but not patiently. He grew even more agitated when Jeaves reported, "Delilah has diverted to investigate an anomaly. Something here is exerting an unexplained influence on the shape of local n-space. It may be of artificial origin."

That was enough to make Li-Jared have to close his eyes to keep them from bulging out of their sockets. He felt a low growl rising in his throat, and had to forcibly turn the growl into words. "She—" *rasp* "—diverted without *asking* us? To steer us *toward* something *artificial*? Which is *changing the shape of n-space*?" Without consciously intending to, he realized, he had begun bouncing up and down on the balls of his feet, with his hands twitching. Controlling his anger with effort, he turned to the others. "Did we approve of this? Were any of you asked if it was okay to do this?"

Ik looked disturbed and indignant, and Antares troubled. Bandicut had a faraway expression; but after a moment, he jerked his head and said, "No. And Charli tells me, Deep senses something there that reminds it of the thing it destroyed when we first met. The Mindaru, if that's what they're called."

"Rrrm," Ik said in a deep voice. "Is Deep going to neutralize this thing the way it did the other?"

It had better, if we're flying toward it, Li-Jared thought tightly.

"No," Bandicut said. "It's too big. Too powerful."

"Too powerf—" Li-Jared began, but choked on his words before he could get it all out. *Jeaves!*

Bandicut said it first, and he sounded angry. "Jeaves, you said you were giving us control over this mission! Did you mean it or not? Can you turn us and get us the hell away from that thing?"

Jeaves looked very busy for a few moments, then said softly, "I'm afraid I can't." Over his head, the halo darted back and forth, chiming in alarm. Then it streaked out through the wall.

Li-Jared started to advance on Jeaves before the robot added, "Delilah has released control; that's not it. The problem is, we appear to be caught in a field of some kind. And it is, unfortunately, drawing us toward the center of that disturbance. I am attempting to analyze . . ."

*

"It doesn't look to me like a force-field," Bandicut said a few minutes later, in puzzlement. "It's more like a strange landscape carved out of n-space, with ridges and valleys, and we just haven't figured out how to move over it yet."

Li-Jared was still clearly angry. "It exerts a force, and it has field lines that we're trapped in."

"However you want to describe it," Jeaves interrupted, "we're going to be getting a closer view, whether we want it or not. We might experiment with different angles of thrust, to see if we can maneuver across the field lines. But I recommend, for now, that we try not to generate unwanted attention."

"Do you believe the—what are they called?—Mindaru?—are creating this?" Ik asked.

"Until we learn more, your guess is as good as mine. Let's see if we can get a clearer view," Jeaves said. "I can adjust the display . . ."

The wisps of the distant, glowing nebula faded, giving way to a tracing of gossamer-thin lines that formed a pattern like grid lines on a topographical map. Overall, the lines revealed the shape of the nebula, including the curved gravity wells surrounding the stars, and the local n-space channel they had been following toward the nebula. To the right, but much closer, there was a coiled pattern of gravity lines, vaguely menacing in appearance. Near its center was a tiny fleck.

Bandicut asked, "Can you magnify that? Is that the source of the pull?"

"Yes, and yes," said Jeaves. "Let's see what we can do with that image. Of course, as it draws us closer, the image should become clearer."

"Wonderful."

The view crinkled and zoomed in sharply. An object only a little less black than space itself became visible. It had a complex, irregular shape, which seemed to change with a quick blur every few seconds. It had angles and spines, and whatever else it looked like, it was clearly artificial. Around it, the n-space gravitational lines spiraled in tightly, then became blurred close to the object.

"It would seem," said Jeaves, "that this object is causing extreme distortion to the local shape of n-space. In fact, it seems to be drawing n-space *toward* it."

Bandicut puzzled over that one for a moment. "You mean it's *moving space*? How? And what the hell is that *crinkling* I see out there?"

"I believe you're seeing the quantum movements—quick jumps—of spacetime," Jeaves explained.

"Losing me," Bandicut said.

"Imagine you were trying to get players to move down a long playing field," Jeaves said. "But the players didn't want to move. They might even be trying to move in the opposite direction. If you were clever, you could shrink the field at one end and expand it at the other—in small increments, a few times a second, when nobody was looking."

Bandicut blinked hard. "So that thing is moving space, and we're moving with it?"

"Closer and closer, yes. You've heard of *frame dragging*—a spinning black hole dragging the fabric of spacetime around with it as it spins? Well, this object is dragging the lines of space *inward,* as well as *around* it. Very hard to get out of."

As Jeaves spoke, Bandicut heard Charlene-echo saying through Charli,

<<< *The only time Deep has felt*
space shaped this way,
there has been at its heart
an agent of the enemy,
like the ones you call the Mindaru. >>>

Li-Jared, meanwhile, was saying, "So what do we do? We're not going to fly into its arms without a fight, are we?"

"Not if you ask *my* opinion," said Jeaves. "But it might not be aware of us yet. We should try to avoid notice until we decide on a course of action."

"If Deep can't help us, what about Dark?" Ik asked.

"Dark is out ahead, beyond communication range right now," Jeaves said. "Unless Deep . . . John, can you ask whether Deep can make contact for us?"

Bandicut muttered assent. But after asking Charli and Charlene-echo, he reported, "Deep believes Dark may come back soon—and may be able to pull us away. But we're off course. So Dark could have trouble finding us."

"Enough!" Li-Jared cried, hands in the air. "Time's wasting while we stand here talking! The hell with whether we're attracting attention—let's see if we can fly out of this thing before it's too late. John Bandicut, do you want to do it or shall I? You're the pilot, but if you don't want to, I will." Li-Jared strode forward as if to take the controls.

Bandicut already had his hand on the joystick. He lifted his chin toward the others. "Antares? Ik? All right, then. Let's try. Jeaves, give me some directions."

"Very well. Let's try some right angles and see if we can slip out . . ."

"Here we go," Bandicut said, squeezing the control. The ship began to turn. But when he applied thrust, there was no change to their course, at least not in the right direction. He tried another angle.

Ten minutes later, he stopped. They had exhausted every suggestion Jeaves could come up with for reversed or angled thrust, corkscrew maneuvers, and thrust *toward* the object. That last *did* move them faster toward the strange object, and Bandicut cut it off at once. But nothing seemed to help, and they were now visibly closer.

"Look at this," Jeaves said, opening a display window in the upper left corner of the viewspace. "It's a false-color enhancement. It shows the movement more clearly."

In the display, all of the n-space gridlines were showing a

slow, rippling movement toward the center. Combined with *The Long View*'s sideways movement, it produced a net inward spiral. "That's the wide view. Now watch," Jeaves said. The image zoomed in, revealing a small spaceship icon. "That's us." The gridlines around the spaceship were narrower and more focused, and moving faster, like water speeding up through a channel.

Bandicut cursed softly. "We're a swimmer caught in a riptide."

"Except this riptide is reacting to our attempts to escape," Jeaves said. "It's tightening around us."

Bandicut exhaled noisily. "Ideas, anyone?"

Antares ran her fingers back through her hair. "How single-minded do you suppose that thing is? Could we distract it?"

Li-Jared swung toward her, eyes bright. "How?"

"I'm not sure. Is there some way to—I don't know—shoot something out there to draw its attention away from us?"

Bwang. "You mean like a missile?"

"*Anything.* A missile, a blob of n-space." Antares waved her hands. "Can we create blobs of n-space?"

"I can think of nothing that would fit that description," Jeaves said. "Nor do we have missiles. The only thing I can think of is—"

"The scout!" Bandicut blurted. "We could launch the scout craft, couldn't we?"

"To what purpose?" asked Jeaves. "It doesn't have enough power to break free."

"No, but suppose we launch it, as if it were trying to escape. It might try any number of maneuvers. The point would be to get our friend out there to worry about it instead of us."

"We could even launch it *toward* the center object," Ik said. "Make it think we're coming after it. Distract it until Dark can come and pull us away."

"What," asked Li-Jared, "is going to make something as powerful as that object get so distracted by a little scout module?"

Bandicut heard a reply in his thoughts.

<<< *Possibly we could create
a time-distortion bubble around the scout.*

That might exaggerate its apparent size and power,
and serve to alert Dark at the same time. >>>

"That may be where Deep can help us," Bandicut said, relaying Charlene-echo's thoughts. He glanced nervously at the graphical display, which showed them drawing steadily inward toward the center object. "It's a long shot. But we have to act fast. Does anyone have a better idea?"

Bong. "I'm convinced," Li-Jared cried. "Let's do it! Before it's too late!"

"How soon could we launch?" Bandicut asked.

"The shipboard AI is preparing the craft now," Jeaves said. "But who is going to fly it? We can't operate it remotely. Even if we can get a comm channel open in this environment, it won't make it through the time distortion."

Bandicut's stomach took a sudden lurch. He'd just assumed it could be flown remotely. He hadn't thought about someone actually having to get aboard and fly the thing. There was only one person who was even remotely qualified.

Antares grabbed his arm and yanked him to face her. "John!" she said fiercely. "You aren't thinking—?" She tilted her head, eyes alight with fire. "This scout won't be coming back, will it?"

Bandicut's voice felt thick. "I don't know. I guess it's not very likely—but maybe not impossible."

Copernicus rolled into view. When had he come onto the bridge? "Milord, I will go. It might be possible for me to communicate with Napoleon, through one of our alternate comm systems."

"That could work," Napoleon said, stepping up behind his fellow robot. "It would be a risky mission for my friend. But he is stout and courageous, and it would be an honor for both of us to serve you in this way."

Bandicut felt a rush of contradictory emotions. Copernicus might indeed be a good candidate. And logically, it made far more sense than *his* going. And yet . . .

"We're—" *bwang* "—running out of time," Li-Jared said. "Either he flies or I do. You're needed to fly *The Long View*, Bandie."

"As your servant, I would be honored," Copernicus said.

Bandicut drew a sharp breath, fists knotted. "All right, Coppy," he murmured. "Get down to the scout. We'll work on a plan while you get ready. Call us when you're there." Smacking the robot firmly on the metal nose, he quickly turned back to the control panel.

/// John, you're bottling off some strong emotions.
Do you want me to—? ///

/Shut up? Yes. I don't have time for emotions . . . /

✳

Listening to the discussion, Delilah felt a shock of responsibility. Strange aliens or not, her actions had gotten them into this. Perhaps her actions should get them out.

Perhaps we'll die, regardless; but perhaps if we do we should die learning; learn what this thing is that sends its roots down into the many-dimensional layers; learn its thoughts; learn if it is the ancient killer; learn why it hates so . . .

Learning was good; learning was why they had come. And defeat might not be the only outcome.

The Mindaru might yield up its secrets.

But I must act now; act at once; they can manage this ship without me if necessary . . .

✳

"Copernicus, are you almost there?" Bandicut called, glancing into the display window at the lower left, where Jeaves had provided a view of the scout hangar.

"Almost, my captain," came the robot's reply.

In the display, Bandicut saw the scout suddenly glow yellow, and begin to vibrate. "Jeaves? What's happening?"

Jeaves was motionless for a moment. Then: "Delilah has taken the controls of the scout. She is launching . . ."

"Captain, I cannot gain entrance to the hangar," Copernicus called.

The glowing scout was now floating in the center of the hangar bay. It began to move. It passed through the far wall of the hangar and vanished. "Scout is away," Jeaves reported tonelessly, and changed the monitor window to show the scout accelerating away from the ship. It looked like a luminous oval, spinning off into space.

Bandicut started to protest, but the sound died in his throat.

Delilah was flying the scout. Was that bad? "Um, don't we need her here to help fly *this* ship?" he asked softly.

"We can manage," Jeaves said. "Delilah left this message . . ." A ringing chime sound filled the bridge for a few seconds, then faded. "She says she caused this detour, and she feels she should get us out of it. Besides, she has the best chance of any of us to gain useful information, and maybe even make it back."

Bandicut and the others stared at each other in astonishment. Copernicus squawked on the intercom, asking for instructions. "Well . . ." Bandicut said, then called to Copernicus, "you can go next time, Coppy."

"But—"

"Come back to the bridge."

"My friends," Jeaves said, "what direction do we want Delilah to fly in?"

"Her judgment is as good as ours, probably," Bandicut said. "It's not like we know." Even as he said it, he felt a query, across the divide bridged by the quarx:

<<< *May we go ahead and create the time bubble?* >>>
/Yes, I think so./

In the display, the dwindling image of the scout shimmered, blossomed slightly, then scooted with unexpected speed across the gridlines.

"So," Jeaves said. "Now we look for an opening, and hope Dark gets in here quickly enough to pull us out."

"Mm," Li-Jared said noncommittally. "That *was* our only auxiliary craft, yes?"

"Yes," answered the robot.

For a few moments, they stood looking at each other in silence. Then Jeaves said softly, "Well—it's not as if we could have gotten home in the thing anyway."

20

THE MINDBODY

 The chords of space rang insistently with overtones that suggested the presence of parasitic, biological lifeforms. One of the objects had become a blurred presence, neither quite here nor quite there, squirming in and out of the temporal present. That in itself was an oddity. The nature of the parasites was unknown, and therefore so was their purpose. The potential for trouble was clear, however. The Mindaru Mindbody presumed a high probability of interference. It was good that the web had pulled them in.

Not in quite a long time had the Mindbody encountered any biological lifeform, much less anything so odd. The closest was the life infesting the star-fires, which was not exactly biological. It might be useful to study this new form, or mixture of forms, to gain information against future encounters. The potential benefit needed to be weighed against the more conservative approach of destroying or encapsulating the specimens at once, before they could become a problem.

Nanoseconds passed, as the Mindbody pondered. Finally it decided: it would neutralize the intruders, yes, but first it would gather information.

It would begin by drawing them closer. It would peer inside. And it would learn just what it was that dared come near.

*

Antares had sensed the presence of Delilah on the dwindling scout craft, but the presence had blurred and vanished, behind the temporal bubble. So much for her hopes of monitoring Delilah's progress that way.

"It appears," Jeaves said, "that Delilah and the scout have attracted attention. The scout is turning toward the center object. That might be intentional on Delilah's part."

Antares felt a shiver of fear for Delilah. She tried to extend her senses more widely, in hopes of gleaning something about their nemesis ahead, but she found nothing.

Li-Jared, arms crossed, but looking as though he were about

to spring into motion, studied the display. "Should we light our engines and make a run?"

"Hrrm," said Ik. "Is not the idea to stay quiet until Dark finds us, and hope she can pull us out? Do we have any reason to think we're freer to move than before?"

We might not have much time, Antares thought. Delilah was falling inward fast. How long could she provide a diversion? Antares let her feelings search outward for signs of Deep and Dark. She sensed Deep nearby, tracking Delilah, but she couldn't locate Dark.

And then she did. She heard . . . it sounded like a *song,* somewhere in the distance. It reminded her strongly of something, though at first she couldn't decide what. After a moment, it came to her. It was like the sound of *goythen* trees in the wind, in a valley far off—their closely spaced trunks vibrating like the strands of an enormous string instrument. The memory lifted her momentarily back to the Thespi woods where she'd grown into her youth, where the mother-who-bore-her said her last farewells and passed Antares on to the teacher-mother, a less gentle and maybe less strong woman . . .

"Can you hear anything? Antares, can you feel anything?"

Antares started. What had triggered that sudden reverie? Ik was speaking to her. "Yes," she murmured, angling her head slightly. "Yes, I hear Dark. *Feel* Dark. It is moving this way. But—" she hesitated "—I can't tell what it's intending to do. Or even for certain if it's located us."

"Hrrm," Ik said, leaving Antares thoughtful and worried.

★

Bandicut had heard Antares's words with half his attention. He was trying to cut through the static of confusion that Charli was experiencing with Charlene/Deep. /Anything?/

> /// *The time-fusion is making it difficult*
> *I cannot quite tell what is happening. ///*

/Keep trying./

> /// *Do you mind if I rotate out of*
> *your dimensional plane for a few minutes? ///*

/Uh—I don't know. Is that okay to do?/

> /// *It may be uncomfortable. ///*

An instant after the quarx spoke, Bandicut felt a flutter, and then a sudden, haunting emptiness in his heart and stomach. /Charli?/

"The scout is actively maneuvering now, trying to change course," Jeaves said, bringing him back.

The small craft, visible only in a highly magnified display, was stretched out into a blur of light. It was swerving and maneuvering at high speed, too fast to follow; in fact, it was blurring around turns. It did not appear to be trying to escape, though; if anything, it was maneuvering to make a direct dive onto the central object.

"It's the time-shift," Li-Jared said. "Delilah's time is moving faster, so that's why she can maneuver so fast. But *what* is she trying to do?"

"Kamikaze mission?" Bandicut said suddenly, heart sinking.

"A what?" asked Antares.

Bandicut stared at the blurred image, unable to pull his gaze away. "Old Earth expression. A suicide dive on a target. I think that's what Delilah's doing. Trying to buy us time, maybe."

"Oh," Antares said, her voice dropping off.

Bandicut felt an unexpected lump in his throat. /Charli? Can you hear me? *Charli?*/

∗

Delilah found it strangely exhilarating to feel her own actions leap ahead far faster than the time-flow on the outside. *Temporary advantage; the field is beginning to adapt; it is changing more quickly than before. This could be to our advantage; may mean the adversary is paying more attention to me than to the ship; if so, this is good.*

One thing she could not do was pilot anywhere she wanted to. Certainly it was unlikely she could return to the ship. Therefore . . .

Don't go straight; make it follow you. But dive at it before you're through; pass it or glance off it or hammer it; try to make the jump over, you are not fractal for nothing; if you can get in, who knows what you can learn.

Was she about to commit suicide? She didn't expect the

scout ship to survive. She didn't expect to survive herself, in her present form.

But I have no intention of dying...

∗

Dark appeared at last, a faint shadow gliding across the field lines. It was not coming exactly *toward* them. If anything, it was veering to pursue the scout craft now shooting in a blur toward the central object. Was Dark going to help the wrong ship?

Antares sensed Bandicut gripping the control pedestal, wanting to reach out and change things. But he was as powerless as she was. Something had happened to Charli; Antares could sense no presence of the quarx, though she hadn't sensed a death, either.

Pushing that question out of her thoughts, she tried to focus on the distant scout. She could read nothing empathically, but the scout was now pulsing with rapid, strobelike bursts of energy. Was that something Delilah was doing on purpose? Or was the scout under attack? Antares strained to read . . . nothing.

The pulses of energy blurred into a long brushstroke of white light. John Bandicut drew a loud breath. "Does anyone have any idea—?"

Before he could finish his question, the image of the scout burst apart into a line of spattered droplets of light, spanning the spectrum from red to indigo. For an instant, Antares couldn't breathe, because she suddenly felt the distant touch of Delilah— and then, as suddenly, she felt it no longer. She felt as though Deep had stopped time right here in this ship. What had she just felt? *Fear. Hope. Determination.*

In a single heartbeat, time unfroze. All of the droplets of light that were the scout sprang inward and vanished into the object at the center of the field lines. A faint spray of light blossomed back out of the center, then faded to darkness. There was no other sign of the scout, or of Delilah. No sense in her mind, no nothing.

"Jeaves?" Bandicut said softly.

The robot was silent for a moment. Then: "I am checking all sensor bands. But I find nothing. I am afraid the scout, and Delilah, are gone."

Antares gave an involuntary cry, and she and the others stared at each other in shock. Shock at Delilah's sudden fate, and at the implications for them.

The silence was finally broken by Li-Jared, who, having already bonged in dismay, now quite practically said, "What now? Weren't we waiting for Dark to come pull us out of here?"

Bandicut answered in a gravelly voice. "We were. But I'm not sure what Dark is doing now." He pointed toward the graphical display. Having passed *The Long View,* Dark was circling around near where Delilah had met her end.

Soon, though, Dark turned sharply, apparently rounding back toward them. Copernicus—when had he gotten back?—said, "I believe Dark may be trying to map the layout of the field lines."

"*I* believe Dark may be trying to find a way to get us out," Jeaves said.

Bandicut shot Antares an inquiring glance. But she had no answer.

★

As Dark approached, the viewspace became shadowed. The ship suddenly shook—not with an impact, exactly, but with powerful vibrations. Bandicut staggered—they all did—and then the shadow swept away from the viewspace. It returned from another angle, and the bridge shook once more. "Dark seems to be trying to grapple us," Jeaves called out, "but he can't do it. I think the space around us is shifting too much."

"What about Deep? Where is Deep?" Bandicut asked, while under his breath he called, /Charli? Can you hear me? Charli, we need to know what's happening!/

"I'm not sure," Jeaves admitted. "I'm seeing a fluctuation near Dark; that *may* be Deep."

Bandicut stepped in front of the small control console and forced himself to breathe. /*Charli,* where the hell are you?/ And at that moment, he felt a sudden great whirlwind of vacuum around his ears. And an instant later, the quarx was back in his head. /Charli? *Jesus!*/

/// I'm here. I'm here. I've made contact.
Deep couldn't stop what was happening to Delilah.

Dark's been working on finding a way to get you out.
You're not going to like what she found. ///
Bandicut felt a great weight on his shoulders. /What am I not
going to like?/
Charli hesitated.
/// Dark can't pull us out. ///
Bandicut choked. /Can't—/
/// That's not the part I meant, though. ///
Bandicut practically exploded. /What could be worse than
that?/
/// There may be another way to get out. ///
Bandicut raised his hands in exclamation. /That's good./
/// Maybe. ///
He was aware of Antares staring at him, waiting for him to
communicate. He raised a finger. /I'm listening./
/// You need to fly toward the center.
Somewhere in that direction is the way out. ///
Bandicut opened his mouth to speak, but for a long time no
words came out.

★

The Mindbody was puzzled. After the parasitic lifeform had di-
vided into two, one part had continued as before, showing no
significant change, while the other part began moving across
the n-space web in that blurred, not-here, not-there way that
made it difficult to follow. It swelled in apparent energy, but at
the same time seemed to be losing its temporal anchor. The
Mindbody watched, wondering what it would do. It was com-
ing closer.
  And suddenly—for no apparent reason—the object flung
itself at the Mindbody. Was it attacking? Probing? Suffering a
malfunction?
  Whatever its intent, it broke apart like a comet diving on
a gas-giant planet. Its pieces physically struck the Mindbody's
outer carapace, many of them disintegrating. The remaining
pieces were swept up in the net and drawn in close for analy-
sis, but so far even the Mindaru logic-core at the Mindbody's
center had found nothing remarkable. Was that the end of it?

Many strands of the Mindbody thought it was, but the logic-core was not so sure. It felt an irritant, as if something remained that it couldn't account for.

Still, no need to occupy the entire Mindbody on this one puzzle. Several strands of mind could stay with it, and later encapsulate whatever survived. The rest of the Mindbody had a job to do.

The remaining invader vessel had extended a number of long-range sensor-fields. Perhaps these could be put to use—as carrier signals, input channels into the intelligence of the invading parasite.

It would not be a risk-free operation. But knowledge of both the vessel and the biological and how they worked could be extremely useful, not just to use against it, but for the possibility of adapting it into the Mindbody's own systems.

There was some risk, of course, that a counter-probe, using the same carrier signal, might find its way back into the Mindbody collective, or even the Mindaru core. To reduce the risk, the Mindbody set up protective layers along its own sensors. Then it reached out, searching for receptor points—and began to thread its way in.

✳

"Bad news," Bandicut finally managed to report. "Dark can't pull us out."

"Hrah?" Ik's face contorted, but not nearly as much as Li-Jared's. "Why not?"

"It's just what Jeaves was saying. Whatever that thing is, it's distorting n-space so much that Dark can't grab on to us."

Antares's gaze was nearly inscrutable. "So . . . did Delilah—?"

"Sacrifice herself in vain?" he asked. "Maybe not. Here's the other thing Charli told me. There may be a way out . . ."

Li-Jared's head weaved from side to side as Bandicut repeated Charli's report. "Fly *toward* the source of the trouble?" he asked, his voice incredulous. "Just where do you think—?"

Napoleon whirred. "Cap'n. Milord. This suggestion may have merit. But there are some issues about flying in this place that we need to discuss."

Bandicut scowled. "Issues?"

"Yes," Copernicus said, rolling forward. "Force and acceleration do not appear to function normally here."

Bandicut could feel his blood pressure rising. "Explain."

"It is difficult, milords and lady," Copernicus said. He rolled out into the viewspace, as though he were going to launch himself straight off into space. Then he stopped and raised a metal arm. It rose vertically from his side, then bent to point forward. "I believe it is necessary to steer *that* way"—he gestured slightly to the right of the dark central object, then swiveled his arm to the left and raised it forty-five degrees—"in order to go *that* way. It's not unlike a magnetic field, where forces get turned ninety degrees."

Ik rubbed his chest and squinted, saying nothing. "Of course!" Li-Jared said suddenly. "It's like a plasma jet coming out of an imploding star. Everything's at right angles to the magnetic field lines."

"Correct, if oversimplified," said Copernicus, swiveling to face them. "The point is that we cannot see the whole tangle of n-space pathways ahead of us. Charli suggests there may be exit points ahead. But they might only *seem* to be ahead."

"Why would they be toward the center of the attraction at all?" Bandicut asked, trying to control his exasperation.

"Ah," said Napoleon. "We think exit holes may have been created when our friend out there puckered n-space like a fabric. There may be an escape chute waiting for us. The only catch is, we don't know exactly where. But we think the puckers are most likely to occur near the stress. Possibly near the Mindaru object itself."

They all stared at the robots for a few moments. The facade of romance was gone. The metal creatures were completely serious.

"It'll be a little complicated," Copernicus said at last. "Because n-space is so warped here, it may be a very twisty path out. There could be up to nine-and-a-fraction spatial dimensions to steer through before we complete the route." As everyone gaped in dumbfounded silence, he added, "It's fractals all the way down, folks."

21

The Mindbody took its time, modulating the sensor beams to make its entry into the larger invader vessel. With a bit of experimentation, it determined the best frequency for penetration. The invader vessel was proceeding cautiously, which gave the Mindbody time to complete its testing.

The invader possessed a sophisticated machine intelligence of its own. That increased the risk, because it might fight back—but also the potential reward, if the Mindbody could subsume useful parts of the intelligence into itself. The Mindbody understood machine intelligences very well, and considered the chance worth taking.

The pathway into the other was not difficult, though it took a few redirects and false starts to find the way in. The spying threads established a beachhead in a maintenance subsection, and from there began to survey the surroundings. There was no immediate defensive action. The ship continued to move in a satisfactory arc toward the Mindbody's capture fields.

*

Napoleon swiveled his metal head to speak again. "Milord—or Cap'n, if I may—the flying ahead is going to be tricky, with many small corrections. Perhaps, if possible, you should consider jacking into the AI to help you do the job. Can Charli help you do that?"

Bandicut felt a dull pain as he pondered the possibility. How many times had he tried that, and how many times had it gone wrong? But Napoleon was probably right. /Charli?/

/// I'll try. ///

"Okay," Bandicut said to Napoleon. He turned to Li-Jared. "Can you be ready to step in and fly, if something goes wrong? Jeaves, have you set up those backup controls? Can Li-Jared use them if something happens to me, or to these controls?" He gave Li-Jared a questioning look and was answered by an emphatic nod.

"I am activating secondary controls in the common room

right now," Jeaves answered. "By the way, I'm starting to pick up some long-distance probing from the Mindaru object. Nothing I wouldn't expect. But it answers the question of whether Delilah successfully diverted its attention from us."

Bandicut grunted. "Then we'd better get moving. I'm jacking in now." /Ready, Charli?/ He squeezed the handles on the flight controls and felt the shipboard AI surround his mind like an inrushing tide.

✱

It was a shocking echo of the old days on Triton, and even before, when he piloted survey craft by mind-computer link, before the accident that crippled his neuros. He felt an exhilarating rush from the sudden fire-hose of connectivity to the intelligence system. That gave way to a surreal blankness. An instant later, he felt the emptiness buzzing with activity beneath the surface, like the perfect vacuum of space swarming with virtual particles. He clung dizzily to the control panel. /Help me in,/ he thought. /Show me the condition of the ship./

You are connected. How can we help you?

It was the voice of the AI. For a moment, his mind was filled to overflowing with questions, and ways he would like the AI to help him. Then, with Charli's help, he focused. /I am John Bandicut. I am taking the con, and I intend to fly the ship manually, from within the system. Can you provide me with real-time guidance?/

Yes, of course. Napoleon has briefed me on your needs. Would you prefer visual or auditory feedback, or both?

/Both, please. Can you provide me with a control interface?/

A variety of interfaces are possible. Any of them should provide several orders of magnitude faster response than the physical controls . . .

There was a sparkle in the darkness, and floating before him was a matrix of colored lights. He stared at it without comprehension, then said, /Next./ With another sparkle, the image was replaced by a visual replica of the physical control stick and control panel.

This might be more familiar, while eliminating the delay of your physical reactions.

Bandicut touched it tentatively with his thought. /Maybe. What else?/

The third image was a topographical map of the n-space web they were caught in, similar to the display on the bridge, with a simple spaceship icon. /Do I just push the icon the way I want it to go?/

Correct. Do you wish to—?

/Let me try it./ He reached out a virtual finger and placed it on the icon. /Ready when you are./

Napoleon suggests following this course. A glowing line in the display indicated the course. *Turn left forty-five degrees . . . now. Down ten degrees . . . now. . . .*

∗

Ik watched Bandicut turn stony-faced as he connected with the shipboard AI. Something about this sudden plan troubled Ik, though he wasn't sure why. Maybe it was the fact that if John was going to do all of the flying from within the AI, there was no way for the rest of them to know what was happening. And no way to step in if something went wrong. Li-Jared had left the bridge to stand by in the common lounge, but if things went badly amiss here, how much good could Li-Jared do from there?

Ik had been very quiet since the death of the star. Perhaps it was time for him to start pulling his weight. He stepped up beside Bandicut, and placing a hand on the control console, closed his eyes and focused on his voice-stones. /Can you connect me to the shipboard AI?/

∗*For what purpose?*∗

/To monitor what's happening with Bandie's connection. To make sure everything is all right./

His voice-stones seemed to consider that before answering, ∗*We will try. Keep your hand on the console, to improve the connection.*∗

Within a few moments, Ik felt a tingling in his temples . . .

∗

The Mindbody threads had the layout of the invader mapped in a short time, and decided they would go a little further. Rather than just observing, they would risk taking control over one or two subsections, and test the waters for a complete takeover. A good place to start could be the structural subsection they were hiding in now. If that seemed solid, they would test the active control system.

They had just observed a new control process connected to the biologicals; perhaps it would be worth testing there, to find its vulnerabilities. And now a second new one had just appeared. Perhaps the time for a takeover was closer than they had thought.

✳

Bandicut found the piloting interface to be quick and easy to master. But something was erratic about the way the AI interfaced with him, almost as if it were only giving him part-time attention, even though he was at the moment performing the most important function on the ship.

/Are you there? Are you with me?/ he asked, after several seconds had gone by with no directional information. The ship was now gliding on a path that looked as if it would take them straight to the Mindaru object at the center. That could be misleading, he knew, but it was alarming.

The AI finally answered, *I am here. My time is divided among many functions. What is your goal with these maneuvers?*

/What do you mean? Our goal is to escape. We are trying to find a path out of this—/ Bandicut stopped in midsentence, with a sudden reluctance to keep speaking. The AI knew as well as he did what their goal was. /Why are you asking that? Didn't Napoleon make it clear—?/ He stopped again, realizing he hadn't heard any direct communication from Napoleon in a while. Or for that matter: /Charli? Charli, you here?/

Instead of the quarx, he heard a buzzing—more a feeling than a sound. He looked around, and everything had changed. He suddenly felt as if he were in an enclosed space—silent, hot, vapors billowing, clinging to his skin. A blast of steam threatened his face. He felt an oppressive pressure. /What is this?/ In answer, he heard a remote, metallic banging, then silence. It reminded him of undersea sounds. Was he slipping into madness, or silence-fugue? No, this was different. He was rational. Scared, but rational. /Charli?/ He could no longer feel the quarx. Where had she gone?

The ship was still moving, yes?

Yes . . .

/Who is that? The AI?/

Yes . . .

/What direction are we moving?/

Where we must go.

He felt a chill, in spite of the steam. /Why aren't you giving me directions?/

There has been a change. We have suspended your control while a check is made for system corruption.

/System corruption? What kind of corruption? Why wasn't I informed?/

It was only just detected. Please wait while we perform some tests.

Bandicut wanted to protest, but he felt a strange cottony full-ness in his head. /Can't wait . . . / Steam continued to coil about him. /Char—/ He could not finish the call to Charlie, and he couldn't do anything to protest the AI's preemptive action. He was boxed in.

Enveloped by steam.

∗

Li-Jared was lost. How could this be? He was just going to the common room. But no sooner had he left the bridge than the corridor started to morph violently—lurching like an earth-quake and contracting and twisting. "Stop it!" he yelled, turning to charge back to the bridge. But the route to the bridge was closed off, and the glowing corridor now kinked and looped backward like a serpent.

Terrified, Li-Jared turned around. Twenty paces in the direc-tion that *had* been the way to the common room, the corridor now ended abruptly, in a doorway that looked out onto open space. Li-Jared staggered to a halt, hearts hammering. And then a side passage opened to reveal a normal-looking passageway. He dove that way and ran, not knowing in the least where he was going.

∗

Progress was encouraging. The Mindbody had probed deeply enough in the control system to interrupt the activities of one of the biologic elements. The biologic was a likely chaotic attractor, and it was vital to establish the ability to control it, or at least remove it from the control loop. It had not surrendered voluntarily, but the Mindbody had locked it out.

The Mindbody threads sent an imperative back to the Mindaru core: prepare a docking space in the salvage area. The invader was interesting enough to keep.

*

"Lady Antares—you seem ill at ease." Copernicus rolled forward.

The Thespi woman was touching John Bandicut's arm, and leaning to peer at his face, and the face of Ik, standing still as ice on Bandicut's other side. "Yes. We are no longer maneuvering. And look at John Bandicut." She reached up to touch his unresponsive face. "He looks unconscious. And now Ik. Copernicus, I fear something is wrong."

"We've missed three important turns," said Napoleon. "I am recalculating on the fly—but my instructions no longer seem to be reaching him."

"Can one of you norgs enter the system and see what is happening?" Antares asked.

"At once," Copernicus said. He spun and rolled to the nearest wall. *Provide hard jack at this location,* he requested of the system, speaking through a low-gain comm-link. A small, oval outlet appeared in the wall. *Monitor things out here,* he said to Napoleon.

Use caution, answered Napoleon. *But also speed.*

Of course, Copernicus thought. He remembered his experiences back on Shipworld, when there were dangerous AI conditions. And he remembered the steps he had taken to protect himself. He took several long microseconds right now to generate a condom protocol across the interface.

Then he jacked into the AI.

*

Bandicut, waiting for Charli's voice, was startled by the sudden presence of a robot nearby, somewhere among the clouds of vapor. /Napoleon, is that you?/

Copernicus, Cap'n. We lost contact with you. Are you unharmed?

/Well, I'm . . . not sure. The AI cut me out of the flying control loop—said it was investigating a possible corruption./

Corruption? Can you refrain from action for a few moments, while I investigate?

/I have no choice. The AI froze me out of the system./

Really. That is very strange. Cap'n, perhaps you should withdraw from your link while we sort this out. Copernicus's voice faded to a low rasp, as though he were hurrying away.

/Well, I don't—wait!/ Bandicut said, finding he could *not* pull out of the system. A block had dropped into place. From the AI? Or some automatic safety?

Copernicus returned. *John Bandicut—are you still there?*

/I can't move./

Copernicus faded, muttering incomprehensibly, into the distance. Bandicut heard a crackling sound, almost a clashing, like gates opening and slamming. A struggle? Copernicus and the AI at odds? He heard a squeal like quarreling squirrels; then Copernicus was back. *There is a malfunction in the system. I've severed piloting control from the AI and will be transferring it back to you. First I must get you out so you can fly by hand.*

/Copernicus, wait—/ Bandicut's mind was spinning. How could he be sure it was the AI that was malfunctioning and not Copernicus? He remembered all too clearly Copernicus's shaky episode in the midst of the boojum crisis on Shipworld. /Aren't we communicating through the AI?/

Through an isolated channel. Cap'n, I'm going to try to cut you loose. Get ready.

Bandicut felt a sudden clunk, like a knife blade dropping. Gasping for air, he found himself standing in his own body again, arms clutching the control console.

/// John! John, are you all right? ///

/Charli! Jesus! I think so. Where the hell were you? I couldn't find you the whole time I was in there./

/// I was protecting you.
At first I was just maintaining the link.
But something in the AI didn't seem right,
and it took all I had—///

The quarx was interrupted by Antares, on his right, shaking him and calling, "John!" On his left, Ik, standing very close, jerked his hands in the air and jumped back as if he'd been shocked. "Hrah!"

Bandicut breathed deeply, trying to pull himself together. He called to Copernicus, jacked into the wall. "Can you talk, Coppy?"

Napoleon answered for him. "He's busy figuring out what's wrong with the AI, Cap'n. We're on our own for the flying."

"Right." Bandicut glanced outside, where n-space was growing more and more savagely distorted. *Fractals all the way down.* "We're getting awfully close to that Mindaru thing. Have we missed any crucial maneuvers?"

"Yes," said Napoleon. "But I believe we can make up for them. I'm ready to feed you directions."

"Why don't *you* just fly it?"

"I'm not a pilot, Cap'n. You are. Now, with all respect, let's do some flying. And let's hope . . ."

"Hope what?"

Napoleon hesitated, as though drawing a breath. "Just hope. Ready now? Apply the n-vector thrust at half, turn three-zero degrees left and twenty-four down . . . *now,* Cap'n!"

Bandicut did as the robot asked. The ship rotated briskly on its axis, and began to slip across the n-space field lines.

★

The invader had some unexpected tricks, then. After infiltrating the vessel's intelligence core, the Mindbody suddenly found itself on the defensive, pursued by an altogether different intelligence. It seemed to have come out of nowhere, and it aggressively intervened against the actions of the Mindbody—first cutting the AI flight control, then releasing the bio-form from the cell the Mindbody had created around it. Finally it had begun a search-and-destroy mission, though it probably did not know what it was looking for.

So there were multiple, independent *intelligences aboard this vessel. The Mindbody had underestimated their adversary. The infiltrating threads were still in communication with their home logic-core, but in this fight, they were on their own.*

And they were being hunted.

*

Bandicut blinked sweat from his eyes and forced himself to relax his white-knuckle grip on the joystick knob. *That's no way to fly.* He gave the knob a more deliberate squeeze. It gave slightly and recontoured itself into a more comfortable shape.

"Cap'n, turn right eight-seven degrees *now*," Napoleon snapped. "And two-zero degrees down . . . *now.* Hold for six, five, four . . . ready to roll ninety degrees to the left . . ."

Bandicut followed Napoleon's instructions without hesitation. He had no idea what course they were following—some invisible thread through the labyrinthine n-space field of their adversary. The instructions were coming faster and faster. /Help me stay with it, if you can./

He could feel the quarx working to speed his coordination. As the robot's directions came in a continuous stream, his hand on the control twitched left, down, up, left, right, in tiny adjustments. The ship was slewing in perfect sync, following Napoleon's course. He realized he was holding his breath, and forced himself to breathe.

/// Napoleon knows what he's doing . . . ///

/Yah . . . / Breathe in, out, follow the mad course . . .

Soon he was scarcely thinking about what he was doing, just reacting to Napoleon's commands.

There was a sudden, loud outcry from Li-Jared. Bandicut responded slowly, turning his head to look around for the Karellian. But Li-Jared's voice was coming from a speaker, and there was panic in his voice. *"What are you doing to the ship?"*

"John Bandicut is flying it!" Ik roared. "What's wrong?"

"Everything's going crazy!" Li-Jared yelled. *"It's all changing! I can't get to the backup or the commons, and I can't get back to the bridge!"* The Karellian yelped, then shouted: *"The corridors are collapsing and twisting! I can't even tell where I am."*

"Jeaves!" Ik boomed. "Can you find out what's happening?"

Bandicut, trying not to be distracted, steered shakily as he heard Jeaves say, "The shipboard AI is changing the contours and layout of the ship. Copernicus is trying to find out why."

"What was that? Say again!" Bandicut was struggling to keep course changes separate in his mind from the rest.

Li-Jared called again, and his voice was a little steadier. *"If you can hear me, I'm in some kind of arm, sticking out into space. It's just a narrow little corridor, and I'm at the end of it. There's a door here with a window, and it just looks out into space . . . people, it's weird, I can see the nebula and . . . moon and stars, that thing we're falling into. You're steering around that, right?"* Bong. *"I feel as if this thing could fall off the ship any second . . ."*

"Li-Jared, you'd better get out of there!" Ik called. "We think the AI has gone crazy, and it's—"

"Left ninety degrees *now*, Cap'n! And down thirteen," Napoleon interrupted. "Then ready on thirty to the right . . . *now.*"

The Mindaru object loomed. "I thought we were going to steer clear of that thing."

"It'll be close. Hold this heading until I say break . . ."

✳

The explanation had become apparent to Copernicus, but not the solution. The shipboard AI was corrupted, all right— corrupted by an outside intruder. Copernicus had found data pathways open between the ship's long-range sensor arrays and some control kernels that had nothing to do with the sensors. And a quick scan of the data moving through those pathways suggested nothing resembling sensor data.

The ship was being invaded, and the invader had gained at least partial control over the shipboard AI. Copernicus had little doubt that the source of the invader was the same as the creator of the n-space web they were caught in.

Copernicus retreated briefly to consider. He had no time to lose, but every action had to count. He made his plans quickly.

He began with a lightning stroke to cut off the flow of data through the sensors. The stroke was successful, but only for an instant. The connection was remade with alarming speed, and he couldn't afford to be tied up keeping it severed. He was already doing that with the flight controls, and it was costing him. Worse, the invader was now aware of his presence. The best thing to do was keep moving, be a small target, and hold nothing back. He couldn't intervene everywhere the enemy was at work, but he could make its existence here as uncomfortable as possible. Live or die, succeed or fail, he would give it everything he had.

The AI, under Mindaru influence, was changing the ship's physical layout by the moment—threatening, in fact, to tear the ship apart. Copernicus focused on protecting the bridge and the vital propulsion and life-support systems. But as for the *shape* of the ship . . . its normal lozenge shape was already distorted, sprouting pseudopods, with holes opening in various places, like tears in stretched pizza dough. Li-Jared was caught in one of the extremities; now he was sprinting down the spindly hallway, trying to get to safety. The best Copernicus could do was to keep the section from splitting off into space. There was no safety to be found, not there, nor anywhere else on the ship.

And how was all this shapechanging affecting their flight? Copernicus had to talk to Napoleon.

✶

There was a buzzing at the edge of Napoleon's awareness. For a few microseconds, he let it go unanswered; he was busy with navigation. Finally he grabbed a picosecond to answer the other robot.

We've got an emergency, Copernicus reported. *The AI is infested with Mindaru programming. It's altering the shape of the ship faster than I can counter. Can you still fly?*

Napoleon spun through half a million navigational computations. *Yes,* he said at last. *We're practically in a controlled freefall right now. I don't think changes to the shape of the ship can affect our trajectory much. But we're going to need maneuvering capability when we reach the central object.*

Reach the central object? Copernicus asked sharply.

We're going right down the muzzle of that thing.

✶

"Hrah! Has the AI turned against us, then?" Ik asked.

Napoleon swiveled his head. "There's an infection. We're trying to clear it out."

"Infection!" Ik barked.

"And *I'm* trying to determine whether Copernicus himself has been compromised," Jeaves said.

"Rrrl, how do we know *you* have not been compromised?"

"You don't," Jeaves said. "That's why *you* four are making the decisions. I'll advise, as I can. I *believe* I am not infected, but that cannot be proved. Your robots may not be infected, but *that* cannot be proved. You must use your own judgment. You can't run the ship for long without the AI. Let's hope the damage can be localized and contained, and that the AI is robust enough to survive."

★

Bandicut could not escape the feeling that he was driving straight for a train wreck. Maybe they'd just auger in, and do as much damage as possible. He drew a ragged breath. "Napoleon, what's your plan for avoiding that thing?"

"Cap'n, look up at the map."

Bandicut did, and saw white filaments of field lines converging on the center. Between the filaments were darker regions, dull red shading to black. "Okay . . . what's it mean?"

"It's like a fishnet, Cap'n. The outer part drags you in. Near the center, all the strength is in those lines that are pulling it together. But there are narrow gaps. If we're fast we can dart through, right under its nose."

Bandicut blinked. "If we can keep the AI from tearing the ship apart, you mean."

"Yes."

"Is this supposed to encourage us?" Antares asked. "Because it's not."

"It is the only encouragement we have, Lady Antares. It is the only encouragement we have."

22

The center of the grid was growing rapidly. Bandicut had a firm grip on the joystick, waiting for the moment of breakaway.

The condition of the ship was another matter. An invisible battle was raging between the AI and Copernicus. The bridge quaked violently every few minutes, and for one instant, Bandicut felt the joystick turn to liquid in his grip, before firming up again. The rest of the ship appeared in the monitor views like a drunken amoeba, squirming and contorting madly. Li-Jared was still trying to fight his way to the backup controls.

"John Bandicut, we may have a problem," Napoleon said.

Bandicut blinked sweat out of his eyes. "Do tell."

"I'm not certain the bridge is still attached to the rest of the ship."

Bandicut's breath caught.

"I'm getting ambiguous readings, Cap'n. Some of them suggest we may have come apart. Have you heard from Li-Jared?"

Not in the last few minutes, he tried to say, but couldn't get out.

"He could tell us better. But here's what the visual sensors are showing . . ."

On the far right and left of the viewspace, monitor squares blinked on, displaying views of the ship—interior and exterior, the latter presumably viewed by a camera out on a strut somewhere. Bandicut's stomach churned. Portions of the ship were billowing out like tattered shirtsleeves. *"My God,"* he croaked. "Is the AI doing that? Or the n-space fluctuations?"

"Uncertain, Cap'n. However, I don't see any choice but to keep going."

Bandicut nodded, swallowing. "Jeaves, are you—?"

"I'm here," said Jeaves in a subdued voice. "Napoleon's right. Signals from the rest of the ship are sporadic, and I don't know if we've come apart or not. Copernicus's battle with the AI has burrowed down to a level I don't dare interfere with. But I'd say our lives are in your hands and Copernicus's now. Keep going and pray."

Bandicut grunted, and tightened his grip on the joystick.

✶

The object at the center of the grid began to take form. "Can you magnify that?" Ik asked Napoleon.

"Yes, but you may find it disturbing," the robot answered.

The image grew, becoming grainier. The object loomed out of the murky shadow like an enormous sea urchin in a deep-space cave, its spines waving treacherously. Bandicut thought he could see a cloud of small objects around it, like floating detritus. /Damn, but I don't want to go in there./

/// Who would?
But Napoleon says the faster we go in,
the better our chance of
a clean breakaway. ///

/Yah,/ Bandicut whispered. /Damn the torpedoes, full speed ahead./

/// Human expression? ///

/An appropriate one,/ Bandicut said, refocusing on the course. He tried to think like a fighter jock from an old war holo, maneuvering his shot-up plane through the stormy sky . . .

"Cap'n, we're on our final approach," said Napoleon. "We can expect our velocity to pick up. It's about to become challenging."

"The ship is holding," Jeaves reported in a distant voice. "By a whisker."

With that, the floor seemed to drop away. The ship plummeted in a broken zigzag, the fractal shape of the field blossoming outward. The ship, with Bandicut twitching the stick this way and that, followed the zigzag like a broken field runner, following sudden changes in the shape and dimension of n-space with hypnotic speed and instinctive movements. He was terrified the ship would get away from him, but it didn't.

The shroud of debris surrounding the adversary was taking on a sullen red glow. Bandicut also felt a buzz around the edge of his thoughts. /Do you feel that?/

/// Yes. But John—do you see what I see? ///

/What do you—?/ And then he saw it, in the glow. He saw what the debris objects were. For a moment, he could not draw a breath.

The objects were broken spaceships. They were approaching a graveyard of spacecraft, hulks of dead ships gathered in a drifting cloud around the spiny array that bristled from the Mindaru object. "Napoleon, do you see it?"

"Yes, Cap'n. We're going to have to steer around them."

The view zoomed in as Bandicut watched. He heard Antares gasp as she, too, realized what they were looking at. There were dozens of vessels—broken and burned and blown to pieces, floating in slow orbit. All wrecked by the Mindaru? Over what—millions of years? That was what it looked like. None showed any sign of life; some looked as if they were crumbling to dust . . .

"Cap'n, keep flying!"

Bandicut drew a sharp breath and jerked his attention away from the mesmerizing sight. They were going to pass very close to those wrecks.

/// John, is that our scout craft I see? ///

/I don't think so, do you think so?/ Bandicut squinted. He wasn't sure he would recognize the scout ship even if he saw it, but . . . *damn,* that did look like . . . pieces of what he remembered . . .

/// Caught, not destroyed.
At least not completely. ///

His breath went out in a rush. /Yeah./ He didn't even want to think about the implications of that. What if Delilah were still alive? He absolutely did not want to think about that. Because even if it were true, there was nothing they could do to help her. Nothing at all.

✳

Relentlessly, the AI kept trying to alter the shape of the ship, and just as relentlessly Copernicus worked to stop it. The robot had already come to the conclusion that there was only one way to *really* stop the AI, but knowing it and figuring out *how* were two different things. Plus, he would have to do it at exactly the right time, or the result would be disaster.

Still, the AI's resources were not infinite, especially since Copernicus had managed to close down seven of the subsystems. But the ship's structural integrity was seriously in question; if he did not take the difficult step, he might well be trying to save a ship that was literally pulling itself apart. That was as good a reason as any he could think of for throwing caution to the winds.

*

Li-Jared paused, panting. This was ridiculous—running in a dozen different directions, always with the same result. He was no nearer to the bridge than he had been before, or to the commons where the backup controls were. He had passed through the hangar section, where an empty docking bay had reminded him of the scout, now lost, with Delilah.

But what was this now? He had just stumbled into a chamber that was almost all window—in fact, it was a clear bubble on the surface of the ship. He was standing, practically, in open n-space. *Bong bong bong . . .*

He could barely breathe.

He tried to think. It couldn't *really* be a bubble, could it? He could see the hull of the ship, and it looked like tattered, disintegrating fabric. And in n-space itself, he could sort of see movement. Yes, bits of debris were floating past: pieces of wrecked spacecraft. Gasping, he tried to focus more clearly. N-space as it appeared here wasn't empty or entirely dark; there were visible striations, as though he were peering through multiple layers in the depths of a clear blue sea.

This was different, though. *We're in n-space. Are those dimensional layers? Is this a view of where we're going . . . or no, where we've been!* He forced himself to move closer and look out, though he was nearly sick with vertigo. Yes, he could see faint traceries of . . . well, it was almost like a wake, behind and a little overhead, as though they were descending through the strata as they moved forward. Whatever was creating this bubble must be translating information visually and—

What is that?

Something was moving out there, moving beneath the surface . . . not really a *surface,* but that was how it looked, like something following underwater . . .

Like something rising from the depths.

He opened his mouth and tried to speak, and he couldn't. Shaking, he leaned out even farther to get a better view—and yes, indeed, a quick and shimmering shape was pursuing them, and was definitely moving upward toward them. And that wasn't the only thing that terrified him.

The bubble he was standing in was starting to peel from the side of the ship. It was rocking and swaying, and he could see the place where it attached to the hull beginning to pull away. Very soon it would rip all the way to the door he had stumbled through. He was about to lose his escape route.

He glanced back at the thing in the depths and shouted, *"Ik—Bandicut—anybody—if you can hear me, there's something coming after us!"* Then he dove through the doorway, rolling as he made it back into the main body of the ship. He sprang up and looked back to see the opening silver over just as the bubble beyond ripped away.

Gasping, he tried to repeat his warning call. "Can anyone hear me?" He had to get back to the bridge! *"Napoleon! Copernicus!"*

Faintly, as though echoing down the rippling corridor, he heard the voice of Copernicus answering, *"Li-Jared, if you can hear me, follow my voice! I need your help!"*

You need mine? Li-Jared thought in astonishment. But he sprinted down the corridor toward the sound of the robot's voice.

✳

The quarx was trying to get Bandicut's attention, which didn't make him happy while he was trying to fly.

/// Charlene-echo seems to be saying,
they're sensing Delilah's presence somewhere
in the wreckage . . . ///

That took him a few moments to absorb. If it was true, that meant . . .

/// I don't know what it means, John. ///

/Is Antares sensing it?/

/// I don't know. ///

He didn't have time to think about it. They were speeding

through fractal-shaped patterns of n-space distortion, and he had to keep flying. Napoleon called out a warning, "Cap'n, in five seconds, break left hard and—"

"Break left and *what,* Napoleon?" No answer. He hazarded a glance sideways. *"Napoleon?"*

The robot's LEDs were flickering rapidly. Was he overloaded? Or worse, shorting out? Had the AI gotten to him? Oh shit. Five seconds . . .

Bandicut frantically scanned ahead, through the lines representing descending dimensions of n-space. There were some patches of darkness in the web, off to the left. Was that where Nappy wanted him to break? Through the gaps in the fishnet? *Five seconds . . .*

Drawing a deep breath, he selected a patch of darkness, counted one more second . . . and, blood pounding, steered hard over. The opening loomed abruptly.

At the same moment, in the other direction, the sullen red aura of the Mindaru object became brighter. The spiny structure grew visibly—and he felt a sharp tilt of the n-space field, trying to reel them back in toward the Mindaru object. For a moment, he couldn't tell whose strength was greater; he thought they might tumble straight back into the graveyard of ships between them and the Mindaru. A shattered alien hulk sailed by on the right, and another was dead ahead. Terrified, he cut harder to the left and swerved into the gap of darkness.

The draw of the n-space field suddenly diminished. The Mindaru and the wrecked ships drifted away to the right as *The Long View* dropped into the gap.

/By God,/ he said to Charli, and then shouted, "We're going to make it! We're going to make it!"

Ik and Antares began to answer, but Jeaves spoke first, urgently: "I'm making connections with several of these wrecked ships. Some of their intelligence systems are still active and full of information about the Mindaru. Can you keep us close to the ships just a little longer, while I download?"

Bandicut had no time to wonder at what Jeaves was saying. *No,* he couldn't keep the ship close to the graveyard, for God's sake! He was trying to get them *away,* and they were dropping like a stone now through the opening that Napoleon had found for them. At least he hoped it was the right opening to get them away from this web of power . . .

★

Li-Jared hurried through what he assumed was the power section. Clear walls flanked him on either side. Behind the walls, curtains of plasma glowed and moved in intermittent eruptions of turbulence. He shivered at the sensation of raw power surrounding him, and wondered what lethal radiations were pouring into him. But he had no time to worry about that.

"Copernicus!" he shouted at the top of his lungs.

"Yes, Li-Jared, yes—"

"Copernicus, you have to warn them! Something following!"

"Li-Jared, I can't hear you very well, but I need you to throw a switch for me!"

"Copernicus, did you hear me? There's—"

"Li-Jared, please run into the next section and look to your right for an opening."

Li-Jared was practically jumping out of his skin as he ran. "What are you talking—?" The floor was pitching up and down beneath his feet. He was about to have two simultaneous heart attacks. *"Copernicus?"*

"Do you see a narrow opening on your right? Can you slip through it?"

Crouching, Li-Jared found an opening half his height. A white light flickered from inside it. *"Hurry,"* Copernicus said. Li-Jared squeezed through. He felt a tingle as he slid through the opening. He was now in a very low chamber, whose walls appeared lined with platinum inlays and thin, translucent filigreed strips flickering with the white light.

Copernicus's voice now seemed to come from close by his ear. *"Look for switches or breakers. I'm going to make the cables visible . . ."*

The walls quivered, and suddenly opened to expose a cluster of fine silver and gold ribbons snaking along the walls above the platinum inlays. Li-Jared was stunned. Somehow, he hadn't expected a ship like this to have something as straightforward as *wiring*.

"I'm trying to make several of them visible," Copernicus said—and as he did so, three of them flickered. *"I can't shut them off remotely. The AI infection is controlling them. These are control circuits for changing the shape of the ship. Can you see if they lead to any sort of switches or junctions?"*

Li-Jared peered, breathless. "Not that I can see. Copernicus, can you hear me?"

"Now I can, yes."

"I don't know what this is about, but you've got to tell them on the bridge—"

"I have already passed that on, but if we don't cut these circuits, the ship will twist itself to pieces. Please look hard for switches. Anything."

"Anything? If we break these circuits the ship will stop tearing itself apart?"

"I hope so. It's the only—"

"Well, frickin' moon and stars, why didn't you say so?" Li-Jared leaped at the wall and grabbed the ribbons in his hands. He felt a pulsing throb, but not too much to bear. Bracing his feet against the wall, he yanked with all of his strength. The ribbons pulled loose from somewhere. With a burst of molten light, Li-Jared flew backward across the chamber, and a great shudder passed through the floor and walls. A quarter of the lights in the chamber went dark.

But the floor was no longer pitching.

★

"John Bandicut! Cap'n, pull up! Now!"

Bandicut blinked, twitched the joystick, and raised the nose of the ship just in time to keep from veering into another piece of space wreckage. After he was past it, he dropped the nose again. *I thought we were past this stuff.* And then he had time to react. "You're back! What happened?"

"I was attacked," said Napoleon. "If you hadn't distracted it by diving through that opening, I might still be fighting."

"That's great. But you know something? I'm not sure we've actually escaped anywhere." It seemed their dive through the gap in the web had only taken them in a detour around the largest cluster of ancient, disabled spacecraft. He could still see the ominous fire-glow of the Mindaru object away to the right. "Nappy, are we getting away from this thing or just circling around it?"

"Cap'n, I thought we were escaping. Now I'm not so sure. It seems this maze of dimensional shifts we're in is just bringing us back around again."

Bandicut hissed out a tight breath and veered past another piece of spaceship debris. Then he heard a sudden declaration from Charli:

/// I feel Delilah's presence.
It's very strong in this sector. ///

Bandicut knew he should be happy, but . . . /Charli, we can't stop and look for her, you know. Even if we had any clue how to do that. Can you communicate with her?/

/// Not so far.
But John, I'm picking up sensations of pain,
great pain from her encounter
with the Mindaru. ///

Antares was suddenly back at Bandicut's side. "John, what's happening?"

"I'm trying to fly. But Charli says she can feel Delilah."

"*Yes!* I can feel her, too! As if she's crying out. John, can she still be *alive*? Is she in that thing out there?"

"How the hell would *I* know? I don't know what kept her alive *here*. Napoleon, I have no idea where to go! Do you see a way out?"

"Working on it, Cap'n. I'm not really sure, either."

Charli wasn't finished talking about Delilah.

/// She feels alive right now.
But I'm getting all kinds of echoes:
sensations of being pulled in, colliding with something,
torn apart by an energy field, maybe.
Some of this happened a while ago.
I can't separate the replays from the present. ///

/You and Antares need to talk. I need to fly./ Jerking his head around, he said to Antares, "Can you grab my arm and talk to Charli? Napoleon, did you say something?"

"Cap'n, Copernicus reports something following us. Something Li-Jared spotted." As the robot spoke, a sudden jolt passed through the deck. "That would be Li-Jared, helping Copernicus regain control of the ship's structure."

Bandicut squinted up at the display that showed the ship's exterior; it appeared to be holding together. "What about the thing following? Any sign of it on the display?"

"Not yet . . ."

As they spoke, Bandicut could feel Antares's probing touch, and the quarx moving to speak to her. But then Jeaves suddenly spoke up, as though continuing a conversation with Napoleon. "Are you getting the download from the wrecked ships, Napoleon? This second one is responding very strongly, lots of information. Grab it fast, or we're going to lose it . . ."

Information from wrecked ships?

Bandicut's head was spinning. Napoleon seemed preoccupied with the information from dead ships, and Bandicut saw another gap, a place where he might slip through with the ship. He angled that way and snapped over . . .

★

Delilah, or what survived of her, somewhere in the matrix of the Mindbody's outer circles, was trying to call out to the struggling spaceship. She could see or at least track the spacecraft, see that it was caught in a maze of interdimensional pathways that would only lead it back, over and over, to the waiting Mindaru mind-complex. She could see the shadowy thing that was pursuing her people, and knew that if the ship got caught, there would be no escape, ever. But Delilah also saw a way out for the ship—if only she could communicate it to those on the ship.

But Delilah did not know how to make herself heard. The scout was shattered; and Delilah, broken and bruised, was no longer there in any case. She was now a part of the outer layers of the Mindaru, the Mindbody. A part of, but not a part of. Delilah did not fully grasp the situation; she felt confusing, over-lapping perceptions, like two different kinds of music overlaid and clashing. The Mindbody was not in control of her, not yet. But it had her isolated. And that isolation was what she needed to break.

What else was moving out there? Wrecked ships of bygone eras. Debris and detritus. Deep and Dark. *Deep and Dark . . .*

The two were indeed out there, spiraling around, almost as though they, too, were trying to find their way out of the Mindaru maze. Could they convey information to the ship? Could she make contact with them?

✴

Daarooaack felt repeatedly frustrated in her attempt to help the quick-ones through the maze. And now she couldn't quite find her own way through. What was it about this place, about the disturbing thing at its center that seemed bent on drawing everything to itself? Since the small vessel had been destroyed, and the main vessel of the quick-ones had begun moving evasively, Daarooaack had stopped trying to stay too close. She was wary of interfering.

But she felt something odd—a presence she thought had disappeared with the destruction of the smaller vessel. Was it still alive? She thought the being might be attempting to communicate. She called to Deeaab, and asked him to reach out and sense what she was feeling. Maybe Deeaab could understand.

✴

Bandicut felt a sudden tension from Charli. /What is it?/

/// I'm feeling something . . .
Delilah trying to communicate with Deep.
There's some translation difficulty . . .
Deep doesn't speak halo.
The stones are trying to help. ///

There was a sound like a rush of wind around Bandicut, and a tingling sensation in the wind, and in his wrists. He heard, (. . . follow . . . way out . . .) more rushing sounds (. . . nothing . . . no help . . . flee . . . flee . . .)

Bandicut was speechless for a few moments. And then, because Antares was looking at him questioningly, he blurted out what had just happened. "Delilah's alive, and trying to show us a way out. But I can't understand much of what she's saying, and I have no idea if it's genuine. Napoleon, are you picking up any of this?"

The robot clicked a few times. "Negative, Cap'n. If Delilah has instructions for you, I am unable to translate or evaluate them. I am sorry I cannot help. Recommend pitch up twenty degrees and left ten."

Antares said suddenly, "I can help." Bandicut blinked and looked at her. "*I can feel* Delilah trying to speak, to guide you. I may be able to sense what she's trying to say."

"Can you translate to flying directions?"

Antares stood close behind him, with a hand gripping his shoulder. Her breath sighed close to his ear: "I'm getting it—not in words, but a feeling—a tactile image. Down, and a little more to the left. More . . ." As Bandicut moved the stick cautiously, he could feel her body language. "Now ease to the right, and down a little more . . ."

Napoleon maintained silence for a few minutes, and then interrupted only to say in a strained voice, "Cap'n, we've picked up the pursuer now." A new display window opened at the bottom of the viewspace. A coil of light was spiraling out of the darkness. It was following them, and it was growing in size and brightness as they watched.

"*Damn.* What is it, Napoleon, can you tell?"

"Unknown, Cap'n. It seems very energetic. Probably dangerous."

"How long till it catches us?"

"At present speeds, three to four minutes."

Bandicut tightened his grip on the stick. *Three minutes . . .*

Antares's grip on his shoulder tightened, too. "Delilah thinks if we don't make any mistakes, we might be able to evade it. Ready to pitch up, and a hard right, not yet . . . *now.*"

Hard over. Following her pressure, Bandicut took the ship tightly through its turns, sweeping through an invisible course under the sullen glow of the distant Mindaru object, as the coiling snake of light pursued.

★

Li-Jared bounded through the twisted corridors, trying to make his way back to the bridge. He had picked himself up off the floor and gotten out of the little service chamber in time to see the squirming corridors stabilize. But though they'd stopped tearing themselves apart, they remained a twisted mess. He was running through a funhouse maze, with the occasional direction called to him by Copernicus, who otherwise seemed very busy.

At last, he turned a corner and realized he had found the arc that held their quarters and the commons. And down at the end of it should be . . .

He burst onto the bridge with a shout, and found his companions almost funereally quiet. Bandicut was hunched over the controls; Antares was hunched over Bandicut's shoulder; Ik was crouched, staring at the images of glowing adversaries in the viewspace. Ik's hands were trembling, and going repeatedly to the stones in his temples. "I'm back," Li-Jared said. And then he saw the fiery pursuer growing in the display window, and recognized it at once as the thing he had seen earlier, only closer now. A *lot* closer.

Falling into place between Ik and Napoleon, Li-Jared watched Bandicut's precise flying maneuvers and thanked the moon and stars that he was not the one flying.

∗

Bandicut was having trouble breathing—not because of the difficulty of the flying, but because through Antares he was feeling the distant presence of the doomed Delilah. He felt the sadness, and the loss, and the determination to see the ship safely away. And the fear that the Mindaru thing would get to them first.

He could almost visualize what they were trying to do now, threading the labyrinthine path through the Mindaru web. If they made each turn just so, through the twists of the dimensional layers of n-space, they might just make it out ahead of the pursuer. A roller-coasterlike turn was coming up, and at Antares's nudge, he dipped and climbed and banked over, flying almost wholly by images Antares channeled into his mind.

"Cap'n, I'm detecting Deep and Dark, at eleven o'clock high and low!" Napoleon called.

Bandicut glanced—and saw Deep at the lower position, streaking along something that looked like a dull red river. Bandicut was tempted to follow. But that was Deep's path, not theirs, and when the impulse came from Delilah and Antares, he swung away to the right. A glance backward showed the spiraling light still gaining on them.

"Cap'n, I'm reading a major power spike in the core section. We may be in danger of—"

In the middle of Napoleon's words, the viewspace went blank. The bridge lights dimmed. Bandicut felt the response in the joystick stiffen, then go dead. "Mokin' A. *Nappy!*"

For a heart-stopping moment, the only sound was the soft intake of Antares's breath, and Napoleon's ticking. At last the robot answered, "Cap'n."

"Yes!"

Tick tick. "Copernicus has shut down the AI."

★

Time stood still while Bandicut's heart hammered out of control. Finally he shouted, *"What do you mean, he shut down the AI?"*

A blue-green LED flickered on Napoleon's face in the near-darkness. "I'm sorry, Cap'n, but it was necessary to prevent the AI from destroying the ship. The AI was initiating a power overload."

Bandicut opened his mouth to speak, but a great vise around his chest kept him from saying anything. He looked down in the dim light, broken only by the emergency strips, and stared at his hand, still gripping the dead joystick.

"He stopped the overload, and . . . zeroed out the AI. Cap'n."

"We have no AI? No control?"

"He's hopeful he wiped out the infection," Napoleon said, in a rapid-fire voice. "He is working on reestablishing controls. Which do you require first—viewing, maneuvering, or life support?"

"View—*no! Maneuvering!* Then life support!" Bandicut forced himself to focus. "Antares, don't stop. We have to do this blind."

Antares had never let go of his shoulder or moved from her trancelike concentration. "Turn coming up," she whispered.

"Quickly, Napoleon, I need this control stick *working* . . ."

In about one second, Antares whispered in his thoughts.

"Hold . . . yes, Cap'n . . . *now.*"

Following the image in Antares's thoughts, he angled and twisted the joystick ever so slightly. Though the viewspace remained dark, he could see in his mind's eye the coiling serpent of the adversary, almost upon them—and then, directly before them, a steep drop like the universe's tallest roller coaster, into the narrow funnel of an n-spatial gravity well. He snapped the joystick forward and they pitched over and shot down the long raceway.

Though he could see it only through Antares's eyes, or perhaps Delilah's, he felt the spiraling arm of the enemy reach out for them—and *miss,* as the ship rocketed through the tiny opening in the Mindaru web. With an almost tangible *whoosh,* they shot through the funnel, and down a river of space and time. He had no idea where they were going, but he felt the Mindaru web vanish in the distance behind them, and he felt the connection with Delilah vanish, as well.

The last thing Bandicut heard before a dizzying twist of n-space fogged his awareness was Napoleon's voice, muttering, *"Oh shit . . ."*

23

THE TRANSLATOR SPEAKS

 Julie Stone listened with tangled emotions as the translator spoke. The four who gathered close to the artifact in *Park Avenue's* cargo bay mostly just listened. The two crewmen in back stood like statues. Lamarr had tried once or twice to interrupt. Julie felt a certain sympathy for his lack of success; she had questions to ask, too. But the director was now listening politely, though with an expression of skepticism.

The translator had been explaining John Bandicut's efforts to save the Earth.

". . . His claims might have seemed extraordinary. But John Bandicut intercepted a massive object on a collision course with Earth, and he saved your world from near-certain disaster. He gave up his life as he knew it to rescue your planet."

Julie's stomach clenched. There it was again—John Bandicut gave up his life *as he knew it?* What was that all about? John had slammed into a comet. How was that anything but "giving up his life," period?

John Bandicut is lost to your solar system, the stones said softly. *But his work may not be ended, nor is ours. There are more dangers. Dangers we must act on . . . *

Julie closed her eyes. /What do you mean, lost to our solar system?/ But the translator had moved on, explaining what it had been doing since its arrival on Triton.

". . . We joined Triton while it orbited the fifth planet of another star system, half a billion years ago. It was the world of the Rohengen. And it was their war, a war we tried to stop, that knocked Triton out of that orbit and into interstellar space. For eons we floated in the cold, before finding your sun and Neptune. As we watched the evolution of your solar system, we also watched the emergence of your civilization. We saw eras of life on your world destroyed by asteroid impact. We knew the same could happen to your species—whether by chance or by deliberate action. The latter most concerned us, though we had no clear evidence it had happened, even when we sent John Bandicut to intercept the comet."

"What do you mean, no clear evidence?" Lamarr growled, speaking for the first time in a while.

"We knew the comet's trajectory, but were unsure whether there was an intelligence guiding it. We're still unsure. But we know this—there is an agent in the solar system representing an unfriendly power, and it was observing. When the comet was eliminated, this agent began moving."

"What sort of agent are you talking about?" Lamarr asked. "How can you know all this, if you were buried in the ice on Triton?"

"While we were underground, we observed."

"It seems like that would be pretty difficult."

"We used slagged metals dispersed through the Triton crust to effect a large sensor antenna. That enabled us to monitor movement of objects throughout the solar system."

Lamarr cocked his head. "We have hundreds of instruments studying interplanetary space. Are you saying that this method detects things that we can't?"

The translator's black and iridescent balls whirled through one another. "You do not observe in the interstitial layers of *n-dimensional space, as we do.*" Lamarr's mouth opened, but he said nothing. Julie felt a moment of dizziness. *"In three-space, it would indeed be nearly impossible to see this object. We tracked it by certain signature ripples on the fabric of n-space. Even so, it only became visible when it initiated a course maneuver shortly after the comet was destroyed. That behavior alone was enough to identify it as almost certainly one of the Adversary."*

Lamarr glanced at Julie as though to ask, Did you know about this? "Adversary? Who or what is the Adversary?" He stood very still for a moment, as if the full meaning were just sinking in. "Are you saying we're involved in some interstellar—?"

"War, yes. A struggle that has been going on for more than a billion years. A struggle that has cost the lives of more than a thousand planetary civilizations."

Julie drew a sharp breath. She tried to absorb that, and found it impossible. "*What* are they, these—what did you call them?—the Adversary? Where are they from?"

Lamarr interjected, "And what would they want with us?"

"We do not know precisely where they are from. They are a collection of forces with their locus of power near the center of this galaxy. We have never pinpointed their exact place of origin."

Lamarr looked as if he were having trouble maintaining his facade of skepticism. The translator continued without pause.

"There is much to tell about the Adversary, and much more we do not yet know. Perhaps later we can discuss this in depth. But for now: we believe the Adversary is an artificial lifeform, and one that threatens organic worlds throughout the galaxy. It has destroyed or tried to destroy nearly three hundred worlds since your species reached its hunter-gatherer stage. The Adversary does not intend to allow your world to become a starfaring race—or to survive at all, for long."

Julie closed her eyes, trying to shut out a roaring in her ears. "Why?"

"The reasons are complex, and rooted in deep history. But they appear not to wish to share the galaxy with organic life."

"So—are you saying that John's sacrifice was wasted, because they're just going to kill us anyway?"

"No. John saved your world from imminent danger. It was a heroic deed, and your people owe him a great debt. But the victory was not permanent. It may never be permanent. There is always another danger. In this case, the new danger is following unusually quickly. And we must act quickly, to preserve John Bandicut's victory."

Lamarr was rubbing his right temple, as though he had a headache. When he spoke, his voice was low and careful. "This is all, to say the least, very disquieting. But you haven't shown us any evidence—or told us what you want us to do. Not meaning any offense—but how can we be sure that you're on our side, and this other thing isn't?" When the translator was silent, he went on, "I mean, what sort of a craft *is* this object? If it threatens Earth, it must be huge. If we knew where to look, would we see it?"

"As for the former question, only you can decide whether to trust us. As for the latter, it is an excellent question. Perhaps we can test it. We estimate the craft to be between one millimeter and one meter in diameter."

Julie rocked back as if a gust of wind had hit her. "Are you sure you converted our units right? That's tiny."

"The units are correct. You must not equate physical size with power."

Lamarr rubbed his thumbs and forefingers together nervously. "All right, I will grant you that power can come in small packages. Clearly you are a living example. But even the most powerful nuclear bomb couldn't come close to destroying a planet. So I don't understand—"

"Wait," Julie interjected. "Is it . . . some kind of black hole? A quantum black hole?"

"That description is imprecise. But the object does control a small singularity, and that is the peril."

"A singularity?" Lamarr was clearly struggling to absorb all this. "That makes it sound like—well, let me put it this way— what could *we* possibly do about it? Look at us!" He gestured around the cargo hold, a cramped compartment holding crates and mesh bags. "We don't exactly control cosmic forces here. Can *you?*"

"If we interpret your intended meaning correctly . . . yes, we believe we can intercept and neutralize the threat."

The intercom buzzed, and a voice called out. It was the ship's master, Captain Iacuzio. "Are you doing something down there that could be affecting our instruments on the bridge? According to my navigator, the radar and lidar transmitters have just come on by themselves. They're sending out pulses in frequencies they're not supposed to be capable of using. Do you know anything about that?"

Lamarr's eyebrows shot up. "Let me check, Captain." He asked the translator, "Did you hear that?"

"Yes. We are performing long-range scans to see if we can confirm certain information about the Adversary intruder. We will be finished shortly."

"Hmmh." Lamarr turned toward the intercom. "Captain, the translator is indeed making use of your instruments. It will be done shortly."

There was a pause long enough for someone to have assimilated that statement and perhaps sworn silently. "Come talk to me when you're finished down there, would you please?"

"Affirmative," Lamarr said. To the translator, he said, "Will you let me know when you're done?"

"We are done."

Lamarr acknowledged, rubbing his jaw. "Was that a demonstration of power? I think we all know that your powers greatly exceed our own. But our lives depend on that navigational equipment. We would appreciate it if you didn't—"

"Understood. We will need to use the equipment again tomorrow—with your permission."

"Do you mind explaining why?"

"To confirm course and velocity measurements on the object."

"You—" Lamarr caught himself. "Are you saying you just detected the object with our equipment?"

"That is correct."

Lamarr swung away, frowning, then swung back. He started to speak to the translator, then instead called to activate the intercom. "Captain Iacuzio? Are you free to come down here?"

★

Captain Iacuzio was a short, trim man in his late forties, with streaks of gray in his hair. He had bright blue eyes and a no-nonsense manner. "I'm here," he said, loping toward them with the ease of someone to whom low gravity was home. Henry made the introductions, and Iacuzio faced the translator. "I meet our guest at last," he said. "I'm honored." He smoothed his navy-blue uniform jacket. "Would someone be so kind as to brief me? Dr. Lamarr—when you called, it sounded urgent."

Lamarr summarized, then invited the translator to elaborate. This time the device wasted no time. *"We must intercept the object and destroy or neutralize it before it can cause harm to your planet."*

"Well, we on *this* ship don't have the capability to do that," Iacuzio said. "But we can pass on any information you give us to the authorities and the military. They'd be in a better position to take action."

The translator spun and twirled, as if it had been doing so forever. *"Your authorities cannot respond in time. And their ships would not be able to neutralize the threat."*

Lamarr made an *urk* of frustration. "They have nukes, and speed. If that's not enough, then I don't know what—"

"Your nuclear weapons would be ineffective against this foe."

As Lamarr stuttered in exasperation, Julie tried to hold back a rush of fear. She suddenly knew exactly what was coming. Damn. Oh, damn.

"The way to deal with this threat," the translator continued, *"is to divert this ship to intervene. In our scan a short time ago, we narrowed the position and likely orbit of the object. If we take another scan tomorrow, we can narrow it further. But we will have to move quickly to intercept it."*

Captain Iacuzio shook his head. "With *this* ship? That's impossible. Our orbit is planned down to the kilometer, and that's what we have fuel for, plus a modest reserve. I'm afraid this isn't a holo-thriller. We can't just change course and zip around the solar system."

"We are aware of your ship's ordinary limitations. We would not divert using your current methods of propulsion."

"What, then?" Iacuzio asked sharply. "Are you about to share a technological secret with us?"

"We would use spatial threading."

Julie closed her eyes. *Spatial threading.* John, in his transmissions from *Neptune Explorer,* had said he was threading space.

"The science is complex. But the procedure is quite safe, and the available energy more than sufficient."

The captain looked like a professor puzzled by a student's question. "I'm sorry, but what energy source were you thinking of? Our fusion drive doesn't—"

"We're not referring to your ship's fusion energy, but rather to quantum vacuum energy."

"Energy from the vacuum? We've been trying to do that for a century. Are you going to show us how?"

"Perhaps in time. Right now, our only concern is diverting this ship and intercepting the object."

"Ah." The captain clasped his hands together, clearly trying to decide just how to respond. He puffed out his cheeks and blew into his cupped hands. "Well. You know, it's not like I *want* to turn down a request from our first visitor from the stars—especially when you're trying to help us. But . . . as I'm sure you know, my first responsibility is to the safety of this ship and the fifty-four people aboard. Without understanding exactly what you're planning to do, I'd have a hard time agreeing to—well, pretty much anything that could put my ship in jeopardy."

"And what about the jeopardy to your homeworld?"

Iacuzio blinked hard. "I guess I don't know enough about that yet. We have only your statement. I'm not saying I don't believe you. But can't you give us more information?"

"If you will permit us to use your sensor equipment again tomorrow morning, we may be able to provide that evidence. Will you grant permission?"

"It didn't seem as though you required my permission last time."

"Apologies. We do prefer to work cooperatively."

"All right. But could you please give us advance warning, before you take over the grid?"

"Agreed."

Lamarr cleared his throat. "May we take the opportunity to confer with our headquarters and discuss this question among ourselves? We have a lot to think about."

"We will take no further action before the next measurements. But time for deliberations is short."

Lamarr turned. "First thing here tomorrow, Captain?"

"Oh-eight-hundred hours, everyone. And no one is to speak of this to the crew or passengers. Is that understood?"

✶

It was late—their conversation with the translator had begun after dinner and lasted for several hours—and Julie fervently wished she could go straight to sleep. But back in the cabin, in her bunk, she found her mind churning—and her roommate bursting with questions. She could hardly blame Arlene; all this time Arlene had been observing from the outside, and to suddenly be put in the presence of the translator, and then to hear it talk of doomsday machines roving the solar system . . .

Arlene seemed torn between disbelief and terror. She brushed her hair almost violently, shaking her head in agitation every few seconds. "Do you think it's as serious as the translator said?" she blurted finally. "That the whole human race is in danger? Isn't that . . . *extreme?*"

Julie laughed hollowly, staring up at the ceiling. "Extreme? Oh, yes. It certainly is. But that's not the question, is it?"

Arlene looked up at her with frightened eyes. "What do you mean?"

"The question is, is it true?"

Arlene murmured something inaudible and climbed into the bottom bunk. Then she said from below, "I suppose the question is not *just* is it true—but if it *is* true, is it really up to us to do something about it?" She breathed noisily for a few moments, before adding, "Oh dear."

"Oh dear," Julie said softly, "is precisely right. Let's get some sleep. Good night, Arlene." She switched off her reading light and closed her eyes. /Stones,/ she thought, /are you going to do to me what you did to John?/ When the stones did not answer immediately, she felt as if she might throw up. /You told me we were going to Earth. Was that a lie, or are you changing the agenda?/

We indicated we were ready for the journey. We did not specify Earth.

/You bastards. You lied to me!/

We gave incomplete information. For that we are sorry. But it was necessary.

Julie grunted silently. After a moment, she shivered. *What the hell am I doing here? Following in John's footsteps—but with a whole ship full of people? Dear God, will I ever see Earth again?* Exhaling stiffly, she forced herself to stop that line of thought. But immediately another thought appeared. /If we do this thing, will I see John again?/

There was no answer from the stones. She rolled over and tried to go to sleep. Impossible. She stared at the backs of her eyelids and thought about what she wanted to say to people back on Earth, if she ever got another chance. *Mom and Dad and Thomas.* Her parents and her brother would never understand, but she needed to say things, anyway. *And Dakota Bandicut: I never said it right to her.* She had sent a couple of holo-messages from Triton, but had never gotten across what she wanted to say—that she felt a special kinship with the girl even though they'd never met, that Dakota should be proud to bursting of her uncle. *And what about John? /Are you going to tell me? If he's alive, where is he?/*

Her stones were silent.

/Why won't you *tell* me, damn it?/

We don't know the answer.

Julie muttered a curse. Below her, Arlene was tossing, obviously still awake. Julie tried deep breathing, and found that all she could think about now was the thing that might be out there waiting to kill them. For the considerable time it took her to finally fall asleep, her thoughts were filled with images of caroming planetary bodies, tiny and large—and some of them intelligent and alive.

★

Breakfast was a quiet affair. Julie and Arlene ate in near-silence, joined halfway through by Henry. Lamarr came into the galley to pour a cup of coffee, but said little, beyond hustling everyone off to the cargo hold.

Captain Iacuzio was already there, gazing thoughtfully at the translator. He nodded briefly to the others, then said to the translator, "Would you care to tell them what you just told me?"

The translator spun rapidly. *"We have just completed our second set of measurements, and the data are alarming. The object has moved faster than anticipated. We believe we can now predict its intended course with a high degree of confidence. Please observe."*

A holo-image blinked on in front of the group. It depicted the solar system, with a pea-sized sun and tiny planets scattered about it in the plane of the ecliptic, their orbital paths traced by faint arcs of light. A winking spark was identified as the *Park Avenue,* partway across the gap between the orbits of Neptune and Uranus. A third of the way across the solar system, near the orbit of Saturn though far from the planet itself, was another spark. *"That is the object, currently crossing the orbit of your sixth planet, outbound from the sun."*

"If it's threatening Earth, why is it moving outbound?" Lamarr asked.

"We project its course as follows: we believe it is en route to intercept and deflect this comet—" the translator paused as yet another spark blinked, between the orbits of Uranus and Neptune *"—and this comet—"* and still another spark appeared, this time outside the orbit of Neptune *"—and possibly even this comet—"* outside Pluto's realm, and within hailing distance of the dwarf planet Eris . . .

Before the translator finished, no fewer than ten comets were blinking, the closest between Saturn and Uranus, and the farthest near the outer edge of the Kuiper Belt.

For a few heartbeats, they all stood in silent shock. Then the captain asked, "Why so many?"

"Redundancy. The more comets sent inbound, the greater the chance of a comet strike on the Earth. And the more comet strikes, the greater the chance of destroying humanity."

They stood in shock for an even longer time.

Finally Lamarr spoke. "That would be . . . devastating. Are you saying you can stop it from doing all that? With our ship?"

"If we can stop it near its present location—yes, we likely can stop it from doing all that. Afterward, if we are successful, we can resume your course—and if you wish, even speed you home more quickly."

Lamarr had trouble drawing a full breath. "How far away did you say this object was?"

"Approximately twenty astronomical units."

Julie calculated rapidly in her head. How far had John traveled in his headlong flight? Neptune was about forty AU out from the sun, and he'd made it all the way in past the sun and in a loop behind it. So what the translator was saying was plausible if you believed what John had done, and completely implausible otherwise. Lamarr was staring at the floor, scratching the back of his neck. Reassessing John's claims?

The captain cleared his throat. He was pressing a finger to a receiver in one ear. "Hold on, please. I sent a message to headquarters last night. We have an answer coming in right now." He nudged Henry toward a wall console. "Could you go read it to us, please?"

Henry scrolled up the text, then read aloud: *"We have reviewed your report. We cannot approve a mission change at this time. Please forward complete tracking data and all available information on the hypothetical object. In the meantime, observe all safe operational practices. Your first priority is to bring the translator safely to Earth. Huntington, John D., for MINEXFO Operations Command."* Henry turned. "That's all of it, sir."

Captain Iacuzio nodded slowly. "Thank you, Lieutenant Cohn." He drew a breath. "Well, there you have the official response. You'll note that they're very concerned for *your* safety." He nodded toward the translator.

The movements of its spheres became more agitated. *"We cannot overemphasize the urgency of this. The new measurements make it clear—we must change course, and soon."*

"Can't you transmit the information?" the captain asked. "You're asking for a big leap of faith here. To them, we're proposing to sacrifice a valuable ship, passengers and crew, and the first extraterrestrial visitor we've ever had, for the sake of a futile gesture."

One of the translator's globes flickered. *"We have transmitted the data. But it will not come in time. We do not ask that they approve of the mission, but that you approve of it. The time for hesitation is past."*

Captain Iacuzio's brow creased with thought; his eyes closed to slits. "You're asking me to disobey my orders and risk fifty-four souls, not counting yours."

"To save your home planet. Yes."

"But with no evidence! Either of the danger, or that this thing can be done!" The captain was finally letting his exasperation out.

Lamarr raised a calming hand, then spoke, but more softly than usual. "You must understand the captain's position. Can you not show us some proof?"

"Your sighting logs of Neptune Explorer *reveal that John Bandicut traveled much farther to intercept that comet, and in a similar time frame."*

"Well, we found those sightings . . . ambiguous. Still, given the stakes, *I* would have to say yes to your request. But tell me— why do you need our ship, or us, at all?"

The globes spun hypnotically. A dozen heartbeats passed. Then: *"For two reasons. One, we require a solid vessel for the spacetime manipulations we must perform. Two, we assist your world with one condition: we require the willing personal participation of at least one member of your civilization."*

Julie could not speak; her heart felt as if it had stopped. She had been expecting exactly these words. But expecting them was not the same as hearing them spoken.

Captain Iacuzio stepped forward. His face had changed; he had reached a decision. "I'm sorry," he said. "I would like to say yes, I really would. If it were just me, I'd do it in an instant. But I simply cannot put this ship and its passengers at such risk. Not without clearer proof. I'm very sorry."

"In that case, it may already be too late to save your home planet. We, too, are sorry."

Julie felt a stab in her heart. She met Arlene's devastated gaze for a moment, and Henry's—and finally even Lamarr's. She had not expected him to come around.

But it was the captain's voice she heard, saying softly, "The rest of you will speak of this to no one. We don't need a panic on our hands."

"But, Captain," Arlene began.

"But nothing." Iacuzio looked straight at the translator. "Surely there must be another way . . ."

24

INTO THE HEART OF STARMAKER

 The Long View had vanished through the hole in n-space, exactly as Delilah had intended. It was a rewarding feeling, one of the most satisfying in her hundreds of years of life as a *rengaalooo,* halo. And by far the most wrenching.

In the thing that mattered most, she had succeeded. She had helped her people escape from the dreadful grasp of the Mindaru. And that was good. It also filled her with grief—because *she* had not escaped, not even into death. Time for that had run out.

The Mindaru logic core, seeing what she'd done, had responded instantly. *The Long View* was gone, but the Mindaru had Delilah, and it snapped the confinement shut like a trap.

Delilah knew she was finished. No more was she *rengaalooo,* soon to metamorphose into *k-k-k-k-reee,* shadow-person. In that instant her future was gone.

There would be no escape into death. This was worse. Her memories began to wink out and reappear elsewhere, in the Mindbody complex. Her identity was not dying, but dissolving and becoming part of something large and terrible.

Deep, she thought with the last gasp of who she was, *will you remember our last contact? Hold on to what you have of me . . .*

✷

When Bandicut's head cleared from the wrenching twist of the n-space passage, the first thing he realized was that Delilah was gone from his thoughts. The second was that the viewspace had come on again, and *The Long View* had tumbled out of that strange, warped passage away from the Mindaru object, and was now sailing through clear, luminous n-space toward a cluster of four brilliant stars. And stretched behind and all around the cluster was the glorious, star-spangled cloud of the Starmaker Nebula.

Then a third thing came to him. He turned to Napoleon. "What did you mean when you said, 'Oh, shit!' a minute ago?"

Napoleon clicked a few times. "Apologies for the language, Cap'n, milord. But I was startled by a piece of information that came to me from one of the ships in the graveyard."

That made him blink. "A piece of information from a dead ship made you say, 'Oh, shit'?"

Napoleon clicked more rapidly. "Milord, I do apologize for the outburst. But I had just completed the translation. What the library of that ship was saying was that the Mindaru Complex is, as I suspected, a huge hive-mind of artificial intelligence."

"Yeah? So—"

"And it is implacably bent upon the elimination of all organic life from the galaxy."

"Uh—" *Shit.* Bandicut swallowed hard against the knot that suddenly threatened to rise up from his stomach. "*All* organic life? From the *galaxy?*"

"Yes, um—Cap'n."

"But *why?*"

"No explanation was offered. I have some speculations on the subject, but I think perhaps that should wait, if you don't mind. Right now, if we don't finish getting the AI restored, we could be in worse trouble than we just got out of."

Jarred, Bandicut remembered the fourth thing: Copernicus had shut down the AI. His companions were all staring at him, having just heard what Napoleon had said. Did they think he had knowledge that would get them out of this? "Nappy, uh—what do we have to do to get the AI running? I thought when we got the view back here, that meant—"

"It meant Copernicus restored that particular function, Cap'n. The AI is still down, and Copernicus and I are handling the housekeeping tasks." Napoleon gestured to Copernicus, still plugged into the far wall.

Bwang. "Where is Jeaves?" Li-Jared asked suddenly, pacing. "He vanished when the AI went down."

"Actually, he switched off even before that," Napoleon said. "He was coming under attack and was in danger of being corrupted by the Mindaru, so he sealed off and went into safe mode. He doesn't have the same defenses we have, and he had no time to explain."

"Oh," Bandicut said, not sure whether to be glad or worried.

The bridge lights abruptly dimmed, then brightened. A few seconds later, they did it again.

"Are you doing that, Napoleon?" Bandicut asked. "Or Coppy?" Copernicus was flickering, but he hadn't spoken.

"Cap'n—" Napoleon raised one mechanical finger "—it's Copernicus, trying to reboot the AI. He says . . . he's tried nine times with various parameters, and it hasn't worked."

Bandicut shivered. Without the AI, they were as good as dead. They couldn't run the ship for long without it—and even if they could, there was no way they could complete their mission, or get home. The only question was which would kill them first, a fatal malfunction or the Mindaru?

Napoleon cocked his head as though listening. "The problem seems to be that only a portion of the AI's physical core is working. Apparently the attack damaged some of the underlying strata. Copernicus is now developing an alternate approach . . ."

Bandicut found himself suddenly thinking of all the ways these robots had changed and grown since they'd started this strange journey with him. He gazed at the horizontal can on wheels that was Copernicus and wondered, with some awe, what was going on inside his metal shell. Antares stepped close and squeezed his arm.

"We'll know more shortly," said Napoleon. Before Bandicut

could ask him to elaborate, the robot added, "I think it's working . . ."

The lights on the bridge flickered again, and the holo-views blinked out, then recomposed themselves. The next voice Bandicut heard was Copernicus's. But it came, not from the robot's own speakers, but from the bridge speakers—and it sounded flatter and more somber than Bandicut remembered. "Captain and crew, milady and lords, the AI has been reconstituted. It appears to be functional, and in control of the ship. However, you may still call me Copernicus, if you prefer . . ."

It took everyone a few seconds to react to that. Charli spoke first:

/// John, he's joined himself to the AI. ///

/What's new about that? He's been helping out all along./

/// Not just helping out. He's actually—///

"I've melded myself with the shipboard AI," Copernicus continued. "Too many components were damaged; I couldn't fix them. But I could replace them . . . with myself."

Bandicut was shaking his head now. "This is too—do you mean you copied parts of yourself into the ship?"

"Negative, Cap'n. There was a need for active control, without delay—and the existing hardware would not have served. The part of the AI that was still working is now part of me, and is mostly in my hardware. I believe it may have to be a permanent arrangement, Cap'n. But it was necessary."

Bandicut fought back a rush of dizziness. "Am I—?" Was he losing Copernicus? "Then you're not . . . you mean you're a permanent part of the ship, now?"

"Yes, Cap'n, I think so. I'm still me. But I'm something else now, too."

Li-Jared strode toward the robot. *Bong-g.* "Then you're . . ." He hesitated, uncharacteristically at a loss for words. His head weaved from side to side for a moment, as though he were trying to triangulate on the robot. "Are you running the ship now? Can you hold it together?"

"And," said Bandicut, "did you get rid of the intruder? The Mindaru?"

"I'm fairly sure that I can, and that I did," Copernicus said, still speaking from the walls. "When I shut down the AI, I isolated and zeroed out a lot of memory space. Of course, we must all remain vigilant . . ."

"Coppy, you've—" Bandicut's voice caught as he interrupted the robot, and he could only finish his thought silently: *You've sacrificed your identity . . .*

/// *To save us. Yes.* ///

Bandicut swallowed hard, nodding to Charli. Beside him, he could feel Antares echoing his sadness. And Ik seemed puzzled, perhaps not entirely sure what to think or feel. "Well . . . *thank* you, Coppy. I guess, while you're getting the feel of the ship, maybe the rest of us had better figure out what exactly we're hoping to do next . . ."

✶

It was only a little later that Jeaves reappeared, as a small, still holo hovering in the air. He reported that the internal realm seemed safe again. "I apologize for leaving so suddenly," he said. "But I thought you'd rather have me absent than infected by the Mindaru."

"Hrrm, yes," said Ik.

Li-Jared made a twanging sound. "And are you?"

"What?" Jeaves asked.

"Infected by the Mindaru."

"I believe I am free of infection," Jeaves said without expression. "I have asked Copernicus to run a scan."

Li-Jared shot an anxious glance at Copernicus.

"I believe he is free, insofar as one can tell," the robot said. "I can't spare the bandwidth to give him a full-motion holo-presence right now. Forgive me, but . . . shouldn't we be looking at what's ahead of us? Our escape from the Mindaru trap moved us a good distance toward our destination, and I think we can see some pretty interesting features in front of us now."

Bandicut squinted forward. They were indeed flying through a spectacular region, a volume of luminous space walled by distant gaseous clouds. On the far side, the diamond-shaped group of four blazing stars beckoned them forward . . . or perhaps guarded the next passage, depending on how one chose to view it.

Copernicus continued, "As you can see, we are in a region of extreme ultraviolet and X-ray activity. We are crossing a large bubble, essentially a cavern of open space that has been hollowed out of the nebula—burned away by the intense radiation from the four large stars ahead."

/// I believe this is the region
which your astronomers call the Trapezium,
at the heart of the Orion Nebula.
Is it not? ///

Bandicut cocked his head, studying the four stars. /I think so. The angles are different, so it's hard to be sure./ "Napoleon, that is the Trapezium we're flying toward, right?"

Napoleon bobbed his head. "I believe so, milord. We're coming into the nebula from behind, so to speak. But after correcting for that, this cluster seems to match well with Earth-based star charts for the Trapezium."

"It's certainly energetic."

"Under normal circumstances, I would say it is *dangerously* energetic," Copernicus said, a hint of warning in his voice.

At that moment, Ik slapped his hands to his temples and cried out in pain. *"Hrahhh!"* He lunged forward toward the viewspace, then suddenly dropped to a crouch, groaning. The others ran to him. *"S-stones!"* he managed to cry, before choking to silence. He kept his hands clamped over his temples, as if holding his head together. His face was contorted by pain, his eyes drawn together.

"Let Antares help him," Bandicut said urgently, restraining Li-Jared, whose eyes were focused brightly on his friend.

Antares already had one hand on Ik's arm and another on his shoulder, her eyes shut, concentrating. After several seconds, she said, "He's in pain, but I think it's easing. Something in his knowing-stones, I can't tell what." Speaking to Ik, she said softly, "Can you tell us what's wrong?"

Very slowly, Ik raised his head. "Rrrmmmm," he gasped with obvious effort. He lowered his hands cautiously. "It is . . . better. I am . . . sorry, it . . ." He paused, struggling to breathe. "A struggle. Something in my stones, trying to express itself. Not sure what."

Li-Jared leaned close. "My friend, was it trying to hurt *you*?"

"I . . . don't think so." Ik sighed. "But it . . . I think perhaps the passage near that sun, and—" he looked up, catching Antares's gaze "—and the *death* of the sun—and then this Mindaru thing we just went through . . ."

"What, Ik?" Bandicut asked. "What did those things do?"

"Not sure. Hrah. Injured, maybe. Damaged." Ik shook his head, as if to clear the remaining pain. With his long fingers, he massaged the area around his stones. "I think—they were fighting to clear these things." He breathed slowly and softly for a minute, until his face returned to normal. "I believe I am . . . able to function now."

Bwang. "Well, that's good," Li-Jared said. "Because we need you functioning, my friend."

Before Ik could respond, another voice filled the bridge, this one reverberating like a series of timpani. *"I-I-I wassss afrrraid-d-d-d youuu had beeeeen lossssst-t-t!"*

Bandicut nearly jumped out of his skin. "Ed?" he called. "Ed—is that you?" He swung from side to side, searching.

"There!" said Antares, pointing to the ceiling.

The hypercone was almost directly over his head, like a hanging, transparent stalactite. It was vibrating visibly, and glowing with a pale green light that pulsed as it vibrated. Bandicut reached up, felt a pronounced tingling in his fingers, as though they were encountering an electrical field, and stopped short of touching the being. "Are you okay, Ed?"

"Pleasssse . . . c-c-c-can you stop-p-p the ins-s-s-tability in that-t-t star-r-r?"

Bandicut felt his breath go out in a rush. He opened his hands as if seeking answers. "We're going to try, Ed. If we can figure out which—and how—"

Before he could stammer any further, Ik interrupted him by howling, *"Hrahh-luu-luu-luu! It will be a—"* rasp *"—hypernova! That is what it is doing!"* Ik sprang up from his crouch, snapped to attention, and pointed straight ahead. "That way! If we keep going, we will find it. The Mindaru *hypernova!"* Then he clamped his hands to his temples again, reeling in pain.

Antares was back at his side instantly. Bandicut pushed forward to join her. *"Hypernova!* How does he know that? Can you find out, Antares?" Bandicut's voice was shaking as he spoke. If they were flying into the teeth of a hypernova . . .

"Yessss. It-t-t will-l-l destroy-y-y my homeworld-d-d."

Bandicut glanced back at Ed. "Yours and a lot of others, if Ik's right." He leaned to murmur to Antares. "It's really important that you find out why he said that, and how he knows."

"I will try," she promised.

Ik was grimacing, much as before. But when Antares voiced the question, Ik turned his head to look at Bandicut with eyes so haunted they gave him an almost skeletal appearance. "The Mindaru . . . my stones heard . . ."

Shocked, Bandicut asked, "When did you hear the Mindaru?"

"In the . . . AI," Ik managed, before his words were choked off by another apparent wave of pain.

Antares spoke without looking up from Ik. "He went into the AI after you did, to make sure you were okay. We couldn't see what was happening, but he seemed to disconnect quite abruptly." She closed her eyes and focused on Ik for a moment longer. When she raised her head, her eyes shone with fear. "John, he was in contact with the Mindaru, inside the AI. His *stones* were in contact. *Oh, no . . .*"

Bandicut blanched. "Are they damaged, or injured? Can you tell?"

B-dang-g-g-g. "Are they *infected*?" Li-Jared asked bluntly, swinging to where he could peer into Ik's eyes.

"Damaged, yes," Antares said. "Infected? I don't know. I'm not sure I could tell." Her gaze narrowed, and it seemed to Bandicut that she was trying to keep her fear to herself.

"How-w-w will-l-l you stop-p-p the star-r-r?" Ed asked in a vibrating voice that jerked Bandicut's thoughts back to the other problem.

"I once helped *make* a star explode," Jeaves said, as though in another conversation altogether. "That was another time, another place. And the circumstances were different. But perhaps my experience can be helpful in *stopping* an explosion, if what Ik is saying is true."

"Listen, I don't—"

Copernicus interrupted Bandicut to say, "Let me change the view. If there is an impending hypernova, we might be able to see the signs."

"Someone please tell me—*what is a hypernova?*" Antares

asked, looking from Ik to the viewspace to Bandicut. "You sound like it's—"

"A massive stellar explosion," Bandicut said. "You know what a supernova is, right? When a star's core collapses and it blows itself to smithereens?"

"Sort of," Antares said.

"A supernova produces things like neutron stars and black holes." Bandicut swallowed hard. "A hypernova is even bigger. Jeaves, can you—?"

"An extreme release of energy," Jeaves said, picking up smoothly. "Short of the Big Bang, there's not much that comes close."

"But what causes—"

"Sometimes a collision of black holes. But *sometimes* a very massive newborn star will collapse abruptly in a gigantic explosion. It's called a hypernova, and also may be a gamma-ray burster, because the shock wave of gamma rays is so extreme it outshines the whole galaxy for a few seconds. Copernicus, can you show an image?"

Two windows appeared in the viewspace. One showed a star, one a galaxy. The star suddenly blossomed with intense light, and with a shock wave that billowed out into surrounding space. In the galaxy view a bright point of light erupted, and grew until it was brighter than the rest of the galaxy. After a few seconds, it faded from view.

"I assume that would be . . . *dangerous* to us?" Antares asked.

Napoleon clicked and answered. "Not just us, but every life-bearing star system within a couple thousand light-years."

Bandicut felt as if he'd been slugged in the chest. "Earth . . . is fifteen hundred light-years from here."

"Yes," Napoleon rasped. "There is a chance that much of Earth's ecosystem would be fried, fifteen hundred years from now, when the radiation got there."

Bandicut had no voice to answer.

∗

"If you could all please look forward for a moment," Copernicus said. "Deep and Dark are leading us across the hollowed-out cavity of the Trapezium."

Bandicut squinted into the luminous space, but Antares said, "I cannot see them."

"Look about a hundred seconds of movement ahead of us, Deep to the right, and Dark to the left. Let me adjust the view."

The viewspace zoomed in. Two dark patches became visible against the distant, glowing nebula walls. Bandicut felt an almost immediate tickle in his brain as Charli reached out to make contact. /Anything?/

/// Yes. They're trying to hurry us along. ///

/Do we know *where* they're leading us?/

*/// Straight across
toward the four stars of the Trapezium.
I think our next destination
is one of them. ///*

/Ah./ Bandicut cleared his throat. "Those four big stars ahead," he said to the others, "are apparently the ones Deep and Dark want us to see next."

"Hrah," Ik said in a strained voice. "Is one of them *Nick*? Isn't *Nick* the star that *Brightburn* told us to see?"

Bandicut consulted with Charli. "We're not sure. Possibly one of them *knows* *Nick*."

That produced some puzzled expressions. But Copernicus said, "Let's adjust the frequency blend, and see what's *behind* the Trapezium, beyond that cloud wall. I'm adding some radio and infrared wavelengths . . ."

The image darkened in some places and brightened in others, and became more saturated with color. Something new became visible through the far nebular clouds: a handful of stars, and in particular, a pulsating stellar object with flickering jets of light shooting out from top and bottom. "That appears to be a newborn star," Copernicus reported. "*Highly* energetic. And highly . . . unstable. It may be a hypernova candidate."

Bandicut felt his heart stutter. "Is *that* *Nick*?" he wondered aloud.

Antares had another question. "Am I the only one who's afraid of all this radiation we're flying into?"

Bwang. "You are not."

Copernicus answered, "The levels are low inside the ship.

Outside the protection of the n-space hull, of course, the bath of radiation would be quite deadly. But your fears are entirely reasonable. If that newborn star is headed toward a hypernova explosion—and it might be—I'm not sure we could survive it even within the n-space envelope."

Bandicut looked around at his silent companions. "I think you just put a damper on the party, Coppy," he said hollowly.

/// But the good news is,
we have time to prepare
while we make the crossing.
Of course, while we're flying across the cavern,
our hides will be in plain sight. ///

/???/

/// You know, in case
the Mindaru come looking. ///

Bandicut shuddered, then conveyed what Charli had just said. Speaking to the robots, he asked, "If, you know, this turns out to look like a bad idea—do we have an out?"

Napoleon clicked a few times, but did not answer. Jeaves and Copernicus both seemed to have gone mute.

"That's what I thought," Bandicut said with a sigh.

25

IK'S STONES

 It looked as if they might have a few days of relative calm as they crossed the cavernous interior of Starmaker, following the two black clouds. Their goal was to get across to the Trapezium as quickly as possible and learn what they could. If they were in danger from crossing the cavern in the open, there wasn't much they could do about it. Copernicus worked on refining his control of the ship, while the others rested, helped the robots sift through the information gleaned from the derelict ships back in the Mindaru trap—and worried about Ik and his stones.

Ed remained with them much longer than he had in the past,

but intermittently. He kept disappearing and reappearing, breaking up, and re-forming himself. Apparently the radiation flux surrounding the ship gave him problems in tracking them, or in penetrating the folds of n-space that enveloped the hull. Eventually he more or less stabilized himself, looking like a small column of fire, floating at the front of the bridge. Bandicut liked the stability, but the column-of-fire part made him a little uneasy.

Antares asked Ed where his homeworld was. Was it in the part of the nebula they could see?

"Close to that wall of cloud. Beyond the four. Can you see?"

"Rrrm, there are very many stars," Ik said.

Indeed, with refinements in the view, they could now see a large number of stars in the glowing cloud wall behind the four bright stars of the Trapezium. It was impossible to tell which Ed was referring to. In addition, they could now see, scattered throughout the nebula, dozens or maybe hundreds of proplyds— pre-stellar globules of condensing matter that in a few million years might become new planetary systems.

If they were not destroyed by the impending hypernova.

That monster—and increasingly they felt that they had identified it—was glowering in the fog beyond. Just now it seemed to Bandicut that it was being guarded by the four stars blazing like the Four Horsemen of the Apocalypse.

"The star . . . must visit . . . great one atop . . . the one that shines hottest."

"The top one of the four?" Bandicut asked.

"Top . . . star . . . brightest . . . call it ∗Thunder∗."

And with that, the column of fire went out, and Ed was gone.

∗

Ik, at some point in the last hour, had become aware with some alarm that he was feeling weirdly removed from the room around him. Everything was beginning to feel dreamlike. And not all of the dream pieces fit together in his mind.

Just now, Li-Jared was talking to him. "Rrrk-k, what do our options multiply against our chances helping Ed's dilemma?"

Ik tilted his head, trying to follow what Li-Jared was saying. He hadn't sounded at all like himself, just then.

Bandicut, looking as if he were about to say something,

instead closed his eyes and sighed heavily. He steadied himself against the flight console. Antares noticed and reached out to him. "Band-d-d-d-ie, are you incapacitated?"

"Just depleted."

"Shall we go to refuel? Or refurbish?"

"I would."

That hadn't sounded like either one of them. Was there something wrong with his—

We are experiencing difficulty . . . translation difficulty.

Ik growled softly to himself. *Hrahhh.*

"R-k-k-k-k," said Li-Jared, "are you effecting cognitive—"

"My stones. Something wrong," Ik muttered. He could hear his words coming out distorted. Groaning, he rubbed his temples, where he could feel the stones pulsing.

Li-Jared's eyes burned bright. He was speaking to the others, and Ik's stones didn't even try to translate. The three gathered around Ik, and seemed to be urging him to leave the bridge with them. "Yes, all right," he said, walking along with them. "But is it safe to move around the ship now?"

His friends looked at him uncertainly. But Copernicus/ship answered in words he could understand, "Safe . . . it is safe now." Ik muttered something in reply and followed his companions off the bridge and down to the commons lounge, glad at least for the change of surroundings.

The lounge, in fact, had changed utterly from its previous appearance. It was now a place of bluish light and shadows. Tree branches arched overhead, and protruding limbs poked inward from where the walls must have been, creating almost a geodelike effect, but in wood instead of rock. It was very cozy, more shelter than light. Ik sighed through his ears in pleasure. This was a very good simulacrum of a small den on Hraachee'a; he even heard a soft undercurrent of Hraachee'an music. But how—?

The astonished voices of the others drowned out his questions. Bandicut, Antares, and Li-Jared were walking around touching the branches, peering into the little areas of seclusion, talking among themselves. Copernicus spoke from somewhere in the walls. "Welcome to a touch of Hraachee'a." That startled Ik more than anything. The robot had spoken in his native Hraachee'an tongue, and done a pretty good job of it.

"Copernicus! Have you learned my language?"

"Some, milord. I thought everyone might enjoy a little visit home, and a visit to each other's homes. I started with your world, using images your stones gave me a while back. Do you like it?"

"Hrrm, yes. It's . . . wonderful! You can just call me Ik, though, instead of . . . that other."

"As you wish. Please—all of you, make yourselves comfortable. I can adjust it any way you like. And I'll do my best with food. Why don't you all find a place to sit."

Ik, dizzily trying to absorb it all, pointed the others to a table nestled among the branches. They gathered around it, on a circular bench seat that was a little odd, but in the right spirit. Soon a basket of Hraachee'an food sticks appeared on the table. Antares passed it around, and they each took one, perhaps to express solidarity with Ik. Bandicut, after munching a little, seemed to perk up. Maybe he just needed food. Maybe he would be easier to understand now.

That hope didn't last long. "Must be essentials," Bandicut said, "that hindrance negativity—Ik's—"

Ik shuddered. "Copernicus, did you understand that?"

Copernicus replied in Hraachee'an. "He's saying they want to help you with your stones."

Ik rumbled to himself and searched inward. He thought he sensed the voice-stones searching for words. Or perhaps searching their own thoughts in the matter. Finally they said: *May require an . . . active . . . (rasp) . . . intervention.*

/You mean what?/

They seemed reluctant. *Another . . . (rasp) host . . . notation . . . potential danger.*

/Danger to them? To you and me?/

(Rasp rasp) Both neither unknown. There was some static in the stones' reply, and Ik felt almost as if they were in disagreement with each other, struggling somehow. He had a feeling of something slowing his thoughts, some thickness in the air. What was *that* from?

But this much he understood: he was going to have to put

one of his friends in danger, if they were to help him. He resisted
that suggestion. He glanced from one of his companions to another, as they talked among themselves. Antares's eyes caught
his gaze; she was aware of his feelings. /What is the danger? Do
we have to join stones?/

    Affirmative (rasp) may inflict . . . damage . . .*

Antares was reaching across the table now, to touch him. He
saw his own arm pulling away from her, as if by its own volition.
He forced it back; it was difficult, and required concentration.
Antares was speaking to him. "Ik-k-k . . . is it . . . trouble . . . your
countenance?"

Ik realized from the feeling of coolness in his face that his
skin was probably turning bluer. Could she see that, or was she
talking about his feelings? He tried to answer her, but he could
see the deep puzzlement in her face. "Copernicus?" he whispered at last.

    "Here," said the robot, speaking out of the tabletop.

    "Help me! My friends can't understand me anymore!"

    "Tell me what you want to say to them. I will translate,"
Copernicus said. Ik told him what his stones had said—that they
needed help from another—that they needed a joining—and
that any joining would involve risk to both Ik and his friends.

Everyone began talking at once, until Ik clapped his hands to
his temples in pain. Antares reached out and drew his left hand
down and held it in both of hers, startling him. He had felt her
touch on his shoulder and arm before, but never like this, hand
to hand. It felt strangely intimate. But he had seen Antares and
Bandie touch this way without harm.

The heaviness still clung to the air around him. Finally he
squeezed back against Antares's grip. He was aware of a slight
tightening of Bandicut's face, which he thought perhaps was an
indication of approval. An instant later, he felt a tingle in his arm,
and an answering tingle in the voice-stones in his temples. Were
his stones connecting to hers?

    "Ik," she said softly.

    "Hrah."

The words that followed seemed to come in echoing layers,
as though his ears, his stones, and perhaps *her* stones each took

a turn at trying to render her meaning. "Ik-k-k, we musst not fear-r-r. If you let me tr-r-ry, I will see if my stones can help-p-p yours-s-s." As she spoke, he clearly sensed her fear. Fear of the contact? Or of what she might find? What was she risking, by putting her stones in contact with his? *Are the Mindaru behind this?*

But he was even more afraid to have to face it alone.

"Yesss," he whispered, at last.

*

Bandicut was filled with a turbulent mixture of fear, hunger, and weariness. His initial hope that Ik would rebound, surrounded here by echoes and memories of his home, had faded as they'd gathered for conversation. His friend's efforts to talk were growing more and more frantic, and the translation more garbled. He was pretty sure it was Ik's stones malfunctioning and not his own; the others were having the same problem.

Then Copernicus interrupted to translate for Ik and explain what was needed. Before Bandicut could even blink, Antares had reached out to make contact—not just with their friend Ik, but with his stones. The knot in Bandicut's stomach tightened. He could feel her fear, and also her determination. She would risk whatever it took to help Ik.

/// John, you've got to trust her. ///

/I do trust her. But what if Ik's stones are infected?/ He touched her shoulder and whispered her name.

She glanced in his direction, but only for a moment. And then she focused exclusively on Ik.

Bandicut drew a deep breath, waiting, and saw Li-Jared stirring, as well. /Can you tell what's happening?/ Ik was muttering something, and Antares moved around to sit close to him.

/// According to your stones,
you need to give them breathing room.
Privacy. ///

Bandicut cleared his throat softly.

/// I gather . . . three's a crowd. ///

Bandicut blinked, stung by the implication that this was somehow about Antares and Ik alone. Li-Jared had already gotten up and was pacing around the lounge. Maybe he had gotten the point already. Antares and Ik were in a strange embrace now; Antares was guiding Ik's head onto her shoulder.

/// His stones are in his head.
Hers are in her throat.
They may need close contact. ///

/Right./ Bandicut flushed, nodded, and got up to join Li-Jared. After a few steps, he glanced back to see a translucent force-field, a privacy-curtain, shimmering around the space where Antares and Ik sat. /Right./

/// I'm sure it's fine. ///

/Yah./ Turning away again, he saw Li-Jared watching him. "So," he said, before Li-Jared could speak, "I hope Antares will be able to help fix his stones."

The Karellian rubbed his chest for a moment. "There's more food on the table over there. Hraachee'an, I guess." He gestured over his shoulder—but gazed at Bandicut with blazing, electric-blue eyes. "I am unsure what to think. About Ik. About what could go wrong. Do *you* think it's just . . . damage . . . and not . . . ?"

Bandicut blinked uncertainly and shook his head. It was not like Li-Jared to be so tongue-tied. He was worried—*really* worried—about his Hraachee'an friend. "I don't know, either. I really don't."

Bwang. "The stones have done pretty well in the past. I think we can trust them to . . . and Antares . . ." Li-Jared's voice trailed off, and he made a finger-twitching gesture that Bandicut took as a shrug, and then he turned around, studiously surveying the Hraachee'an lounge.

"Yes." *And if it's the Mindaru . . .*

/// We'll still have to trust them,
won't we? ///

Nodding, Bandicut followed Li-Jared to the small buffet table. And he tried to ignore the steady tightening of his throat.

*

Antares had never felt anything quite like the joining of her stones with Ik's. Her stones had connected with John's to enable communication; but this was deeper, a diagnostic connection. Her stones were probing Ik's, seeking out the source of his trouble. It was a stuttering connection, trying to get past the damage in Ik's stones, at once intimate and distant.

Ik's pain was a hollow, bony kind of feeling, impossible to soothe away with her empathic touch. But beneath his distress she sensed Ik's sinewy strength. /Ik? Can you feel me here?/

/Here. Risking. Your stones—/

/They know what they're doing. You must relax./

/—can't tell—/

/Is it just the stones causing you pain, or is it more?/ *Are you infected, Ik? Will I become infected from touching you?*

/So hard—cannot tell—/

Antares felt a sudden rush of memories from Ik, as if he'd kept them bottled up and could hold them no longer: shock from the encounter with *Brightburn*; the awakening of memories of his own sun's death; fear reverberating from the encounter with the Mindaru; the loss of Delilah. But beyond the fear, something more.

*Damage to the core programming . . . investigating . . . *

And all the while, rushing beneath those feelings were echoes of others: the loss of his Hraachee'an friends, waves of affection and concern for his friends here, a shivering bond growing toward Antares . . .

She trembled in turn. /Ik, we're all . . . with you. We won't stop until you're . . . /

/I am fine./

A hope? Be very careful . . .

*Probing for evidence of infection . . . please wait . . . *

Nothing she could do *but* wait. She tried to search her inner awareness for her stones, to gauge their progress; but she only felt a buzzing, and then a blurring sensation as though everything were shifting slightly out of phase. She felt frenetic, desperate activity, but she could decipher none of it.

Wait. Be patient.

She felt as if she had been patient for a very long time. She was floating, uncertain. But there was still that pain, coming in waves. /Stones, talk to me! What are you doing?/

The reply, when it came, jolted her:

*Search of the program-core complete. Mindaru infection present but in remission. We have isolated areas of damage, and are attempting repair and removal of infection. Remain alert . . . *

✱

Bandicut and Li-Jared picked at the food and poked about anxiously. It was too bad Ik couldn't enjoy the lounge with them. He might have explained what some of these strange-looking plants were, and why these three seats were attached to the walls, leaning at odd angles out into the foliage. He might have told them whether it was safe to pet the knobbly-skinned animal that sat in a tree gazing serenely into space, with unblinking orange eyes.

But Ik and Antares remained behind the privacy-curtain. Twice, Bandicut started toward it. Each time he stopped. There was nothing he could do. Antares was better equipped. But he was scared of what could go wrong and hurt Antares as well as Ik.

/// Scared that Ik and Antares are getting personal? ///

/I didn't say that./

/// You were thinking it. ///

/Maybe, on some level. But I didn't say it./

/// So you told me. ///

/I'm concerned about my friends. Both of them./ He sat down on a bench, facing the buffet table. "Li-Jared, what can we do if there's an infection from that . . . Mindaru thing . . . still on the ship?"

"You mean—"bwang"—in Ik?"

"That's one possibility. And what about Antares? She's in close contact. She could get it, too. Any of us could."

Li-Jared looked thoughtful, biting off a bread stick. "I think we had better start learning all we can about the Mindaru."

Bandicut considered that for a moment, then said, "Jeaves! Napoleon! Can we talk?"

✱

Napoleon was reluctant to leave the bridge, and Bandicut and Li-Jared were reluctant to leave their friends, so after declining an offer from Copernicus to meld the two compartments into one, they settled on a holo-conference. The robots reported on the information they'd gained from the ships they'd passed in the Mindaru graveyard. Though they had found nothing definitive, there was a great deal that was suggestive. All three robots agreed that the Mindaru were almost certainly a pure AI, and quite possibly descendants of the combatant AI from the ancient wars.

Bandicut found that more frightening than helpful. "Where the hell is it *from*? Not in ancient times. *Now.*"

"I'm not sure that's a meaningful question," Jeaves said.

"Well, does the cursed thing report back to its superiors, or is it a free-roaming agent?"

"It may be a little of both," Jeaves said. "We found no logs connecting that Mindaru installation to any higher control. But then, we only got snapshots. It seems most likely to be a group mind, or colony consciousness. But whether it links to others in real-time somehow, or is simply a free agent on a million-year mission, I can't say. It does seem likely it's one of many agents at large—which would be consistent with the activity we've observed moving outward through the galaxy."

Bandicut swore, and Li-Jared made twanging sounds under his breath. They both started to speak, and Bandicut jerked his head to prompt Li-Jared. "So," said the Karellian in a tone that suggested that he was *really* getting fed up, "what's this about them wanting to exterminate every lifeform in the galaxy? Which I assume includes us? What's that all about?"

The robots hummed and ticked for a moment, and then Napoleon answered. "That was a message that the oldest of the three ships we contacted kept repeating. It was really the only message it had, milords."

"Nappy—knock off the milord crap, will you?" Bandicut said in annoyance. Napoleon hummed and bowed acquiescence. Bandicut sighed. "Thank you. Now why would the Mindaru let it broadcast that information?"

"Perhaps it doesn't mind if we know its intent."

"It wants us scared?"

"Perhaps, Cap'n," said Napoleon. "At the same time, it's clear that we survived at least partly because it wanted to study us before it destroyed us."

"But—" *bong* "—destroy us *why*?"

Jeaves seemed almost to draw a breath and let it out. "I think it might be an anger that's been held so deeply for billions of years that it's part of the essential Mindaru programming." Jeaves turned his head to Napoleon. "You were studying the details from the second ship . . ."

"*Rage,*" said Napoleon. "That's what I deduce. A self-righteous rage, and a pride bordering on hubris."

Jeaves sounded surprised. "You found that in the second ship's—?"

"No, I found a detail in the second ship's logs that seemed to resonate with information from the Maw of the Abyss, which I glimpsed as we were leaving the Neri world. At the time it meant nothing to me—an image of an awesome power, raging against all of creation, or at least living creation. It was not the power that sent the Maw," Napoleon said, anticipating Bandicut's next question, "but a power the Maw knew tales of."

"Then why didn't you—?"

"I didn't connect it until now, because it was classed by the Maw as a myth. A story. But this ship caught by the Mindaru was also owned by 'the Others,' the ones who sent the Maw on its journey. And it told me it had been caught by a myth. It was, more than anything else, astonished by that."

For a moment Bandicut could think of nothing to say. Li-Jared was twitching and rubbing his breastbone. Then Charli spoke, and she seemed breathless.

/// There's more to it than that,
I'm almost certain. ///

/Huh? What?/

/// Something I just realized.
I got it from Delilah when she was captive,
as she was connecting with Deep.
There is something practical in the
purpose of the Mindaru.
Deadly but practical.
The Mindaru want to populate the galaxy
with AI life like itself.
That's why they're destroying stars—
not just to eliminate organic life,

which they view as a threat,
but to build up the supply of heavy elements
in the galaxy! ///

/Uh . . . / Bandicut rubbed his cheek thoughtfully, then told Li-Jared and the robots what Charli had just said.

"They want more heavy elements to create more of themselves!" Li-Jared shouted, jumping up. "More hardware, more AIs. They want a universe friendly to them and hostile to us."

/// And heavy elements— ///

"Heavy elements are created in supernovas. And . . . hypernovas," Bandicut said. "Oh, Jesus . . ."

✱

The conversation turned to a discussion among the robots of *how* the Mindaru might be trying to trigger the hypernova. They seemed to be getting nowhere, so Bandicut walked back to the privacy-curtain. "Copernicus, do you have any way of knowing what sort of progress Antares and Ik are making? Are they likely to be in there for a while yet?"

The tree beside him said, "They seem very still, and their stones are communicating at a high speed. I think they may be there for quite some time yet."

Bandicut sighed. "Do you think we should stay here, in case they need help?"

"Cap'n, I think you should go and try to get some sleep. You'll be more help to everyone that way. I'll call you if you're needed."

"Are you sure?" He was, in fact, struggling to fight off sleepiness.

"I'm sure," Copernicus said. "Li-Jared, you too."

The Karellian looked up from a flower he was inspecting. "You may—" *bong-g-g* "—be right." He dusted his hands and looked at Bandicut. "You, Bandie?"

Bandicut nodded. "Let's go."

✱

It was lonely in the sleeping room. Copernicus had fixed the room up with some Earthlike touches—a raised bed, pillows, and a comforter; but it felt too different. And it wouldn't be right for Antares. He asked Copernicus to change it back. He dropped with a sigh onto the low sleeping pad.

He found it impossible to sleep, though. Despite his weariness, he was now wide awake and restless. The lights were dimmed but not out, and he let his gaze run up one ghostly wall, across the ceiling, and down the opposite wall. Then he'd pick another spot and do it again. On about every third run, he imagined Mindaru in the wall. He knew it was nonsense, but it was alarming nonsense. He became angry at his inability to go to sleep, and that made him more awake.

/// Do you want me to help?
A little alpha wave or something? ///

/I don't need help./

/// Yes, I can see that. ///

Bandicut snarled softly and closed his eyes again.

Eventually, he calmed down a little, and in time he must have dropped off to sleep, because he started awake when Antares slipped in beside him. "Hi," he said.

"John Bandicut," she answered, her voice sounding strained. He woke up enough to realize that she was radiating strong emotions. Distress and relief and need and worry. It was hard to sort them out.

"I'm here. Is he—is Ik okay?"

"Put your arms around me."

"Huh? What's wrong?"

"Put your arms around me."

He rolled and did as she asked. Something in her gave then, and she melted against him, shivering with jangled emotions. He was definitely awake now. "John," she whispered, and sighed into his shoulder.

"Is it all right? Is Ik—are *you*—?"

"I'm okay."

"Are you really? Are you sure?"

"Yes, but Ik—it was hard. So much pain from watching stars die. Did you know he's unusually sensitive to stars? His stones were damaged; my stones helped repair them."

He pulled back just enough to see her face. "Was that all there was? Damage from seeing stars die?"

Antares shook her head. "The Mindaru—they infected his stones, too—not as badly as they did the AI, but enough to make it difficult for him to function. My stones worked long and hard. They think they rooted it all out."

"They *think?* Don't they know?"

"It's impossible to know for sure. But they're pretty sure."

"And you?"

"I'm okay, but—" she sighed softly against him "—it was exhausting. To watch. And to share with Ik. I think it did draw us closer together." She shivered a little. He couldn't tell quite what she was feeling.

At that moment, his own embrace felt inadequate. "Oh. I guess I—"

"No," Antares said. "You *don't* see."

"Huh?"

"He's our friend. We must stay close to him—all of us. He may need help again. He *probably* will. We must be ready." She hugged him more tightly. Her touch sang with need, fear, confusion, passion.

His head was now spinning.

"John . . ." Antares rested one thigh against his and hooked his calf with her ankle. "John, I think I need you right now."

His confusion ebbed away. "I'm here." He slipped his fingers into her hair, stroked her soft mane, sank his hands into the thick, rich hair between her shoulder blades. Her stones were flickering in her throat. "I'm here," he whispered.

She practically enveloped him with cascading emotions. Grief and fear and gladness and urgent desire and restlessness and anxiety. "John, will you make love to me, please? Now? Slowly?"

He closed his eyes and drew a long, silent breath. Then he touched Antares's chin and raised her face to his. Her small nose quivered as she breathed; her eyes probed his with their black orbs, deep wells encircled by golden halos. He bent to kiss her, brushing his lips to hers. She pressed back with humanlike urgency, her lips not letting him pull away. Her fingers tightened on his shoulders as she moved against him, and the waves of her emotions washed over him like an incoming tide.

★

For Antares, it felt like slipping from a tangled jungle into a cool, blue sea, like the sea of the Neri, salty and refreshing. With each

274 ★ JEFFREY A. CARVER ★

of John Bandicut's caresses, she felt a little more able to breathe after the frightening experience she had just been through, more able to open herself to his touch. She was aware of his jangled emotions, and she tried to offer solace, but right now she needed far more than she could give.

This was all wrong, she knew, by all that her training had made a part of her; wrong that she should be joining this way; wrong that she would be *taking* so much right now, and giving so little. *But I just gave all I had. I cannot give more, cannot be all things all times to all people. Not even one I love. And yes, I do love him.* All that she had done for Ik was right, just as she had been trained. Why should she feel it a weakness that now she should *need*?

John's arms enveloped her, and that was what she needed. She shivered with pleasure at his erection pressed against her, and she shivered at his lips and hands touching her breasts and shoulders and back, and she shivered to feel his acceptance and his love, washing over and enveloping her.

She wished it could last all night.

★

As Bandicut lay tangled with Antares in long afterglow, he studied her eyes, trying to locate a window into her emotions. She was nibbling at his fingers, with which a moment ago he had been tracing circles around each of her four breasts, noting how like and yet how different they were from human female breasts, smaller but with larger tips, nipples he supposed. Antares clearly enjoyed his touch. But now she was gently biting his fingers, stopping him from continuing the touching. Was she laughing? Or was it something else? He thought he sensed something welling up inside her. Worry. Fretting. Something was wrong. "What is it?" he asked.

"John." Definitely wrong. Was she wondering if she should have done this?

"Yah?"

"I have to go now."

He grunted, closed his hand, felt a stinging in his cheeks.

"I'm sorry. I have to go back to Ik."

He swallowed and nodded. "I understand."

She raised herself on one elbow, making no attempt to cover

herself. And yet something in the aura was gone. She was no longer open, no longer—what? Available? "Do you? I hope so. I needed . . . and I thought perhaps you needed . . . and I am glad . . . very . . ."

"Yes."

"Glad."

"But . . ."

"Ik is in a fragile state. His stones and, I think, Ik himself. I need to be there in case he needs me."

I need you now, he thought. *I love you.*

"So—that's why I have to go."

/// Tell her what you just thought! ///

/Not right now. She doesn't need to hear it now./

Antares sat up, pushing back her thick mane of auburn hair. She had never looked more desirable. She got to her feet, slipped her clothes back on. Sighing, she bent and touched her lips to his. He reached up for a moment to caress her cheek. And then she slipped out of the room.

He stared at the closed door for a long time, and then at the ceiling for an even longer time, unsure just exactly what he was feeling.

26

DISTANT MEMORIES

 Ik passed the night in a kind of dream state, not quite sleeping and not fully awake. He was aware, but felt unable to influence what was running through his mind, or between his mind and his voice-stones. It was a strange, timeless state; he knew some kind of healing or repair or change was taking place, but it was beyond him to know what kind. He felt occasional flashes of pain. After a while, the pain became less frequent, but in its place came a hollow, ringing sensation, like a reverberation in a large steel chamber. With it came . . . he wasn't sure what. A sense of striving, maybe. But striving for *what?*

As the room lights brightened with ship's morning, he slowly came to, wondering where he was. He shifted his eyes. He was sitting cross-legged in . . . sleeping quarters? If so, they no longer looked the same. It looked like a Hraachee'an comfort den, a place where a Hraachee'an on holiday or in transit might rest for a few nights. The smooth walls were curved asymmetrically, like the interior of a natural cave. On one side, however, a wide window appeared to look out over a rugged mountain slope. *Rrrm,* he thought. *Am I hallucinating? Or have the stones gone mad?* And then he remembered the lounge last night, transformed into Hraachee'an form.

He heard his name, and turned his head. Antares was sitting up on the padded floor, a long arm's reach away from him. Had she been here all night?

"Hrah," he murmured. "Hello."

"How are you feeling? Can you understand me?"

"Yes, I seem to be able to now." And he gasped, suddenly realizing what that meant. He placed his fingers to the sides of his head. He could hear and understand Antares's spoken words; he could also sense her thoughts and feelings, hovering around the edges of his own. /What is our condition?/ he asked his stones.

✳Improved. Major traumas appear to have been corrected. Functionality has been restored to the verbal translation module. Linguistic accuracy may now exceed ninety percent.✳

/That's good. Was that the only problem?/

Hesitation. *✳Still evaluating.✳*

They hadn't mentioned what he most worried about. The Mindaru. He felt reluctant to mention it himself. He realized Antares was still gazing at him expectantly. "It seems you have done, hrrl, remarkably well in repairing the damage."

"And how do you *feel*?" Antares repeated.

He honestly didn't know how to answer that question. For a moment, he felt the ringing sensation again. How *was* he doing? The connection between his inner sensorium and the stones was definitely clearer, as was his thinking. Was this all due to Antares's efforts? It made him lightheaded just to think of it. For a moment, he was carried back to the undersea world of the Neri, where he'd used his stones with John Bandicut to guide the sick Neri back to health, guided their minds and bodies to heal themselves. Was that what Antares's stones had done for him?

No. There was more. He *had* been infected, or his stones had. And Antares's stones had worked half the night rooting out the infection.

But it wasn't just his stones that were hurting. What of his heart and soul, where the memories still burned? They had been reawakened by the star earlier, reawakened to a fire he had not been able to put out. In the presence of the stellar inferno, he had been wrenched back to the destruction of his homeworld. For so long, he had managed not to think of it much. But now, it burned and burned in his mind. *Hraachee'a.*

So many losses. So many people to remember. Onaka, his lifebonder. He missed her desperately. His young heirs, offspring of his egg-brother Aon. He'd cared for Edik and Sar as though they were his own. But they were gone, too. They hadn't deserved to die. Had Onaka, had Aon, had the young ones gone quickly, quietly? Or had they endured terrible pain in the holocaust of an exploding sun? Why had he been spared?

He and Onaka had planned and hoped for a groupbond one day. During his long, solitary sojourns in space, he had often thought of what such a groupbond might have been like, if he and Onaka had found one. Even after his arrival on Shipworld, he'd wondered if perhaps one day he would find his own kin among the millions of beings in that strange place. But that hope was stretched thin now, very thin.

Somehow entwined with the remnants of that hope was the reality of this company, his new friends, Hraachee'an or no. He felt now just how much a family this company had become. He gazed at Antares and thought of Li-Jared and Bandicut. There was much good they had done together, the four of them. Li-Jared, for all his bluster and excitability, would throw himself in front of a charging bull-mammoth to save any of them. And John Bandicut: as trustworthy and courageous as anyone Ik had ever met. Even his robots had become friends. And Antares. Before, she'd kept herself at a distance. But she had just risked her own stones to help him in his need. They were now joined by their stones—and more, by a personal bond. There was healing in her touch, as there had been healing in his and Bandicut's touch to the Neri. But Antares's healing touch seemed a part of her fundamental being, and not just something made possible by her voice-stones.

"Ik?"

He shifted his gaze. Antares had been waiting patiently the whole time he'd been lost in his own thoughts. "Hrah. I am still sorting out . . ." As he spoke, his head filled again with the hollow ringing. He could feel his face tightening.

"I'm here to help," said Antares.

"Thank you. Thank you for what you have already done," he said softly. "I believe . . . the rest may be up to me."

*

Jeaves felt that it was up to *him* to conduct some serious thinking and analysis during this quiet interlude, while *The Long View* crossed the cavernous hollow at the center of Starmaker. There were some questions that really had to be answered soon. Foremost was, what exactly were the Mindaru doing to bring a star to the brink of violent explosion? And what could they on *The Long View* do to stop it?

Jeaves, in another time and place, had been present for the triggering of a supernova. That had been a carefully orchestrated event: collectors siphoning mass from a companion sun; satellites within the star's atmosphere reflecting neutrinos back into the core to make it hotter and hotter; and an n-space connection to a cosmic hyperstring, strengthening the gravity at the heart of the star. Even with all this, it had amounted to little more than an extra push, tipping a star that was already on the cusp over the edge.

Could this be something like that? It felt different, though Jeaves could not pinpoint how. Soon they would arrive at the Trapezium, and try to contact the one of the four called *Thunder*. That was good; but he needed more information, he needed everything the ship's sensors could give him about *Thunder*, and even more so about the one floating in the mists of the cavern walls beyond, the one called *Nick*. Without knowing *why*

✻Nick✻ was on the verge of exploding, they might as well be flying into a deathtrap.

✻

Li-Jared had gotten up early, unable to sleep with Ik murmuring to himself, and Antares coming and going in the middle of the night. She had spent a long time sitting very, very still, and maybe that was what kept him awake. He kept waiting for her to do something. But she didn't; she just watched Ik, waiting for *him* to do something.

Li-Jared could have asked Copernicus-ship to create a separate sleeping room for him, but instead he went to the common lounge, looking to the robot for company. "Would you like me to change the décor into something from your own world?" Copernicus asked, providing a platter with a good replica of a soma-fruit, a long, slender pod filled with a salty nectar.

Li-Jared bit off the end of the fruit and looked around at the vision of Hraachee'a that Copernicus had created last night. "Why not?"

"Could I ask you to step into the hallway for a moment?"

He complied. As he waited, he peered up and down the glowing red passageway, remembering when he had been lost in these corridors, afraid for his life. He was suddenly aware of how alone he felt, and not just alone but lonely. His friends were in adjacent compartments, and yet, in this weird, weird ship, they could be miles away.

The door opened and Li-Jared gratefully stepped back into the lounge. He stood stock-still, his hearts hammering in sudden wonder. The room was utterly transformed. It was Karellia— *home with green, beautiful, perilous sky*—almost exactly as he remembered it. Karellia at the onset of night. A grassy sward was surrounded by tall-spire trees and fog-bushes. The sky overhead was light-filled darkness: the green-tinged dark of night, with a blazing star and nebula field splashed across it like luminous paint. The sky was an artist's playground, a thing of joy and beauty. It was a nightmare of radiation, a thing of deadly peril. Karellia was located in a region of dense stellar activity. Bathed in radiation, it was a wonder the planet managed to support life at all.

And yet, thanks to a strong magnetic field, it did. It was fertile with life. It was also fertile with extinctions. Many were the species that had come and gone in the planet's history. Many were the changes that the years and orbital instabilities had brought to the world.

Li-Jared's mind exploded with memories. He was, for a few heartbeats, transported back to Karellia, surrounded by ghosts of his own people.

The Karellians had always been vulnerable to mutations from the radiation. Over time, they had learned to protect themselves against climate shifts and stellar fluctuations. They had explored their own planet, but only sporadically gone into space, into the "perilous sky." Beyond the protection of the atmosphere, the radiation was truly horrific, and even automated probes required heavy shielding. Only in Li-Jared's time had work begun to find ways of creating energy shields against radiation. Li-Jared, through his mathematical research, had been a part of that effort.

He tipped his head back and gazed at the fiery night sky. Copernicus had done a fine job creating the effect, and Li-Jared was almost convinced. Once he looked for star patterns, of course, he could see the limits of what Copernicus could extract from his stones, which in turn had drawn it from his memories. But as long as he ignored the fine detail, the look of the sky was dead on.

"Would you like to have a proper Karellian breakfast?" Copernicus asked.

Li-Jared turned and saw a holo-image of the robot, standing behind a counter suspended between two trees. On the counter were several plates of food. *Bong.* "Everything else looks so real. But where'd this counter come from?"

"Ah—I was afraid this wouldn't match up," said Copernicus. "I didn't have any images of food service on your world, so I took this from a human setting."

"We would never have a long surface like that," Li-Jared said. "We'd have a lot of small holders sticking out from trees or posts—" he demonstrated, extending a hand palm-up from a half-bent arm, as though he were holding a tray in the air "—and there would be a bowl on each holder. People would walk among them, taking what they liked."

"Ah. Would you like to step back while I try it?"

Li-Jared backed up.

The countertop blurred, then was gone. Several new trees appeared, and from each tree, several supports arched out, holding small shelves. A moment later, bowls appeared on the shelves. "Is that better?"

"Yes," said Li-Jared. "Thank you." He walked among the offerings, selecting a small, round fruit and two bread-fingers. "Very authentic." He ate slowly, savoring the earnest attempt to duplicate Karellian flavors.

"Li-Jared?"

"Yes?"

"How did you leave your homeworld?"

Li-Jared felt a momentary flash of fire in his throat. How had he left his homeworld? Quite abruptly. The stones had come first . . .

It had started with the landing of what first seemed to be a meteorite, in the field near his home. It hit with a loud concussion—*whoom!*—but not the massive explosion that one would have expected. When he got there, he found the site enveloped in a glowing halo of bluish plasma. After waiting for the glow and obvious magnetic effects to subside, he cautiously approached. The cratering was minimal; this was no ordinary meteorite. A haze continued to obscure the immediate surroundings. But he saw—too late to duck—the burst of violet plasma that slammed him in the chest and knocked him flat. When he sat up, he smelled ozone and felt a tingling in his chest. Embedded in his skin were two tiny crystals, flickering with light.

Copernicus stirred almost the way Bandicut might have, his metal arms gesturing. "That must have been very exciting!"

Li-Jared made a rude, rumbling sound. "It was *terrifying!* And once I knew what they were, it was infuriating!"

"Why?"

"That—" *ngngngngng* "—aliens took it upon themselves to blast me down and put these stones in me!" He could feel himself growing hot all over again with the remembered emotion.

Copernicus made a ticking sound that was probably intended to be soothing. "What did you do?"

"I tried to get them out!" Li-Jared's hearts thumped; his hands went to his chest; his thumbs rubbed at the jewels that he had frantically tried to claw out, until it was clear he would only hurt himself. And that was when the voices first spoke in his head. "It was the voices that stopped me. Have you ever heard voices in your head?"

"I *always* hear voices in my head," Copernicus said mildly.

Li-Jared jerked his head in surprise, then shrugged with his fingertips. "You wouldn't know the difference, then. You don't realize how shocking it is to have someone suddenly talking to you that way. And to know that the speaker is actually inside you."

Copernicus's LEDs flickered. "I must try to imagine that."

"Yes, well, when the voices spoke to me, I wondered if I'd lost my mind. But it did make me stop trying to dig the things out of my chest."

"What did they say to you?"

"Stop trying to dig us out of your chest."

"Is that really what they said?"

Li-Jared made a burring sound. "More or less. I think actually they said something like, 'Please do not injure yourself. We cannot be removed that way.' After I got over being scared witless, I started talking back to them." Li-Jared sighed at the memory, and poked at the nearest food bowl with one finger. "We talked quite a long time that night. Of course, we spent a lot of that time just trying to figure out *how* to talk . . ."

"You were contacted by an alien race! Weren't you excited?"

It felt like a million years ago, it felt like yesterday. Li-Jared's hearts went momentarily out of sync. "Yes, of course! Eventually. But that didn't mean I wasn't annoyed at the way they did it." He didn't mention that he was also half convinced that he had gone crazy and was hallucinating the whole thing.

Copernicus clicked. "You're in good company in that."

Bong. "Yes." I *am* in good company, he thought grudgingly.

"Both the captain and Ik have indicated feelings of . . . would *resentment* be the right word?"

"Don't ask me what the right word is," Li-Jared said. He drew a slow, whistling breath. "Still . . . I suppose there's good that's come out of it. I mean, we've helped people. And been given an unusual chance to . . . serve, I guess."

"Indeed you have. *We* have, I suppose."

Li-Jared looked up. He'd been studying his fingertips, without seeing them. "Yes, I would definitely include you in that."

"How long was it before you knew the stones' intentions?"

Li-Jared laughed hollowly. "Before I *knew*? I still don't know. I mean, they seem to have taken Bandie as a kind of payment for saving his world. And I think they *tried* to save Ik's world, or at least part of the population, even if they failed. But *my* world? I don't know. Was it in danger? I suppose so; there was always danger. That's why we call it the 'home with a perilous sky.' But was there a *specific* danger that we were saved from?" Li-Jared flicked his fingers in bewilderment. He picked up a biscuit-fruit and nibbled at it.

"How did they take you, in the end?" Copernicus asked.

Li-Jared ate half the biscuit-fruit before answering. The memory of the new stones was so vivid it made him shiver. The memory of being taken was just the opposite; it was a ghostly afterimage, a shadow on his brain. "It was the very next night. I'd gone back home." He could see the clustered compartments of his little house in the woods as clearly now as if it were yesterday. "We'd had a very long conversation, not all of it harmonious. I hadn't told anyone about the stones. In fact, I never did get a chance to tell anyone." Li-Jared touched his brow. "Even now, I doubt anyone knows about my contact with an alien life, or where I went. They probably all think I vanished into the air. Which I did, sort of."

"How did it happen?"

"It was night, but getting close to dawn. I stepped out of my house—I lived at the edge of the clearing. I wanted air; I wanted to look up at the sky; it all seemed so unreal. I hadn't taken more than five steps, and I looked up, and suddenly realized I had passed through a *boundary,* because I was looking up through a *golden haze.* It was all around me, almost like a star-spanner bubble, not that I knew anything about *them* yet. I had just enough time to be surprised, and then—*fffffft-t-t.*" He snapped his fingers and made a gesture of shooting off into space. He'd lost consciousness, though he had a strange sense of blazing star-clouds passing by. When he awoke he was in a transparent golden tube arrowing across the stars toward what turned out to be Shipworld, with the galaxy he'd left behind spread out across half the sky.

"Reminds me of John Bandicut's and my arrival at Ship-world," Copernicus said. "Do you know why they picked you?"

Li-Jared uttered a low growl. "I know they waited to make sure they had good communications before they grabbed me."

"But why *you?*"

"Do you think I didn't ask that question? Sometimes I think it's because of what I knew, or knew how to do. But really, you know . . . mostly I think it was just because they knew I was alone. I guess they knew I wouldn't really be leaving anyone be-hind." His voice dropped slightly. It was an old wound, one that was likely never to heal.

The robot hummed in thought. Finally he said, "I guess, in truth . . . the same thing could be said about me. And about Napoleon. And I wonder . . . John Bandicut?"

Li-Jared took another bite and stared at the metal robot, thinking, Is that why we're all so expendable? Is that why we've just been tossed toward an exploding sun?

27

⋆THUNDER⋆

 Over the next several days, *The Long View* crossed the eerily glowing void and drew steadily closer to the Tra-pezium, the blazing diamond-shaped cluster of stars that marked, as much as anything could, the heart of Starmaker. Copernicus was growing into his position as ship-board AI, and Napoleon and Jeaves continued to work tirelessly, and futilely, to determine what the Mindaru were doing to ⋆Nick⋆ and the spacetime continuum. Twice, the ship passed through hypergrav shock waves, and during the second event they finally managed to get a fix on the point of origin of the disturbance. It was indeed the star behind the Trapezium, the one they were calling ✷Nick✷.

As for the crew, Ik's stones seemed to be working, and everyone at last had a chance to rest and regain their equilibrium. In Bandicut's case, the time was not altogether restful. The dreams had started up again—the visions of the wheat field and the towering thunderstorms and the combines bearing down on him—and he still didn't understand them. He was increasingly unsure whether they were wholly dream or partly memory; but their persistence was getting on his nerves. Charli had started having her own dreamlike experiences: memories surfacing inexplicably, quarxian memories linked somehow to her longstanding questions about the fate, ages ago, of her race. Charli was sure there was something important in those memories, but she had no more idea what it was than Bandicut did about his dreams.

On the fourth day of their crossing of the central cavern of the nebula, Ik announced on the bridge that he was sensing the mind of the nearest Trapezium star, ✷Thunder✷. Shortly afterward, Charli informed Bandicut that Deep was beginning to make contact with the star.

/// I'm feeling something around the edges myself.
I think this star is in distress. ///

When Bandicut passed this information on to the others, Ik affirmed the impression.

"Why?" Li-Jared asked. "Does the star say why?"

Ik let out a long sigh. "I cannot say that it *speaks,* as such. Right now I only sense waves . . . ripples of feeling. No clear details. There is something very strange and disconnected in this, I don't know what. I hope as we get closer . . ."

They were still some distance away. Copernicus was making course adjustments, but the intense radiation flux forced him to navigate with caution. It would be a little while yet before they were close enough to the star for meaningful contact.

"This radiation makes me nervous," Antares said, gazing at the great arching walls of glowing gas that surrounded the ship in its passage across the cavern.

"Understandable," Napoleon said. "It is the radiation from the

Trapezium stars that hollowed out this whole region of the nebula and gave us such a clear view. It is strong stuff."

"Is that unusual?" Antares asked.

"Not really," Napoleon said. "New stars often produce huge bursts of radiation—and when the shock waves hit other parts of the nebula cloud, they can do two things: trigger the birth of still more stars, or burn out a big cavity in the nebula surrounding it. It's like a new power on the block, clearing the neighborhood of competitors, if I may use an Earth metaphor."

"Nevertheless," Copernicus said, "these stars will be minor powers in the block, compared to *Nick*, if *Nick* explodes."

"That's very cheering, Copernicus," Bandicut said.

"We are nearly across the bubble now, so I would expect the quality of contact to improve soon."

"Rrrm, not soon enough," Ik murmured.

★

Before another day had passed, they were drawing near to the uppermost star in the cluster. *Thunder* was now a billowing blue-white ball of immense size. Perhaps it only seemed so because of what Bandicut knew, but it also looked alarmingly *alive* against the background of the nebula. The viewspace was now presenting a radically altered view for their benefit, since a "true view" would have blinded them instantly.

Deep and Dark flanked *The Long View* as they drew closer to the star. Charli was in contact with Charlene-echo, and Ik sat in a near trance, opening himself to whatever communication was possible. Antares sat nearby, ready to assist as needed.

Bandicut felt as if he should be doing something. The flight controls were deactivated, since Copernicus was doing the flying. "Napoleon, are we scanning to see if anybody else is in the area?" If the Mindaru were involved, it wouldn't do to be too cavalier about watching their backs.

"As a matter of fact . . ." Napoleon paused and seemed to be checking something. "We've picked up an object in close orbit."

Bandicut felt a chill run up his spine. "Ah." *Damn.* "What do we know about it?"

Napoleon clicked. "Not much. We'll have to get closer if we want more data."

"How much closer?"

"Uncertain, Cap'n. The readings are devilishly strange. It appears to be a very small object, less than a meter across."

"Really."

"But it seems more massive than its size would indicate."

"A *lot* more massive? You mean, massive like collapsed matter?"

"I think not. There are definite hints of a complex internal structure. More than that, I can't say."

Bandicut frowned. /Any chance Deep could take a look?/ he asked Charli.

/// Deep has his, er, hands full already.
He's establishing time-fusion,
so that we can talk to the star.
But Dark is trying to probe the object.
The word I'm getting via Charlene is that
it has n-space structure. ///

/Oh . . . / He peered again and saw that Dark had indeed sped on ahead and was circling around some invisible point.

/// The object is not just floating in n-space.
Its form and structure appear to be
shaped from n-space. ///

/You mean like our ship?/

/// I think so, yes.
Except apparently there are some long streamers
extending from it. ///

Bandicut conveyed that information to Napoleon. The robot made a rasping sound. "It must have its structure better concealed than ours."

"What do you mean?"

"Well, any fool could look at *The Long View* and say, of course it extrudes into n-space and uses n-space boundary layers as a hull."

"Any fool."

"But this object . . . well, the readings are a lot more ambiguous. I think maybe it's a normal-space structure that's been rolled up somehow into n-space, so that most of it is hidden. I can't tell for sure. And I'm not picking up any suggestion of streamers. I wish there were a way for us to probe it directly."

"Can you at least tell if it's Mindaru? If it is, maybe we should be thinking of how to take it out—or at least stay away from it. You know what happened the last time we approached one of those."

"That's a reasonable speculation," Napoleon said. "But speculation nevertheless. Obviously, we don't know what the results would be if we destroyed it, assuming we could find a way."

"I understand that. I was speaking hypothetically, Nappy."

Charli cleared her throat.

/// Mostly hypothetically? ///

Bandicut shrugged inwardly. /What do you suggest?/

/// Charlene-echo says Dark can't go any closer
without setting off alarms,
assuming she hasn't already.
I think we've got to go in and take a look.
And hope we're less obtrusive. ///

/That's what I was afraid you were going to say./ Bandicut relayed Charli's thoughts to everyone on the bridge who was listening. But before asking Li-Jared to help him decide—and the Karellian looked as if he was anything but amenable to approaching a Mindaru object—Bandicut called out to Ik and Antares. "Are you getting anything from the star? Any sense of whether this object might be involved in the trouble?"

Ik appeared lost in his trance, but Antares looked up and blinked her golden eyes. "It's all quite vague. We're still just making contact."

"If we move in to investigate this thing, do you think it will interfere with your contact?" Bandicut asked.

"I think our movements will not cause a problem. If we do come under attack . . . well . . ."

"Yah." Bandicut started to turn to Li-Jared when Charli suddenly yelled something. He couldn't understand, and had to ask her to repeat it.

/// That's it! Damn it, that's it!
I know what it's doing! ///

/What? What's it doing?/

*/// I've been getting this hazy image of
this star being caught up in a web of some kind,
but it didn't make any sense to me.
Ask Napoleon if he can do anything that would
make dark matter visible. ///*

/Dark matter? Charli, we can't *see* dark matter. That's why it's *called* dark matter./

*/// Just ask him. Or Jeaves.
If not dark matter, then n-space channels.
Ask them! ///*

Bandicut put the question to the robots. Napoleon wasn't sure, but Jeaves jumped in to say, "Exotic dark matter is nearly impossible to image in normal-space, but if it's passing through n-space channels, then we should be able to do something to light it up. Yes—I think I understand now. Not again! Why didn't I see that?"

"What do you mean, not again?" Bandicut asked.

But Jeaves was busy working with Napoleon to change the view. After a few moments, the image of the huge star flickered, then darkened as though a violet-black filter had dropped into place. Now it was no longer just the sun; threading from the surrounding space into it were a number of fine, glowing strands, a little like streamers of lightning playing from the center of a toy plasma globe. "That's it, they're feeding in the direction of the object," Jeaves said. "But where are they going from there?"

"What are those—?" Bandicut waved in bewilderment toward the streamers.

"Still trying to fine-tune the sensors," Jeaves said. "I believe Charli is right—those are streams of exotic dark matter being channeled through n-space. Wait a sec—here." The view lightened and turned bluer, and now the threads were thicker and looked like ghostly streamers of something flowing.

Li-Jared stood crouching with his hands on his hips. "Dark matter, eh?"

"Are we all talking about the same thing—the undetectable stuff that keeps the galaxies from flying apart?" Bandicut asked. "Because if we are, then I really don't understand what's going on."

Bong-ng. "Neither do I," Li-Jared said. "But you may be right. I hate to say it, but we may need to take a closer look."

"I *might* understand," Jeaves murmured.

"If you know something, tell us," Bandicut said.

"It might be the way they're attacking the star. But I could be completely wrong. Let me finish processing the information we're getting before I speculate, okay? Can we ask Copernicus to bring us in closer? We'll have to penetrate the star's outer atmosphere to get near the object."

Bandicut cast a frustrated glance at Ik and Antares before nodding yes.

∗

∗Thunder∗ was now a massive wall of light, filling most of the sky. The presumed-Mindaru object was floating in the star's photosphere, so they had little choice but to go on in themselves. The n-space fields would isolate them, as usual; if the fields failed, they would hardly have time to know the difference.

"I'm not sure what we're going to do once we have this object where we want it," Bandicut said, with a shiver of apprehension.

"I'm not sure, either," said Napoleon. "But it does appear to be of a different nature from the last."

"How do you know? I can barely see it."

"The last Mindaru object projected an n-space web that was clearly intended to trap and destroy spacecraft. This one appears to have other fish to fry."

"What sort of other . . . fish?" Li-Jared asked.

Napoleon flickered. "It *appears* to be involved in—and possibly *creating*—conduits through n-space. Conduits carrying dark matter. I can't tell yet where the conduits lead, but I think we might all have the same guess."

" ∗Nick∗?" Bandicut asked.

"That's *my* guess," Napoleon said.

Jeaves emitted a gentle sigh. "It would be consistent with a situation I once encountered, in which . . . sentient intervention . . . was causing a star to build toward supernova. It would have been very difficult to stop." He seemed to draw himself up. "We must be extremely creative in our response."

"Exactly," said Napoleon. "Captains, we really need to move

in for a close-up look, if we are to have answers. Do we have your permission?"

Bandicut glanced at Li-Jared, who assented with a flick of his fingers. "Sur-r-re. What have we got to lose? But be careful, all right?"

"Aye-aye, Cap'n."

*

It was very strange . . .

Ik felt his body turning to gossamer, to a wispy translucence. He was evaporating from the bridge of the ship. What was happening? A wave of panic rushed through him, then faded as quickly. He was floating through spacetime. He flew toward Deep, and toward the swelling star.

The star. It was a huge, luminous thing, filling the sky. It ought, logically, to have felt dangerous; but he did not sense heat from it, or radiation. Or danger. What he sensed was something, *someone*, aware of his approach.

Ik also felt a growing awareness of *time*—not as a flow or a past/present/future, but rather as a great diaphanous ribbon stretched out across . . . he didn't know what to call it, eternity maybe, or the timeline of existence. Whatever it was called, the star occupied a much greater swath of that ribbon than he did. Millions of Iks, or Ik-lifetimes, could be stretched end to end within the ribbon that the star occupied. Clearly the star was alive and aware, but how could it possibly commune with one so tiny? It was, Ik knew, Deep's work making that possible; the time-fusion sang through this vision like electricity through a wire.

And through that singing, faintly, came the voice of *Thunder*, very different from *Brightburn*. Ik could not make out words or expressions from *Thunder*, but he did detect a feeling, he thought. It was a strong emotion, an undertone to the electric song.

Thunder knew they were here. And she was not glad to see them.

*

The gases of the star's photosphere glowed whiter and bluer and brighter, ever brighter. They were gliding through *Thunder*'s atmosphere. Bandicut knew it was a translated image—they were still in n-space and would hardly have seen that view even if the ship had had windows—but he nevertheless felt his throat tighten as he watched. Ahead of them, the Mindaru object was now visible as a dark speck. When magnified, it was still an indefinable shape, a severely pixelated image. Standing nearby on the bridge, he sensed that Ik and Antares were being drawn further and further into contact with the star. He wished he knew what they were seeing and hearing. /Can you follow any of it?/

/// Only a little.
I get the feeling this star is angry. ///

/About—?/

/// About small, invading bodies. ///

Sorry he'd asked, Bandicut turned and spoke to Napoleon. "How close do we need to get to that thing? And do you see any danger signs?"

"As close as possible. And none so far."

No danger? That seemed unlikely. "Can you tell yet what it's doing?"

"I can confirm the flow of dark matter through a channel in n-dimensional space." A window appeared in an upper corner of the viewspace, revealing a false-color image in God-knew-what wavelength. Several ghostly streamers converged on a clear bubble surrounding the Mindaru object, then diverted inward into the star in one stream. "This would not be detectable from normal-space using any means familiar to us," Napoleon said.

"So the dark matter is being directed into the body of ∗Thunder∗?" Li-Jared asked.

Jeaves answered, "Yes, but I don't believe that is its final destination. Our scans cannot penetrate far enough to confirm, but I believe the flow is being redirected to another star."

"To ∗Nick∗?" Bandicut asked.

"I can't think of where else. My guess is that dark matter is accumulating in ∗Nick∗'s core," Jeaves said. "Precisely how, I'm not certain. But that buildup is probably what's causing the hypergrav disturbances. The intent must be to push ∗Nick∗ to the point of hypernova."

/// That's exactly the point, ///
Charli said, and there was anguish, grief, and anger in her voice.
Bandicut blinked in surprise. /How are you so sure?/
/// Because . . .
that's how my homeworld was killed. ///
/Charli? Are you sure?/
/// An hour ago, I wasn't.
But the memories that have been
coming back to me . . .
I know now, I remember it. ///
Bandicut swallowed hard, thinking. /You mean—that the
Mindaru destroyed your homeworld?/
/// Our sun was . . . like ∗Thunder∗.
Made to contribute to the explosion of
a neighboring star. ///
Bandicut closed his eyes. /And then wiped out by the super-
nova?/
/// Yes. Cosmic murder.
So this setup is not only giving ∗Thunder∗ a bellyache,
it's threatening the life of every star nearby,
and doing it deliberately. ///
Bandicut gulped. "Okay, Napoleon," he said at last. "Take us as
close as we need to go. Let's see if this thing has a weak spot."
"Aye, Cap'n. Doing so now."

∗

It took several hours for Copernicus to maneuver *The Long View*
close enough to give them a good view of the thing. It was a black,
prickly sphere, like a floating mine. So far, there had been no sign
of hostile activity, which was puzzling. "It's possible," Jeaves said,
"that this device is designed to perform just the one task. The others we've encountered may have been sentries and protectors."

"And they may have big brothers nearby," Bandicut muttered.

"So how do we distract this thing from its one true task?" Li-
Jared said, scratching his breastbone. He had been very quiet
throughout the approach, apparently unbothered by their plunge
into the sea of fiery radiation. Bandicut didn't know whether it
was good or bad for Li-Jared to be so calm.

"Well, we don't have any ship-to-ship weapons on board,"

Jeaves said. "Just some small arms. I believe we have some n-space disrupter grenades, and that sort of thing."

"So-o-o . . . ?" Bandicut asked.

"We probably need to dock," Jeaves continued. "Board it. Shut it down from the inside, if possible. What do you think?"

"That you're nuts?" Li-Jared said.

"Probably," Napoleon said. "We should be close enough to dock within the hour. Shall we prepare our boarding party?"

Bandicut could only stare at him.

28

BOARDING PARTY

 There were at least sixty reasons Bandicut could think of *not* to attempt a boarding of the Mindaru satellite— or whatever it was—starting with the fact that they were inside a star, and if the Mindaru didn't kill them, the star probably would. But the Mindaru was a marauding murderer that had to be stopped, and he couldn't think of any other way to stop it.

"No indication of defensive force-fields or hostile weaponry," Napoleon reported. "It may be that the fact that it's in the atmosphere of a star was considered defense enough."

"Yah," Bandicut said. "Or maybe its big brother will be paying us a visit." *So who's going in? What am I saying, the thing is the size of a beachball! Unless we have some really tiny probes . . .*

"I have identified a possible service-entry port," Copernicus reported. "I am going to attempt a semihard dock, and attach a boarding tunnel extrusion."

"Coppy, the thing is tiny! How are we supposed to—?"

"We will have to drop into three-space," Copernicus continued. "This may cause a change in the aspect. In any case, we have automated probes that will fit nicely through that port— assuming we can get it open."

Bandicut's heart was suddenly pounding with relief; or maybe it had been pounding all along and he hadn't noticed.

/Thank God, we don't have to turn ourselves into spaghetti to get into the thing./

/// For the time being.
But a probe isn't going to be able to interpret
what it sees the way your stones might.
Or I might. ///

Bandicut scowled but didn't answer. Napoleon was already saying, "Depending on what the probe finds, it is logical that I would be the next to go. Shall we proceed with rendezvous and docking?"

There was a sudden vibration in the deck, and the image in the viewspace changed subtly, as though the sensors had shifted to a different wavelength. The Mindaru satellite appeared darker, closer, and more ominous.

Copernicus announced, "We have dropped into three-space, folks. Normal-space, if you prefer—though of course we still have the n-space layering of the hull for protection."

"Then why—?"

"To simplify station-keeping and docking with the other vessel."

Bandicut glanced around nervously. "Then shall we go ahead and—"

There was a perceptible bump, then a click. "We are docked," said Copernicus.

✳

Ik was both surprised and moved by the upwelling of sound around him. It reminded him of the Maw of the Abyss from the Neri ocean-world as it distorted and twisted gravity in a futile attempt to complete a stargate operation. It was also like the rushing of wind he'd experienced in one of the sectors of Shipworld where huge air masses swept, moaning, over a hot desert. And it reminded him of the star-spanner that, long ago, had pulled him and his little ship to safety from his exploding sun.

/Hello?/ Ik tried to say, and the result was a translation into a gentle *gong-ng-ng-ng-ng-ng-ng* sound, reverberating into space. To his astonishment, there came in reply a deeper, almost seismic groan. Words? Or at least syllables? Were the stones translating?

*We are attempting . . . it is difficult . . . *

Besides his own stones working frantically to understand the star, he could feel Antares's stones trying to help . . . and all the while, he could feel the *presence* nearby, the star trying to understand what this new thing was. There was still anger, Ik thought, and fear or alarm. The star didn't know what they were, but it knew small intruders were harmful.

/Hello,/ he offered again, and hoped that this simple sound, and the benevolent wish behind it, might somehow be conveyed to the star.

Gong-g-g-g-g-g-g. And with the sound, an expanding wave front of crimson-orange light.

Ik felt a sudden burst of activity in his own head, a buzzing that ricocheted back and forth from one side of his skull to the other—the stones, consulting with each other on the exquisitely difficult problem of translation.

A fresh groan welled up from the star. A response to his hello? Maybe. But he was a long way from verbal communication. That, Ik thought, might take a very long time.

∗

For Deeaab, this was a more difficult time-fusion than any he had yet attempted. Time, in this region, flowed in subtly different streams and currents; it was altered by the many channels of n-space that the Mindaru had created. The sun clearly was in distress, no doubt because of the strange matter burning through those channels. Charlene-echo said that it seemed angry. The faint memory-echo of Delilah said that it was in pain. Perhaps both were true.

Deeaab considered taking immediate action, perhaps disrupting the n-space channels by direct force. But neither echo supported this thought. The results could be unpredictable; and in any case, he could not disrupt all of the channels at once.

Instead, he focused on what he was good at—bending time and trying to help the large life and the slow life to talk. He just had to accept that it was going to be hard.

∗

"The boarding tube is pressurizing," Copernicus reported. "The probe is ready. We are attempting to crack the code on the access hatch."

"You're still watching for defensive threats, right?"

"Of course, Cap'n."

"Good. Uh—listen, as you probe this thing, check to see if conditions are suitable—you know, in case one of us has to go in." Bandicut shut his eyes; he couldn't believe he was even thinking it, much less saying it.

"Certainly, Cap'n. But does it make sense for you to risk yourself if our probes can explore the area? Napoleon can go if we need greater capability."

Bandicut drew a breath. "Just call it a premonition. Maybe we won't have to, and that would be great. This is purely hypothetical." He realized Antares was looking in his direction. Even though she was mostly focused on the star, she apparently had heard him.

Copernicus said, "Code resolved. The port is opening. Probe now entering the Mindaru vessel. Readings are coming back." Napoleon pointed to a display window in the viewspace, where they could see the camera's eye view of the probe floating into the dark interior of the alien device. Angular shapes of machinery loomed in the probe's lights.

"What are we getting?"

Napoleon answered. "Atmosphere is confirmed, one-half sea-level Earth normal. Thirty percent argon, seventy percent helium. If you should decide to go in, you would need to take air, assuming you'd like oxygen."

"I accept the recommendation. What else?"

Napoleon took a moment to study the telemetry. "Local illumination is starting to come on, Cap'n, seemingly in response to our probe's presence. Also, it would seem that the interior space is expanding to allow room for movement. Interesting."

Bwang. "Why would it do that?" Li-Jared asked, looking more troubled than pleased.

"Perhaps it is designed to accommodate servicing visits," Napoleon suggested. "It may be like our ship, and able to expand at need."

/// Excellent.
That will be very helpful in the event
we decide to go in person. ///

/Mm./ Bandicut squinted at the images coming from the probe. "It's pretty hard to tell what we're looking at here. Nappy, can you decipher any of it?"

The robot clicked briefly. "Not very specifically, Cap'n. There appear to be large masses of solid-state circuitry, and possibly some moving parts. I cannot determine the function of any of it." A little later, he added, "I recommend I turn this analysis over to Jeaves, and prepare to enter the space myself."

Bandicut nodded, working his jaw for a moment. "I probably should prepare to go with you. In case it seems necessary."

"Cap'n, I don't see the purpose in risking your life," Napoleon said, and his words were echoed a moment later by Copernicus.

"The purpose is: if we can't interpret what's inside there, and determine what the hell it's doing, then we aren't going to be able to stop it, are we?"

Jeaves spoke up. "Do you think you could do that better than Napoleon? Enough better to justify the risk?"

Bandicut glanced at Antares and Li-Jared, both of whom were staring at him. "Not really. But—" he tapped the side of his head "—Charli might. And don't forget my stones. Between us, yes, I think we have a better chance."

"Bandie," Li-Jared said, "it would really make more sense for me to go—"

"No, it wouldn't. I mean, it might if we were talking about sending the smartest person. But Charli has memories that are connected to this business. And she's smarter than both of us combined. So no—if anyone goes, it should be me." Bandicut put a hand on Li-Jared's coarse-haired shoulder. "You know it's true."

Li-Jared's eyes narrowed, but he didn't answer.

"Folks," Copernicus said. "Sorry to interrupt, but we just lost the signal from the probe."

✳

Things were happening in Ik's mind, things he didn't understand. He felt as though he had come to a cliff edge, and gazed out onto a nighttime vista of stars, and become aware of something or someone much larger than himself moving and thinking and feeling in that vista. His sense of time, and space, and the boundaries of his body were all changing. He had lost nearly all awareness of the ship around him, and wasn't even completely sure it was still there, or that he was on it. He felt as if he were floating on a river of time, a stream flowing from time's beginning to time's end. He had always been on that stream, but now something was different; he was *stretching* along the stream. He could see many parts of it, though the end stretching into the future was obscured.

The sensation was dizzying. Behind him, sharing the view, was the great, luminous presence of the star, and also the darkly mysterious cloud of Deep. He couldn't *see* either of them, but he knew they were there, sharing this space. What he saw, they saw; what he felt, they felt.

His vision began to change again. He was starting to glimpse what ∗Thunder∗ saw in the time river . . . cold gas swirling and condensing and forming into balls of proto-stellar matter. The globules remained that way, like eggs, until a shock wave from a supernova slammed through the clouds, compressing the gases and igniting fusion.

∗Thunder∗ was reliving these moments, replaying them with perfect fidelity . . . as a new sun burst into life. With it came a dazzling brightness, and a billowing wind of radiation, blasting and scouring surrounding space. The shell of searing radiation hit other knots of coalescing gas—and some of them blew apart to the winds—and some of them, compressed by the shock wave, also collapsed and fused, and thus even newer stars were born from the chaos. And in many of them, *thought* emerged.

The stars whispered among themselves, telling tales, tales of the passage of years, of transformation, of newlife becoming oldlife and oldlife becoming death. Sometimes death came in cataclysms, and sometimes sooner rather than later. Some suns burned hot and fast, living their lives with intensity. One such was ∗Thunder∗. She knew her life would be measured by its blazing brightness, not its duration.

Even so, there had come to be a wrongness at work, stars

300 * JEFFREY A. CARVER *

dying young, dying because they were invaded, infected. There was a killer among them, poisoning the birthing grounds. A killer small and deadly . . .

Ik absorbed all of this in a billowing, wordless cloud. He felt a sense of timelessness in his knowing, a sense in which he felt he had *always* known these things, and always *not* known them. And a sense in which he had always, and never, asked the question he now found himself speaking to the star: "We are here to help. Can you tell us how to stop this killer?"

To his astonishment, a response came:

Lives
    created
    lost
So many things passing
    passing away

The words jolted him, coming fully formed through his stones. He was momentarily speechless. The stones had found a translation key.

"We are here to help," he repeated. "We want to help."

There was a sudden change in the air; he couldn't say what it was exactly, but the winds whirling around him seemed to have changed direction. And he heard more words, embedded in the sound of a clear bell, ringing deep from the bottom of an un- fathomably large space:

Grieved
    We are grieved
Filled with pain
    So much pain
      Why are you here ?
Are you here to cause more pain ?
      More death ?

Ik was staggered by the suffering and anger. Why *should* it trust him? He could only repeat what he had said before. "We have come to help. Do you know how?"

    We are uncertain
    What you are
      What are you ?

"I am Ik. Call me Ik."

The star's reply began with a softer kind of gong, and then . . .

Ik-k-k . . .

Ik rocked back, stunned by the confirmation that it really had heard him.

Why are
>**you here ?**

Are you sent by ∗N-n-ck-k-k-k∗ ?

Ik breathed in through his ears, his excitement growing. If he could convey their intentions; if they could genuinely communicate . . . "We have spoken with ∗Brightburn∗. ∗Brightburn∗ told us of ∗Nick-k-k∗."

∗Brightburn∗ is dying

"Yes," Ik said. "But she told us of ∗Nick-k-k∗."

The ringing and gonging of the star began to grow louder and faster.

∗N-n-ck-k-k-k∗ is dying
>**The serpent passes**
>>**through us**

Help
>**Help**
>>**Help**
>>>**Help**

>**Yes ?**

Ik whispered, "Yes . . ."

∗

"Any idea where the airlock is?" Bandicut asked Napoleon.

"I will take you there, while Copernicus sends another probe in," Napoleon answered. "We have made no decision that you will enter the object, are we agreed on that?"

Bandicut chuckled darkly. "Yes, Napoleon."

Napoleon stood between Bandicut and the door leading from the bridge. "Cap'n, just so we are clear about this. I have, at your request, stopped addressing you in the manner of respect that you are due. But that does not mean I have abandoned my fealty to you and your company. I will not let you needlessly put yourself in danger."

Bandicut opened his mouth but didn't know how to reply.

Finally he said, "Thank you, Napoleon, I appreciate that. But trust me, I have no intention of entering that damn thing unless it's absolutely necessary. Now, can we go?"

Napoleon bowed and turned to the door.

Bandicut looked back at Antares and Ik; it seemed unlikely that they were aware of what he was doing. He told them the plan anyway. "I'll be near the airlock, watching the second probe go in. If you learn anything, let me know. If . . . I have to go in . . . I'll try to stay in contact, but make whatever decisions you think are best."

Antares blinked slowly and squeezed his hand. "Use care," she murmured. "Ik is speaking to the star." It took a moment for her words to penetrate. *Ik is speaking to the star.* He blinked, dumbfounded, as he watched Antares return to whatever realm she was inhabiting with Ik.

Finally he turned his gaze to Li-Jared. "I guess you're in charge here. Pay attention to Ik and Antares, okay? They're . . . speaking to ∗Thunder∗."

Li-Jared made a soft hacking sound. "Yes," he murmured. "Be careful, Bandie John Bandicut."

"Yah." He strode off the bridge, following Napoleon.

The airlock was, surprisingly, only a short distance away. Jeaves followed them on audio, reporting on the progress of the second probe. *"Nothing yet that we didn't see with the first one."*

"What equipment have you got for me if I need to board? You said something about n-space disrupters—whatever those are. I don't suppose we have any high explosives, do we?" Bandicut asked. He had never touched a high explosive in his life, but right now, it seemed like a good idea to have some.

"The small n-space disrupters might be more useful than you think," Jeaves said. *"But we're not a warship. Mostly what we have is our intelligence, a certain ability to manipulate n-space, and Deep and Dark."*

"Mm." Bandicut looked around to see where Napoleon had brought him. They were in a small compartment, the right-hand wall lined with storage units, the left wall blank. In front of him was a round portal with a window in its center. He stepped up to peer through it. He could just make out the interior of a narrow tube, large enough for something about the size of a grapefruit to pass. He couldn't see very far into it. "What are we learning from that second probe?"

Napoleon raised a mechanical hand and touched a flat, metallic surface on the left wall. "Let's see if we can pick up the transmission." A moving picture appeared. It was a fish-eye-lens image from the probe. Strange-looking structures on all sides swelled and distorted as the probe moved through the interior of the Mindaru vessel. "There's not much I can interpret from that."

"Can't you get any—?"

"Wait!" Napoleon pointed. "Look!"

Bandicut was looking, but it took a few moments before he could make out what Napoleon was pointing at. Just coming into view, past a lot of jumbled, shadowy shapes and structures, was a faint horizontal halo of light, like the first light of dawn hazing up over a line of buildings. "What is it?"

"Unknown, Cap'n."

"Well, can you get a—"

Before he could finish his question, the image swung dizzyingly, then broke up and went blank. The voice of Copernicus informed them, *"We have lost contact with the second probe."*

"Any sign of what the trouble was?"

"None, Captain. No prior indication of trouble."

Bandicut swore. He felt a knot in his stomach. /The probes are failing. Does that mean we should go in, or that we'd be crazy to go in?/

/// I hate to say it, but . . . ///

/Yah./ He tipped his head back and called to Copernicus, "Do you have *any* clues? Because Napoleon and I are getting ready to go in."

"Unfortunately not," Copernicus answered. *"The signal weakened rather abruptly, and then went out. I'm afraid I can offer no advice on the possible risk to you. Captain, I think you should consider letting Napoleon go alone, at least to begin with."*

"Negative, Coppy. We don't know when that star could blow,

and the probes aren't getting the information we need. I'll look out for Nappy and he'll look out for me. Right, Napoleon?"

"Unfortunately, I cannot argue," Napoleon said. "But I do plan to improve our chances of maintaining contact, by dropping small transmitter-relays along the way."

"Good," Bandicut said. "Besides, I'll be protected by . . . come to think of it, I don't *see* any spacesuits here. Jeaves?"

"If you look to your right . . ."

Bandicut turned, and saw stuck to the wall a set of sand-dollar-sized, pewter-colored objects. "These?" He tugged at one and it pulled easily off the wall. Turning it in his hand, he said, "Don't tell me—"

"That's it. Stick it to your belt, or wherever it'll fit."

Bandicut pressed it to his belt, and it stuck like a magnet. "Okay, I—" A flash of silver suddenly bloomed up around him and quivered into place, enveloping him in a billowing transparent bubble.

"Now press—ah, you did already," said Jeaves.

"Yes. But how am I supposed to *do* anything from inside this bubble?"

Jeaves hesitated a moment. *"I'm not sure. Stand by . . ."*

While he was waiting, Bandicut squinted through the airlock window, and saw that the tube to the Mindaru vessel was visibly expanding. It was already almost large enough for him to float through. He took a slow, deliberate breath.

/// Chin up. I'm with you. ///

/Right. Thanks./ And to Napoleon, he said, "Are *you* ready?" He extended a hand, and the force-field bubble billowed silver.

"Yes. Could you touch that little plate on the right-hand side of the portal, please?"

As Bandicut's finger touched the plate, the force-field around him suddenly contracted and coated him like quicksilver. He held up his gleaming hand and turned it one way and another, examining it. "Hello. Was that supposed to happen?"

Jeaves answered, *"I think so, yes. John, if you look in a small compartment next to the suits, you'll find several packs of n-space disrupter units."*

"Grenades, I think you called them," Bandicut said, picking

up what looked like a wide-but-too-short belt with three slender egg-shaped devices stuck to one side of it. "How do I—never mind." He had tried, experimentally, pressing the belt section to his waist, and it was instantly attached. "Okay." He picked up a second belt and offered it to Napoleon. The robot took it, but instead of attaching the belt to himself, he simply pulled the eggs off and stowed them out of sight on or in his metal body.

"Okay, we're armed. Let's go." Bandicut straightened up and was surprised to see that the airlock portal had vanished, replaced by an open tunnel. It looked just large enough for him to pass through headfirst.

Li-Jared's voice filled the airlock. *"Bandie John, can you hear me?"*

"Loud and clear. I'll do a comm check as soon as we're over."

"Cap'n," said Napoleon, moving toward the opening. "I shall go first. I am the more expendable."

"Mm, okay."

"You'll be right behind me, though, yes?"

"*Yes.* Now move it before I run you over."

Napoleon strode forward into the tunnel. Bandicut followed, with an *oof!* as he went unexpectedly weightless. He bounced off the tunnel walls, his force-field suit glimmering as he ricocheted gently from one side to the other. Of course; why would a self-contained, robotic AI module a third of a meter in diameter need artificial gravity? *Keep moving.*

Napoleon had made it out the far end of the tube and was hovering just inside the Mindaru vessel, eyes turning this way and that, sensors obviously working at top capacity. Bandicut squeezed out of the tunnel behind him and floated motionless while Napoleon did his scans. He seemed to be in a wide, low cave, with very little headroom. If there had been gravity, he would have been crouching. "Li-Jared, can you hear me?"

There was a moment of silence. Then: *"We're getting both voice and images. Can you ask Napoleon to hold at least one of his cameras still? He's making me dizzy, swinging back and forth like that."* No sooner had he spoken than two of Napoleon's eyes abruptly stopped moving. *"That's better. What are we looking at?"*

"We are at the edge of a low, cavernlike space that extends farther than I can see into the distance," said Napoleon. "I suspect this interior may have the capacity to open wider, as needed. The question is whether it will close behind us as we progress deeper into the structure."

Bandicut had a sudden vision of dark storm clouds crowding in around him—he imagined a sharp flash of lightning, and the familiar farm image, harvesting machines towering, bearing down on him. He felt his knees buckle, and for a moment was unsure whether it was his real knees or his dream knees. Charli rushed to intercept, suppressing the power of the image.

/// John, that's a memory surging up.
But that's not what's here in this place. ///

He blinked back to reality with a gasp. /Right. But . . . was I on the verge of silence-fugue just then?/

/// I think so, yes.
It has a powerful hold on you.
There must be some reason why it keeps
coming back like that. ///

Bandicut drew a deep breath. /Well, until we figure it out, do what you can to keep me wired to reality, okay?/ He glanced around, and had the sudden weird feeling that he was diving through a congested, underwater factory space. Most of what he saw looked like very strange machinery, some of it squared-off and angular, and some melted-looking. It all felt threatening.

Napoleon was continuing his verbal report. "Since this compartment is crafted out of n-space, our original size in normal-space terms might be irrelevant. Possibly *all* that we see here might appear larger, if translated back to normal-space. As to why there's room to move around, I speculate it's for maintenance, and also for cooling, with the helium atmosphere."

Bandicut cleared his throat. He supposed that might make sense. But he still worried that they were swimming into a trap. "Let's get moving, all right?" Napoleon kicked off to float forward. "What's that?" Bandicut snapped as a spark dropped away from Napoleon and floated back past him.

"Transmitter-relay, Cap'n. Remember?"

Bread crumbs. Good. He followed Napoleon as the robot

moved deeper into the gloomy realm. He was reminded of the star-spanner factory back on Shipworld. This machinery was quite different, but he could almost smell the ozone and oil and strange chemical compositions of the semiconductors and super-conductors and quantum-conductors and whatever other damn things might be here. He wished they had the shadow-people with them.

"You were wondering about maintenance units?" Jeaves said, causing Bandicut to rotate in place, looking for him. *"No, I'm speaking from the ship. But I'm getting a good feed from Napoleon. Take a look ahead, and to your left. Do you see that thing crawling along the wall?"*

Bandicut squinted, and finally saw what Jeaves was talking about. A discus with numerous insectoid legs was scuttling along a low wall, tiny sparks of light coming from beneath it as it moved. He tensed, wondering if the thing had detected their presence. Should they try to disable it, before it noticed them?

/// I think that might sound the alarm,
if you tried to harm it. ///

/But surely *something* is going to notice us here./

As if reading Bandicut's thoughts, Napoleon said, "I recommend we leave mech units like that undisturbed. I think Copernicus did a pretty good job of thinking like the Mindaru when he hacked the entry system. I see no indication that we have been noticed as an intruder."

"Let's keep going, then."

Napoleon pushed off again, and Bandicut hastened to follow. "We seem to be on the edge of a fairly intensive operation here," Napoleon said. As they passed over some dark walls—Napoleon dropping another relay-spark—the space ahead seemed to open out to reveal a wider area. Light flickered as though from distant welding torches. And then the glowing halo appeared, the light they had seen from the probe. "I think we're moving in the right direction."

They floated among massive, curved structures that might have been transformers or capacitors or n-space field generators, or for all he knew, cubicle walls for mechs. As they drew nearer to the glow, the jumble of machinery that passed for a floor opened up, and Bandicut saw the source of the light. They had just come over a rise, and now were looking down into a kind of river valley. A *long* river valley. And flowing in that valley was a river of ghostly, sapphire light, a glowing plasma.

Bandicut could not help shivering with awe, even though he thought he knew what it was.

/// The flow of dark matter.
This must be one of the streams we saw
feeding into the star.
Or maybe all of them, combined.
Why is it channeled through here? ///

/That's what I'm wondering./ Bandicut instinctively reached out to find something to hold on to, for fear of falling into that ghostly place. His hand touched something *moving,* and he jumped when sparks shot from his hand. Rotating to look, he saw that his silver-coated hand had come down on the back of a robo-mech similar to the one they'd seen before. And his hand was stuck, as though held by a magnet. "Napoleon!" he cried, trying to yank his hand free.

/// John, don't pull away!
I think the stones are getting information
from it. ///

/From a maintenance mech?/

/// Yes. Give them a little longer. ///

He felt a wave of dizziness. Napoleon came up on the other side, and he steadied himself with his right hand on the robot. "Thanks," he gasped.

"Are you injured?" Napoleon asked. "What has happened?"

The force holding him to the robo-mech suddenly let go with another shower of sparks. The maintenance unit backed away. Bandicut shuddered and let out a long breath. "We had a momentary link, I think. I'm okay." /Am I? Are the stones?/

/// They're fine, but . . . busy processing.
I think they're trying to crack the code
of the language. ///

/Infection?/

/// I don't think so.
It seemed like a limited intelligence. ///

"We should keep moving. I'm getting a lot of EM and quantum activity in this area," Napoleon said, gripping Bandicut as he kicked off.

"Yeah," Bandicut said, taking a deep breath. He squinted toward the river of light. "I'll bet there's a lot of n-vector shit going on down there."

"I have *no* idea what you're talking about," Napoleon said. "But we are certainly seeing n-spatial manipulation on a large scale. That is no doubt one of the channels feeding mass to the star."

/// Did you make that up, just now?
N-vector shit? ///

/I honestly don't know./ Bandicut leaned closer to Napoleon. "So that *is* dark matter, that river of light?"

"I can't identify everything in it, but that plasma is primarily tiny-mass neutrinos, moderate-mass neutralinos, axions, and a lot of heavy particles that stump me," Napoleon said. "That sounds like exotic dark matter to me. Doesn't it to you?"

"I don't know. Why isn't it dark?"

"It's concentrated, and in a high-energy state, compared to its usual free-floating condition. So it's emitting light." With a long metal arm, Napoleon pointed down the river to the left. "It's flowing in that direction."

Way off to the left, the river disappeared into a kind of luminous haze. Napoleon began moving in that direction, flicking out another transmitter bread crumb as he went. "Li-Jared, are you still with us?" Bandicut called, following the robot. He took a moment to report.

"Affirmative. Any sign of the probes?" Li-Jared asked, his voice a little fuzzy with static.

"I see one of them ahead of us now," Napoleon said. He slowed and hovered near a small, drifting, ovoid object, which looked just as alien to Bandicut as anything else they'd found here. After a moment, the probe suddenly began moving, and scooted off to the right, paralleling the river in an upstream direction. "It's fine," Napoleon said. "It became disoriented and lost its position and signal-lock. It was confused by the recurring convolutions in the shape of n-space here. I've sent it scouting in the other direction."

"Convolutions in the shape of n-space?" Bandicut murmured. "*We'll* be very careful not to become disoriented by that, won't we?"

"Indeed," said Napoleon. He pushed off and glided along the upper ridge of the river valley. Bandicut kept pace, eyeing the flow of dark matter to his right and "below" them. As they floated parallel to the stream, the hazy view ahead slowly began to resolve. It became clear that the plasma stream was flowing into a tunnel that led out of the cavern.

"Nappy, can you tell where that tunnel leads?"

Napoleon dropped another bread crumb. "At first I thought it connected this cavern to another farther on. Now I'm not so sure." His sensors were twitching and blinking. "I'm thinking it goes a *lot* farther." He slowed as they approached a low wall; they paused and peered over it like a parapet.

The river of plasma entered the cavern wall through a round opening. It lit the inside of the tunnel, which looked like an extremely long, straight tube that stretched off to infinity. At the vanishing point, Bandicut thought he saw a diamondlike glint. "Collimated n-space channel," Napoleon muttered.

Bandicut squinted and bit off a sarcastic reply. "Naturally. Can you tell where it goes?"

Napoleon ticked, like an engine cooling. He shifted position, trying to align a sensor on the end of a telescoping arm. A dazzling light flared through a lens on the sensor, and Napoleon jerked back. "Bright. Sorry. I think this channel leads straight from this star into the heart of the next star. Into ✳Nick✳."

Bandicut tried to think how to respond to that and finally, very softly, just cleared his throat.

29

 The walls of the message-recording booth felt like a cell around Julie Stone as she sat silent, frozen, unable to think what she had intended to say in any of her messages. Captain Iacuzio's last words still echoed in her ears: *Surely there must be another way.* And the translator's answer: *Perhaps. We will speak again shortly.* And her stones, as she'd stood there watching the translator go silent: *Are you willing to do what must be done?*

Yes. I'm willing. You knew that before you asked. But it doesn't mean I have to like it.

She sighed, staring at the wall of the booth, clearly visible through the star-vista incompletely rendered by the VR equipment. *You don't have much time. Let's get this done.* She clicked on the icon to begin a recording to send to Earth. When the tiny red light came on, she drew a breath and began, "Dakota, this is Julie Stone. I've never really managed to say the things I've wanted to say. I've been looking forward to meeting you on my return to Earth. But our meeting might have to be delayed . . ."

She couldn't really tell Dakota *why*, of course, just as she couldn't tell her parents and brother. But she could let them know she was thinking of them. And perhaps set their minds at ease that she hadn't lost her marbles. Besides, there was always the chance that she'd make it back if things went well. A chance.

Now she was hurrying to finish; she'd spent too much time already. Clicking to send the holos, she rose and exited the recording booth. And bumped into Arlene, who was waiting outside. "Ah! Hi!" Julie said, her voice half an octave too high.

Arlene managed a wan smile. "I guess we had the same thought," she said awkwardly. "I feel like I need to say hi to my mom, or *something*. Keeping quiet about all this—that's going to be hard."

Julie tried to will her heart to stop thundering. "Yah. Well, I'm on my way to talk to the captain. He wanted to see me."

Arlene nodded and started into the booth.

"Listen," Julie said. "I might be . . . late for dinner tonight. So go ahead and start, don't wait for me." She grabbed Arlene's arm and squeezed it impulsively. Before Arlene could reply, she turned and fled up the passageway.

The captain's quarters were just aft of the bridge. She knocked hesitantly, and heard his muffled voice tell her to come in. She slipped inside and shut the door behind her. The quarters were only modestly larger than hers, but far more cluttered, with zero-gee bookshelves, photographs, and various official-looking pieces of equipment. The captain was seated at a small desk, with a tablet, a computer, and several open books arrayed in front of him. "Sit," he said, gesturing to the only chair. He closed his books and turned off his tablet, facing her.

Julie sat with her hands folded in her lap. She wasn't sure what to expect of the captain. She knew what *she* had to do. But the captain was an unknown.

He ran his fingers back through his gray-streaked hair, looking tired. "Have you finished all the messages you wanted to send?" he asked. She nodded. "And you kept this business to yourself? Because we need to check all messages before we transmit. Not just yours, but everyone's." Iacuzio sat back, glanced at a framed image of a dark-haired woman—his wife? daughter?—and scratched his jaw. "Listen, Miss Stone. I've been thinking a lot about the last thing I said to the translator. Perhaps you can tell me—*is* there another way?"

He knows. Will he let me do it?

He cocked his head, and she wondered if he was reading her mind. "You know," he said, "that we have a small maintenance craft docked to our hull, yes? Now, I don't know if . . ." His voice trailed off, and his jaw went to one side, and he seemed to be having doubts as he watched her reaction.

Julie let her breath out—had she been holding it?—and said, her voice unsteady, "Yes, the translator told me that it *could* try the mission using the service craft. It would be more difficult, because of its lower mass, and more limited supplies, and the chances of returning are smaller. But I—that is, *we*—were going to—"

Iacuzio rocked forward. "No, *you* are not going to do anything," he said flatly. "Unless you're holding a pilot's rating somewhere that you haven't told anyone about."

Flying experience will not be needed, the stones murmured.

"Nor am I going to send any of my crew on a one-way mission. But there's nothing that says I can't go myself." The captain was rubbing his thumb and forefinger together, studying his hand.

"But your ship—your responsibility here—"

He looked up, his clear gaze framed by his graying hair. "I have a highly qualified executive officer who is perfectly capable of looking after this ship without me. But I would need your cooperation in working with the translator."

We require you and your stones, not the captain.

Julie exhaled, shaking her head. "Captain, that's—not what the translator needs. It needs me." On an impulse, she pulled back her sleeves, raised her hands, and showed her wrists to the captain. Her stones glowed accommodatingly. "And it needs these."

Iacuzio stared at her wrists as if *they* were the translator. Then he looked up again. "No," he said.

Her voice started to shake. "What do you mean, no?"

"I mean, *no.* You have no training and it would be a dea—" He caught himself and shook his head. "The risk would be far too great. Unacceptable. I will not send an untrained young woman into deep space to her . . . almost certain death. Translator or no translator." He glanced again at the photo. Definitely a daughter.

She sat for a moment, her head spinning. *What about the risk to Earth?*

Before she could say anything more, there was a sharp jolt through the deck, followed by a heavy vibration and loud klaxon sound from the corridor. *What the—?*

The captain's gaze snapped around. "Stay right here!" he ordered and clicked on his intercom. "Bridge! Captain. What's going on?"

"Major power fluctuation in the fusion drive, Captain!" The voice from the intercom was tight but steady.

"How bad?"

"Way in the red. We have to shut her down."

"Do so at once." Another alarm sounded, there was a softer jolt, and acceleration cut off. Julie began to rise in her seat, weightless. "Are we stable?" Iacuzio asked, still speaking to the intercom.

"Pressure in the reactor has dropped into the green. We're stable."

"All right. I'll be there in a minute. Start assembling a repair team for EVA." Iacuzio turned to Julie. "That one maintenance craft is the only way we have of getting to the drive for repair. So it looks like neither one of us is going. Now, if you'll excuse me—"

"Captain, wait!" Julie grabbed awkwardly at his desk to keep from floating into him. The stones were buzzing in her head. "The translator has something—"

The captain had one hand on the door. "Make it fast."

She blinked, listening. "The translator has monitored the malfunction. It's a critical one, and needs immediate attention. But the translator can repair it. *If* you send me out in the craft."

"Send *you*—why you?"

She gulped, listening as the stones spoke rapidly. "Because it will need the stones on the scene, and because—"

"Fine. You can go as a passenger."

"No, I have to go alone, because . . ." She flushed. "It wants to continue on with the mission—with me—after it has repaired the reactor."

Iacuzio's blue eyes widened. He growled, "Is the translator trying to blackmail me?"

"No, sir—it's offering a deal."

With a soft curse, Iacuzio turned back and forth from the door, then said, "Stay here while I go to the bridge." He flew out of the cabin.

Julie followed him; the bridge was only a short distance. The alarm had stopped, but crew members were hurtling urgently up and down the passages. She paused at the entrance to the bridge when she heard the captain growl in dismay. She peered in. Captain Iacuzio was engaged in a heated technical discussion with the bridge crew. He turned and scowled when he saw her. But when he spoke, it was to snap to a crewman, "Then that's what we'll have to do! Don't argue with me. Get the craft ready!" He turned again, and shouted, "Lieutenant Cohn, where are you?"

"Here, sir." Henry was at the far end of the bridge, hunched over a console.

"Henry, follow me." Both of them barreled toward the door where Julie was waiting, and would have plowed into her if she hadn't backed away hastily. "Henry, get Miss Stone down to the maintenance craft on the double."

"Captain?" Henry's face went from worried to stunned.

"*Fast*, Henry. Get her aboard the craft, and make sure she has everything she needs. Air, food, extra of everything. Understood?"

"Sir, is this a—?"

"Not a joke, no. She and the translator are going to repair the drive. So says the translator—and further, it says it can fly the craft. Is that right, Miss Stone?" Captain Iacuzio turned to her with blazing eyes.

She swallowed. "Yes."

"Then, Miss Stone, you need to know that we have a critical overload building in a secondary reactor chamber. It could rupture and destroy the rest of the drive. I don't know how it happened, and I *would not* send you, except that we have no choice. *We* can't fix it in time."

"Yes, sir."

"Now, move—both of you! God help you, girl."

"Thank you, sir. And please don't—"

"*Get going!*" Iacuzio roared.

✷

/What about the translator? Is it coming?/ she asked the stones as they pushed off down the passageway. /Do I need to see it first?/

It is preparing to join you there.

"Julie, please tell me you're not doing what I think you're doing," Henry said, gliding beside her and giving her a slight correction with a nudge.

"Which way? Are we almost there?"

"This way." Henry caught her arm and pulled her through a side passage and into a different corridor. They went past a bulkhead door, and suddenly were in a ready room filled with lockers and cabinets, spacesuits, air tanks, and other gear. Two crewmen were scurrying in and out through a hatch with supplies. "Julie—" Henry said, and the words started flying from his mouth. "Do you have *any* training in a craft like that? Do you want me to—?"

She made a sharp gesture with the flat of her hand, cutting him off. "Henry! No more questions! Just get me ready."

Henry nodded and spoke quickly to the crewmen. He turned back to her. "All right. There's a fully charged spacesuit already on the craft, in a locker. You'll only need that if you lose pressure for some reason. There's air for five days, for two people. There are some emergency rations on board, but here—" he flipped open a storage pod and gathered up an armful of food packets "—take these, just in case. And here, water."

"What's going on here?" one of the crewmen asked. "I thought she was just going to fix the reactor."

"She is. If it's ready, let her board."

The crewmen moved out of the way, but didn't look happy about it. "Captain's orders," Henry snapped. "Julie? Come on."

Laden with supplies, Julie ducked through the airlock into the cramped, musty-smelling cockpit of the maintenance craft. She found a place to dump the supplies and worked herself into the pilot's seat. "Okay." She stared uncomprehending at the bank of controls. "Where are the communications?"

Henry reached in and pointed. "Masters, comm, propulsion, life support. Turn them all on." She snapped the switches in quick succession, which brought lights and sounds to life in the cabin. Henry seemed suddenly to lose his voice. Clearly he wanted to say something. "You okay?" he said finally.

Julie nodded and closed her eyes. /Are you almost ready?/

Affirmative. The translator is moving at this time. It will be attached to the outside of your craft momentarily.

Julie reached to fasten her seat restraints and said to Henry, "Can you seal me in, please?"

"Yah—right." Henry pulled away, then stuck his head in one

more time. "Listen. Whatever you have planned . . ." His brow was furrowed in a scowl.

"Shut the hatch, Henry!"

"Right." He slapped a control. "Be careful!" he shouted as the hatch slid shut. He waved through the window.

Julie bit her lip, reading the inside of the hatch by her right shoulder. Stenciled on the lip of the window was the inscription:

MNT DPLY UNT 1

/We're in the army now. There *is* only one maintenance craft. Okay . . . / She ran her fingers along the controls. Rows of indicator lights had come on, most of them turning from red to amber to green, as the automatic systems booted up. She leaned to her left, and through the window saw two curved sections of hull—one, part of the main ship, and the other, curving tightly rearward, the hull of this craft. Behind it all was the black of space. She jerked herself back and turned on the comm. A voice was blaring: "*. . . Artifact analysis team to the hold at once! The artifact has disappeared from monitors. Repeat, the artifact is no longer visible on monitors.*"

I'm sorry, Dr. Lamarr, she thought. I really am. /Where is it now?/

She was answered by the slightly deeper voice of the translator itself. *We are attached to the outside of your craft, near the propulsion unit. Please make ready to undock.* Out the left window, she glimpsed a faint flicker of light. She felt a sudden, shivering sense of electricity around her. Something very powerful had come to life around the craft.

/What should I do?/

Prepare to separate.

The next voice from the comm caught her by surprise. It was Captain Iacuzio. "*All hands, the translator is assisting us with this emergency. Is Maintenance One ready? Lieutenant Cohn, are you ready to release Maintenance One?*" She glanced over her shoulder and saw Henry's face through the window one last time. "*Release Maintenance One.*"

She felt a jolt, and the craft began to float gently away from its docking cradle. Out the cockpit window, Julie saw a gap opening between her craft and the *Park Avenue*; more and more of the mother ship was becoming visible. Thrusters fired. They were drifting away, and to the other ship's stern. /What now?/

We must gain a clear distance from the ship.

/And the emergency?/

We are in the process of restoring the reactor. There will be no further malfunction.

Julie could feel her eyes bulge. *"Are you saying there was never—? Why, you son of a b—"* She bit off her audible curse and snarled inwardly, /You put this whole charade on to get me away in this little tin can?/

It seemed the only way.

"Damn!" she yelled. *"Fuck!"* She snapped off the comm.

It really did seem the only way.

She cursed a silent stream and snapped the comm back on. The ship was calling her: *"Miss Stone, is there a problem? Can we help?"*

"No. I'm fine. I broke a fingernail. How's that reactor, is it calming down?"

"Affirmative. It is stabilizing. How the heck is that possible?"

"Dunno. But keep me posted." She pushed her head back against the seat and watched the ballet as the craft glided toward the stern of the *Park Avenue*. On the comm, she heard someone on one part of the ship yell to someone else that the maintenance craft was dangerously far from the ship, and shouldn't they do something? The captain's voice came back on and said, No, it was part of the plan, don't worry. Another voice was paging Julie Stone to the cargo hold.

Julie drew a long, slow breath as her stomach did a somersault. She didn't feel any acceleration, but the *Park Avenue* was moving away faster. /Is this going to be a one-way trip, like John's?/ she asked suddenly, the frightening thought slipping past her guard of optimism.

That is a possibility. We do not know what will happen.

She swallowed hard. She was going to spend a long time

processing this, she knew. She hadn't even really gotten over losing John, and now she was off to do the same thing. She did not
think of herself as a particularly brave or self-sacrificing person.

*Sometimes people learn what they are capable of only
when—*

/And sometimes people need to close their eyes and pretend
that none of this is happening,/ she muttered. And she did just
that, as the two vessels continued moving apart.

*

Her retreat didn't last long, but it helped. Now the comm unit
was blinking insistently and buzzing at a low volume. She
reached to turn the volume back up; she didn't remember having turned it down.

The bridge comm officer was calling to her. "Miss Stone, can
you hear me? Are you able to scan the reactor area from your
present location?"

She peered helplessly at the control console and appealed to
the translator. *The malfunction is corrected. We have made
several adjustments to reduce the risk of future drive failure.
They should prepare for a restart.*

Julie relayed that information.

A moment later, the comm officer said, "Miss Stone, Dr.
Lamarr would like to speak to you on a private line."

Julie told him to go ahead. He could make her feel bad
maybe, but he couldn't stop her. The comm crackled, then she
heard his voice.

"Miss Stone, when the translator spoke of . . . another
way . . . this wasn't exactly what I thought it had in mind, taking you in a small craft that wouldn't even get you to . . ." His
voice seemed to catch.

"No, Dr. Lamarr," she answered. "But since we couldn't risk
the whole ship, this was the only other option."

"Yes. Is the translator with you?"

"It is. As soon as we have confirmation that your fusion drive
is working, we'll be on our way."

"I see. You know, we'd had hopes . . . well." It was a done
deal, and he seemed to realize it.

She remembered how surprised she'd been when Lamarr had

voiced a willingness to go along with the translator's original plan. "Dr. Lamarr—thank you for being willing to support the translator in the end. Even if it . . . even if it's not the way we'd hoped."

There was static for a moment, before he answered, *"Yes, well—I guess I'm there with you in spirit. I hope we see you again, and . . . Godspeed."*

Julie felt a lump in her throat, but before she could answer, Captain Iacuzio came back on to say, *"We're preparing a restart of the drive, as soon as you're at a safe distance to observe."*

The translator muttered to her, and she echoed to the captain, "You may go ahead."

They were now behind and to one side of the *Park Avenue*, at a distance of perhaps a kilometer. The drive units were clearly visible. She could hear the captain issue an all-ship warning, and a few seconds later, the tail of the ship began to glow scarlet, then orange. Then, as if with a quick flick, the fire turned diamond-white. The ship began to accelerate away from her.

She swallowed, keyed the comm, and said, "Everything looks fine from here. Good-bye, *Park Ave.*"

An answer started to come from the ship, but was cut off by a knife-stroke, as a bright ring of light sprang up around her craft, encircling it at the middle, maybe fifty meters across. Julie craned her neck to see. She suddenly realized that the *Park Avenue* was receding impossibly fast. It dwindled in a few seconds to a twinkling point, and then it was lost in the starry darkness. *My God. What have I done?* She turned to look the other way, and was stunned to see a series of wide, concentric rings of light stream out behind the craft.

∗We are threading space. Radio communication is no longer available.∗

She blinked, trying to clear the mist from her eyes as she peered into space, wondering where exactly she was going, and how fast. Against the darkness, the sun was brighter than the rest of the stars, but not by much. All the stars seemed very distant, very cold, and very lonely.

30

 "So you really think that stream of dark matter is shooting straight across half a light-year to *Nick*?" Bandicut asked, crouching low while he tried to think this through.

"That is how it looks to me," Napoleon said. "A straight tunnel through n-space." He was doing something Bandicut couldn't quite see. His left mechanical arm was raised and cocked, as though he were about to throw something. "I think, Cap'n, our best hope is to try to find where all of this is controlled. If we can turn it off using *their* controls, instead of trying to disrupt it by force . . ."

"What's that in your hand?"

"Probe. I'm going to try sending it into the tunnel. Is that acceptable?"

"Sure. Fire away." Bandicut raised his head to watch. "Where'd *you* get things like probes?"

"Part of the latest upgrade," Napoleon said, anchoring himself against the nearest support. His arm pivoted fast, in a flinging motion, and something rocketed from the end of it and streaked toward the opening of the tunnel. "Probe away." The point of light vanished into the tunnel. "Getting a signal. No, wait. Temperature's spiking. I'm losing—I've lost it."

"Burned up? That fast?"

"Yes."

"That sort of argues against going much farther that way, doesn't it?"

"It does. Cap'n, there might be a better way. Maybe we should follow the track *upstream,* to see if we can stop it where it comes in."

"Well—that's still the thing, isn't it? *How* can we stop it?"

"Control interfaces. That's what we need to find."

"And if we do, can you talk to them?"

The robot, crouching in the eerie light of the cavern, suddenly looked to Bandicut like a gnarled, half-starved man wearing mirror shades. He swiveled his head to peer back at Bandicut through his shades. "I suggest we find that bridge before we cross it."

Bandicut rose, floating away from the wall of machinery. "Lead on, kemosabe."

*

For Ik, things seemed to be heating up. He felt surrounded not just by the voice of the star, but by its heat and light as well. The feeling was intense, though he knew logically that he was still on the bridge of the ship. But something was happening inside this star, something beyond the normal fusion-fires, something strong and deep. Something that felt *wrong,* not just to Ik, but to the star.

Can you stop the pain
Make it stop ?
It will kill
is killing

Yes, Ik wanted to say. They were trying. But . . . "The pain," he whispered. "Is it just yours, or is it that other star's, too? Which of you is it killing?"

N-n-ck-k-k-k
Killing *N-n-ck-k-k-k*
killing
through me
Making me kill

Ik slowed his breathing very deliberately and tried to focus. Making me kill. *What* was making *Thunder* kill? The thing John and Napoleon were investigating? Almost certainly. "How can we make it stop?" he whispered to the star.

There was a thunderous reverberation—and then a dazzling image that froze across his vision for an instant like a bolt of lightning: the star surrounded and penetrated by a great web of ghostly strands, and a tremendous but pale stinger that shot out from its body. Far away, another star brightened, apparently on the receiving end of the ray.

Must stop
that, you must stop

Ik, stunned, did not know what to say. He felt Antares also

reeling from the image. *John Bandicut, you must succeed.
Somehow you must succeed...*

✳

Li-Jared glanced from time to time at Ik and Antares, wishing he
could guess what was happening in their inner worlds. Meanwhile, outside the ship, Bandicut and Napoleon were moving
deeper and deeper into the Mindaru object, and farther and farther from any chance of his helping them.

Li-Jared was fit to burst from the feeling of helplessness.

Jeaves interrupted his thoughts. "You had better take a look
at the long-range scanners. Something is coming our way."

Li-Jared turned to look, hearts suddenly burning in his chest.
"Oh no."

"Oh yes."

✳

Deeaab was captivated and sobered by what was happening between Ik and the star. Thanks to the quarx-echo bridging the gulf
to Ik's organic consciousness, Deeaab was able to follow some
of the communication. The star's thoughts Deeaab could fathom
more easily, as it bore greater resemblance to Deeaab's own consciousness. This star's pain was harder to bear than ✳Bright-
burn✳'s, perhaps because ✳Thunder✳ was young and not near the
end of its natural life, as ✳Brightburn✳ had been. The long cords
of strange matter running through it and joining it to the more
distant star would lead to mounting pain for this star, and violent
death for the other. And ✳N-n-ck-k-k✳'s death would cause a
cascade of violent death for ✳Thunder✳ and many other stars.

Deeaab was all too familiar with death. In another time and
universe, Deeaab had witnessed great violence, multiple cas-
cades of death. Indeed, only by slipping from that universe to
this had Deeaab—and, separately, Daarooaack—escaped that
death themselves, a death of the universe itself, a winding down
of all energy and life. Slipping through a rare, fleeting connection between universes, they'd found their way to a place where
life still lived, where death, while everywhere, could be held
back for a time. Deeaab greatly preferred life to death. And he
did not want to be alone again.

Now, as the small, quick life did their work, Deeaab thought hard about how this particular pain, this impending death, might be stopped.

It would not be easy . . .

Even as Deeaab thought this, another hypergrav shock wave passed through, coming from the direction of ✳N-n-ck-k-k✳. Were those waves coming more frequently? He feared so. He feared they were a sign of something nearing completion.

✳

As they floated back along the ridge overlooking the dark-matter river, Bandicut began to feel as if he were on a long quest in some phantasmagorical land, searching for a magical *something.* He didn't know what. He had the feeling that if he slipped on a rock and fell into the glowing river to his left, the waters of the river would dissolve his body and separate his soul from it within moments. Which probably wasn't far from the truth. He felt an acute sense of vulnerability; so easy to lose control and slip . . .

/// *What's really bothering you?* ///

Bandicut grunted. /For one thing, the fact that we're getting farther and farther from the place where we came in. I'm not sure I could find my way out, if anything happened to Nappy./

/// *Good reason to keep a sharp eye out*
for Napoleon's safety. ///

/Yah./

/// *John, maybe you need to slow down*
and take a few deep breaths.
You're very tense. ///

/You think?/

At that moment, his surroundings began to vibrate violently. "Cap'n, hypergrav shock waves," Napoleon warned.

Bandicut felt his own body shake. Reaching out to grab the nearest support, he missed, took a bad bounce off a melted-looking piece of machinery, and caromed unexpectedly to the left. Before he could catch himself, he was floating out from the ridge toward the river of dark matter. "Shit!" he yelled. "Help—Napoleon!" He flailed his arms. There was nothing to grab on to. "*Napoleon,* can you—?"

Something grabbed his ankle and jerked him to a stop. He gasped with relief. Now he was being pulled back. Twisting around, he saw that Napoleon was anchoring himself with two or three grippers, and reeling in a rope that was coiled around Bandicut's ankle. "What the—is that Ik's rope?" he asked as Napoleon brought him alongside and released the rope with a final tug.

"It is a copy," the robot said, retracting the line. "The ship made it for me. That was a pretty strong shock wave we just felt. Likely it is a sign of growing instability."

Bandicut grimaced as they continued on. The hardware landscape began to open out, as though they were emerging from a valley into a plain. They passed over a low rise, and the view before them took Bandicut's breath away. The dark-matter river, on their left, emerged from the valley and took a sharp turn so that it looped to the right to cut a glowing swath in the landscape before them. It divided into numerous branches, until it looked like a great meandering estuary system. But the branch-streams, instead of draining into an ocean, rose up from the landscape and climbed like spider-web tendrils into the darkness of a starry sky.

The movement of the ghostly stream was clearly visible—coming *down* from the sky in the many individual streams, and joining to become the great river that flowed past Bandicut and Napoleon, and continued behind them to the n-space tunnel and on into the heart of a star.

Bandicut remained poised, scarcely breathing. Finally he murmured, "This is it, then? This is where it's brought in from all over space and funneled together? Into ✳Thunder✳ and then ✳Nick✳?"

Napoleon ticked slowly. "It would seem so, Cap'n. This is what will kill ✳Nick✳, if we don't stop it."

"And do you see any way to do that?"

"I can only hope that somewhere down there is something that controls all this."

Bandicut nodded. "Any information from the probe you sent this way?"

"Nothing useful so far."

Bandicut sighed. "Shall we go have a look, then?"

✳

"Copernicus, what *is* that thing that's moving toward us?" Li-Jared rubbed the control panel nervously with two fingers. He was pretty sure he already knew the answer.

"Appears to be another Mindaru object, doesn't it?" said Copernicus.

"I was hoping you'd tell me I was wrong."

"Not this time, no. It appears," said Copernicus, "that we have drawn the attention of the local Mindaru bouncers."

Bwang. "What?"

"Local guardians. Sentinels. Trouble. There's a good chance we're going to want to move quickly. I recommend you consider recalling John Bandicut and Napoleon."

Li-Jared made a gravelly sound. "I don't know if you noticed, but they're in there trying to stop a *star* from exploding."

"I know that," said Copernicus. "But it's no good having us all dead, is it?"

"No, but—" Li-Jared dropped the hand he'd raised in protest and keyed the comm. "Bandie, what is your status?"

There was a long pause before he heard anything, and then, distant with static, Bandicut's voice: *"We're trying to find the control point to alter the stream of dark matter. What's the ship's status?"*

Bong. "Not much happening here. Except Copernicus has detected what he describes as a Mindaru 'bouncer' approaching. He suggests you might want to come back to the ship. We may have to move quickly."

Bandicut's voice sounded even more strained. *"We need every minute you can buy us. It could be critical."*

Li-Jared drummed his fingers on his chest. "Do you have a time estimate?"

"No, I—wait, Napoleon is communicating with Copernicus—"

Li-Jared turned and looked at the robot, half-embedded in the wall. "Well?"

After a moment's delay, Copernicus said, "Napoleon suggests, if necessary, we may have to leave them temporarily behind—if we're forced to move to evade the Mindaru sentinel."

"We will do no such thing," Li-Jared growled. "We will hold our position. Right here. Is that understood?"

Copernicus seemed to hesitate before answering. "Understood."

★

Bandicut followed Napoleon into a narrow cleft, which cut off the view of the river of light. He felt as if they were surrounded by living rock as they passed between the walls of the cleft. There was an electricity in the air, and quick flashes of light along the walls, like firing synapses. Napoleon pushed on ahead without hesitation, and as Bandicut followed, he felt an odd *crinkling* sensation.

"N-space transition," Napoleon reported. "We've gone a dimension or two deeper. And . . . we've lost contact with the probe."

Damn. "All right, that means we're now *where?*" Bandicut looked around uneasily. Everything had changed, or at least shifted around. He rolled slightly, and was shocked to see the ghostly glowing river flowing over his head. He suddenly realized he was looking up as if through the bottom of an overhead aquarium, with the dark-matter streams moving *above* him. It was an extremely disorienting sensation.

Napoleon was examining the surface of the wall, where there had been glimmers of light a moment ago. "I am attempting to find a control interface. There are surface points here for the local intelligence system, but I cannot seem to find a linguistic common ground. I am at a loss."

Bandicut scowled, thinking. He mentally paced in circles. They didn't necessarily need to understand the whole control system, if they could just make a small change, in the right direction. It was a problem in plumbing, really. Hydraulics, maybe— or fluidics. It was a problem on a cosmic scale, but the same principles might apply. "Nappy? Is it possible we could influence it in some *very small way?*"

An idea was beginning to form, and he hesitated before mentioning it to Napoleon. "Napoleon, what if . . ." and he hesitated, and looked within to Charli and the stones for confirmation. /Can we do this?/

We are ready to try.

"Suppose *I* tried to make contact with the control. I mean the stones, not me, but I would have to make the contact. Maybe they can translate where you—"

"Where I could not. Because they learned some language from that mech. It is a promising idea, but a risky one, Cap'n." The robot turned and eyed him with pale-glowing sensors.

"Yes, it is. But if we don't succeed, that star's going to blow up and take us with it, anyway." Bandicut surveyed their immediate surroundings; they were still in what felt like a rock passage. He floated into position and hooked his feet on something to steady himself, and reached out to touch the spot Napoleon had just been probing. /Are you ready for contact?/

Proceed.

Taking a deep breath, he pressed the silver-coated palm of his hand to the wall. At first he felt just a tingle, and then a sputter. He resisted the urge to pull away, quelled the fear of electrocution . . .

And then a flash of purplish blue light passed over him. And a second flash, at a different angle. And with a rush, he felt himself buzzing with dancing electricity, and voices, and rapidly thrumming strings. For about ten heartbeats, he was completely out of his body, and unable to control so much as a thought. *Something* was happening between the stones and the interface. Then all the sensations vanished as abruptly as they'd come, except for a burning in both of his wrists. And that, too, faded and he came back to his senses, peering at Napoleon. "I— I just—oh, my God, I don't know what I—"

/// That was . . . very strange.
John, the stones took a jolt.
I don't know what they learned,
or did . . . ///

The stones were silent. It was impossible to tell if they had accomplished anything. Napoleon was asking, for the third time, if he was okay. He didn't know. But there was something else—a deep, thrumming reverberation that shook him like the pulse of some gigantic creature. *"What the hell is that sound?"*

"Cap'n, I'm not picking up any unusual sound," Napoleon said. Bandicut cocked his head, puzzled. He began to experience a strange kind of flickering, as though a strobe were nearby. Images began pulsing in his thoughts—dreamlike, but broken and stuttering, as though someone or something were rifling his memories. "Napoleon, I—" he began, and then, /Charli—/

/// I'm . . . trying . . . ///

There was a sudden *snap* and Bandicut felt another change within himself. A slippage. A shifting of internal gears. A blurring . . .

/// John, are you—? ///

Silence-fugue. Oh God.

His mental space ballooned outward, and along with the terror, he felt a sudden airless clarity. *Yes.* Now he saw things that before had been hidden from him, as though by obscuring layers of dust. This was the way to view reality, the saner way; he could *see* the razor-sharp focus of the other intelligence around him, like an enormous network of flickering tendrils. And he could see other things as well: Napoleon's thoughts in the midst of a small cyclone, as threads of the other tried to probe Napoleon's mind-space . . . and now a looming presence that was at once alien and familiar, emerging from a deeper dimension.

/// Hold tight, John.
I'll get you out of there . . . ///

/Wait, no . . . I think it's—/

Before he could complete the thought, Charli's grip was on him like a hand on his collar, yanking him back from the precipice. The world rotated around him, and his own mental space hardened again into something that felt like frozen space. He was back in his own mind again. *Damn.*

/// I wanted to get you out before anything
else could go wrong. ///

/Uhhhh . . . no . . . no, Charli, I . . . / Bandicut was struggling with chaotic thoughts. There had been something he was on the verge of recognizing. /Charli, I—was almost—/ He tried to clear his head, blinking and shaking. /Charli, there was something I was seeing, that I can't see now—/

/// Li-Jared and Jeaves are yelling for you. ///

There were voices in his ear, agitated voices. Li-Jared, frantic. *"John Bandicut, you've got to get out of there!"*

"Why?" He couldn't remember what was happening outside.

"There's a Mindaru sentinel craft coming down on us! We're going to be its lunch meat!"

Oh. Yes.

"Are you almost done? I'm hanging on as long as I can. But we need to move!"

Bandicut squeezed his eyes shut. Earth was going to be lunch meat. Not to mention *Nick* and *Thunder*. And Ed's world, wherever it was.

Ed!

He shook himself suddenly like a dog coming in from the rain. *Ed!* /Charli, it was Ed I saw in there! In the silence-fugue. I was on the verge of something when you pulled me out. Can you send me back in? Right now?/

/// What do you mean?

How could you see Ed in the silence-fugue? ///

/I don't know, I know it sounds crazy, but I did. Maybe the fugue lets me see across dimensions, I don't know. But send me *back*, Charli! Send me *now!*/

/// I don't understand— ///

/But I do!/ And to the robot: "Napoleon, I've got to go into silence-fugue! Watch my back."

"Cap'n?"

"Trust me. Li-Jared—hang on! I'm trying to get Ed to help us!" As he spoke, Bandicut felt Charli reaching into his mind-space and undoing the work he had just done. He felt his mental control slipping away, as far in the distance, Li-Jared twanged in protest; he felt the wild yawing sensation of veering into perilous inner territories, and the looming presence of the Mindaru. He felt simultaneously a thrill of excitement and a wrench of fear . . .

It wasn't quite the same as the fugue of a few moments ago. The intelligence of the machine-world was whipping around him like glowing strands; but other things were stirring, too, in this altered world. There was a big oval of light—faint, transparent, but enormous—vibrating like the head of a drum. And through it, like a cascade of mirror images within mirror images, other disks of light just like it. They were all calling, calling to him, calling to anybody, to stop the shaking. Their calls were haunting him; it was hard to think in the din.

One other thing came into focus, though, a whirling shape like a tornado of fire, emerging from some deeper dimension. Familiar, it was familiar. But he was dizzy in the midst of all this, and he couldn't place it . . .

It seemed to be calling to him.

/// John, that's Ed—and he is calling to you! ///

Who? Ed? Oh yes, he remembered someone named Ed. But that person was a fried egg. /Why would I want to talk to a fried egg, Charli?/

/// That's why we're here, John.
Can you hear his voice?
Can you? ///

Voice . . . yes . . . he thought he could hear a voice . . . Dreamily.

/// Focus, John! ///

Calling to him for help?

No. *He* wanted to ask *Ed* for help. /What did I want to ask him?/

/// The dark matter flow.
We need to change its course. ///

/Of course I . . . / But his thoughts were still reeling, he couldn't help thinking of someone charging on a horse across a plain, lance leveled, assaulting a distant windmill.

No, he realized with a start. His vision began to turn clear as crystal: dimensions opening up in space before him, square turning into cube, cube into tesseract, and tesseract into an n-dimensional jewel of light. And he began to glimpse the depths of Ed's reach. In these dimensions, Ed was no longer a mere column or circle of fire, but a starfish radiating into a thousand dimensions with long, luminous arms; and his reach was long indeed.

But Ed couldn't see what Bandicut was seeing. He didn't know what to do.

"*Great pain here . . . great peril. What can I . . . ?*"

Bandicut felt a sudden jolt as he realized Ed could reach into places he, Bandicut, could not reach, and perhaps even place one of his long arms along the edge of a flow . . .

/// Yes! That's it!
Even a subtle shift might be enough . . . ///
"Ed!" Bandicut cried. "Do you see a glowing river?"
"Yes . . ."
"Can you stop it, or deflect it?"
"Don't know . . . can try . . . will it stop the pain . . . ?"
"Maybe . . . maybe." Bandicut was speaking not out of any certainty, but out of faith and hope. *Looming storm clouds and the giant mechanized combine, bearing down on him; a dog darted across its path, triggering the collision-avoidance, and it veered, just enough to steer it past the boy hidden in the tall field.* A tiny change, in this version; but it was enough. "Yes. Yes, I think so. Can you do it?"

From the shimmering circle, a sighing voice. *"I will try."*

Bandicut nodded. Yes. Yes. They would try, they would do it, they would rule the stars.

"What . . . should I do?"

Think. Think. "Can you . . . somehow stretch across the stream and—" he windmilled his hands in the air, groping "—do anything to the space, change the flow of it—change its direction?"

The Ed creature made a low humming sound. Bandicut grimaced, trying to focus; he was on a carousel, turning without moving, disoriented. He was trying to think how to explain the concept of *bending space* . . .

There was a flash of light and a shudder in the continuum. Bandicut furiously tried to see what had just happened. Had the multidimensional creature simply *placed a foot in the stream of dark matter?*

The stream shifted slowly as he watched; it was rechanneling itself.

/// The stream is changing course, John. ///

/Away from the other star?/ He could feel his thoughts unwinding and coming back together. The fugue was lifting.

/// I can't tell. ///

"Napoleon?"

The robot appeared confused. "John Bandicut, I don't know

what is happening, but I believe you have either diverted or blocked the stream."

"Good. Very good. Ed did it, you know."

The robot barely missed a beat. "Ed? Well, it looks as if he's significantly altered the flow, Cap'n. Significantly."

Bandicut's head was clear; the fugue was over. "Good. Then let's get the hell out of here."

31

A VISIT TO A STAR

On the bridge, Li-Jared frantically wished for a clearer image of the black object that was coming toward them in the glow of ∗Thunder∗'s atmosphere. Jeaves and Copernicus were certain it must be a sentry of some kind—but what would it do when it reached them? Did it carry weapons to vaporize them? Would it assimilate them, as that Mindaru graveyard had tried to do? Did they have *any* defense? Could they at least outrun it?

He had a strong feeling that the answer to all of those was: *Whatever's bad for us.*

"Copernicus, anything from Bandicut or Napoleon?"

"According to their last transmission, they were having difficulty finding the exit."

Bwang. "Damn!"

"Li-Jared."

"What, Jeaves? Or do I already know?"

"I think you do. Have you decided at what point you will leave them, if necessary—to save the ship, and the mission?"

"I have not. I am going to play it by ear, as Bandie would say."

"Play it by ear?" Jeaves said. "Does that mean you are intending to make a snap decision? I appreciate your loyalty, but is that the best way to make a decision that affects the whole mission?"

Li-Jared rubbed his chest with his fingers. "You don't think so?"

"It's for you to decide, not me."

Li-Jared breathed deliberately several times before answering. "Well, Jeaves, that's what I'm going to do. And if you think it's wrong—tough shit, as Bandie would also say."

The robot was silent, but Li-Jared continued to fume to himself. He knew the robot was right. But he'd be damned if he'd decide right here and now that when x became y, he'd up and abandon his friends.

He turned his scowl to Ik and Antares, still huddled unmoving off to one side. What was he going to do about *them*? They were almost certainly unaware of the situation. He closed his eyes for a moment to resynch his heartbeats. Then he strode over to crouch in front of them. "Ik! Can you hear me?"

Ik's only response was an incomprehensible mutter. He seemed to have heard, but his eyes were angled away from each other and up, as though he were looking deep into space at something no one else could see. Beside him, with one hand on Ik's arm, Antares was rocking forward and backward, her eyes tightly closed. She looked as if she were in pain. Li-Jared spoke to Ik twice more, then Antares: "Can *you* hear me? *Antares?*"

Her murmur was almost inaudible. ". . . In contact with the star . . ." *Do not interrupt,* her impassive expression said.

Li-Jared paced back to Jeaves. "How far away is that thing?"

"One light-hour and closing fast. I believe we have at most twenty minutes to initiate action."

"And have you come up with a recommended action?"

"Getting out of its way would be my recommendation."

Li-Jared rubbed his fingers together rapidly, in frustration. "Are you working on an escape route?"

"We are," said Copernicus. "But I just received another transmission from Napoleon. They have encountered something unexpected . . ."

✶

Getting out had turned out to be as hard as Bandicut had feared. Napoleon came to a stop and turned to face him. "Cap'n, something's wrong. I'm not seeing the same landscape we passed on the way in, and I can't find any of the bread crumbs I left for us. I'm not sure we're on the correct n-space level."

Bandicut kept his voice neutral, ignoring the chill in the back of his neck. "Are you saying you can't find the way back?"

"I can't retrace our steps exactly, no. But I think we're . . ." Napoleon's voice trailed off as he floated a little ahead of Bandicut. "Cap'n, you'd better have a look at this."

That didn't sound good. Bandicut caught up with the robot. "Oh, jeez."

"Yes."

Bandicut groped for something to hang on to. "What *is* this?" He was poised in an opening in another parapetlike wall. Beyond the opening was a sheer drop-off into the darkness of space. It looked like a wide loading bay high on the side of a vast skyscraper. Beyond it was space—but impossibly close by, a great orb floating in the void. It looked like a planet. Or no—it was glowing a sullen crimson, and there was a granularity in the fire. It was a *star,* alarmingly close up, viewed through a powerful filter. "Nappy? What *is* this?"

"I think . . . that may be our hypernova star. I think it's *Nick*."

Bandicut blinked hard. "I thought we were half a light-year away."

"We are, in normal space. But we're embedded in n-space inside this thing, with all those channels. Distances may be very different. *Look at those inflowing streams.*" Napoleon pointed with a metal hand, first to one part of the dark sky, then to another.

Bandicut squinted, at first seeing nothing. Then, gradually, he began to make out what Napoleon was talking about: a few thin, ghostly streaks of deep blue and violet, originating from somewhere out in deep space and converging on the star like threads of a tattered spider's web. He thought he could guess what they were. As his eyes grew more accustomed to the lighting, however, his heart began to sink. There were not just a few, but *dozens* of the streams, and they all looped in from somewhere in the starry darkness to plunge into the great sullen orb. All except one, fainter than the others. That one originated in a vague and almost indefinable haze from the very structure upon which he and Napoleon were standing.

"Are you thinking as I am, Cap'n, that the stream directly below us must be the one Ed has stopped up?"

"It looks like he's slowed it, but not eliminated it."

In his head, the quarx was recoiling. There was recognition in his fear.

/// Look at all of those streams!
It's coming in from stars all over.
We've barely touched the inflow.
It's just like . . . like . . . ///

Bandicut felt a powerful anxiety from Charli. /Is this . . . it's not how your homeworld ended, is it?/

/// I think it might be.
I have a memory—can't be sure—
but I think it happened just this way.
We tried, my people did, but
we had no idea . . . ///

Bandicut shivered. To Napoleon, he said, "Charli's homeworld . . . the same way. They thought they were stopping it, but . . ." His voice caught. "If that's ∗Nick∗, then we've hardly accomplished anything."

Napoleon ticked softly, not answering directly. "Do you suppose the central control for *all* those streams may be somewhere over there? Near ∗Nick∗, where it all converges?"

"I don't know. You?"

"I do suppose," the robot said. "It's the most central location."

Bandicut gazed across at the threatened star. It looked as if he could step out and float across to it. "If the control center *is* there, what the hell can we do about it?" He felt at his waist for the small cylinders, the n-space disrupter grenades. It felt pretty silly to think they'd be much help. "Could we blow it up?" /And probably us with it?/

/// Probably. I'm willing to try, though. ///

"Cap'n, if we attempt to blow anything up, we need to warn Li-Jared, so that he can get the ship out of the way. With us or without us." Napoleon was carefully scanning every section of the view. "I think I may see a way over there."

"Yes?" Bandicut said cautiously.

"It's a little hard to see. You might have to trust me."

"I always trust you, Napoleon."

"Yes, of course. That minor untruth aside, I would like to present a possibility."

"I'm listening."

"I suspect there *is* a pathway between us and the star. I cannot precisely image it. However, I believe that this view of the star arises from an n-space connection between this point and what *may* be a central control nexus, over there."

"And you think we could somehow—?"

"Travel along the pathway, to reach the control nexus."

Bandicut drew a breath. "Which we would do by—"

Tap. "By stepping off this ledge." *Tap tap.* "That's where you'd have to trust me."

Bandicut suddenly felt dizzy, ill, peering out into the vertiginous gulf with the sun hanging in the middle of the darkness . . . and beneath them, nothing but blackness and distant stars. "You want me to . . . step off into . . . nothing."

"As I said, you have to trust me."

/// Yes! Please. ///

At that moment, the comm came alive, and Li-Jared's voice filled Bandicut's ears. *"Bandie, are you almost out yet?"*

"Uh, we're—" Bandicut's voice caught "—uh, we've found something that may give us access to the central controls."

He could hear the anguish in Li-Jared's voice. *"Bandie, I have to move the ship soon."*

Tightly, Bandicut said, "I know. But this could really be it. You should take the ship and go. Circle back for us later. In case we . . . survive." The words left him feeling sick. *Antares, I don't know what to say. I'm sorry.*

"Bandie, I'm not sure we'll be *able* to come back."

Struggling to draw a breath, Bandicut turned to Napoleon. He thought he was going to say, *Do we really need to do this?* But what came out was, "Can you explain to Copernicus what we're trying to do? So he can explain it to Li-Jared?"

"Already done, Cap'n."

"Then, I guess—let's—" He stopped, then forced the words out. "How do you see this happening?"

"I detect a curvature of n-space, Cap'n. I believe it is an

338 * JEFFREY A. CARVER *

indication of a pathway, and when we step off this ledge, we will find it. I hope it will carry us to . . . the other end."

"You mean, to *Nick*?"

"Or near it. But in n-space, remember. I hope the conditions at the other end will be nonextreme."

"We won't be burned to a crisp?"

"Correct."

Bandicut closed his eyes, then opened them. /Crazy./ "All right. Whatthehell. Let's go. Together?"

"I should go first," said Napoleon, flicking out some bread crumbs.

"And leave me here, to try to find my way back alone? No thanks. We'll risk it together. On three, before I lose my nerve. One . . ."

"Very—"

"Two . . ."

"—well."

"Three." They pushed themselves off the wall into space. Bandicut felt an odd sensation of falling and being lifted at the same time, as the vista of space distorted around him. The next sensation was of an odd disjuncture, a feeling that time had slipped by unaccounted for; and then the distortion was gone. He blinked hard, looking around.

The place where he had been poised was gone. No, there it was—way over *there,* across the blackness. It looked like an enormous, slab-sided building, dotted with lighted windows and beacons in the night. It reminded him, strangely, of that first view he'd had of Shipworld, as he'd approached it in his earthly ship, *Neptune Explorer.* He rotated, and drew a shuddering breath. His back had been to a wall of fire, a vast, glowing, undulating tapestry of fusion-fire. It looked now as if he could reach out and touch it, in all its terrifying glory. He glanced down to see what he was standing on—and he was *standing* now, not floating—and he wished he hadn't. He and Napoleon were on a barely visible, glimmering ledge, without sides or features. He instinctively wanted to back up against a solid wall for safety, but there was no solid wall. Beside him, Napoleon was gathering information, his sensors flickering frantically.

But they weren't being consumed by fire. Napoleon had gotten that right.

He swallowed, hard. "Nappy—?"

The robot sounded distracted. "I imagine you are wondering where we are?"

"Yeah."

"As near as I can tell, we're in a pocket of n-space that's *very* close to the sun, while protecting us from it. I think we must also be very close to the central control. I can *feel* that it's here somewhere."

"Feel?"

"I don't know how else to describe it, Cap'n. I can sense that there are . . . data pathways . . . nearby. I can hear it like faint crosstalk in a circuit. But I can't find access."

Bandicut squinted at the view of the sun, where the fires of destruction were being stoked hotter with each passing second. For a terrible moment he flashed ten years into the past, to the memory of a burning apartment building, where his friend was dying, beyond reach of firefighters. He felt the wrenching pain all over again, the horror of being unable to help his friend. Nick's death in the fire had given him nightmares for a year. He pulled himself back with an effort. "If you don't find access to that, there'll be no way for us to turn off the flow of dark matter." *And we will have come all this way and failed.*

"I'm still searching, but . . . no. Not yet."

Bandicut nodded and forced himself to look away. He stared instead at the thin, ghostly streams of dark matter flowing into the sun. He felt Charli do something, and the view improved. Now he could see the streams more clearly against the darkness. He felt that he was standing in the center of a plasma globe, with a fantastic array of glowing whiskers of electricity streaming toward them, toward the central ball. They looked beautiful and harmless; they were killing the star.

Napoleon swung to look at him. "Nothing, Cap'n. *No, amend that*—I *do* detect another pathway. *Into* the sun." He pointed tangentially toward the blazing body.

Bandicut squinted. He thought he saw an extra little glimmer of light, but who could tell. "That's it?"

"It's the only thing I can see."

Bandicut drew a breath. "Then let's try it, shall we?"

"Aye, Cap'n."

They stepped together.

The transition was much the same as before. But this time Bandicut had a feeling of being surrounded by silent, billowing walls of flame; and when the transition ended, he was enveloped in a storm of fire, and a thunderous roar that shook him to the bone, like standing inside a rocket launch. Napoleon touched him, and must have done something to his force-field suit, because the roar decreased, until it was more like standing a hundred meters from a waterfall. The fire was undiminished, though; he was surrounded by a blowtorch, a blast furnace, a continuous hydrogen bomb explosion, pulsing, blinding. He couldn't move.

/// Breathe, John—now! ///

He gasped, fearing he would die from inhaling the maelstrom. But he did not die. He was protected by the suit, or by n-space, or both. But he sensed something else, something that made him shiver. /Charli, do you feel that?/

/// A presence . . . ///

/Yes./ It was a tingling sensation wrapped around his mind, a little like the feeling of his first encounter with the translator, and Charlie. But different. More . . . massive.

/// John, I think it's the star. ✶Nick✶. ///

That was what he thought, too. "Napoleon?"

"Yes, Cap'n, we're inside the star. I really thought we might find the control center here. But no sign."

Bandicut drew a deep breath. "I think I *feel* the star."

Napoleon swung quickly. "Is there a problem with your protection?"

"No—I mean, in my mind. I feel its presence." He hesitated, shutting his eyes to focus—and suddenly felt strobe flashes going off in his skull. With each dazzling burst of light, he felt a powerful rush of *fear,* or *confusion,* or *pain.* For a dizzying few seconds, he thought he was falling into another fugue.

/// It's not fugue. It's the star. ///

/I can't make sense of it! We need Ik! Or Antares!/

/// Or Deep, to fuse
the difference in time scales. ///

Bandicut felt a whirlwind in his mind. The strobe flashes had given way to jets of fire, flying around like leaves in a fall wind. /Can't you or the stones help?/ he cried.

/// Trying . . .
I don't think it's really aware of us. ///

Bandicut tried to focus on the thought: *We are here to help, to save you.* But the thought seemed to just bounce around the inside of his skull like an EineySteiney ball. Finally he gazed at the star again. His eyes, or the filter, were adapting. He could see cells of turbulence churning in the nuclear fires. It was like watching the star's heartbeat. He turned to the left a little. /My God./

The streamers of dark matter were visible again, only now they were rivers of shadow, not light, coursing through the sun glare. The streams dove straight down through the body of the sun. Squinting, he tried to see what was down there in the sun's core. Charli helped, tweaking his vision slightly. Then he saw it: a shadowy sphere submerged deep in the heart of the star, and the dark matter playing down into it like streams of water in a fountain. It was beautiful, in its way. And it was deadly. "Napoleon?" he murmured.

"I see it, Cap'n. It's a reservoir of dark matter, contained by an n-space field. I don't quite understand it. I suppose when enough has accumulated to make the star collapse, it'll implode and the Mindaru will have its hypernova."

"Jesus."

"Quite so. Captain, I cannot determine how close it is to the point of collapse. But I *can* tell you, there's a lot of dark matter down there. And I think we're looking at the source of the hypergrav shock waves. I see a lot of vibration down there. I'll bet it periodically gives a big shudder as it adjusts to the buildup."

Bandicut absorbed that. "Do you see anything we can do to stop it?"

Long pause.

"Nappy?"

"Captain . . ."

"What?"

"I don't. No. I don't see a way. I'm sorry."

Stung, Bandicut was silent. /We've come all this way. And by now, Li-Jared has probably taken the ship out of danger. At least, I hope so. Sort of./ Charli didn't answer. Streaming plasmas thundered in glorious chaos around him as he struggled to think it through. Finally he shouted, *"We're in the middle of this star and we can't get at the controls to stop that? What the hell's this pathway for, anyway?"*

Napoleon seemed almost pensive. "An inspection portal, maybe? There's a lot here I don't understand, Cap'n."

Bandicut fingered the small cylinders at his waist. "What about these little n-space disrupters? Could we lob a few of these into the core?" It sounded dumb, even as he said it. They'd brought them along for demolition inside the Mindaru vessel. They were grenades, not super-bombs.

"Flea bites, Cap'n. They'd probably just disrupt the bubble that's keeping us alive."

"Bad."

"Yes. Unless . . ."

"Unless *what?*"

"Well, I suppose it's *possible* that if we somehow managed to get these disrupters down onto the wall of the reservoir . . . they *might* prick the wall like a balloon and cause it to release the dark matter prematurely. It's definitely a long shot."

Bandicut felt suddenly very cold, in the midst of this fury. "And what would that do?"

The robot turned to face him with its dark electronic eyes. "I imagine, Cap'n, that it would destroy the star."

Bandicut closed his eyes again. "Bad."

"Bad," agreed the robot. "But if we release the matter before there's enough to trigger the hypernova, the star might become so unstable that it dies—and it might even explode. But it might not send out such a massive blast of gamma radiation. It might not destroy a hundred other worlds, as the hypernova would."

Bandicut drew a slow breath. *Sacrifice the star—and ourselves—but save the Earth?*

*/// Not too different from a choice
you already made once. ///*
/I shouldn't have to make it again!/
/// No, you shouldn't. ///

Bandicut winced inwardly and said to Napoleon, "It sounds like a better plan than nothing."

"Except that I have no idea how to do it," said the robot. "Get the grenades from here down to the core, I mean. Plus, there's always the chance that we would only trigger the hypernova ourselves. Just a little sooner."

Bandicut clenched his hands helplessly, and glared at the cathedral of fire around him. Pressure was building in his forehead. "Isn't there any way to *tell?*"

"Not that I know of. Do you feel lucky, Cap'n?"

"No. There has to be another way."

"Perhaps so. But none that I can see from here."

"So we go back empty-handed?"

"*You* do."

"What the hell does *that* mean?"

"It means, milord, that I should stay. It is the only reasonable course."

Bandicut felt a burning sensation in his forehead. "You just explained why there's no reason to stay."

"No, I explained why we might not want to use the grenades now, even if we could. The odds are too uncertain."

"Then—"

"However, it may be that I will think of a way. And it may be that you will fail to find another method. And it may be that, in the end, this is our only hope. If it fails, and causes a hypernova, then that was going to happen anyway." The robot was turning back and forth in the tiny area that they had to stand on. "But it will be better than doing nothing. It won't save me, and it won't save the star, and it might not even save Ed's world. But it *might* save Earth. And who knows how many other worlds. Isn't that worth giving my life for?"

Bandicut slowly nodded. "Then I should stay with you."

"No, you should not. Because you have to get word out, and

help your friends. And because you should get back to Lady Antares. That's why."

"Napoleon—"

"And if it all works out, maybe you can swing by and pick me up on your way out. Like you just told Li-Jared to do."

"Yeah, but I didn't believe that when I said it to Li-Jared."

The robot cocked his head and gazed at Bandicut. "Maybe I don't, either. Now, get out of here, Cap'n. Before I push you out."

Bandicut blinked, hard. His vision was blurred.

/// He's right, you know. ///

/Easy for you to say./

/// No, it's not. ///

Bandicut opened his mouth, then closed it. He faced the robot and gripped its metal hand. "Napoleon, I don't like this one damn bit. But okay. You stay, hold the fort, bring up the rear. Are you in touch with Copernicus?"

"Cap'n, get moving. Before they leave."

"Can you hear Copernicus?" Bandicut shouted.

"No. But quit worrying. Let me be the great romantic hero. Now, *go.*"

"Okay." Bandicut was trying to think of some last thing to say. But it didn't matter, because at that moment, Napoleon's powerful hand gripped him, spun him around, and shoved him off into the thundering heart of fire.

32

IN FLIGHT

 Julie spent a long time staring out the window of the little service craft, wondering where all this was going to end. Wondering if this was how John had felt when he flew off in pursuit of a comet. Wondering if this was really going to be a one-way trip.

It seemed likely. The translator wouldn't commit—just told her that if it *could* take her home safely, it would. But it didn't seem like a very good bet.

For several days now, they had been hurtling away from the *Park Avenue*. Her emotions had been careening around at roughly the same rate of speed. For a while, she'd been accepting of her role, if a little numb at the thought of the sacrifice she was making. But that cover hadn't lasted long, before being torn open by seething rage. Rage at the injustice of what was being done to her life. Rage at the threat to her home planet. Rage that both she and John had been asked to do this, but not together.

The rage, in time, had given way to disbelief. This wasn't really happening. She wasn't *really* being taken for a fool, chasing after some ghost in the night. She was going to wake up any moment now, for sure. When that didn't happen, she bubbled for a while with quiet resentment.

The resentment was mostly drained away now, replaced by exhaustion and sadness. She wondered when she was going to start feeling noble.

/How soon are we going to be there?/ she asked, breaking a long silence with the stones.

We expect to intercept the target in approximately seventeen hours.

Seventeen hours? That was impossibly fast—and yet she could hardly stand the wait. The feeling of helplessness was becoming intolerable, the cockpit becoming a jail cell. She placed her hands on the console, gazing out at the star-speckled blackness. /Can I send messages from here?/ She might not feel so damn *useless* if she could at least get reports out to . . . well, someone.

To what purpose?

/To let them know we're still alive and on course! To have *some* contact with humanity! What the hell purpose do you think? Can it be done?/

The stones hesitated to answer. But finally, they said, *It may be possible. Difficult, but perhaps not impossible.*

/Difficult, why? Because of the distance?/

Because of the spatial threading. We dare not interrupt it. But possibly we could transmit in microbursts during the interstitial fractions, when we are in normal-space.

She blinked, and stared at her reflection in the cockpit window. /Are you trying to make me feel stupid?/

We are threading space: weaving in and out of normal-space hundreds of times per second. During each interval that we are outside of normal-space, we translate forward much farther than we could in normal-space. Thus our apparent speed.

/Oh./

It may be possible to send transmissions in a stutter-burst, during the normal-space intervals.

Julie closed her eyes and thought of the alternative, to sit here feeling helpless and utterly cut off from humanity. "Let's try it," she said out loud.

*

It took her two hours to compose and record four messages—a situation update to the *Park Avenue* and the authorities in general, a more personal message to her parents and brother (probably her last, futile attempt to convince them that she knew what she was doing and was still of sound mind), one to Georgia on Triton, and one to Dakota Bandicut. Of the four, the last somehow cut the deepest for her, probably because it felt like her only remaining link to John. Maybe that was why, in what started as a personal statement to the young Dakota, she finally just started talking and didn't stop until she'd described everything that had happened, from her first meeting with the translator till now. The message might or might not ever get to Dakota, but at least she was going to get it all on the record. She talked for quite a long time . . .

Do you wish to transmit to your ship or directly to Earth? Our chances of clear reception to the ship may be better.

She came back from a reverie that had followed her recording. /Uh? Can you do both?/

We will try. Please remember that this is experimental. And we may have no way to hear an answer. Are you ready?

Julie thought a moment and nodded. /Yes./

Very well. Pause. *All four messages are sent.*

/Thank you./ Julie sighed deeply, reclined her seat, and went promptly to sleep.

*

When she woke, the console was flickering with instrument readings. "What's going on?" she asked in a hoarse voice.

The long-range imaging screen came on. It seemed to show

only a dark star field. As she looked more closely, she saw a tiny object in the center of the screen, twinkling and turning. "What's that?"

Our quarry. A highly enhanced image. The actual object is quite small, and dark. We are still calculating its mass, but measurements indicate it has a diameter of one point four millimeters.

/One point four *millimeters?*/

Correct. Mass indeterminate. Readings vary from several tons to one grain of sand. Readings may be inaccurate.

Julie stared at the screen, trying to divine what the stones were talking about. /Can you give me the simplified version?/

Supposition: the object contains encapsulated nano-structure intended to enable it to reconstitute itself into a machine that can attack your homeworld.

/You mean it's going to make a weapon? Or become one?/

Affirmative: method uncertain. It may simply gather and control mass. It is not hard to destroy a world, given sufficient mass and orbital energy. Observe Miranda, moon of Uranus: blasted to pieces millions of years ago, then drawn back together by gravity. Probably a natural disaster, but it could have been a test run for the Adversary.

/Why would they want to do that?/ she whispered, a chill creeping in between her shoulder blades.

To prevent humanity from advancing to the stars.

/How much of this do you know for sure?/

About their intent: much, but not all. About the object: we can detect complex structure within it, but not read details. Analogy: we can observe that your cells possess DNA, without being able to map its instructions.

Julie blinked. /How did you even *find* it?/

We detected its spatial threading signature.

/Of course. How foolish of me. How are you planning to stop it? The same way as the comet?/ She closed her eyes as she asked the question, trying to shut out the image of a suicidal collision.

No, it's harder to destroy than a simple comet.

She wrestled back her dread. /How, then?/

We are planning to grapple it.

Julie imagined slinging long chains around the grain-sized object. /Uh-huh. Then what?/

Then we are planning to drop it into the sun.

✷

Hours passed, and they drew close to the object at last. It was too small to be seen out the window, but in the screen it looked like one of those electron microscope images of a speck of soot or pollen. Julie's nerves were on fire, waiting for something to happen.

It may try to evade us by threading space. May we suggest you fasten your seat restraints?

Julie grunted and groped for the buckles. On the screen, the target suddenly started to move in small, darting movements. She felt a vibration pass through the deck. The ship became momentarily transparent. Fear flashed through her from head to toe. "What the hell was *that?*" she yelped, crouching down in her seat.

There was no answer. The ship became solid again. But then it *squirmed* forward, stretching and contracting with a quiver. Julie's heart was jumping. She felt dizzy. On the screen, the target was jumping around wildly. *Shift. Squirm. Flicker in and out of solidity.*

"Stones! Talk to me!"

She felt a surge, and the ship stretched *long,* then *longer,* and with a sudden outrush of breath, she felt herself suddenly *streaming forward.* When she focused, terrified, on the screen, she saw the target swelling in size. She gulped a breath, and in that instant, the object vanished from the screen, and she felt a shudder through her seat. /What was *that?*/

The stones answered at last. *Capture. We have the Adversary in our capture-field, in the cargo pod of your ship.* A new image blinked onto her screen: the same object, enveloped in a purplish glow. The inner walls of the cargo pod gleamed faintly around it.

Her heart was pounding. She didn't know where to put her fear. /How did you *do* that?/

Spatial threading. We had greater power—and perhaps, the benefit of surprise. We suspect it was not aware of us until we were very close.

She closed her eyes in gasping relief. /And now?/

And now we set course for your sun.

*

What troubled her, she thought the following day, wasn't so much that they were now diving toward the sun with their captive, as her fear of what this thing nestled in the belly of their ship, in the cargo pod, might be doing. Perhaps not idly accepting its captivity. In the screen, it looked unchanged—motionless in the violet force-field. Or did it?

We're uncertain of its degree of sentience, the stones said. *Its evasive maneuvering might have been automatic.*

/Can't you find out? Study it, now that you've got it?/

There is risk. It may be awaiting sensory signals to awaken. Probing might trigger a more dangerous state.

/So you're going to just hold on to it, until it's time to drop it into the sun?/ She eyed the growing orb of the sun in the screen. They were moving inward impossibly fast. They had long since shot past the *Park Avenue,* though at too great a distance to make any real-time contact. She had sent another transmission, reporting their capture of the object, but received no reply. The translator had predicted that reception might be problematic through the threading environment, but it was frustrating not knowing if her reports were being received. /Isn't this exactly what John had to do, make some insane dash inward?/

It is similar, the stones conceded, then fell silent.

More time to kill. Julie composed more messages to Earth, sending all the info she could think of.

"Dear Earth. Time is growing short now, as the translator and I head for the sun to drop this thing into it. We hope to obliterate it completely. I fear that it will come alive suddenly and fight us. But as far as I know, it hasn't tried to do anything like that yet . . ."

She now included requests that all of her messages be copied to MINEXFO headquarters, to her parents and Georgia and Dakota, to the *Park Ave.,* and to the New York and London *Times,* and Al Jazeera. No more than ten seconds after she had sent this last message, she saw blinking lights on the instrument panel. /What's that?/ When there was no answer from the stones, she started querying the computer. *"What the hell?"* she muttered when the systems-status board started filling up with warnings about hull integrity in the area of the cargo pod. *"Translator, what's happening?"* she yelled, banging on the panel. On the screen, she saw a much larger version of the ball of light, and it seemed to be surrounded by a haze of dust.

She felt a buzzing sensation in her wrists, as though the stones were very busy with something. Finally:

We have a problem with our captive.

/Really./ The console now reported a failure in external lighting.

We're working to restore encapsulation.

/What?/

It appears the object is awake, has found a way to penetrate our encapsulation fields, and has begun to react in ways we did not anticipate.

Julie blinked to look back and forth between the growing image of the sun and the screen image of the captive grain of soot now pulsing with a reddish light. She felt her throat constricting. "What exactly didn't you anticipate?"

We didn't expect it would begin disassembling the ship.

She clenched her eyes shut.

Breathe, Julie Stone!

She gasped in a sudden breath and realized she'd nearly passed out. "Did you say . . . disassembling the ship?"

Apparently so. It seems to have defeated our spatial field encapsulation by using the interspatial intervals of our threading to slip outside the containment. In its immediate vicinity, it is attacking the cargo hold on a molecular level. We believe it is trying to accrete the ship's mass to itself. It may be trying to escape, or it may have started the process of building whatever it was planning to build.

This was unbelievable. Impossible. Very, very bad. Julie said softly, /How long before it dissolves a hole in the hull?/

We cannot give a definite answer. We are slowing its progress. We hope to halt it.

Julie felt as if she had been punched in the solar plexus. She had gotten accustomed to thinking of the translator as invulnerable, nearly omnipotent. It came as a terrible blow to think that it could be defeated. Swinging forward to face the control console, she said to the computer, "New transmission. Quote. *Anyone receiving this message: the enemy object has begun attacking the structure of our craft. Our mission may be in jeopardy. If we fail to destroy the object, Earth will be in danger. Keep a track on our course. The object appears to be a nano-constructor, and it may be attempting to build a weapon out of the mass of this ship. I will transmit updates when possible!'* Unquote. Translator, please send that to all previous recipients, and repeat at three-minute intervals."

She sat back, catching her breath. /Okay, now what can I do? Can I help fight this thing?/

We suggest you wear protection against loss of life support. Meanwhile, we are accelerating our threading toward your sun.

Julie glanced out the window at the sun, shuddered, and went to the equipment locker at the back of the cockpit. She pulled out a musty-smelling spacesuit and wondered how long it would protect her if that alien thing turned her ship to dust. Would she die first from the vacuum and cold, or from being turned to dust herself?

She started to unzip the suit, then paused. /How long do you expect me to stay in this thing? What's the time frame here?/

At our current rate of threading, we should reach the surface of the sun in about three days.

/You expect me to keep this stinking suit on for three days? How am I supposed to sleep, or go to the bathroom? Forget it. Can I trust you to give me advance warning if the hull starts to come apart?/

That way entails greater risk.

"I'll take the risk," she muttered, tossing the suit into the copilot's seat.

Keep the equipment close. The activity of the Adversary is beginning to creep outside our new containment.

/Again!/

✶It is proving difficult to contain.✶

Julie closed her eyes. /How long? How long before it empties out the air—or turns all of us to dust?/

✶If we cannot stop it . . . we estimate three days.✶

She shuddered. /Is that three days exactly? Or three days, give or take?/

✶Give or take.✶

She slumped in her seat and closed her eyes. /Sweet Alabama . . . /

33

SENTINEL

Li-Jared was growing frantic, watching the approach of the Mindaru sentry. Very soon he was going to have no choice but to leave Bandicut and Napoleon behind. *A few more minutes—I can give them that much.* Copernicus had plotted a series of possible escape trajectories, but none of them held much hope if they kept delaying. "Jeaves, how can we tell if this thing is going to attack? What do we look for?"

"I think we're about to see," said the robot, notching up the magnification on the view, where the shadowy sentinel grew steadily against the glowing atmosphere of ✶Thunder✶.

Bwang. "Oh, hell." The sentinel was changing, like a flower unfolding—a black, carnivorous flower. Arms and petals were opening outward, and in the space within the petals there seemed to be a more consuming darkness, with fine, radiating glints of something shiny. Li-Jared rubbed his fingertips, hard, against his chest. "Do we have any idea what it's doing?"

"Analyzing now," Jeaves said. The image snapped rapidly through a series of enhancement changes, leaving Li-Jared with a dizzying series of afterimages of the Mindaru vessel. It ended on the original view. "Inconclusive. But probably it's a strike posture of some kind."

"Well, yeah—*damn*—all right, let's get ready to move." Bandie, Bandie, I am sorry.

"Signal from John Bandicut," Copernicus said, interrupting his thought. "He's on his way out. Without Napoleon."

Bong. "What—?"

★

Bandicut had scarcely felt the transition as he stumbled out of the star onto the tiny ledge. He gulped a breath, looked back . . .

/// Keep going! ///

. . . and stepped out into space. An instant later, he was back inside the mechanized station, staggering in the direction he thought was the way they'd been heading before. He shouted on the comm, and was stunned when Copernicus answered. "Coppy, can you give me a signal—something I can home in on?

After a beat, Copernicus said, *"I've just sent in a probe. It's got a homing beacon and a strobe."*

/// Let's get past that ridge, John, ///

Charli urged, nudging him to his right, where a narrow path through clusters of machinery led straight up a slope.

Bandicut pushed off hard. He felt a tingle of dimensional shift as he crested the little pass. Then he heard a beeping in his comm, and a floating red arrow appeared before him, pointing the way. /Did you *know* or was that a lucky guess?/ he asked Charli, breathing hard.

/// Not sure myself.

There's the probe! Do you see it? ///

/Yes!/ He kicked again and soared in a low arc toward the pulsing white strobe. "Coppy! Li-Jared! We see it!"

Li-Jared's voice rang in his ears: *"Bandie, we've got company! How much longer?"*

"I see the exit!"

"Tell me the instant you're out."

Bandicut didn't answer until the flashing probe and the airlock tunnel loomed before him. He dove into the tunnel. It seemed to take forever to get through it. As he fell into the ship's airlock, he gasped, "I'm in! *Go!*"

★

"Go!" Li-Jared shouted to Copernicus. He braced himself as the ship detached from the Mindaru satellite and accelerated away.

Moments later, they dropped back into n-space. Li-Jared watched with growing alarm. "Copernicus, are you taking us *deeper* into the sun?"

"That's the idea," Copernicus answered. "By the way, John Bandicut is on his way to the bridge." A window in the view-space showed Bandicut stumbling through a corridor.

"Show him the way, will you? Did he say what happened to Napoleon?"

"I expect the captain will share that with us."

Li-Jared tried not to gnaw his knuckles as he waited. He called to Ik and Antares that Bandicut was back, but Antares responded only with an upturn of the eyes and a low hum.

A minute later, Bandicut ran onto the bridge. "Did we get away in time?" Taking in the view, he looked shocked. "Are we heading deeper into the star?"

"Just what I was asking," Li-Jared said. "Copernicus, what's your plan?"

"Captains, we are making a slingshot maneuver inside the sun's atmosphere. I am hoping to pick up extra speed from the star's gravity as we loop around it, and hope that the Mindaru can't go as deep into the sun as we can. This is all happening in n-space."

Bandicut appeared to be still catching his breath. He squinted at the sight of the star's roiling inner layers drawing closer. "Is it working?"

"I think so," Copernicus said. "We're increasing our lead at the moment, but . . . oh . . ."

"Oh, what?" Li-Jared asked.

"I think our pursuer just sped up."

✴

Floating together in a place where space and time intertwined in ways perhaps best described as *different,* the two quantum fluctuations tried to follow the unfolding events among the ephemeral ones. Daarooaack could see that the stream of strange matter from ✴Thunder✴ to ✴Nick✴ had been partially blocked. The curious being they had seen intersect with the ephemerals from time to time, the one called Ed, was visible now and seemed to have played a part.

"It is too little. It cannot save the star. And there's a new threat!"

Deeaab's voice echoed across the gulf. *"Can you remove the threat?"*

"The new one and the quick-ones are very close. Uncertain I can intercede without harm."

"Can you not place yourself between them?"

Daarooaack hesitated. She felt so wary of making matters worse; she was far younger than Deeaab, and wished that the older one could do it.

A sigh rippled through Deeaab. Daarooaack knew Deeaab's attention was on the time-fusion between *Thunder* and the small ones. Daarooaack really should do it; she was in a better position, and had the stronger command of energy. But Daarooaack was afraid of endangering the ephemerals while trying to save them.

"You must try to pull the attacker away. And I must end the time-fusion."

Daarooaack spoke reluctantly. *"I will try."*

*

Ik's head was so full of images from the star, they were hard to keep straight. It took time to realize that *Thunder* was experiencing a new distress. The flow of dark matter had changed, and it was building up a knot of indigestion in *Thunder*'s own belly. What was happening? Was this John Bandicut's work? He must ask *Thunder*. That's what he was here for, was to gain understanding, to learn how to help. /If you can hear . . . what is happening? We are trying to help you and the other star./

Stop

it must stop

Can you not help ?

Ik struggled to understand. He could not. Then Antares, nearby, nudged him to look at something. /What?/ Finally he picked a detail out of the images: a complex network of threads converging on a star. But this wasn't the streams of dark matter going into *Thunder*, a lot of little streams joining to make one large stream. No, this was a network going into *Nick*—a lot of *large* streams from *Thunder* and *many other stars,* joining to become the flood that would kill ✳Nick✳. Was that what Antares wanted him to see? Was there more?

/Uhhhl . . . *look.*/

The nearby stream from ✳Thunder✳ was attenuated, because of the blockage. *Ed?* And something was trying to free it. The stream was twitching like a high-pressure hose. There was a node of some kind, a center down close to ✳Nick✳, maybe even inside ✳Nick✳—and that was where the efforts were coming from. He could see it the way ✳Thunder✳ saw it, little pulses of light, persistently trying to get the flow restarted, like someone turning the water on and off in a hose, trying to clear a kink.

/Is that—? ✳Thunder✳, is that what's controlling it all? Is *that* the control center? Over there inside ✳Nick✳?/

> **Source**
>> **source of the pain**
>>> **there**
>> **Must stop . . .**
>>> **can you not stop ?**

Ik was stunned into silence. The stream from ✳Thunder✳ was just one in a *myriad* of dark-matter streams pouring into ✳Nick✳. Their efforts here were futile. Moon and stars! He focused on the control node. *That* was what they needed to get to. He felt a moment of dizziness as he tried to fix it clearly in his mind. /I think . . . I see . . . we will . . . / And then he stopped again. He had a sudden feeling that his thoughts were no longer reaching the ailing star. The images were flattening out, losing clarity, dissipating. He could no longer hear the star's thoughts. He felt Antares begin to pull away.

It was ending. /✳Thunder✳ . . . / But it was too late. Whatever Deep had done to enable the contact had disappeared.

Ik opened his eyes. He was almost shocked to find himself still on the bridge of *The Long View.* How long had he been in the joining? His limbs ached. He slowly stretched his arms, moved his legs, and blinked his eyes back into focus. Beside him, Antares was doing the same. He saw Li-Jared a dozen strides away, pacing, talking to Bandicut.

Bandicut was the first to notice Ik, and he rushed to help Ik and Antares to their feet. He was full of questions, but Ik waved the questions off for the moment; he was too overwhelmed with thoughts and images. "What has been happening here?" he asked in a rasp.

Bandicut looked just as overwhelmed. He gestured at the viewspace. "We're just trying to get away from our new *friend* out there." Ik looked again and drew back. A menacing-looking object—*not* the satellite where they had been docked—was silhouetted against the star.

"Hrrr! Are we fleeing?"

"Yes we are," Li-Jared growled, sounding preoccupied. Then he wheeled around, apparently registering Ik's voice. *Bong-g-g.* "Ik! You're out!"

"Yes."

"What happened in there? No wait—Bandie was about to tell me what happened inside that Mindaru vessel, and why he had to leave Napoleon behind."

"Vessel? Left Napoleon?" Antares had just staggered to her feet, and was leaning on Bandicut's arm for support. "John, do I remember . . . did you tell us you were going *off the ship?*"

Bandicut turned to glance anxiously at the pursuing Mindaru. "I'll have to say this fast, because we're dealing with a lot. Napoleon and I tried to reach the central control, but we couldn't. We think it's in orbit around ∗Nick∗."

"Hrah! Yes! *Inside* ∗Nick∗!" Ik exclaimed. "We saw it."

Bandicut started visibly. "You *saw* it? Napoleon's *over* there in ∗Nick∗'s atmosphere now—"

"*Uhhll?* How?"

"Hrrl—?"

"N-space connector—Napoleon's there now, waiting to see if we can find some other way to shut off the dark matter. If we can't, he's going to try to blow up the star before it reaches the critical mass for a hypernova."

Antares's eyes opened wide. She looked at Ik, who looked at Li-Jared, who said to Bandicut, "I thought you said you'd stopped it."

"We thought we had, or Ed had, but—"

"But, rrrr, you didn't," Ik interrupted. "There are *many* stars pouring dark matter onto *Nick*, not just *Thunder*."

"Exactly," Bandicut said, explaining what he and Napoleon and Ed had done.

The part about Bandicut and Napoleon jumping across to the hypernova star, while the rest of them were inside *Thunder*, left Ik speechless. How could that be?

His thought was interrupted by the voice of Copernicus. "Folks, I'm pleased to have you all back, but while you've been talking, we've just completed a slingshot maneuver close to the sun. And I'm afraid we've got a problem."

*

Daarooaack made her move as the quicklife began their plunge around the body of the star. It seemed clear they were attempting to outrun the pursuer. They were widening the gap, possibly enough for Daarooaack to slip across and make contact with the enemy—perhaps enough even to *grab* it and pull it away. She wasn't sure how to destroy it, the way she knew Deeaab had once destroyed one of these objects, but if she could just give the quicklife some room to flee . . .

Darting, she caught up with the enemy and engulfed it. She tried to pull it onto a new course, but it felt like . . . she wasn't sure what. It felt like nothing she had ever known, a solid un-life, but an un-life that behaved and reacted like life. It squirmed; it was hard to hold, too compact, too dense. It was trying to follow the quicklife in a tight loop around the sun. Daarooaack tried widening the object's arc; but somehow it slipped out of her grasp and steered even tighter to the sun.

Daarooaack dove after it. The currents of space and time were tricky here. She seized it again, caught it in her downward swoop, and tried this time to carry it straight down into the core of the sun, where surely it could not survive. Deeper and faster she took it. But again it spun in an unexpected direction and slipped from her grasp. This time, however, she had given it speed in the wrong direction. It was now cutting an even tighter arc through the sun, and it was gaining fast; it was now nearly upon the ephemerals' ship.

And it was now too close for her to intervene without

risking her friends. Daarooaack veered away in fury and frustration.

✳

"I think Dark just tried to help us," Copernicus said.

Ik and the others turned to look. "Oh, mokin' A," Bandicut said. A black cloud, presumably Dark, was flying up and away from them. The Mindaru was now emerging from the glowing mist of fire, and was a lot closer than before, and growing fast.

"I believe Dark just tried to drag the sentinel into the sun," Copernicus said. "Unfortunately, it failed."

"Worse, the Mindaru has managed an even tighter loop than ours," Jeaves reported. "It's gaining fast. I can only suggest to fly evasively if you can."

Ik could see that Copernicus was trying, but the Mindaru sentry was closing rapidly. It now loomed over the viewspace balcony like a great crablike thing, all angles and extensions. Parts of it seemed darker than night; other parts blazed brighter than the star behind it. Long, jointed appendages erupted from it and arched forward, as though to pluck them each right off the bridge. Ik stepped back involuntarily, and grabbed in the air for support as Copernicus attempted a last, desperate course change. "Hrachh!" he cried. "Copern—"

But before he could finish calling the name, a crashing jolt passed through the ship, sending Ik slamming into Bandicut, and all of them sliding across the deck. As Ik struggled back to his feet, he looked up to see a flashing array of shadow-and-light, great jointed claws of metal or energy, encircle and snap closed around their ship.

34

CAPTIVE

 The Mindaru entity known locally as Starburster was wrestling with an unexpected challenge. Instreaming data told of multiple invasive activities nearby—all threatening the mission of creating a

massive overload of exotic matter in the star at the heart of the nebula. The Starburster Mindbody strove to weave together an understanding of the situation. Organic life-structures were attempting to disrupt the matter-gathering enterprise. Default response called for parasitic lifeforms to be caught and examined. One set had just in fact been captured, possibly the same lifeforms that had recently eluded one of the outer sentries.

Their presence had caused minimal harm, but not trivial. One thread of the Starburster mass-gathering project had been compromised. It was a small percentage, but worrisome because it was unexpected. They could not be allowed to survive, but it was essential to learn more about them, especially their places of origin.

The inner sentinel would arrive soon with the captives. Two other, quite different, entities were approaching, however—cloudlike spatial discontinuities that displayed certain lifelike characteristics. Their nature and purpose were unknown. One had briefly interfered with the sentinel, but the interference had turned to the sentinel's advantage. For now, the Starburster Mindbody would simply monitor the strange beings; it had no means of acting against them.

Behind all of this lay the mission of the Survivors. The Survivors were relentless in pursuit of their goals, and so therefore were the Mindaru, their servants. The Starburster Mindbody would stay here until the work of the Survivors had been done. Eons of work had already been completed; but eons more remained, before the transformation of the galaxy would be complete.

*

Daarooaack watched in dismay as the hostile entity closed its long pincers and physically seized the quicklife ship. The entity began at once to drag the ship onto a new course.

Daarooaack called to Deeaab: *"I could not stop it. I cannot separate them. What can we do?"*

Deeaab drew in from the other side, and they flanked the hostile one as it pulled the quicklife vessel onto a course toward the imperiled star, the one the ephemeral Bandicut, through Charli-echo, had identified as *Nick*.

As they shadowed the joined spaceships in flight through the layers of otherspace, Deeaab gently probed and tested the surrounding fabric of spacetime.

"Too risky to try to separate them now. Let us follow. An opportunity may arise..."

✴

Bandicut reacted in disbelief to Copernicus's report. "It's taking us to ✴Nick✴? *Why?*"

"Unknown, Captain."

"It may be," Jeaves said, "that it simply wishes to assure our destruction when the star explodes."

Bandicut considered. "Or maybe it's taking us to Mindaru Central for an interrogation. I wonder if there's any connection between that and the control center Nappy and I tried to get to."

Ik rubbed the side of his head. "Perhaps the place I saw?"

"Would you recognize it again?"

"Hrrm, I think so."

"And if we are interrogated, what then?" Antares asked, her eyes glinting. "Communicate with it?"

Bandicut shook his head. "I don't think that's a viable idea." /Take it out, is what I was thinking. If we could./

/// You really think we could destroy it?
With a few n-space disrupter grenades? ///

/No, not really./ Bandicut grabbed a handhold as the deck trembled again. "Coppy, what's happening? Are you shaking us free?"

"Testing the restraints," said the robot. As if to punctuate his words, the deck shook again. "I was trying to disrupt the n-space bubble the Mindaru has generated around us."

"I don't think we'll succeed at that as long as it has a physical lock on us," Jeaves said. "Why don't we wait to see if it loosens its grip later."

"You think we should . . . rrm . . ."

"Play dead?" Bandicut said. "Instead of rattling the bars of our cage?"

"Yes," said Jeaves. "Of course, we don't know what it's going to do when it gets us there. Things could go quickly from bad to worse."

"So we need to be alert for even the slightest weakening," Bandicut said.

"Because if we miss it, we might not get another chance. Yes."

Li-Jared glared at Jeaves, then at the shadowy, indistinct shape of the thing that had seized them, obscuring most of the view outside the ship. "If it's alert you want," he growled, "it's alert you'll get. Copernicus, can you be ready to make an instant move, without *looking* as if you're ready?"

"Of course," said Copernicus.

Jeaves made a sound of approval. "But we had better be thinking of a backup plan, if we fail to escape."

Ik made a rasping sound. "Do you mean what I think you mean? How shall I put it—?"

"Whether we should blow ourselves to kingdom come, and hope to take it with us?" Bandicut asked.

"Hrrm, yes."

"Precisely what I meant," said Jeaves. "Because that frankly seems the most likely outcome."

*

Antares had no desire to dwell on that probable outcome, though she had to concede there was little they could do beyond, as John put it, rattling the bars of their cage. Once they had discussed and scrutinized every detail of what they had been through that day, it became painful to remain on the bridge, futilely rehashing un-likely strategies. Ship-day wound to a close with Copernicus esti-mating that they would arrive in the vicinity of *Nick* in about two days.

"If I might make a recommendation," Copernicus said, "it would be that you all get some rest." Antares thought Copernicus was a very wise norg, and eventually they all returned to their quarters, except Li-Jared, who was still too agitated to rest.

Antares, back with Bandicut in their quarters, found that she also was too wound up to think of sleep. While John went to bring some food back from the commons, she sat cross-legged on the sleeping pad, mulling all that had happened. As the min-utes passed, she realized she was having difficulty focusing. She was struggling to shake free of what felt like a cloud of unreality enveloping her. She felt as if she had not quite broken with *Thunder*.

She started out of her daze when Bandicut returned with a platter and a jug, which he set on the small sideboard. She leaned to peer at the selection: an assortment of rolls, cheeses, and fruit. John filled a small goblet with a purplish wine from the jug and handed it to her, then poured one for himself. He popped a small ball of cheese into his mouth and sat down beside her. Raising his goblet, he clinked it to hers. "Cheers," he said, and took a swallow. "I suppose I'd better not drink too much of this. No telling when we'll need our wits about us. But still . . . it looks as if we're going to be prisoners for a while." He took another swallow.

"Uhhl," Antares murmured, taking a sip and gazing at Bandicut. They had been separated for what felt like a long and very intense time. Now she found it as difficult to reenter his emotional world as she did to leave the emotional realm of *Thunder*. She felt the torn edges of John's psyche, wounded by failure and the loss of Napoleon, and afire with fear of what was to come. *John Bandicut, I am here,* she tried to say, but her attempt at communication felt awkward and insufficient. *Can you hear me? Can you feel me here?* She reached out and squeezed his arm. "John?"

He started at her touch, flashing a grimace. He glanced down at his plate with an obvious lack of interest.

"Tell me what you're thinking," Antares said. *Share. I'm missing something. Are you?* She ran her fingers over the back of his hand.

A whisker of a smile played at his features, and she sensed, for a moment, an opening. "I don't know. A lot of things, I guess." He rubbed his jaw.

Antares angled her head. "Charli. Tell me what Charli has to say."

Bandicut's eyes went out of focus for a moment. "She's worried, like me, that she'll never see Napoleon again. But"—he blinked—"she thinks we'll get out of this somehow. Hah!"

Antares straightened. "You don't share that belief?"

Bandicut took another sip of wine. "It's hard to see how.

We're trapped here. And even if we escape, I don't see how we're going to stop the thing."

"What about Napoleon?"

He shrugged. "Maybe he can do something—but that's such a long shot, him and those little grenades. Like trying to bring down an elephant with a mosquito."

She didn't understand the simile exactly, but got the gist. "Have you given up, then?"

"Me?" He shook his head and laughed. "Nah. Though I'll be damned if I know why." He frowned. "What?"

Antares had squeezed his hand and now gazed into his eyes, trying to decipher his emotions as they rose to the surface. They seemed more protected than before. Naturally enough. But there was a storm going on under the surface. Was it because of Napoleon? Or his failure to find a way to stop the Mindaru? She wanted to find a way in. "You . . . are feeling very . . ." She could not find the word, even in her own tongue.

Bandicut tipped his head back and closed his eyes. "Torn. Split in two. I can't make sense of things on the scale of the stars, or even Ed. Certainly not the Mindaru. But the human scale seems so . . . *inadequate.*"

Antares waited for him to say more, but when he didn't, she asked, "Can I help?"

He cocked his head, looking uncertain.

Antares muttered softly to herself. It was difficult; his thoughts were so fragmented, so restless. She caught a familiar memory stirring beneath the surface, and for a moment she could not place it; then it came clear:

His life in danger, in the field. And along with him, a small animal, a dog. Why did he keep coming back to this? There was something else. Another memory. Darker. More terrible. And yet something bright in it. *Fire.* A building on fire. A dreadful memory . . . a friend. *A friend who died.*

/John,/ she whispered, hoping he could hear her through the connection of their stones. /Is that what's haunting you?/

If he heard her, it didn't show in his expression. Perhaps a tiny twitch in one eye. But she felt his response. /Tried, I *tried.* There was nothing I could do to save him. I *couldn't.*/

/Who was it? Why are you thinking of him now?/

Bandicut blinked. His inner voice was strained with the memory of an old pain. /Nick. It was Nick I couldn't save./

"Nick?" Antares repeated aloud. "The friend you thought of when ⋆Brightburn⋆ told us about ⋆Nick⋆?"

"Yes, I . . . don't . . ." His emotions were a blaze of confusion. "How did we get onto Nick, for God's sake? He was a friend when we were teenagers. He died in a fire . . . that someone else started."

Antares took his hand between both of hers, trying to quiet the inner blaze. "I found the thought in *your* mind. Does our situation remind you of Nick?"

His eyes widened. "Yes. My God." For a moment, he could not speak. Then he seemed to deliberately gather himself and crease his face, as though to put everything back into order. His emotions threatened to close off again.

She squeezed his hand. "Bandie, let it go. What's behind it?" She began to shake a little, as her own fears and demons threatened to come out and join his. *No! Mine can wait.* She exhaled slowly, letting her senses flow back toward his. He was struggling with the pain of remembering his friend's death; but at the same time, an edge of determination was pushing through the haze and confusion, a determination that what he had let happen to the one Nick would not happen to the other. His breathing slowed and deepened along with hers, and for an instant she felt the warmth of her friend and lover return.

It lasted only moments. And then all his pain and bewilderment seemed to come back in a rush. Something else was weighing on him, something she hadn't found yet. It was pushing back in as relentlessly as an incoming tide.

She tried to reach to the knowing-stones burning in her throat, to see if they could help her find a clearer vision. /Stones? Can you help me reach John Bandicut?/

She was surprised to sense something like confusion there, too. Finally: *We are trying . . . difficulty with his stones . . . they are overloaded with data. Data from the Mindaru.*

/Mindaru!/ Antares blinked. /What kind of data? Is *he* aware of it? Are his stones infected?/

Not that we can detect.

She drew a sharp breath. "John . . . did you . . . get some information when you were in that place? Something new? About the Mindaru?"

He was clearly straining, brow indented, eyes narrowed. "No, I—" And then his eyes widened and a look of astonishment rippled over his face. "Oh, my God—!"

✳

Bandicut felt a sudden rush of static, as though from a bad neurolink. Dizzying, but not a neurolink. /Charli—?/

/// I'm not sure what.
John, the stones are going nuts. ///

/What do you mean?/

/// Antares is right.
They have a lot of new data. ///

Stunned, Bandicut tried to refocus his thoughts, to see what the stones were doing. It was nothing he could make sense of.

*Experiencing difficulty in interpreting . . . *

/Uh . . . Charli, can you enlighten me?/

The quarx answered slowly.

/// I'm having a hard time following.
It's the download from our connection on that station.
They've been trying to decipher it ever since.
Let me see if they can
produce an intelligible stream for us.
Hold on. ///

Bandicut waited. And then it started. Half visible, half heard, half felt, half understood without words . . .

The Mindaru were indeed agents of the once-decimated remnant of the ancient war, agents of an entity known as the Survivors. The Survivors: highly evolved descendants of tiny fragments of code long thought destroyed, as Jeaves had described. The Survivors apparently lived (best guess) within compact dimensions revealed only in "extreme space"—most likely in close proximity to, or inside, super-massive black holes.

The goal of the Survivors (best guess) was the creation of more black holes—expanded habitat—by triggering supernovas and hypernovas throughout space, particularly in stellar nurseries. Where better to set up starburster chain reactions: each cataclysm producing new rounds of starbirth / stardeath / birth / death / bam / bam / bam? And all of these bursts of stardeath seeding the galaxy with heavy elements, the better to continue building agents (or descendants?) such as the Mindaru. The Survivors' existence (best guess) was both fast and slow. Eras of history might pass for them and their descendant AIs while Bandicut was stirring his coffee. And yet, at the same time, their view spanned the lifetimes of galaxies . . .

Bandicut absorbed all of this in stunned silence. But there was more.

The download contained other details, including the recipe for a galaxy-class hypernova. It was not just a matter of gathering exotic dark matter from the surrounding space and dumping it onto the core of a star. That would wreak havoc—instability and psychosis—and eventually kill the star. But to set off a hypernova and a starburst chain, the star must be carefully selected, and the buildup of dark matter crafted with the artistry of a thermonuclear bomb.

The n-space containment at the center was key. It walled off everything including the gravity from the concentrated matter. The buildup required centuries of patience, until critical mass was achieved. Only then would the signal go out— drop the containment, release the matter, and expose the star's core to the crushing gravity of all that mass. Timing was crucial. Mess up the trigger, and the whole thing would sputter like a firework gone wrong.

"Damn," Bandicut breathed. "Napoleon was right."

Antares murmured her puzzlement.

"If all else fails, and Napoleon can breach the n-space field and let out the dark matter at the core of ✳Nick✳, then the hypernova fizzles."

"And that would be good?"

"Not *good*, exactly. ✳Nick✳ would probably blow up, and we would die, but it would be a much smaller bang." He sat back, puffing his cheeks out in thought.

Then he allowed himself a wistful smile, and he reached out and took Antares's hand.

✳

As John described what he had learned from his stones, Antares was filled with fear and wonder in equal measure. "If the Survivors are implacably hostile to *all organic life . . .*"

Bandicut's expression seemed grave, and yet, oddly, more at ease than she had seen him look in some time. "I don't know if it's because they just don't care, or because they're still really, really angry that organics tried to exterminate them in a war a couple of billion years ago."

For a moment Antares let that seep into her consciousness. "We probably can't do much about a power that reaches across the galaxy and can do things like cause stars to blow up. Except . . . maybe we can, *here.* Now. This time. Do you suppose there are other people like us, in other parts of the galaxy, trying to stop them like we are?"

Bandicut scratched the side of his head. "There's a thought."

Antares shivered with a sudden vision of being sent to the center of the galaxy to confront the Survivors where they lived (maybe), in the enormous black hole there. She drew a breath, realized she was seeing the same worry in Bandicut's eyes.

He seemed to read her thoughts. He chuckled, then looked away. "So now that we know how they do it," he said, "how does that help us stop them?" He met her gaze again. "Maybe for a little while, we shouldn't *worry.*" He reached out to caress her cheek.

She caught his hand and pressed it to her lips. "That is a sensible idea," she whispered.

John began running the fingers of his other hand through her hair, and she breathed with a sudden rush of pleasure and an unexpected ache for him. For a moment, she resisted; then she leaned into him with a sigh and found his lips with her own, drawing him into a most human, and prolonged, kiss. The surge of arousal took her by surprise, but she felt his own feelings rising to match hers—and without another word, they were embracing awkwardly, intimately, passionately. She was only dimly aware of the fading echoes of their fear, and the clatter of wine cups being knocked over, as the urgency of holding each other gave way to a quiet desperation as they made love.

∗

They both slept fitfully through the night. As they lay together in the semidarkness, Antares felt Bandicut's pain and worry gradually seep back into him. In time, it grew too strong to ignore. "Bandie John?" she whispered, reaching to him.

He started to answer, but was interrupted by the sound of a chime. Copernicus's voice called from somewhere in the wall. "A change in the flight dynamics, everyone. I believe we may be approaching our destination ahead of schedule."

"Time to worry again," Bandicut muttered. He held her close for a dozen heartbeats, then got to his feet. He reached down, and Antares accepted his hand in rising to her own feet.

Neither of them spoke as they pulled on clothes and stumbled toward the bridge.

35

INTO THE SUN

 On day two, the translator reported that it was applying force-field reinforcement to the hull structure. That, Julie guessed, meant things were getting a little shaky down there in the hold.

∗*Would you like to see?*∗
/Not necessarily./

The image appeared in the cockpit status screen. It was difficult to make out the image—it was a cloud of particles, shimmering and hard to look at, the way the translator was hard to look at. At its center was a small, shiny nugget. It twisted and turned like a ball of mercury, but looked solid at the same time. *Cancerous,* she thought. It was growing. Visibly. It seemed to have little needle points appearing around its periphery, then disappearing, like a snowflake growing in time-lapse photography. But she knew, because she sensed it from the stones, that this was not time-lapse, this was real-time growth.

The knot in her stomach was growing, too.

"What's it doing?" she whispered.

The stones shifted something, and now she could see thin tendrils spidering out from the nucleus, slipping through tiny openings in the weave of whatever was surrounding it—the translator's force-field?—and then out to a pebbled, pitted surface beyond. Was that the wall of the cargo hold, or had it already eaten that away? She feared it was some part of the ship's belly, where the nano-constructors that streamed out from the enemy took little bites and carried the pieces back to join the cloud of accreting particles.

"Can't you tighten the net?" she pleaded. "The weave? Whatever it is?"

Not without dropping out of spatial threading. If we do that, we can seal it off. But then we delay getting it to the sun. As soon as we thread space again, it will start all over. Remember, we're shifting in and out of your continuum to move. It seems able to use those transitional moments—millionths of seconds—to get through, no matter how fast we go. All we can do is reinforce the ship's fields to make it more resistant.

Drums pounded in Julie's head. She was having trouble thinking straight. There had to be *something* she could do. She put her hands to her temples, trying to shut out the drumming feeling of inexorability. /Can't we—there has to be—/

But the stones had no further answer. And the cancer in the cargo hold was growing. She circled the tiny cockpit interior. Had to be something she could do. *Had* to be . . .

✶

By the end of day two, the sun was a lot bigger, a ghostly pumpkin in the window, where the light was filtered by the threading field. The thing in the ship's belly was still eating its way outward. It had dissolved and absorbed the cargo container. A couple of power conduits were gone, forcing the rerouting of some circuits. There was a constant buzzing in Julie's feet, in her hands, and her head. Maybe it was the vibration of the ship being dissolved, or maybe it was her mind, trying to process what was happening to her—and, finding no way to produce understanding, her brain was shaking like a truck on an unpaved road.

When she queried the stones on the state of the ship, she got no reply; they were too busy trying to hold things together, she supposed.

Quite apart from her fear for her personal safety—and she was surprised how well she was able to compartmentalize that fear—she felt growing concern about whether the translator could actually deal with this threat. The translator was the closest thing she'd ever seen to an omnipotent force. Could this object the size of a grain of sand really be a match for it?

It seemed all she could do was watch the object devour her ship while the translator tried to stop it—and transmit periodic radio reports on her condition, entirely in the blind. That, and live with the fear that she had made a terrible, unthinkable, fatal mistake in linking up with the translator on this mission.

Do not think that, the stones replied, revealing at least that they were still paying attention to her. *What you are doing might cost you your life. But you are attempting to save your world.*

/Yeah, yeah./ She thought she sensed impatience on the part of the stones. /What? Don't I have a right to be scared and pissed and disillusioned?/

Perhaps you do. But consider: even if you fail and die, will you be the first to die in a cause you believed in?

Julie felt momentarily ashamed, but not mollified. /Maybe not. But does that mean I should *want* to throw my life away?/

The stones seemed puzzled. *Would you rather have gone back to a homeworld that was on the verge of destruction, which you might have been able to save?*

Julie knew she needed to get past this. *I was okay with it yesterday, why can't I be today? Things are just a little harder now. And God knows, the stones are right. Is* my *survival the most important thing here?* /All right,/ she said finally, half believing it. /But isn't there at least something I can *do*? I need to be doing something./

There was no answer. "Stones!" she yelled. "*Tell me some way I can help!*"

Finally, after a silence so long she had gone back to staring out the window, the stones answered:

There is something we'd like you to do. It's risky.
/What is it?/
We'd like you to suit up now.
/Why, is the hull getting ready to breach?/
Not immediately.
/Then what?/ On the screen display, the haze seemed to be increasing in the space where the alien object was working away at the frame surrounding the cargo hold. It looked like it was one step away from attacking the main hull.

There's something we want to try, and we would rather you were outside the hull when we do.

That rocked her back in her seat. /Outside the hull?/ There was a very bright and growing sun outside, and they were barreling headlong toward it. I'll be roasted, she thought.

*No, we have a plan . . . *

✶

Julie sealed the helmet and moved to the exit hatch. Her stomach was churning. She had been outside in a suit on Triton's surface, but never outside a small craft in the middle of infinite space. /You're sure this is safe?/

The word "safe" would be an exaggeration. But we'll protect you from the radiation and heat, you'll still be enclosed in the threading field, and you'll be farther from what we're about to try.

She waited as pressure in the cabin dropped. /You mean, you're moving me out of the line of fire?/

Something like that.

The door slid open, and she cautiously floated out onto the doorstep, attached a safety tether, and turned to face the little craft's cabin, a disconcertingly small enclosure mounted on the front of the craft's ungainly arachnidlike chassis. A series of handholds led to the cabin roof and to what Julie automatically thought of, despite the lack of gravity, as the "top" of the craft. A blazing light in the edge of her visor revealed the massive disk of the sun to her right. She avoided looking that way, even though the suit had filters and the stones had promised to protect her. The edge of the disk that she glimpsed had a shimmering quality through the spatial threading.

Please move to the top. Carefully.

She took the handholds like rungs of a ladder and floated hand over hand onto the roof. Once there, she rearranged the safety lines so that two were clipped to cleats on either side of her. She bobbed slightly in a standing position on the roof of the cabin, looking around. Despite being encased in a spacesuit, she felt naked and vulnerable outside the ship. Vertigo threatened her around the edges. From here, she could see just about the entire maintenance craft except for the cargo pod hidden beneath the cabin and the service section amidships where fuel tanks were clustered. The translator was nestled between the service and rear propulsion sections, just peeking out with its revolving cascade of black and iridescent globes.

/What do I do now?/

As if in answer, something quivered in her peripheral vision. She looked quickly, and saw a half-silver bubble pop into existence around her, then slowly fade into transparency. /What was that?/

An extra measure of protection.

That was undoubtedly supposed to reassure her. And yet, the vacuum of space surrounded her with its diamond hardness. If anything, the bubble seemed to filter out the shimmer of the threading, making the sharp emptiness of space as stark as if she were simply floating in the void. And here she was, on the roof of her spacecraft, sunbathing under a *very* tropical sun in a secondhand spacesuit. /What about that *thing* down there that's eating through my ship? Can this bubble keep me safe from *that*?/

Unknown. Please refrain from conversation now.

The translator brightened momentarily. Then, through the cabin roof, she felt a vibration. There was a flash and a jet of light, white with blue-green flares, out one side of the cargo area. Startled, she bounced up against her tethers. The flash and jet repeated—and again, four times. /What are you doing?/ she asked when she could stand it no longer.

Focusing bursts of solar radiation on the object, hoping to disrupt it.

/And did you?/

Unclear. It deflected some of the energy out through the side of the hull.

/Was that why you wanted me out of the way? Jesus, mother of—!/ She glanced back at the sun. *Are we going to make it? Are we going to dump this thing in the lap of the sun? Or is it having us for toast?*

It will be close. We're going to lose more of the ship going in.

She shut her eyes. /Can I back out now? No—forget I said that. If we're going to die, let's make damn sure we take *it* out with us!/

That's our intention.

Julie turned to face the sun. Screw the glare, she'd trust the filters. She could clearly see sunspots on the face of the sun now, like irregular black moles, and the curling turbulence of an electromagnetic storm. One day to go. /Is there any hope we can still drop it in and try to get away?/

Uncertain we can jettison. Our powers are being strained. Containment and speed are our sole priorities.

Julie closed her eyes to slits. Maybe *you* can't jettison with your fancy fields, she thought. But that thing's in a mechanical cargo pod. *I just wonder* . . . She called to her spacesuit heads-up display for information on the layout of the craft.

*

Time passed more quickly than she'd have thought possible. By the time she'd figured out most of what she needed to know, she was very tired, and the sun loomed large in the sky. She must have dozed off, because the sun's disk seemed to have grown when she wasn't looking. She remembered holding her bent arm up to the sun, and being able to span the sun's diameter with her forearm from elbow to fingertips. That was no longer true. The sun was now swollen to cover a third of the sky.

By this time, she thought, the skin of the ship ought to be glowing like a horseshoe in a blacksmith's fire. It wasn't, so she guessed the translator—or the spatial threading—was protecting it from the heat. She peered cautiously over the edge of the cabin roof to see what condition the ship was in now, and was shocked to see dancing rays of light and sparkling dust billowing steadily from below. /What's that mean that I'm seeing?/

The stones answered gravely, *You will not be able to return to your cabin.*

/You mean it's being destroyed?/

Unfortunately.

Damn. *Damn.* And now . . . just knowing that her living space with all of its amenities was gone, she felt a sudden, urgent need to pee. Forget it, kid. Hold it. That's how you're going out. Try not to pee in your pants when you fall into the sun.

Does this help?

The pressure in her bladder suddenly went away. She blinked, and thought for a moment she saw a glitter in the distance. /As a matter of fact, it does. What did you do with the pee?/

We removed it.

/Damn. *Really?* Did you dump it on that thing's head down there?/ That would give her some satisfaction at least, pissing on the thing that was trying to kill her.

What an odd notion. No—we didn't want to give it the mass, so we vented it to space.

Julie sighed in disappointment. She felt oppressed by the sun, vast and sullen through the filtering field. How much longer? She had a sudden vision of just the three of them left, falling in a cluster into the sun: the mass-gobbling alien object, the writhing translator, and her in her force-field bubble.

Not so far from the truth. Look to your right.

She looked. Where the translator had been nestled into the framework of the ship's midsection, it was now far more exposed. The portion of the ship's hull beneath it had been eaten away, and it now looked like what it was, a very strange, semi-iridescent object hitching a ride on the side of a steel framework. Its perch was disintegrating in a soft haze. *God damn it. God damn that thing!*

Understand, the translator is not a fighting machine, and never was. It can manipulate space, but was not created to do battle against a malicious foe. If it had, the Fffff'tink might have survived.

The Fffff'tink? She caught a mental glimpse of a civilization self-destructing, a civilization that both the translator and something called a quarx had labored to save. And now the fight had moved . . . to this little craft, a battle to save *her* civilization.

We only have to hold a little longer.

She gulped a breath, staring down at the half-eaten hull. /Aren't we close enough to the sun now that we could drop it like a bomb, then get away before it destroys us? Could it escape at this point?/

Probably not. But to release it, we would have to relax our containment fields. And we dare not risk that, not yet.

Julie stared thoughtfully into space for a moment, then resumed studying the diagrams in her heads-up display.

*

Had she dozed again? She was definitely tired. Being out in the hot sun in a threading field must do that to you. The sun now filled most of the sky. She was very thirsty. She sipped from the suit's meager water supply and surveyed the wreckage of the ship at her feet. Perhaps it was time to put her own plan into action.

/I need to move down toward you,/ she said.

Do you mean toward the translator?

/Yes. Can you protect me while I move?/

We can, but . . . it is less safe.

/I thought you said "safe" wasn't a word that applied here./

What are you planning?

She began readjusting her tether lines and inching her way toward the back of what was left of the cabin. /I'm planning to drop a payload into the sun. The hard way. By hand./

Please clarify.

Julie wondered if John had had to talk his way around the stones. /Watch and see. I'm just going as far as that little ledge down there./ She pointed a gloved hand toward a jutting metal step on the side of what was left of the cabin. The thing she wanted to reach was supposed to be accessible from there. It took some careful maneuvering, but eventually she was perched—awkwardly—not more than a meter from the venting plasma. She peered into the shadows. There it was: a large, upside-down U, a handle that looked as if it might take both hands to pull. Tough in zero gravity.

Julie?

She centered herself in front of the handle. Bracing herself with one hand, she gripped the handle with the other, and pulled.

This is a manual release for the cargo pod.

/Right./

You can't release it just by doing this, you know.

/I know./ The handle budged, ever so slightly. She relaxed a moment, then strained again. It moved a little more. /There are three more spaced around the cabin section. I'll take them one at a time, and release the last one when we're sure we're close enough to the sun. Can you help me?/

We're uncertain about this.

/I trusted you, now you trust me, okay? I promise not to jump the gun. Now let me get this done and move on to the next one!/ She pulled again, and this time the handle came, rotating out and away from the hull's surface. She felt something, a slight clunk, as the latch released.

*Julie . . . *

/Just tell me when it's safe to cut it loose, okay?/

She felt some far corner of the stones acquiesce as she began making her way to the second release. It seemed the translator was unwilling to force her into something she didn't want to do. It might be in charge, but it insisted on working *with* her rather than in spite of her. That was good. Because she had a lot to do here. The sun, she could have sworn, was swelling visibly. She wanted to have a little bit of her pride left as she plummeted to her death.

/We *are* going to die, right?/ she asked matter-of-factly, as she attached her tethers in front of the second manual release lever.

That is a possible outcome. Just now we want to focus solely on ensuring the destruction of this object.

/Could flying it into the sun make it stronger?/

We have considered that possibility. We believe it has not yet reached a stage of being able to transform solar energy into propulsive energy. It is laboring to survive. The bursts of solar heat we have focused on it are taking a toll. It is suffering.

Julie considered that. /Are *we* suffering from the heat, too?/ *Not as much.*

/Good./ Gripping a handhold with her left hand and placing her right on the second release lever, Julie pulled with all her strength, and with a great gasp that echoed in her helmet, hauled the handle to the open position. /You said it *might* develop the ability to fly out of here on solar energy—if it sucks enough material from us to sprout wings or something, right? So aside from what I want, it might be better to boot the thing off into the sun if we can, anyway? Right? To deprive it of more of our matter?/

Possibly so. In its current state, we do not believe it could survive outside our threading field. You may be right.

I'll be damned, she thought. I may be right. Even if I am about to become toast. Unfastening and refastening her tether lines, she began making her way across the top of the spacecraft. Beneath her, the cargo pod seemed to be vibrating. Half the releases were open. Was the sun bigger than it was ten minutes ago? Who cared? *Gonna be a hot time in the old town tonight. Yeah.*

She was maybe halfway to the third release mechanism when the stones' voice penetrated her consciousness: *Please respond!*

/Hah—?/

Are you in distress?

/What—?/

Julie Stone! Are you in distress?

/What . . . distress . . . ?/

She blinked away sweat from her eyes, and realized that her heart was pounding, and she felt a little lightheaded. /Fine . . . I'm fine./ Except for a dizzy, sweltering euphoria. The sort of feeling one might get if one were spinning around. Or too hot. Or going hypo . . . hypox . . . *hypoxic* . . .

She blinked hard and tried to focus. She was holding one end of a tether in one hand, and the other end was attached . . . where? To her waist. That was right, wasn't it? One to the hand, one to the waist . . . ? She felt herself floating . . .

Attach the tether! Now!

She looked at the tether in her hand, looked down at the cleat from which she was slowly drifting away. That did not seem right. She was turning slowly, coming to face the wall of the blazing sun. *No . . . gonna float away . . . not even have the ol' translator to die with.* A jerk at her waist brought her back. The second tether had come to its end and stopped her escape. But she was rotating now, swinging around, out of control.

Pull yourself in! Do you need more oxygen?

Panting, she grabbed for the other tether, and nearly wrapped it around her neck as she struggled to arrest her movement and pull herself back. /Oxygen? Might be good./

We are trying to analyze. We think your regulator has malfunctioned. We are trying to—

She felt a sudden gust of wind inside her helmet. She drew greedily on it, like a deprived smoker on a cigarette. /Jesus, that's—/ And then it stopped, and she gasped again. /Why'd you turn it off?/

Can you adjust it inside your suit?

/I—maybe—/ She pushed at her chin control and felt a little more air coming. /Is that—am I—uh!/ She slammed into the side of the cabin, and grabbed for something to hang on to. She slid downward. Toward the cargo pod. Again she grabbed. Missed. Her feet were dangling toward the cloud of disintegrating matter coming out of the ruptured cargo hull. Nothing else to grab.

Pull the tether in your other hand!

/What?/ She yanked hard with her left hand, surprised to find a tether still in her grip. With a jolt, she began to float back toward the roof of the cabin. /OK. OK. OK. What about my air?/

You were running low. We have set up a transfer from another tank. Hold on.

Like emptying my bladder, but in reverse? She tried to pull herself back to where she'd been, and finally got her second tether hooked on a cleat. The airflow started to feel okay, and her vision was clearing up. She hadn't even noticed the tunnel vision before. She breathed in great lungfuls of air. Jesus, that was close. When she felt steadier, she resumed moving toward the far side of the cabin. /How long was I out of it?/ How much bigger was the sun?

Not long. Long enough. Can you pull the handle?

She planted herself, sucked a deep breath, and pulled. The release opened. /Got it. Is that the last?/

One more. Can you move more quickly?
She grunted. /We getting close to the dive, are we?/
*We think we detect new organization forming in the alien object. Some of its mass is boiling off in the sun, but it's pulling from us faster than it's losing . . . *
/Say no more./ She began moving to the last handle that would jettison the cancerous monster. It seemed to take a very long time. Then her hand was on the handle. *Brace yourself. Pull.*
It didn't move.
She pulled harder. Still nothing. /It's not . . . I don't know why . . . if I can't get this . . . / Biting her lip, she put both hands on the grip and braced her feet on either side of it, so she'd be lifting from a squat. *Pull!*
Let's try this.
The craft beneath her feet suddenly jolted, as if with a change in acceleration. The handle gave with a lurch, and she sprang involuntarily away from the hull with her feet, and an instant later was hanging on by the handle as her body flew out and twisted. She struggled to pull herself back and grab something solid. /Did it—did it work?/
Look down.
Something was shaking where she was holding on. She bent her head down to peer past her feet. /God damn!/ The cargo pod was sliding out of its docking adapter and separating from the service craft. Or rather, what was left of the pod was separating from what was left of the craft. It was a hazy ball of dust and light, drifting away from a badly moth-eaten hull. It all seemed to squirm in her vision.
It's trying to hold on. We're going to make a slight change.
As the stones said that, something happened in the spatial threading—and the spacecraft seemed to change velocity rather abruptly. Julie had a sudden sensation of the brakes being put on, while the detached cargo pod went flying ahead of them. Flying ahead of them into the fiery heart of the sun . . .

✷

The sun. It *was* most of the sky now, and the stones advised her that they would be making their entry over the next few minutes. She was going to have to ride it out, right where she was perched, on top of the remains of the cabin. She had moved closer to the translator. /There's no way for me to get a message off to anyone now is there?/

Not really. Look.

She looked. The alien object had disappeared in the glare. But a point of bright light flared, dazzling even against the intense fire that dominated the sky. It blazed for about one second, then disappeared. /Was that it? Is it gone?/

It is gone. We monitored its disintegration. A few more hours and it might have been able to protect itself. It wasn't complete enough to survive the intense heat.

Julie looked a little longer, then turned to look back at the dizzying view of the translator, where it was attached, squirming, to the skeletal remains of the spacecraft. /You sound sad./

We'd hoped to take it with us to study. There is much we would like to know about its creators.

/A shame,/ Julie said, making the most insincere statement of her life, as she tried to swallow her ballooning fear. *Take it with us, right.* /Where is it we think we're going?/

Hold tight, said the stones.

With that, the ship plummeted into the heat and light and thundering inferno of the sun.

36

IN THE FIRE OF A STAR

Racing to the bridge, Bandicut and Antares found Copernicus working with filters on the sensor images, and Li-Jared pacing back and forth in front of the viewspace, apparently trying to decide what he was looking at. All Bandicut could see was a blazing sun mostly hidden behind the limbs and struts of their captor. "Is that *Nick*?" he asked, thinking of Napoleon out there, somewhere, inside the star. Wouldn't Napoleon be surprised to know they had traveled here from *Thunder*.

"It is," said Copernicus.

"What—rrrm—is it doing to us?" Ik asked, arriving just behind them.

"✳Nick✳ is doing nothing to us," Li-Jared answered. "But that *thing* out there seems to be bringing us to its parents." Li-Jared raised his chin a little, gazing first out ahead of them and then back inside at Copernicus. The Karellian looked as if he hadn't slept. He swayed as he asked Copernicus, "Can you replay the image we saw before?"

The viewspace flickered, and showed them farther from the star. For just an instant, as the angles changed, something became visible past all the struts and legs, a shadowy object at the edge of the star's atmosphere.

"Hrah!" Ik exclaimed. *"That's it, that's the control center! That's what we saw through ✳Thunder✳'s eyes!"*

Bandicut tensed; his hands balled into fists. Was that where the entire dark-matter-channeling operation was controlled—the place he and Napoleon had tried unsuccessfully to find?

Ik turned to Antares. "That's what you saw, isn't it?"

Antares cocked her head at Ik. A strange expression passed like a shadow over Ik's face, only for an instant. "Ik, are you okay?" Bandicut asked. "Are you sure it's the control center?" The Hraachee'an looked puzzled by his question and bobbed his head. "Good," Bandicut said. "Then we're going right where we need to be."

"Glad to hear *that*," Li-Jared muttered. "What now?"

Bandicut drew a breath. "We find a way to disable it, I guess."

Copernicus restored the current view, which didn't show much. "I am still monitoring for any change in the sentinel's grip on us," the robot said, "but so far I have found no weaknesses."

"I don't think escape is our goal right now," Bandicut repeated. Antares touched his shoulder; he felt her thoughts, urging him to persevere. In his head, meanwhile, Charli was scanning for their allies.

/// I feel Charlene-echo nearby. ///

/Did they both follow us here? Deep and Dark?/

/// I believe so.

But I don't know if they have a plan, either. ///

"What?" Antares said, watching him.

"Charli says Deep and company are out there."

"Can they help us?"

"Wouldn't we all like to know."

∗

An hour later the ship lurched, and Copernicus announced, "Our captor has dropped us out of n-space."

"Is it moving us to a dock?" Bandicut asked.

"Not that I can tell. But we're still being held."

Bandicut strode forward and pointed to the upper left of the view. A patch where the sun had been visible was now partially blocked by a shifting darkness. "Is that the Mindaru control center structure?"

"Yes. We're being probed, by the way."

Bwang. "Probed by what?"

"Magnetic, gravitational, neutrino-beam, X-ray, gamma ray, tachyon . . ."

"Is that all?" Bandicut asked.

"No, I am also detecting AI threads trying to penetrate my system."

Ik's eyes seemed to harden, and he stepped forward, growling softly. Antares, eyes narrowed, stayed close to him. Bandicut felt a twinge of her sudden concern.

Li-Jared was bristling. "Can you shut them out?"

"Yes, but here's the problem—we must study them if we want to find a way to stop them," Copernicus said. "Jeaves and I have developed a set of what we believe are robust protective protocols."

Bong. "Robust, you say? Strong enough to withstand an assault from *that*?" Li-Jared sounded doubtful.

Jeaves answered. "Let's just say, if the assault is strong enough to overwhelm our defenses, we will have already lost. Does that reassure you?"

"Not much," Bandicut said.

"My point is that we have a pretty good defense."

Bandicut glanced around, noting that Jeaves's reassurance seemed to be meeting with a mixed reaction. Ik's eyes glinted—with worry? "What do you think *its* game plan is?"

"One presumes," Jeaves said, "that it wants to study us as well, perhaps before destroying us. It did go to the trouble of bringing us all this way. So—"

"I am detecting a loosening of the gripping arms," Copernicus interrupted.

"Are you ready to break?" Li-Jared danced forward into the viewspace.

Before Copernicus could answer, there was an abrupt change outside the ship. The sentinel arms pulled away, revealing a blinding light from the star, which the filters chopped back at once. Between the ship and the sun was a curtainlike thing of black and dazzling silver; it almost, but not quite, enveloped *The Long View.* Bandicut squinted, trying to decipher what he was seeing. Mindaru control station, enforcer, star destroyer—maybe all at once—it rippled like a silver-and-shadow ghost between *The Long View* and the roiling sun. The star's light seemed to shine partially through it. "What *is* that? Physically, I mean."

"I cannot measure much," Jeaves said. "But if this really is the control center—"

"What do we do, now that we have it right where we want it?"

/// Be very, very patient, I should think.
Wait for a proper opening. ///

Antares shot him a quizzical gaze. Bandicut repeated Charli's comment.

Bwang-g-g. "Charli's right," Li-Jared said, startling him.

Copernicus tapped twice. "Actually . . . I had already arrived at that conclusion, and so I did not attempt a breakaway just now."

Li-Jared spun, eyeing the robot.

"Hrah-h-h," Ik drawled.

Antares touched his arm. "Is it the star? Are you in contact?" She closed her eyes. "The time-fusion is starting. I can feel it. That's what Deep is doing . . ."

*

Ik felt at once that *Nick*'s pain was different from *Thunder*'s. *Nick* had a fierce knot in the pit of his stomach, a knot that was growing steadily harder and tighter. And it was going to kill him if it wasn't removed soon.

That's life, Ik thought—and then caught himself with a jerk.

Why had he thought *that*? He wanted to offer assurance to the star. /We are trying. Trying as hard as we can,/ he whispered. It didn't seem like much.

To his surprise, there came an answer:

Trying ?

How ?

It grows

gnaws

kills

Seeks death

Where is hope ?

How ?

How can I ?

How ?

Which left Ik groping for an answer.

Soon

will end soon

I feel-l-l

And Ik sensed a long, reverberating sigh that seemed to carry from one eon to the next. If there was any hope in the sigh, he could not feel it. He wasn't sure he could offer any, either.

*

Deeaab had an idea. It was an extreme solution, more extreme than he would have chosen.

Deeaab and Daarooaack had entered this universe from a place far away—at least, when considered in a certain way. Viewed in another way, their universe of birth was no farther than the backside of a wave of sunlight. They had arrived through a discontinuity in the membrane that bounded this spacetime from others. The universe they had left behind was winding down toward its death, dark and chaotic and increasingly formless. It was a place, Deeaab thought, that would suit the Mindaru very well.

Deeaab spoke to Daarooaack.

"This entity kills and kills, and will kill everything it can reach. We must put an end to it. Do you see a way?"

Daarooaack was moving about at a distance from the starship and the enemy object, trying to find a weakness.

"None that does not involve great risk, and probable failure."

Deeaab agreed. And yet . . .

<<<*Your idea could work.* >>>

The quarx-echo lodged in Deeaab's heart spoke with a kind of assurance Deeaab had not heard from it before.

<<< *There is risk to the star and to us.*
But would we rather do nothing? >>>

Deeaab felt an ache of recognition. What the quarx-echo said, and the Delilah-echo quietly reinforced, was exactly what Deeaab had been closing in on. It might be the only way to help their friends. Perhaps it would even make up for the time, long past, when he had *not* been able to help other friends—when he had tried, and failed, to bring more of his kind out of the dying universe.

Daarooaack had begun circling more widely, exploring various dimensional layers. Finally she called:

"There is an opening into the star."

Deeaab looked hard. Then he saw the channel: from the outside of the star down into its center, a channel where once the strange matter had flowed, but was now blocked upstream by the being called Ed. Many other channels were streaming into the star with strange matter. But there was slack in this channel, and Deeaab thought it just might be possible to take a large object down through it . . .

⋆

It was still damnably hard to tell what was happening outside the ship. The sentinel that had captured them had somehow folded itself into the Mindaru control station, but much of their view remained shrouded. Bandicut could see that *The Long View* was trapped in the upper atmosphere of ⋆Nick⋆, but couldn't see much more than that. He wondered if he should be planning another boarding party. Of course, they weren't docked to the control station, and he didn't have Napoleon to accompany him, but still . . .

Before he could get very far in that line of thought, Charli nudged for his attention and said that Charlene-echo needed to talk. Bandicut listened:

<<< *Deep believes we may be able*
to stop the Mindaru
and free you at the same time.
But we need your help. >>>
/I'm glad someone has an idea. What's Deep have in mind?/
<<< *It would be risky.*
We need you to make contact.
Mind to mind. >>>
/With—?/

<<< *The Mindaru AI.* >>>
Bandicut barked a disbelieving laugh, which caused Antares
and Li-Jared to look his way. /That thing is a killer!/
<<< *Exactly.* >>>
/When Ik came into contact with it, it took over his stones!/
<<< *We are aware of the risk, yes.*
But it is necessary for Deep's plan.
And Charli can help protect you. >>>
Bandicut asked cautiously, /What's the plan?/
Before Charlene-echo could respond, Charli said,
/// *I think I see*
what they have in mind.
We need to persuade the enemy
to do something . . . ///
/Well, that's just craz—I mean, the chance of being
infected—my stones—and if I let that thing in my head, how do
we know *I* won't go crazy, or have a silence-fugue, or—/
/// *Yes. Yes. All risks.*
But we've learned a lot about the Mindaru,
and the stones will have a much better chance
of controlling the situation. ///
"John! What is it?" Antares asked.
Bandicut paused long enough to tell them what Deep was
proposing. They were appalled, as he knew they would be, and
they demanded to know more. He spoke to Charlene-echo. /You
haven't told me the plan yet./
<<< *We want to throw the Mindaru,*
and all of the dark matter with it,
out of the universe. >>>

/That sounds good. How?/

<<< *We need you to convince it
to release the dark matter now,
and begin to collapse the star.* >>>

Bandicut felt his mind freeze. /*Begin* to collapse—?/

<<< *That's right.* :>>>

/That'll give it what it wants. Kill the star, kill us!/

<<< *Not if we're successful.
We're going to control the process.
John, this thing's ready to blow.
We need to move fast.
Do you trust us?* >>>

/Yes, but—can't you tell me what you're planning to do?/

<<< *Not all of it.* :>>>

/Why the hell—?/

<<< *Because we're asking you to make
direct contact with the Mindaru.
If it manages to see more in your mind
than you intend . . .* >>>

Bandicut rasped a breath. *Hell's bells!*

/// *John, we don't have a lot of options,
and time's getting short.* ///

Bandicut thought furiously. If he trusted Charlene-echo and
Deep and tried this insanely risky thing—and made even the
slightest mistake—wouldn't he likely just set off the hypernova,
instead of stopping it?

/// *It will happen anyway,
if you take no action.* ///

Pressing his fingers to his eyes, he said to the others, "I'm doing what Deep wants! I can't explain, but it's the only way. And
I have to do it *now.*"

Li-Jared yelped, Antares made a low, unhappy growling
sound—and Copernicus said, "Captains, I have no better idea to
offer. Jeaves?"

"None. If we trust Deep and Charlene-echo . . ."

A new seat suddenly appeared in front of the control console. Bandicut sat in it and placed his hands on a pair of contacts
in the two armrests. He felt an immediate connection as the

stones' reproduction of a neurolink melted into place around him. "John!" he heard Antares call, but her voice faded into the background along with the rest of the bridge.

Bandicut shut his eyes again. /Promise you'll keep me from flipping out and going into fugue?/

/// *I will try.* ///

That would have to be good enough. "Hold the fort down," he said to the others. "Let's go."

The neurolink was alive with energy and activity. He sensed Copernicus and Jeaves nearby, and the translator-stones hovering watchfully over his shoulder. The ship's systems were right there in front of him, and he could sense the Mindaru entity trolling at the outer edges of the network, testing its defenses. The protocols Copernicus and Jeaves had set up were allowing it to probe, within limits. They were keeping it out of sensitive areas, and keeping Bandicut hidden. But that last was about to change.

Are you ready?

As he gazed out at the shadowy presence of the Mindaru, he felt himself suddenly falling . . . his neurolink presence falling, down into a place where he could see and hear much more—and where *he* could be seen.

✳

Frustration was not something the Starburster Mindbody felt as a discrete sensation. But the captive's intelligence system was proving difficult to break into, forcing the Mindbody to enlist more probes, more energetically. The captive had shrewd defenses.

Something was happening, and the Mindaru entity needed to find out what that was. Following the path of greatest probability, the entity narrowed the focus of its probe onto the one bio node that seemed most open to contact. Here, it thought, it might learn what this thing was planning, what sort of meddling with the mission. Images were starting to form, behind a haze of static . . .

✳

He felt the pulsing of multiple streams of thought: the AI's and the other robots'; Charli's, the quarx-echo's, and his own. And the scratchy, rasping nails of the Mindaru trying to claw its way

in. He prayed he could stand up against it. Mostly, he thought it
was beyond his control; it was between the stones and the Mindaru. He tried to still his fear.

*/// John, keep your mind closed to it for everything
except what we tell you, all right? ///*

He had no time to answer, because something banged open
in his mind. It felt a little like the door to silence-fugue—except
there was a presence behind it.

/Stones? Charli? Are you on top of this? Because I'm—/

Without warning, he found himself in another space, a place
where the thoughts of the Mindaru buzzed like angry hornets.
For a moment he felt pinned there; then something yanked him
away. Now he was in a darkened space, a portal. The way to the
Mindaru control center? He shivered as a thread of malicious
thought reached out toward him . . .

—<mode shift>—

There was a flash, a discontinuity, just like in the old neurolink before his accident back on Triton. Suddenly he was
standing in an old barn, or a tractor-shed. The shed was empty,
but in its doorway a shadow loomed. It was the combine, towering, grinding forward toward him. Was it going to finish the
job it had failed to do in the field? A scream rose in his throat . . .

—<mode shift>—

Another neurolink discontinuity. He floated along complex
pathways, all angles and sloping contours. Was this a landscape
of his own mind, or of the alien control center? Was it the landscape on which they would meet? He felt the presence of the
unseen opposing intelligence, like a dangerous animal circling
around him. It was alien and cold, aloof, frightening—like the
combine, about to thresh him into oblivion. /Stones? Charli?/

We are here.

Here, but distant. He felt currents of movement around him,
more than one thing stalking. Faint scratching sounds. It was
more like . . . *rats scurrying in the woodwork.* Charli called
from a distance:

*/// It's surrounding you.
It's trying to filet your mind open.
Don't let it. ///*

Jesus! /Thanks, I'll remember that!/ He was shaking now, as the scratching sounds intensified. *Rats.* Were they actually AI probes gathering around him, preparing to strike, to suck his mind dry? Was it about to learn everything it wanted to know about Earth, and Shipworld?

Probes are indeed approaching. We will protect you as we can. But we too must learn.

Yeah. So what are we going to do here?

—<mode shift>—

Silence-fugue was on him in a heartbeat, forcing him to fight for his sanity. He teetered on the edge . . .

Rat-things crawling over me. Nipping at my hair, squealing. Panic rising, voices screeching in my mind. Try to flee! Can't move! Not rats, more like huge vampire mosquitoes, trying to suck away his memories. The Mindaru. *Swat them away!*

His thoughts and memories?

Don't let it see anything it shouldn't see . . .

The landscape of his thoughts was like a million popping flashbulbs, each illuminating for a split second a different piece of memory. He couldn't control it—something else had control—he could only watch in horror as myriad pieces of himself seemed to detach and be revealed in a spotlight. But some were revealed more than others; some were drowned out by too much light, or hidden by the fog of chaos. The stones?

—<mode shift>—

The field, the combine bearing down on him, thunderheads roiling overhead. The black dog barking frantically. He stumbled and fell, right in the path of the machine . . .

—<mode shift>—

Sputtering images, a galaxy at war. Armadas dispatched to the distant reaches of space, leaving the safety of the galactic core to seek out infested worlds and neutralize them. Stars exploding, sterilizing their surroundings, seeding the galaxy with heavy metals. A treasure: elements to be gathered one day into planets and asteroids, and harvested millions of years later by other machine armadas.

—<mode shift>—

—<mode shift>—

Multiple discontinuities. Combines roaring, machine-monsters bearing down on him. *Why? Why this again?* Had he always known he would someday be facing a threatening machine like this? *Blackie barking frantically, not knowing the danger! Blackie was going to die and it was his fault...*

Or was he? No, he was warning me. Saving my life. I had to trust Blackie and follow him.

—<mode shift>—
—<mode shift>—

Star fuming and building pressure, almost at the perfect point for the release. Almost. And then would come the cataclysm and cascading shock wave.

—<mode shift>—
—<mode shift>—
—<mode shift>—

Charli was trying to get his attention, calling from a distance. Weren't they supposed to be quiet here? Where were the rats? Were the stones keeping them away? For how much longer?

/// Can you hear me, John?
Deep needs you to persuade it now. ///

Bandicut blinked slowly, like a lizard. /Can Deep kill it?/

/// Something else.
When you persuade it to blow up the star. ///

/What else?/

/// The less you know, the safer. ///

He could feel himself slipping toward the edge again, driven by anger and frustration. And fear. Oh yes, fear. /You want me to do this thing, tell me what it is!/

/// John, can you not trust Deep? ///

/Trust Deep? Yes, but—/ Dear God, where was Antares now? She was somewhere off at a distance, keeping an eye on Ik. And Ik? Was he talking to the stars again? What was Li-Jared doing? And poor Napoleon, somewhere down in the star? They were all counting on him to do the right thing in here.

/// John! Can you not trust Deep? ///

He felt his breath, ragged, and remembered. *Trust Blackie to lead me from the danger.* /I trust you, but my friends out there

trust me,/ he whispered. /So *I need to know,* and you'll just have
to help me keep it from the Mindaru. *What are you planning to
do?* Talk fast./

✶

It was simple, really. When the Mindaru released the dark matter, it
would cause an abrupt increase in gravity at the core of the star—
triggering a core collapse. This much Bandicut already knew. And
following core collapse, the star would explode in a cataclysm—
unless Deep and Dark were precisely ready. Dark, at the core,
would use that abrupt spike in gravity to punch a hole out of this
universe and into a dying one next door—a hole in the "brane"
layer, the membrane gap separating the two universes. Only gravity could make that hole, and the core collapse would provide the
punch.

Timing at that point was critical. Dark would hold the hole
open, dumping all the dark matter into the other universe. And
Deep, seizing the Mindaru control center, would hurl it down
through the opening, as well. Let the dying universe have the Mindaru and the dark matter. And with the dark matter gone, and the
hole closed again, the core explosion would self-extinguish before
it got far enough to destroy the star. The gravity-spike would vanish as quickly as it had begun. If they were fast.

Simple. He just had to convince the Mindaru to release the
dark matter. And he had to do it before Napoleon—if the robot
were still alive—found a way to lob those grenades and do it
first, the wrong way.

✶

/And I would persuade the Mindaru by—?/

He didn't get a chance to finish. At that moment, the Mindaru mind-probe rats burst through the screen the stones had
been holding up, and Bandicut's words turned into a scream.

He fought back, throwing up the most vivid image he
could . . .

✶

Antares felt Bandicut's scream in her heart. "John!" she cried,
rushing to him. He sat rigid, eyes clamped shut. "What is it?"
When there was no answer, she stood behind him and placed

the palms of her hands against his temples. She could feel turmoil and fear boiling out of him like vapor. /John, speak to me! What's happening?/

Images flickered: crawling creatures barely held at bay, conversations rising and falling, the stones laboring to keep the walls of silence in the crucial places . . . and deep down, great billowing membranes floating together in space and time, and fusing momentarily . . .

That image was shut off and a new one appeared, and this one was laid open to the probing Mindaru. It showed the star blossoming and exploding. *If you don't do it now, you'll never have the chance,* was the thought she heard reverberating into space, into the hearing of the Mindaru. *Release it now!*

/John—are you mad?/ she whispered, suddenly terrified that he had been taken over by the Mindaru. */No!/*

∗

Ik felt it almost at the same instant Antares did. *John Bandicut is telling the Mindaru to destroy the star!* And at that moment, he felt something strange and unpleasant, as if he were twisting apart into two people. One part of him began to rise and turn, to lunge, to stop Bandicut from betraying them. *He is the one who is infected, it is not me at all!* Appalled at this discovery, Ik tried to move, but he could not; he was paralyzed.

The other part of him erupted with unexpected joy at the thought. *He has been captured, too; he is working with us; you must let him; you must aid him.* Ik was dumbstruck by this thought, and helpless; the Mindaru infection had resurfaced and seized control of his stones. *You must prevent the female from stopping him.*

Now Ik lunged—but for Antares, not for Bandicut. "Hrahh, you must let him do it!" he cried, seizing the Thespi and dragging her away from Bandicut. He felt her stones touch his, with a tremendous flash. They recognized the Mindaru activity and reacted instantly, with a combative strength that astounded him. He threw her to one side and released her physically to break the contact.

"Ik, stop!" she cried from the floor. "You're being controlled by the Mindaru!"

B-gong-ng-ng. "What is this?" Li-Jared shouted, advancing on him.

Ik clacked his mouth shut and turned to grab the control console. He couldn't fly the ship, but he could link to the AI. He squeezed the contacts and his stones shot their tendrils into the computer system. Copernicus and Jeaves were ready, and the stones didn't get far; but they didn't need to. They just needed to flash out a message to the roving Mindaru thread: **Bandicut speaks the truth. There is one inside the sun who can sabotage the plan. Trigger the collapse now!**

By the time that thought was complete, Jeaves had shouted a warning that Ik was a captive of the Mindaru. Ik looked up just as Li-Jared hurled himself into Ik, tackling him. Ik was surprised by the Karellian's strength. But it didn't matter now—the message was out.

*

Bandicut's mind was a place of fury and chaos, the stones maintaining certain barriers, his own volition pouring out images and directed thoughts, straight to the Mindaru probes that scrabbled and scratched for entry. His selected thoughts shone brightly, allowed out by the quarx and the stones. *You will never have the chance if you don't act. Because we got there first. If you do not act, you will lose.* And brighter than any of the words was an image of Napoleon, somewhere in the star, impatiently stroking his n-space disrupter grenades . . . ready to rip open the field holding the dark matter at the star's core. The release wouldn't be shaped right; it would destroy the symmetry of the critical mass; it would prevent the hypernova. *If you want that hypernova, you'd better act now.*

Bandicut felt Antares's distress, but there was no way to explain now. He had to get the message out, and . . . */What the hell? Is that Ik I hear?/*

/// Yes—he's in the system, or his stones are.
They're still infected by the Mindaru! ///
/Then we have to warn—/
/// They know.
Keep your head down and finish the job. ///
Blanking his thoughts, he once more projected the

image: Napoleon preparing to detonate his grenades, deep in the star. After a minute, Charli broke into his thoughts:
> /// *Deep and Dark are going to try to break*
> *the field that's holding you captive.*
> *When they do, turn on your n-space propulsion*
> *and drive toward the core of the star*
> *as fast as you can.* ///

/Toward the *core?*/

> /// *To look as if we're trying*
> *to sabotage their plan.* ///

As he thought his approval, he felt the stones open a channel through the AI connectors to Copernicus and Jeaves, relaying the instruction.

> /// *Remember what Deep is good at,*
> *and be prepared . . .* ///

✳

The time was right, Deeaab decided. The enemy had been given enough hints. Now they would force the matter. It would take careful slicing of the continuum, to separate the ship of the ephemerals from the enemy, but Deeaab and Daarooaack could do that. Daarooaack was terrified of failing again, but Deeaab encouraged her. He called out:

"Shear the field."

Daarooaack spun in and flashed neat as a blade between the ephemerals' ship and the enemy. It was enough to break the spacetime distortion that was binding the two together. The ship began to float free.

Deeaab spoke to the quarx-echo within itself. **"Tell them now."** As he did so, he stretched out and touched the enemy. And with his touch, he froze the flow of time within a bubble surrounding the enemy structure. Just for a moment.

✳

The quarx-echo spoke:

> <<< *Gentlemen, start your engines.* >>>

✳

Bandicut shouted through the link and through the air: *"Go! Now!"*

The ship, released from the Mindaru's grip, sped away into the fury of the star.

*

The Starburster Mindbody was jarred by a sudden disruption in its holding field. The captive was escaping. Its propulsion field flicked on, and the ship started to accelerate.

... *discontinuity* ...

The Mindbody knew that *something* had happened. Somehow the captive ship had traveled much farther than any projection or understanding of its motion could place it. The Mindbody knew it had to apply corrective action at once.

But something else caught its attention—several things.

The vessel was driving hard—not to *escape* from the star, but to penetrate *into* the star. A suicide mission?

Intelligence gathered by the probes indicated that the bio entities had an agent already deep in the star's body. Their intent was to sabotage the balanced critical mass in the heart of the star.

They might have the ability to prevent the starburst.

All these considerations flashed through the dense algorithms of the Mindaru entity, along with the critical-mass status. The dark matter gathered was sufficient. Not with any reserve, but sufficient.

It must be done now. Any delay could be fatal to the mission. Without further deliberation, the Mindbody flashed the signal down the synaptic link: release the field holding the dark matter. Let the collapse begin.

No need to recapture the intruder. It, as well as this Mindbody outpost, would shortly be incinerated, then reduced to subatomic particles.

37

Deep in the fire of the star, from the sheltering n-space bubble, Napoleon watched what little he could see. Too much time had passed since John Bandicut had gone back to the ship; at least, Napoleon hoped he had made it back. By now, Napoleon judged, they should have had time to do what they needed to do. Unless they had failed.

Napoleon watched the dark matter flowing into the n-space reservoir. By his estimate, there was already enough dark matter there to kill the star in a cataclysmic explosion. It seemed likely, then, that it was up to him. He hadn't actually been looking to be a hero when he pushed Bandicut toward safety; that had just been a rationale. And perhaps heroes did not choose their roles as he'd thought, but simply found themselves in a position where it was up to them.

He held one of the three n-space disrupter grenades in a metal hand, mulling the possibilities. He wasn't sure they would go off, even if he managed to put them where he wanted them. And if they did . . . they were so small, what was the chance they would have any effect? And yet he saw no other option. If they created a tear in the dark-matter reservoir, they would probably kill the star—but maybe without the hypernova. His friends would die. He would die. But they were all going to die anyway, if the star went up as the Mindaru planned. And along with them, all habitable worlds within two thousand light-years.

The question remained whether he could get the grenades down to the core of the star and have them survive long enough to work. It was a big if. He'd had time to think about it, and the thought had finally occurred to him that they wouldn't have built this ledge just as a pretty place to stand. If it wasn't connected to the control center, surely it was connected to the reservoir down in the core. Maybe for maintenance. Napoleon couldn't imagine what sort of maintenance the Mindaru could do on the reservoir from here, but what else could it be for? Perhaps there was a provision for sending special mechs down to do who knew what? With that thought in mind, he had undertaken an extremely careful search for a thread, a hint of an n-space connector between the ledge where he stood and the core.

Six hours ago, he had found it. It was literally a thread, more like an anchor line, or a placeholder for a real n-space passage. But there it was. And he was pretty sure that even with the very limited n-space abilities he had from his upgrades, he could pry it open just a little—just enough to pop three grenades into it and send them on a long slide down to the core. The n-space layer should protect them, and the pressure of the sun might even squeeze them downward faster.

One by one, he set the slender grenades to detonate when they encountered an n-space field of a certain strength; the exact setting was a guess. When that was done, he spun up the tiny n-space generator in his third hand, and with great care, dilated the opening of the n-space thread. With one last hesitation, he popped the grenades down the tube. Then he pinched the end of the tube closed.

With a thought that was very much like a prayer, he waited. And figuratively put his head between his knees, as Bandicut might have told him to do.

✳

The Mindaru were taking the bait. Deeaab heard from Daarooaack that a change was occurring in the boundary layer deep in the star. The inflowing streams dropped away. An instant later that shell of spacetime, the boundary layer that had been holding all the strange matter in, was gone.

The dense strange matter was abruptly part of normal-space at the heart of the star. Gravity spiked instantaneously. The surrounding plasma, already fusing furiously, began at once to fall into the steep gravity well.

The star began to collapse.

Deeaab whirled to bring time once more to a near-standstill in a tight cloak around the enemy. He would have slowed time at the core of the star, too, if he could have. But that was more than he could do at once. He was just going to have to work fast.

The ship of the ephemerals had done all it could. Deeaab murmured to the quarx-echo, *"Tell them to flee. Flee for their lives!"*

✶

It seemed to Bandicut that the probing of the Mindaru AI suddenly slowed, as if it had stepped into molasses. The Mindaru's rats appeared frozen, out at the periphery of his vision. They had turned pale, ghostly transparent.

He didn't understand why. And then he did. Remember what Deep is good at, Charli had said. Time-fusion. Was Deep slowing time for the Mindaru? *To let us get away!*

The last of the link with the Mindaru was dissolving. Bandicut blinked back to awareness where he sat, in the middle of the bridge. In front of him was the fire of the star. They were free and diving headlong into the sun. *A diversion. To convince the Mindaru we were serious.* He turned and was stunned to see Li-Jared wrestling on the deck with Ik, both of them shouting. Antares was getting to her feet, shouting, "Ik, this isn't you, it's the Mindaru! Don't let them control you!"

Bandicut remembered with a jolt. The Mindaru infection had erupted in Ik's stones. "My God!" he croaked, and lurched out of his seat.

Antares flew to his side. "John, what have you done? I felt you telling the enemy to destroy the star!" She grabbed his arm in a viselike grip and shook him violently. "Ik's gone mad—have you, too?"

Bandicut struggled to keep his balance. "Deep and Dark—we have to work together with them! You've got to trust us, no, we're not working with the Mindaru!"

"HRAHH!" Ik bellowed, throwing Li-Jared off. He staggered to his feet, glaring at Bandicut. *"You are—not—Mindaru?"* He whirled at Li-Jared, who was picking himself up—then whirled again and strode toward Bandicut. His hands were half curled into fists, as if undecided whether to punch or strangle the human.

"No, Ik!" Bandicut edged to one side, crouching defensively. He hated to think what Ik might be capable of, under enemy control.

"Captains, things are happening very quickly," Copernicus called. "Dark is—*look!*" Copernicus refocused the image in the viewspace. Dark had shot past, a black shadow streaking into the blazing body of the sun. She left a faintly coruscating tunnel in her wake.

At the same moment, Bandicut heard Charli say,

/// *Deep says we've done our part.*
We should flee! Fast! ///

"*Coppy!*" Bandicut shouted. "*Deep says get us the hell out of here! Get out of the—!*"

"NO-O-O!" Ik bellowed, crashing into Bandicut and grabbing him in a powerful bear hug. "Do—not—*leave!* That is the—*enemy talking!*"

"Ik-k-k!" Bandicut gasped. "You're—chok-k-k-ing—m—"

There was a jolt through the ship as Copernicus savagely changed course. Though he could barely see past Ik's head, Bandicut caught sight of Deep wrapping his shadow around the Mindaru control station and swirling downward into the heart of the sun. Then he was blinded by pain as Ik's hands clamped around his neck.

*

It was tougher than Deeaab expected to carry the enemy down into the collapsing sun. Not at first, because he'd slowed the enemy's time and it couldn't fight back—but Deeaab had never before tried to keep a time-bubble stable in the midst of such energetic chaos, and it wasn't long before he felt his grip on that tiny, contained pocket of time begin to slip.

Daarooaack was flying before him, widening the channel down into the sun—whirling first through the outer layers, where magnetic lines whipped through the turbulence of plasma storms. The entire system boiled on the verge of eruption. Light and chaos and convection cells of streaming particles were ordinary life here, part of what made this star a living being. Deeaab arrowed down through it all. Below those layers, everything was radiation and fury. Was there *thought* here? Particles and photons were flying, hammering, heating. They dove through all of that, through the sea of radiant energy, toward the glaring abyss of the core. Toward the fusion furnace at the heart, where the inferno began.

And through it all, Deeaab struggled to keep a grip on his Mindaru captive, and the increasingly hard-to-maintain pocket of frozen time.

As they approached the center, they crossed at last into the hell of the just-released strange matter. *Strange dark matter.* It was the closest thing to insanity Deeaab had ever touched; it was all of the strangeness that he had felt tenuously spread among the stars, now gathered tightly in this one place. Freed from its n-space imprisonment, it was warping the star's time, space, and gravity in a horrific knot that was squeezing the center of the star into oblivion.

Through it all, Daarooaack led the way, and Deeaab with his captive followed. And in the very center, *there was the opening.* Just a pinprick, but an opening into the next universe, created by the spike of gravity that was crushing the star. And Daarooaack, whirling down, exerted her own mastery over space and energy to widen the opening.

Now it looked like a small doorway of darkness in the heart of blinding fury.

It yammered with energy, and glowered with the darkness of the dying universe beyond. Deeaab recognized that glower; it was the same universe he had escaped from, so long ago.

The portal would not stay open, not without help. That was Daarooaack's job. And getting this enemy, the Mindaru, through the opening was Deeaab's job. Already the strange matter was gushing through, into the other universe. But everything had to happen before the collapse brought on the explosion that would light up ✳Nick✳ brighter than the rest of the galaxy combined.

✳

The Mindbody was stunned, incapable of understanding what was happening. It tried to reconstruct the immediate past, but there were baffling discontinuities. Memory loss, then; but the crucial thing was it had gotten separated from its captive, and then had become a captive of something it couldn't fathom. Around it, the star was dying, crushing inward. The Mindaru would fight for its independence. But if the star was dying, in the end it wouldn't matter; its mission was already accomplished.

✶

The strain of freezing time was too much. Deeaab couldn't hold on to that *and* the physical enemy. When he let go of the pocket of time, the enemy suddenly came to life and fought madly, trying to fly this way and that through n-space. Deeaab fought, spinning, and nearly lost his grip. He tried to shape space to force the thing toward the dark doorway, but shaping space was Daarooaack's strength, not his, and it was all Deeaab could do simply to hold on.

Daarooaack couldn't help without letting go of her hold on the portal opening, and that was unthinkable. But Daarooaack cried: *"The star is collapsing! Shall I widen the opening?" "Yes! Yes!"*

Daarooaack whirled, expanding the opening, the portal, the gateway—until it became a funnel of darkness spinning in the middle of the star's core. As the strange matter swirled through it, the portal began to grow bright with the torrent of matter pouring into the next universe. Even as the star's core was crushing inward, the source of the gravity was shooting out through the portal. If the gravity eased quickly enough, the collapse would stop. But would it happen in time?

Deeaab felt the crush of the star around him as he struggled to hold the enemy. He no longer thought he could hurl it through. If he released it, would it escape through its n-space fields? What else could he do? *Carry it through?*

✶

Antares, still disoriented from the shouting and the jolting course change, reeled as the star's protest swept over her. She felt the shock, then the crippling knot in its heart, and finally a kind of numbness. The end was inevitable; it could only collapse inward, and die. /No, don't surrender to it!/ she tried to cry, though she didn't think it could hear.

But as that wave subsided, she came to her senses and realized that Ik was strangling John Bandicut. *"Stop it! Stop it!"* She leaped to grab Ik from behind, and Li-Jared was already pummeling Ik from the side, but the Hraachee'an's strength was enormous. She tried to connect her stones to Ik's, but Ik was moving too violently. *"STOP!"* she shouted, darting around to where she could see his face. *"Ik, think! You're killing your friend!"* She grabbed his sculpted head and tried to force him to look at her.

For an instant, Ik seemed to recognize her. He shook off her hand, but not before she felt the struggle for control inside his mind. The stones in his temples were pulsing like embers. His eyes were wild, tortured in their deep sockets. His hard-lipped mouth opened, letting out a groan.

Antares dug her fingers into his shoulder. */Stones, you have to stop this!/* She felt the connection like a jolt of electricity, her own stones searing in her throat. Ik stiffened.

What happened next she could barely follow. Her stones locked in battle with Ik's—with the Mindaru that had taken control. No gentle healing this time. It was a fight for life. The Mindaru were deadly and swift—and for a heart-stopping moment, they seemed to be coming after *her,* like glowing demons. But they were cut off, their attack caught and turned by the fury of her own stones, flashing like swords. The Mindaru retreated, and turned instead on *Ik.* The Hraachee'an, releasing Bandicut, fell back, choking. Antares followed, keeping her grip on his shoulder. She knew what needed to be done, and she shouted to the stones, /Cast them out! *Cast them out!/*

In the terrifying whirlwind, she felt the moment in which her stones gained control—surrounded and reinforced now by Li-Jared's stones and Bandicut's stones—

—and the swords flashed one more time—

—and Ik's stones flew out of his temples.

"Hrahhhh!" Ik bellowed, and fell to the floor in anguish as two points of fire flew into the air and circled like angry bees over the viewspace balcony.

∗We cannot save them. They must be destroyed!∗ her stones said sharply.

"Copernicus!" Antares shouted. "Can you get those things off the ship?"

"Are you certain?"

"Yes! Now!"

"Fall back, everyone! To the back of the bridge!" Jeaves commanded. They scrambled to obey. "*Now,* Copernicus!"

A shimmering force-field sprang up across the bridge, with the evicted stones on the far side. There was a thunderclap, the viewspace went dark, flashed bright, then dark again. After a moment, it slowly returned to normal. The force-field ebbed away. Ik's stones were gone.

*

It all came together for Deeaab with a strange solemnity, as though he had slowed time around himself while he thought matters through. He hadn't, but the understanding that filled him felt so deliberate and clear that the effect was the same. The truth crystallized like a thing of terrible beauty:

All their efforts would fail unless he carried this enemy through the opening himself. He could not release it or throw it; he had to *carry* it through, into the universe he had once fled. Maybe he could drop it there and get back before the portal closed, and maybe he couldn't. If he didn't, he would be marooned forever in a dying universe.

Was that a fair exchange for the billions of lives he would save? For the universe that had given him asylum for eons? The small voices that carried something of the soul of this universe in a quarx-echo and a halo-echo seemed to agree:

<<< *If that's what we must do . . .* >>>
<<< *There really is no time to waste (chime).* >>>

Drawing his courage, Deeaab tightened his grip on the struggling Mindaru thing and called to Daarooaack:

"I must take it through myself!"

Daarooaack seemed to realize Deeaab was right. Her voice reverberated from where she spun, holding open the portal: *"Quickly, then! Release it and return!"*

Praying he could do that, Deeaab plunged down into the funnel with the enemy in his grasp. As he did, he called, *"Let it close . . . if you must. Save the star . . ."* And then he flew through the thundering opening into darkness—through the twisting wrench of the passage.

And suddenly all of the fire and fury were gone.

*

Bong. "Copernicus?"

Tap tap. "We'll be out of the sun's atmosphere soon,"

406 * JEFFREY A. CARVER *

answered the robot. Bandicut, sitting on the floor in stunned exhaustion, thought he could feel tremendous power surging through the deck. It was probably his imagination, but it gave him a feeling of hope—even though, deep down, he knew that if the star blew, no amount of power was going to get them far enough, fast enough. Beside him, Ik and Antares were crumpled in even greater exhaustion. Ik looked haunted, filled with pain; over and over he brought his hands to his temples, as he stared emptily into the viewspace. Antares looked stricken, but kept her head up, her eyes darting from one friend to another, and to the view of the shrinking sun. She kept murmuring under her breath—words to the star, Bandicut thought.

In the view, the great swollen surface of *Nick* was shrinking as they retreated from it, though it still filled the view. Ghostly in the n-space view, it looked like an emissary from another dimension. *Can't we move faster?*

"What was that?" Li-Jared pointed to where a brief spark had flared, just to the left of center of the sun's disk. There was a momentary shimmer, as though a rock had plunked into still water.

"Hard to interpret," Jeaves muttered. "Wait, we're getting something in X-ray and tachyon. Let me show you . . ."

The image zoomed in, showing fiery, ghostly chaos at the star's core. But there was something else—a tiny black pupil in the midst of the chaos. Jeaves tweaked the image, and a bright torch became visible in the center of the dark spot. "*Very* hard to interpret, but I believe it may be just what you said, John. The dark matter appears to be draining away," Jeaves said. "I can't tell where it's going."

"Out of this universe," Bandicut whispered, more to himself than anyone else. "They're doing it, Deep and Dark."

/// I feel Deep, and Charlene-echo.
They are in pain, something about to happen.
I cannot tell what . . . ///

Bandicut opened and closed his mouth silently. There was another tremor in the star.

/// Charlene—no! ///

*

Whirling around the portal opening, Daarooaack understood perfectly what Deeaab meant in his final cry before vanishing.

The strange matter was nearly gone from the star. But it was not *just* strange matter spewing through the portal; it was also the normal matter, the fusing matter that gave the star life. If the portal stayed open much longer, the star would die a different death; it would simply be extinguished. But it was to save the star's life that Deeaab had taken such a risk.

Daarooaack understood that, and hated it. If Deeaab did not make it back on his own, she could do nothing to help him. All she could do was reach out with her senses to feel the star, and judge when the portal *had* to close to save the star's life. Once closed, she could not reopen it. If that was what it took to honor Deeaab's purpose, then that was what she would do.

✳

Dull red, glowing against emptiness. The strange matter, and part of the star with it, vented into the bitter cold of this dark, dying universe. The gases began at once to cool. Deeaab was dazed by the passage, and slowly came out of it to look around. There wasn't much to see. Space was dark and starless, except for some blotches of dying galaxies receding into the ultimate distance, so far away their light could barely even reach this place.

In Deeaab's grasp was a dying thing. He must still be dazed; he couldn't quite remember why he was holding the thing. Whatever it was, it didn't seem to quite work in the physics here; its solid, near-metal, near-life function was fading.

And then he remembered, a picture rippling back into focus. He had succeeded in exiling a terrible enemy; he had brought this thing from the other universe, to where it could do no more harm. He released it and watched it float away.

But there was something else coming back into focus. *The portal was closing. He had to get back now—if it was not already too late.*

The trouble was, he couldn't really see the portal. Probably it was somewhere in the center of this cloud of dully glowing gas. He searched, with growing alarm and fear. He could find nothing but the cloud, its glow fading, and surrounding it nothing but empty, expanding space for maybe a few billion light-years . . .

✳

"Deeaab! Deeaab, can you make it back?"

Daarooaack's calls went unanswered, as they had for the last eon of seconds. She could wait no longer; the fury of the star was changing around her, as the gravity of the other universe pulled the star toward a different kind of death, bleeding the life from it. If she closed the portal *now*, she could save ✳Nick✳.

"Deeaab!"

No answer. No answer.

Daarooaack spun away from the dark window and savagely pulled at the threads of spacetime to yank the window closed forever.

The portal of darkness vanished.

Daarooaack's hope vanished.

The core of the star rebounded from the collapse, sending shock waves up through the fiery layers toward the surface. But the fusion-fires continued, and the star steadied itself and did not die.

38

REGATHERING

 /Charli, what happened? What happened to Charlene?/ Bandicut pushed himself to his feet and clutched the control panel to steady himself as he tried to make sense of the view. Charli was reeling from something terrible.

"John," Antares said in a shaky voice, "what is it? Do you need me?" She and Ik were slumped against the back wall.

"Don't know. No, you stay with Ik."

Finally Charli managed to say,

/// They're gone.

Deep and Charlene-echo are gone. ///

/Where?/

/// Out of the universe.
They took the enemy and all the dark matter
right through that opening.
But they never made it back.
And now it's too late. ///

And with that, Charli fell silent. Bandicut, in a bruised voice, conveyed that to the others, and Jeaves confirmed that it seemed to be true.

"What about the star?" Li-Jared demanded. "Is it exploding?" He was still coiled for action, standing forward of everyone else with his fists clenched.

"No," Antares said. "I can feel it. The pain is gone."

"But there's apt to be one hell of a shock wave rebounding from the core," Jeaves said.

"Indeed there is," Copernicus announced. "We're retreating as fast as we can, but the n-space shear is slowing us. I'm rigging for extreme turbulence. I suggest you prepare." He went on to say something else in another language. Hraachee'an.

"Hrahhhh," Ik said weakly in response.

"Good," Copernicus said. "He seems to understand me a little." Ik said something else, and Copernicus added, "He says he is sorry."

"Yes," Bandicut said hoarsely. "I know." *He has no stones. His stones burned up in the sun.* Bandicut shuddered, remembering what it was like to be without stones. He had once lent his to a creature in distress, and the experience of loss had been terrifying.

Ik gestured helplessly with his hands and said something Bandicut couldn't understand. Ik sighed through his ears, looked at Bandicut, then stared straight ahead.

Bandicut stepped over and placed a hand firmly on Ik's shoulder. "I understand." Ik's eyes seemed to flicker with comprehension. Bandicut nodded and turned back to the sun. "Coppy, did you see a flash, just before Deep vanished through the opening? Do you know what that was? Could it have been Napoleon?"

"Uncertain, Cap'n. He did have disrupter grenades."

Jeaves interjected, "We will be overtaken by the first shock wave in about three minutes."

Antares looked alarmed. "Is *Nick* going hypernova after all?"

Jeaves turned his holographic head. "No. The core contracted, then rebounded. The star is basically ringing like a bell. But all the n-space channels have collapsed, and we can find no evidence of dark matter flowing. The entire collection system seems to have collapsed with the removal of the control center."

"Is *Nick* still alive?" Bandicut asked. "Able to speak, I mean?"

Antares glanced at Ik, before saying, "I can feel its presence, but without Deep—"

Ik barked something in his own language. Copernicus translated: "I feel . . . its relief. There is joy. And sadness." Ik rubbed the bony ridge above his deep-set eyes and continued, with Copernicus's help. "*Nick* is not . . . gone. I feel . . . its life. But its time . . . not our time. We can no longer speak." Ik raised his hand, as though in farewell to the star.

An alarm sounded. "Folks, we're about to be hammered by the expanding plasma shell," Copernicus said. "I'm going to apply a damping field to the interior of the ship. Get comfortable *now,* because you won't be able to move until the shock wave has passed."

The four scrambled to the bench sofa at the back of the bridge. Antares hooked one arm through Bandicut's and the other through Ik's. A moment later, the deck began to rumble, and Bandicut felt suddenly as if he were in molasses—or back in the star-spanner bubble.

/// That would be the damping field,
keeping us from being turned to mush. ///

Bandicut acknowledged silently, glad to hear Charli speak again. But now that he was sitting still, he was beginning, like Charli, to feel the impact of losing Deep and Charlene-echo. And Napoleon, who almost certainly was destroyed in what had just happened. Then the shock wave hit, and he had the feeling of riding a roller coaster in slow motion. The sensation lasted about a minute, then subsided.

Copernicus called, "Dark is flying out toward us."

Indeed, they could now see the small dark cloud zigzagging as it sped out through the layers of the star. It veered suddenly and disappeared from view. "What's it doing?" Li-Jared asked, his words slurred by the dampening field. "It's not leaving us, is it?"

/// I don't think it's gone. ///

/Then where—*oh!*/ Bandicut looked to the left of Dark's previous position. "There!" Bandicut said to the others, raising a finger with difficulty to point. Dark was again visible, and growing rapidly.

✳

Napoleon was still trying to understand the last few moments of his life. He had lobbed the disrupter grenades down the n-space tube. A tremendous upheaval followed: time disturbances, n-space disturbances, Deep and Dark passing through the star. The dark-matter reservoir letting go. He thought he saw the dark matter disappearing through some kind of opening, much larger than anything he could have created.

Then the shock wave caught him, and he knew he was going to die. Instead, protected by the n-space bubble that surrounded him, he rode the shock wave like a surfboard rider, up through the layers of the sun. He squawked all the way, trying to signal his shipmates—but that was useless, they were back at ✳Thunder✳. It was Dark who noticed him, and Dark who *caught* him by the n-space bubble and lifted him the rest of the way out of the star, into the glorious blackness of space.

✳

Soon Dark was looming large beside *The Long View*. There was a tiny silver sparkle in her interior. Bandicut felt a sudden sharp hope, but it was Copernicus who first cried out in recognition. "Dark has Napoleon! He's calling to see if we can take him on! Listen . . ."

"Long View, Long View, this is Napoleon . . ."

"Nappy!" Bandicut cried.

Bong bong bong. "How?" Li-Jared leaped up from the sofa, and that's when Bandicut realized the damping field was gone and they could move again.

Antares raised the first note of caution. "Uhhl, is it Napoleon as we knew him?"

Copernicus ticked. "As nearly as I can tell. We will scan him thoroughly in the airlock."

Bandicut's heart soared at the thought of Napoleon coming back from the dead. But he felt a chill at the possibility of the Mindaru once more getting aboard the ship. "You'll scan him *really* well—yes, Copernicus?"

"Indeed, Cap'n. In fact, he has requested it."

"Requested it?"

"He reminds us of the time, back on Shipworld, when you had to find out if *I* was still trustworthy."

Bandicut breathed a sigh of relief. *That's the Napoleon I know.*

*

Gathered around the airlock, the company peered in at the robot. "Are you all safe?" the robot asked from inside the airlock. "And where's Deep? Dark saved my life. Where is she?"

"Dark is still with us," Bandicut said, just as Napoleon said, *"Oh."* He had apparently just gotten a silent summary from Copernicus. For a moment, nobody said anything. They hadn't had time to contemplate it much. Deep was gone. Deep had saved them by grabbing that thing and plunging out of the universe with it.

"Then," said Napoleon, "there is no hope for Deep's return?"

Copernicus answered, this time for all of them to hear. "There is no opening. It was a difficult thing to do, puncturing the membrane borders between the universes. Without the gravitational collapse of the star's core, Dark could not have done it. But the dark matter is gone now."

"And the star?" Napoleon asked.

"Ringing, but stable." Copernicus paused. "Captains, I've scanned Napoleon by every means I know. I detect no contamination. Does anyone object to my bringing him back in?"

Bandicut drew a deep breath, thinking. He badly wanted to see Napoleon back with them; but after what they had just been through with Ik . . .

Antares spoke first. "Copernicus, can you let me into the airlock, please?"

Bandicut tensed as the airlock opened and Antares stepped through. Four minutes later, she removed her hands from Napoleon. "My stones sense no presence of the enemy." She looked up at the window. "They were wrong once before, but I believe they learned."

Li-Jared's bright blue eyes were focused, not on the airlock, but on Ik, whose expression was still haunted. Li-Jared blinked as he turned. "Then I, for one, would be glad to have Napoleon rejoin us."

Bandicut let his breath out. "I agree." The door winked out and Napoleon stepped forward. He flexed up and down on his legs in apparent pleasure as they greeted him. "Nappy, am I glad to see you!"

The reunion was interrupted by a call from Copernicus. "I need you back here, folks. We're out of the turbulence, and with your permission, I want to light this candle and get us out of here."

*

Candle lit, they sped away from the still-quaking star. In a few thousand years, Jeaves predicted, the quaking would subside. As they left it behind, Antares tried to tease out a few threads of the star's thoughts or feelings. "I don't really know what it's thinking," she said, giving up at last. "I think it's mostly just in shock. I don't know if it has any idea of what happened."

Bandicut felt torn between immense relief at Napoleon's safe return and sadness at the loss of Deep. Charli probably felt it more keenly than anyone, because she had lost a part of herself as well as Deep. There was little talk of the loss among the group, though once when Deep's name came up, Napoleon rose up on his flexible legs, peered into space as though looking for him, then sank again with a pneumatic sigh.

/Can you read Dark's thoughts?/ Bandicut asked Charlie. /I wonder how she is feeling about losing Deep./

/// I feel her . . . I will call it sadness,
because I have no other name for it.
But I cannot read her thoughts. */// *

Bandicut turned, looking at Dark flanking them in one of the sections of the viewspace. /I wonder if there's some way we could get Dark a set of translator-stones./

/// And some new ones for Ik? ///

Bandicut directed the question silently to his stones. They replied, *Unknown. We are not able to split at present. Dark may be too different. And Ik must heal.*

As though she were reading his thoughts, Antares came to his side and said, "Do you suppose Dark will accompany us . . . wherever we're . . . going?"

"Does anyone actually know where we *are* going?" Bandicut asked. "Copernicus? Jeaves?"

"Though you are in command, Captains," Copernicus said, "I thought we might want to move out of this—shall we say—*hazardous* region of space, and see if we can begin to make our way home."

"Whose home do you mean?" Li-Jared inquired.

"In the absence of a common home for us, I was referring to Shipworld."

Jeaves made a throat-clearing sound and said, "I'm not sure we actually know how to *get* to Shipworld. Or if this ship is capable of making the trip."

Bwang. "Well, that's just—"

"But I was going to suggest, if we can find the way there, we might look in on Ed's homeworld. I'm very curious how Ed's people are faring. And Ed *did* help us at a crucial moment."

"Fine with me," Bandicut said with a shrug. *If we can find our way there . . .*

✻

They were about forty light-minutes out from ✻Nick✻, and in the commons filling their plates with lunch—having by common agreement requested a Hraachee'an setting for Ik. The Hraachee'an was once more, through translation and fumbling gestures, apologizing to Bandicut for trying to strangle him, when Ed appeared—this time in the form of a shimmering entity wrapped like a sunbeam around a Hraachee'an terrace wall. "Ed!" Bandicut cried. "We've been hoping to see you! You can take your toe out of the stream now."

"Wee-ee have stopp-p-ed the f-flow?"

"Yes, yes! Are you all right? Did it hurt you to stop that stream inside the other star?"

"No-o . . . happ-p-y . . . my worl-ld s-safe!"

"How can you tell, Ed?" Antares asked. "Have you traveled back to it already?"

"Of-f cour-r-s-se. Look-k-k. S-see."

At what? Bandicut wondered. Before he could ask, Ed suddenly dilated open like a camera's iris, revealing an image like a strange telescopic view, right through the side of the ship. The group gasped and murmured in unison.

It was like peering down a luminous channel, with sides that hinted at various kinds of landscape all down its length, but without quite revealing them. The far end, however, was zooming in rapidly on a view of the broken, convulsive surface of Ed's world that they had seen, long ago. It was a breathtaking view: brilliant crimson rocks; jagged cliffs; glowing lava pillows; yawning crevasses. But something was different. The lava flows were hardening. The crevasses seemed to be narrowing.

Li-Jared asked, "Have the gravity waves stopped, then?"

"Yes-s-s."

"But how could it return to normal so fast?" Bandicut asked.

*/// I think we're seeing it
as interpreted by Ed. ///*

"*It will-l-l look-k this way-y. Glimps-s-se forward-d. My people-le may be able to re-t-turrrn, now.*"

"Return?" Antares asked. "Where are they now?"

Ed seemed to struggle to answer. Napoleon intervened with a series of incomprehensible chirrups. After a bit of that, Ed tried again. "*T-trap-peez-eezium. Be-t-t-tween stars. Floating-ng. Waiting-ng.*"

Bandicut stared in disbelief. "In the *Trapezium?* With those high-energy stars? How could they live *there,* if they can't survive earthquakes and volcanoes on your homeworld?" The Trapezium was a maelstrom of radiation emanating from the four energetic stars. It hardly seemed a likely sanctuary for any lifeform.

Ed and Napoleon buzzed and chirruped some more. Finally Napoleon said, "Ed's people can survive in gaseous clouds— even plasma clouds. But they need to nest and, I think, reproduce in complex rocky strata. If I interpret correctly, they are drawn to the specific pattern of their homeworld's magnetic field. Rather, I believe, like certain sea creatures on your own homeworld that must return to their home grounds to spawn."

Bandicut found that notion staggering. "Do you know—can you tell where their homeworld *is*?"

More buzzing. "Cap'n—they live on a proto-planet of the star we just saved. Of *Nick*."

"Jesus," Bandicut murmured as Antares drew a startled breath. "Then a hypernova wouldn't have just disrupted their planet, it would have vaporized it."

"Indeed," said Napoleon.

"S-sa-f-f-e now. Our-r-r hom-m-e." The hyper-being, still visible as a glowing iris around the view, shivered—and looked as if he might disappear again at any moment.

"I'm glad, Ed," Bandicut said with a heartfelt sigh. "I really am." *And I'm glad Earth is safe, too, fifteen hundred years from now.*

39

ARRIVAL

 Julie was only half conscious through most of the passage through the sun. To the extent she had any conscious thought, it was the thought that she had died. She was occasionally surprised to realize that she *had* awareness, but that was inevitably burned away by the relentless inferno of gases past her face and body. It all seemed to deny any possibility of living reality.

Then something happened. A soundless *thump* and a low, crackling hiss, and the solar inferno blinked away. She was surrounded once more by the dark of space. Consciousness drifted away again; but eventually, it came back and she heard:

Spatial translation complete. We're threading space again.

That brought her around. It was the translator. Or no—the stones.

Look around you.

I thought I was dead.

We'll be there soon.

This doesn't feel like Heaven.

Open your eyes. We picked up a lot of energy diving through the sun.

Oh yes. She remembered now. It seemed a long time ago.

Finally her eyes came into focus. What she saw took her breath away. She was still looking out through a space helmet, and sitting atop the battered remnant of a spacecraft. But beneath the spacecraft, an entire galaxy stretched out like a carpet of jewels. Or like the view from an airplane, flying over a city at night. Except it wasn't; it really was a galaxy. /Is that a close-up of—what? Andromeda?/

Not Andromeda. Milky Way.

Milky Way? That made no sense, not if this was supposed to be real. There was no way—from the solar system—that one could look *down* on the Milky Way from above the galactic disk. /You don't mean . . . you aren't saying . . . / Suddenly she felt so dizzy she'd have fallen off the remains of her spaceship if she hadn't been strapped on. Except she *wasn't* strapped on, she was *holding* on, to the scorched beam she was straddling like a metal steed. She clutched it harder between her knees. /Stones? *Where are we?*/

There was no immediate answer. She looked off to one side, then the other. In the night, she saw few if any individual stars—just the galactic spiral and, dimly, close at hand, the twisted beams of her spacecraft. As her eyes became accustomed to the dark, she began to make out some small, fuzzy patches at the limits of her vision. Other galaxies? She shuddered. No. This was too vast and weird and terrifying to think about. She wasn't *really* looking at her own galaxy from the outside. *Was* she?

Twisting farther to her left, she managed to look behind her. She was hoping, at least, for the reassuring sight of the translator. /Where is it?/ She had last seen it nestled among some reinforcing crossbeams, and it was not there now. Panic set in. /Stones! *Tell me!*/

The translator is there, but is greatly reduced in size.

/What do you—wait, is that it?/ In the dim surroundings, it was hard to see. She thought she saw a dark sphere about the size of a softball, wedged between two girders. /Is *that* it?/

Yes. It was forced to collapse inward to protect itself. It sustained considerable damage protecting us in the passage through the sun. We are unable to make contact. We are unsure if it survived.

Julie's head reeled at the thought. The translator . . . *dead?* Not possible. It *had* to have survived. It was her connection to John and home and everything that had happened. She tried to hold it together until she had more facts, but against her will, she began to cry. *No, no, this is stupid, you can't afford to cry now . . .*

✳*Julie! Pay attention to your surroundings! Look forward, ten o'clock, high.*✳

/I am paying—wait, what *is* that?/

What it was became clearer as it drew nearer. It was a stupendously large artificial structure. Why should there be a structure of *any* sort out here beyond the edge of the galaxy? And yet it was clearly artificial; it looked like a gargantuan chain, or segmented necklace. It sparkled a little here and there, but mostly it consisted of dark shapes, shadows against the gloom of extragalactic space.

/Is it *inhabited?*/ she whispered, hardly daring to hope. And in the back of her mind, she wondered, *Did John come here? Did he see this, too?*

✳*Some call it Shipworld. Soon you will learn more. Very soon.*✳

✳

The structure grew incredibly fast, mushrooming before her eyes. The overall shape became lost to view, as the nearest segment filled up the sky. Details on the surface began to become visible. Soon those lines and sketches grew to reveal still finer detail of structure. Finally *those* details revealed themselves to contain assemblies of bubbles, tiny windows, maybe even docking ports.

Her pitiful remnant of a ship sped straight toward the side of the massive structure. Finally, when it seemed certain they would crash, a portal irised open before them. It blossomed in size; then she and her ship glided in and floated to a stop, in the midst of blinding, crisscrossing, swiveling beams of light.

After a few seconds, the beams dimmed and went out, leaving her eyes dazzled. When she recovered from the glare, she saw . . . nothing much. The walls around her and her craft—if they really were walls—were a featureless blue-steel *blur*. They didn't look solid, exactly, more like a fog. Julie sat bewildered on the skeleton of her ship and peered out of her helmet in every direction. /You want to give me a hint?/ she asked at last. There was, she realized suddenly, gravity under her. *Gravity.* /Should I get off? Is there going to be something to stand on if I get off?/

Yes.

/That's all you can say?/ Gathering her nerve, she started to swing her left leg around, to climb down from her perch. /I don't mean to bore you with conversation./ She continued her movement, as though dismounting from a very tall horse, in her very cumbersome suit. When it came time to step down off what she thought was the lowest part of the ship (hard to see, with the damned helmet blocking her sight), she hesitated. She couldn't see a thing but fog beneath her. /How do I know this isn't a fifty-foot drop?/ A rush of fear flooded through her, and she clung, trembling.

It's safe.

/Are you sure?/

It is safe.

Okay, she thought. Time to show them what we Earth women are made of. She drew a deep breath and reached down with her left foot. When she didn't find anything solid, she grunted, pushed back, and jumped feetfirst. She dropped maybe a meter, then *slowed*—gently, to a stop. Looking down, she saw a blue fog curling over her boots. She was standing on the same misty "ground" as the ship. She felt heavy; the gravity was at least Earth-normal. She hadn't felt that in a long time; it was going to take some getting used to.

Turn around.

Disregarding a prickling of fear, she turned. She didn't see anything until she had turned completely—and then she jumped with a startled cry. Floating toward her was a tall, oval patch of glowing air—emerald-green in color, but shimmering blue around the edges.

She took a step away from it, and felt her back pressed against the exposed girders of the ship. There was nowhere to go. Before she could protest, the oval passed over her, sparkling as it made contact with her spacesuit . . .

*

For a time that might have been seconds or minutes, she floated in a sapphire glow. She felt a strange sense of *separation,* as though something in her were being pulled apart and put back together again. She wrapped her arms fearfully around her chest—and started again.

Her spacesuit was gone. "What are you *doing?*" she shouted, clutching at her clothing, afraid it would be next. "I need that suit! I *need* it."

Remain calm.

She gasped, "How am I supposed to *breathe?*"

Then she realized she *was* breathing; there was air, and it seemed fresh and good. The glow surrounding her turned pale, nearly white, and she heard the stones again, as though at a distance:

Normalization complete.

She stumbled out of the glow, lost her balance, and fell forward, face-first into thick grass.

*

For a while she lay still, shaking in wonder and fear. Was she losing her mind? The smell of the grass was what brought her around. *Grass?* She raised her head and looked around. Grass, yes. Not quite like grass as she remembered it on Earth—the blades were thinner, softer, bluer. But grass, certainly. *Alien* grass.

You have been normalized.

/Huh?/

You will not get a rash from touching the grass.

That made her get up in a hurry. /Uh. Right./ She brushed her hands off nervously, then suddenly realized—the gravity no longer felt oppressive. Something else occurred to her. /Does that mean I can eat the food here, too? Assuming there is any?/ Waiting for a response, she looked around. She was standing on a gently sloping, grassy hillside with a small knot of odd-looking trees clustered at the bottom. She was on an alien world. *An alien world.*

You will be able to eat the food.

/Good./ She turned around again, to make sure she knew

where the spacecraft was. Not that it was of any conceivable use anymore, but it was all she had.

Or all she *had* had. There was no spacecraft behind her, nor any sign of the docking bay, nor any sign that there had ever been any of those things. *Jesus,* she whispered. *What is happening to me?* She felt a sudden, overwhelming sense of loss. What *hadn't* been taken from her? Her life? Her world? Her *solar system?* They hadn't even left her the shattered remains of the craft that brought her here? /Where is the translator? Is it gone, too? Is it dead? Please tell me *what is happening* to me?/

We cannot answer all of your questions. We hope the answers will come in time.

/In time!/ She gave up and fell to her knees, shaking her head. Finally, heedless of her surroundings, she wept uncontrollably, in quaking sobs.

After a time, when her tears were spent, she wiped her face on her sleeve and lifted her eyes to squint at the sky. /This isn't a planet, is it? Is that an artificial sky up there?/ Of course it was; she'd passed into that enormous structure. The gravity was probably artificial, too. Had John come here? *Will I see him?* What lay beyond this? she wondered. All she could see was the cresting knoll, and rolling land beyond.

No, she realized suddenly—there was one more thing. A small animal had just poked its head up out of the grass, maybe thirty feet away, near the top of the knoll. It was peering in her direction. It resembled a prairie dog—or one of those African animals, a meerkat. It scurried a short distance toward her, then stopped, gazing at her with its head cocked. It chittered briefly, then cocked its head the other way. Its eyes were dark and unreadable. It chittered again, more slowly, as if trying to talk to her.

Julie's heart thumped. The creature's vocalizations gave her, unaccountably, a rush of bewilderment and hope—and an inconceivable grief and anger and longing for her own world—and then something that was almost a kind of joy. Why would she feel *joy*? Because something else was alive on this hill with her? Overcome by emotion, she gasped in a series of long, deep breaths, trying to calm herself.

Finally, she straightened her back and beckoned the creature toward her. To her astonishment, it crept forward to within a couple of meters. It sat gazing at her, and made a sound that reminded her of a hamster. Holding back tears, Julie stretched out a trembling hand and whispered, "And who, my small friend, might you be . . . ?"

40

HOME

 Ed disappeared, with a pop and a sparkle that looped around the commons, making Bandicut blink. A moment later came a much louder *pop* and a bright flash. Copernicus called out, "We've had an unexpected course deviation. The n-space slope we're following seems to have altered toward Ed's world!"

Bong. "Didn't you tell us Ed's world was in orbit around ✶Nick✶?" Li-Jared asked, gaze shifting rapidly back and forth between the view and the holo-image of Copernicus.

"Yes, that's—wait—wait—I'm having to recalibrate. The readings coming from ahead of us are very confusing."

Jeaves added, "I don't quite understand it, either. But I think Ed has done something to enable us to *see* something, or maybe *lead* us to something, that was hidden before. It's not like anything I've ever seen."

As the robot spoke, the view of space began flickering and swimming. "I think we'd better get back to the bridge," Bandicut said, jumping up. The others followed him, at a run. They all lurched down the passageway, as the artificial gravity fluctuated. It was like running on the deck of a small ship at sea. As they cascaded onto the bridge, Bandicut asked the robots for an update.

"I'm still uncertain," said Copernicus. The viewspace was just stabilizing, showing Ed's world much as they had just seen it— cliff faces and volcanic outcroppings—but with something new. The view was going through some sort of transformation, turning transparent and separating oddly, as though instead of looking down on a planetary surface, they were gazing through finely layered transparent images stacked together, each one a little different—many, *many* layers, shuffling and rotating and twisting like a kaleidoscope as they watched.

It made Bandicut dizzy. "Coppy, can't you—?"

His words were interrupted by a sudden vibration in the deck. "What's *that?*" Li-Jared asked. "Copernicus, are we about to fly *through* that—whatever it is?" Indeed, they appeared to be speeding toward the bewildering image.

"Uncertain. Our n-space readings indicate a clear passage ahead, despite what we see. Different from the usual, though. I think Ed is leading us toward an n-space regime that is . . . *quite* different . . ."

"And we're just *following?*" Li-Jared asked. "Aren't you supposed to ask us for instructions?"

"I am indeed, Captains. But in truth it's the shape of n-space that is forcing us—"

Li-Jared made a loud bonging sound. "Is anyone else thinking of that Mindaru trap we fell into once already?"

"I do not believe this is the same," Jeaves answered. "In fact, I think Ed is trying to—wait, there he is again."

Ed had just reappeared as a column of fire at the front of the viewspace. *"I will-l hel-l-p you go h-home!"* he called.

"How?" Bandicut asked.

"You are far-r, far-r-r by your-r means-s. But-t I will ta-a-ake you another-r way-y."

"Ed!" Bandicut said, trying to make a gesture of caution. "We're not really sure what you're *doing,* here!"

Without answering, the column of fire spun itself into an almost-closed circlet of light, like a snake chasing its tail. It shot forward out of the bridge, and reappeared ahead of the ship, leading the way toward what was turning into a transparent-walled tunnel aimed at infinity. *The Long View,* flanked by Dark, flowed after the fire as though pulled on a tether.

The company stood together, for that one moment silenced by common wonder and apprehension. *"Hrabh!"* Ik whispered.

The thing that had once seemed like Ed's world was spinning past them, stretched out of recognition. They were now shooting through a coruscating mix of rainbow and darkness.

Bandicut's stomach lurched, and he grabbed something to hold on to. "What the hell is going on?" he muttered. Beside him, Antares had slid onto a sofa, and was holding her head. The tunnel seemed to take a sharp turn, and they flashed around it without slowing.

"Hrrrmm," Ik said, and this time it sounded like a moan of distress.

We're on a runaway train, Bandicut thought. *But it's running loose through the galaxy . . .*

Li-Jared shouted, "Would one of you robots explain this before we all die?"

/// I think I . . . ///

Before Charli could finish, Jeaves called out, "Ed's homeworld is a little different from what we thought!" He paused as they whirled through a spiral. "It's the tip of a hyperdimensional *tree*. It stretches and branches all through spacetime."

"Is this, uhhl, *good?*" Antares gasped.

"I don't know! If Ed's world touches many places at once, it explains why he was able to contact us at so many times and places."

Bandicut was starting to get his feet back under him. The tunnel was not so clearly visible now, and their movement had smoothed out. /A tree?/

/// A difficult metaphor.
I have seen this sort of thing before, I think.
A multidimensional tree waving its branches,
touching here and there,
throughout the galaxy. ///

Bandicut, uncomprehending, passed that on to the others. Li-Jared stretched his arms out in disbelief. "Why stop with the galaxy?" *Bwang.* "Why not the whole of creation?"

"I don't think it's infinite," said Jeaves. "Probably anchored to the gravitational curvature of large masses. Which could be why it had trouble with ∗Nick∗—with all the disruptions."

"And," Bandicut said, "we are in this tree now?"

"I believe so," said Jeaves. "Look how much distance we're covering!"

"Uhhl, I can't tell *what* we're passing!" Antares muttered, forcing herself back to her feet.

"I can't with any accuracy, either," Jeaves admitted. "But we may have an opportunity here."

Please don't say that, Bandicut thought, wanting to clamp his eyes and ears shut against whatever the robot was about to say.

/// *You don't want an opportunity?* ///

/I just want to go home. I want to relax in a nice, quiet place with . . . Antares. In a hot tub. And not think about any of this anymore./

/// *Did you almost say "Julie,"*
just then? ///

Bandicut's face burned. /No. Maybe./ He breathed slowly. /Maybe I want both./

/// *I just want to understand.* ///

Jeaves was still talking. ". . . May be an instantaneous connection to other parts of the galaxy. If we're able to use it for travel, or communication . . ."

"What—"*bong*"—the star-spanner isn't fast enough?"

Before Jeaves could answer, Copernicus cried out a warning. The deck suddenly shifted like a surfboard on a wave—and smack in front of the ship was a coiling mass of light. Ik gave a throat-wrenching gasp, and Bandicut felt Antares clutch his arm. They all grabbed for support again.

"I think we just branched from one limb to another in the hyper-tree," Copernicus reported. "Hang on!"

The lighting on the bridge flickered, then darkened to a dying-ember red—and finally went out altogether, leaving only the light of the coiling thing before them. It was growing larger, and it looked very dangerous.

"*Coppy!*" Bandicut called, aware of the fear in his own voice. *Tap tap.* No answer. "*Napoleon?*"

Click. "Sorry . . . Cap'n . . . trying . . ."

Bandicut started for the control panel, but there was another surge, and the deck seemed to *ripple.* The hellish light out front brightened until it dazzled—and Antares cried out in pain—and for an instant Bandicut thought he glimpsed Dark out there in that light—and even imagined he glimpsed *two tiny points of light streaking out toward Dark*. Dark seemed to do something, and the hellish light suddenly went out, plunging them into darkness, and silence.

*

The darkness lasted for several heart-pounding minutes, before the lights flickered back up and Copernicus spoke. "Magnetar, folks. A *highly* magnetized neutron star. That was . . . a very dangerous moment."

"Dangerous?" *Bong.* "You don't say! How did that happen? How did we come to be at a *magnetar?*"

"I'm not certain," Copernicus answered. "But the magnetic field destroyed about thirty percent of our internal circuitry."

"How did you get us away from it?" Antares asked.

"I did not. Another force did."

Li-Jared's eyes flared in confusion. "Dark?"

"Possibly. I am not certain."

"If we are entrained in this network," Jeaves said, "we may have no direct control over our choices of destination. It may be that we simply arrived *randomly* at that magnetar. Or it may be that Ed—or perhaps Dark?—is trying to steer us, and removed us from that peril. Is Dark still with us, Copernicus?"

Tap tap. "Yes. Captains, this might sound strange—but is it possible that Dark just acquired translator-stones?"

There was a startled silence. Then Antares said, softly, "Yes." Bandicut spun to look at her, remembering her outcry, and found her holding her throat with one hand. "I am unhurt. Just . . . shaken." Her eyes narrowed, meeting his gaze. She turned to Ik and touched him. "I'm sorry. I don't know why the new stones went to Dark, and not you. But I think Dark responded when I cried for help. I think Dark got us away from that . . . magnetar." She folded herself into Bandicut's arms, shuddering silently.

Ik *hrrm*'d very softly.

"Approaching something else," Copernicus said.

Bandicut and Antares turned together. And then . . .

*

A dense star cluster appeared in front of them, and they soared through it, banking and curving like an airplane. Bandicut felt a distinct sense of questioning, as though someone were waiting for a reaction. *Is this your home?* seemed the unspoken question. *No,* was the unspoken answer, and they fled the place.

★

The view blossomed into a panorama of alien-looking structures, some floating in a debris field, some shattered on the surface of a nearby moon.

/// *Oh my God, no.* ///
/No, what?/
/// *It's the ruins of the Rohengen.*
I was there; I saw them destroy themselves.
No, tell them no! ///

Bandicut blinked and shouted, "Charli says *no,* get us out of here if you can!"

The view blinked away.

★

It flickered back. This time, a view of an astonishing frozen landscape—tremendous soaring cliffs of pure ice. Water ice? Nitrogen? Methane?

No.

★

Blink. Floating hulks, against the luminous gas clouds of Orion. A spaceship graveyard. The prison yard of the Mindaru, the place they had narrowly avoided once before . . .

"No!" shouted five voices, one of them inside Bandicut's head.

★

Wink. A collection of floating spaceships again, but different. There was no nebula, and the spaceships were now a extended collection of linked structures, all silver and spidery, looking as if they stretched in a *long* arc, perhaps all the way around their local sun. Several small, bright slivers coiled and looped their way around the structure, like sea creatures. Bandicut felt a chilling presence of the truly alien.

No.

★

A switch tripped. Enormous long banks of circuitry, pulsing with energy and channeled thought. Artificial intelligence, staggeringly large. An outpost—or the heart?—of the Mindaru? A pervasive feeling of menace.

"NO!" As one.

✳

Somewhere, Ed the hypercone muttered, *"Not-t-t right. Not-t right-t-t! Musssst help-p them find-d . . ."*

And that was when Charli realized, and whispered,

/// Trying to look in our thoughts
for the right picture!
That's how he's choosing,
by looking in our thoughts. ///

✳

There was a sense of a page being flipped over, and a new view . . . sparkling violet light, pulsing in darkness like tiny splinters. A sudden stirring of longing . . .

/// John, this is so much like . . . ///

/What?/ The pang in Charli's voice was heartrending.

/// It reminds me intensely of my . . . home. ///

/Your—/

/// It's not, but look how it— ///

✳

Gone. And in its place, the orangish-glowing structure they had seen once before. How long ago, when they were first setting out?

The interstellar waystation. Or what was left of it. It was in pieces, shaken apart by the hypergrav waves.

Then it was gone, too.

✳

A dozen other places appeared, and disappeared. Twenty maybe. Thirty. And then . . .

It emerged gradually out of the immense darkness of space: the misty, glowing panorama of the galaxy, sprawling before them. Bandicut sensed that they were at an extreme reach of the branches of the Ed-tree. Antares gasped and squeezed his hand. *Is it really?*

And then the ship rotated with exquisite slowness, to reveal a series of enormous, connected jewels stretched across the emptiness of extragalactic space, like a long necklace . . .

"Uhhll—"

"Shipworld," Bandicut breathed. He squeezed Antares's hand as he caught sight of Dark, with two glints of light.

/// Home, ///

whispered the quarx,

/// Yes? Home away from home. ///

/Yes./

"Yes-s-s-s," murmured Ed, from somewhere in the darkness.

EPILOGUE

What a strange, strange closure. The sight of Shipworld has filled me with as much wonder as it did the other members of the company. I did not expect to return. I did not know how, or if, I could bring the company back here, even with the best outcome. Ed! What a creature, and world. I hope we meet him again.

I have in a sense come full circle. Once, long ago by my subjective time, I witnessed the destruction of a star in a supernova. I did not cause it, but neither did I prevent it. Indeed, a part of me became a part of the remnant of that deed. Here, by contrast, I helped to save a star. I knew a little better what I was doing this time, but maybe not that much.

We have saved a stellar nursery of considerable value—a cradle of new stars—as well as many individual worlds. And we have learned much about the Enemy. The Mindaru. The Survivors. Not nearly enough, but much.

Do they know yet that their project in the Starmaker Nebula has failed? Does it distress them? Or do they not even check in for millions of years at a time? Are they so implacably cold and hostile that no setback matters for long, or is there some part of them that questions and wonders? Some part that we could one day communicate with? Or are they hunkered down too deep, beyond reach in their crushed dimensions, in their black holes, or wherever they have hidden?

I do not know. This mission cannot tell us.

One day we will have to learn, though. I don't know whether to hope for that day to occur in my time or not.

I just know that it must.